OAK SEER

CRAIG COMER

CITY OWL
PRESS

OAK SEER
A Fey Matter, Book 2

CITY OWL PRESS
www.cityowlpress.com

Cover Design by Mibl Art. All stock photos licensed appropriately.

Edited by Heather McCorkle.

For information on subsidiary rights, please contact the publisher at info@cityowlpress.com.

Print Edition ISBN: 978-1-944728-88-5

Digital Edition ISBN: 978-1-944728-87-8

Printed in the United States of America

For Martina,
who means everything to me.

PRAISE FOR CRAIG COMER

"A fantastic sequel, OAK SEER, plunges you willingly into the fey underworld of Victorian Scotland." - *Garrett Calcaterra, Author of Dreamwielder*

"Comer weaves a riveting tale of intrigue, magic, and romance in a steampunk-flavored Scotland packed with evil creatures, scheming politicians, and vicious bigots. But the real highlight of OAK SEER is its heroine. Effie of Glen Coe is one feisty freedom fighter!"
- *Wendy N. Wagner, Hugo Award Winner and Author of An Oath of Dogs*

"For a heroic fantasy novel written by not one, not two, but three authors - Garrett Calcaterra, Craig Comer, and Ahimsa Kerp - The Roads to Baldairn Motte is a surprisingly well-structured, remarkably cohesive tale that actually benefits from the different voices, without seeming fragmented."
— *Bob Milne, Beauty in Ruins*

"In The Roads to Baldairn Motte, three perilous adventures are tied to the same epic war, with different people from different walks of life, but, clearly in the same lands, at the same time, speaking the same language, right down to the swear words. It was graphic and captivating. I couldn't put it down."
— *GoodReads Reviewer*

"In The LAIRD OF DUNCAIRN, each character is unique and has a back story that allowed me to develop attachments to them. The story is very well developed and is told in a way that grabs you from the beginning. As the heroine, Effie, comes to know her race's past, she develops abilities that surprise herself, her companions, and her enemies...This book was a great read. I cannot wait for the sequel!"
— *Rita Cline, Reader*

SCOTLAND, 1884

E ffie peered through the window of the steam carriage as the village of Langmire came into view. The buildings—crofters' homes mostly—sagged like slump-backed crones. Grey smoke wafted from blackened chimneys sprouting from thatched roofs. Someone baked fresh bread. She caught it on the wind beneath a perfume of moldy timbers, damp leaves, and rusting iron, all remnants of the heavy spring rains that had flooded the River Teith and left the roads full of boggy ruts and bared stone.

Eager for a warm hearth and a cup of honeyed tea, she licked her parched lips. She'd travelled a full day to reach the village. She'd come because Conall Murray had begged her, because without her an innocent woman would hang.

The thought drew her attention to the heart of the village where a stout oak grew. Muckle Ben, the locals called it, Effie had once heard. They'd carved a Green Man into its bark long ago, during a time when such things held power. Now banners pronouncing some celebration hung from its limbs more often than not, but none remained there currently. Its trunk stood as somber as an undertaker. Chickens picked at worms in the upturned soil near its roots, and a lone hound howled at the rustling leaves as the branches creaked above.

Fergus Alpin hacked into his handkerchief, a wet, miserable noise she'd had to contend with the entire journey from Stirling. The Fey Finder sat across from her in the steam carriage's tight compartment. His wrinkled face was spotted and thin, and he kept tugging his coat tighter about his frail bones. She tried to avoid his gaze, but nothing adorned the compartment for her to study, and she could only stare out the window for so long before feeling rude.

"I'll do the speaking," the man said. "You will remain silent." The quiver at his lip turned into another fit of hacking, yet she still heard his mumbling. "Send a fey to catch a fey, and one with paps at that!"

The steam carriage rocked and bounced, splashing through the muddy road as if fording a stony riverbed. Effie braced herself against the hard, worn benches, the padding flattened from years of service. A lightly stained wood paneling formed the carriage's walls, floor, and roof. The boiler at its rear warmed the compartment, but at the expense of the coal smoke that clouded the air.

She shifted to relieve her sore hips. Her eyes narrowed. "The Fey Finder General bade me accompany you, Mr. Alpin, and not so I would stand and do nothing." She tried to keep the bite from her tongue.

Of Fey Finders, Alpin was a journeyman and not a zealot. At least there was that. He sought not to be bothered rather than possessing the fiery hatred common to his profession.

She pressed her palms into the cushion on either side of her, to steady herself. It still marveled her she could sit so close to a Sniffer, a man the crown tasked with hunting down malevolent fey. *Malevolent, as if they knew what the word meant.* They hunted all with fey blood, and as a Sithling—one with the ancient blood of the Daoine Sith coursing through her—that included her. But things had changed after Caldwell House, and she had a need to trust where once she dared not. The fierce battle there had forced the lords of the empire to open their eyes. They could not rest on centuries of intolerance any longer. They had to welcome the fey into society's ranks and accept a permanent treaty. They had witnessed the fate awaiting them if they did not.

Effie's heart warmed. If the lords of the empire could learn to trust, so could she, and perhaps the Scottish fey would live freely for the first time in millennia.

Alpin's jaw worked. He'd likely never had someone with paps stand up to him. Most Scots of either gender avoided Sniffers as if they carried the plague. "Look here, Miss Effie," he snapped. "I'll not have it. You may dine with the likes of lords, but you're not in some grand procession here. I know the hearts of these gentle folk better than you ever will, and I will not banter with the mind of a devious hag."

"When you see one, I'm sure," said Effie, not knowing whether the man had meant her or the poor Spae Wife they'd come to question. Neither deserved such venom.

He snorted but had the decency to duck his head in a slight nod of apology. The carriage rattled as they hit a deep rut, and Effie had to grab the window sill to keep from tipping over. They'd reached Muckle Ben. Steam exhaled from the carriage's boiler as the driver brought them to a halt. She could hear the man clamber down from his perch above. She'd much rather have spent the journey up there, with its better view of the trees and mountains, trickling burns and muck-filled marsh.

And its lack of hacking fits.

The door opened, and the driver, a freckled young man with ginger locks, offered his hand. She sighed. She'd rather do many a thing differently—wear trousers for a start—but she may as well wish for sheep to shear themselves. Gathering her pale green skirt, she accepted the man's hand and stepped onto the muddy road. She had a respectable image to maintain, even if it did involve underskirts and a high-necked chemisette. At least the copious folds of cloth kept her reasonably warm.

Alpin alighted from the carriage and gestured with his cane. Two men approached, their jackets and trousers of rough wool stained with grass and muck. They carried the walking staves of shepherds.

"A good afternoon ta' ye," said the taller one. He smelled of pipe smoke. His gaze ran over Effie's womanly shape before he bobbed his head to Alpin. "I am John McCreary, and this here's Ewan Keith. Are you the Sniffer? Er, I mean my lord's Fey Finder?"

"I am Her Majesty's Fey Finder," shot Alpin, bristling. He sniffed the air and wrinkled his nose. "Let's see to this business before the sky turns dark. Where are you keeping her?"

McCreary pointed at a cottage down the road. "She's at home under the watch of the constable. But you should see what evidence we did find in the fields first. It'll leave no doubt as to her trickster ways."

Ewan Keith scratched the stubble on his chin. "Ye may wish to avoid such sights, miss," he said to Effie. "'Tis a gruesome thing."

Effie smiled. She remembered how a giant had ripped the Piper of Ceann Rois apart at Caldwell House, the field there strewn with the mangled bodies of the Horned Host. "I've developed an iron stomach for such sights," she said, "and the Fey Finder General himself has asked me to investigate this matter."

The shepherd's eyes widened. "You're the Lady in Green," he said. He took her in again, taking a step back, though he stood a head taller than her.

"Effie of Glen Coe," said Alpin, giving her the courtesy of an introduction, if a bit late.

She wasn't surprised they hadn't known her for a Sithling. With her young woman's stature, she looked like any other Scottish lass. Her chestnut locks fell around hazel eyes and a cheerfully rounded face. What continued to surprise her was that strangers knew of her at all. Tales of her connection to the Duke of Edinburgh and Sir Walter Conrad, and with the matter of the fey treaty, had spread throughout the empire. She hadn't imagined herself as interesting gossip—far less so than tales of pixies, brownies, and giants—but word persisted of the lady in the green dress who'd hung on the arm of the newly appointed Fey Finder General. It troubled her, having strangers know of her. It was such a far cry from the life she'd lived in the twenty-three summers before Caldwell House.

"Let us see the evidence, then," said Alpin. He waggled his cane and bade the men to lead the way.

Their feet slapped wet mud as they trudged through the village. Effie tried to avoid the puddles, but the hem of her skirts became a mess by the time they reached the Spae Wife's cottage. A comfortably lived-in thing, its windows held boxes overflowing with a mix of wild flowers and herbs, and a proper garden was well tended in the yard. McCreary led them around to the rear. A simple wagon sat there, and on it lay two devilish creatures.

"Wulvers," Effie named them. Alpin's brow raised. He covered his mouth and coughed. Not as large as a wolf, the creatures had the ears of a fox and the blunted snout of a boar. Fangs curved beneath their maws, as sharp as any knife. They stunk like a moldy bog. They'd been dead for at least a few days, their shaggy coats mangy, their stomachs bloated.

"Is it true you slew a thousand of these devils to protect the duke?" asked Keith.

"Hardly," scoffed Alpin.

Effie shook her head. "The queen's soldiers did the fighting. They are the heroes. My part was rather small." She held back the truth. Her part had been meant to be small, but it was she who'd wrested control of the Horned Host from the Piper of Ceann Rois and caused his defeat. As many times as she relived the tale, it still amazed her she'd ever been so brazen.

"Enough of that," said Alpin. "Miss Effie has enough wild fancy in her head not to need your exaggerations." He tapped the wagon with his cane. "Now tell me of these creatures. Where did you find them, and how are they evidence against the Spae Wife, this Miss Teasdale?"

"We found them on the riverbank less than a mile from the village," said McCreary. "They was already dead. They must've drown when the banks overflowed a couple nights ago. They killed a couple of sheep before then, scaring everyone with their howling."

Effie frowned. "I don't see a connection to your village's Spae Wife."

McCreary's eye's bulged in disbelief. "Well, Miss Teasdale must've summoned them here, hadn't she? How else may they have come?"

Fergus Alpin chuckled. He planted his cane in the muck before him and drew up his bearing. "Wulvers have been found all over the countryside in the past year. Found, fought, and dispatched by Her Majesty's Fey Finders. They offer no proof that the Spae Wife has acted unlawfully. These are modern times where a fey is not guilty merely for drawing breath, despite their natural proclivity for foul deeds."

He eyed Effie. "Thankfully, I have the means to root out the truth of the matter."

She stiffened. For a moment she had wanted to thank the Sniffer for not readily assuming guilt over such a contrivance, but his final threat was far worse. "You cannot mean to drug the poor woman!" she cried. They'd used such measures against her in the past, before the truce, and she wouldn't stand by while another suffered as she had, having her personal thoughts squeezed out as milk from an udder.

"It won't harm her, only force her to speak the truth. The serum is quite mild compared to those developed on the continent. Or is it you have another means to ensure she speaks no lies?"

"Let us at least speak with her first, and treat her like an honest citizen," Effie pleaded.

Alpin waved his hand dismissively. "Bah, you'll go nowhere near the woman. I know of your Fey Craft and how it strengthens within proximity of another fey. Your presence would lend her the power to trick us all, and then where would we be? It is better you remain out here, watching over these things." He nodded warily at the wulvers, as if they were about to rise from the wagon and attack the village.

Effie swallowed down the urge to bark at the man. He spoke the truth, in part. Fey Craft grew in power when concentrated in a small area. By herself, Effie was barely able to sense a hound across the way, but with only one or two other fey about, she could feel the fleas on its coat from a quarter mile distant. It was why the ancient fey lived in troops, the power of their Seily Courts enough to travel to distant realms and mask themselves from any intruder. Still, she would not concede to the Sniffer. Her presence might lend the Spae Wife strength, but the opposite was also true, and the man knew it. He didn't trust her. He'd spent a lifetime not trusting the fey, tracking them down for supposed crimes against the empire, and despite the promise of a treaty he would not so easily change his nature.

"The Fey Finder General commanded you to escort me here," she said. If she couldn't persuade or charm him, she would calmly force him to see her way. "He will not understand why you refused my help."

Fergus Alpin's lip tugged at the corner, forming a slight sneer. "Conall Murray is the temporary Fey Finder General until one better suited to the task is appointed by Her Majesty. And, Miss Effie, I have escorted you quite far enough." He strode to the backdoor of the cottage and pounded on it with his cane.

As he did, a chill ran along Effie's arms, startling her. The touch crawled along her flesh and snaked up to her head. She started and spun about. *Was it the wind? Or some distant Fey Craft?* The thought unsettled her even more. She reached out with her fey senses and felt the auras around her. It was how she had learned to become aware of other fey blood nearby. Closing her eyes, she scoured the village and the river and the hills, but only a single pulsing aura returned to her. And that came from within the cottage. Fergus Alpin might know a little about Fey Craft, but he didn't realize proximity required neither sight nor touch. She'd felt the Spae Wife as soon as they'd entered the village, a tickling, throbbing sensation in her belly that she'd once mistaken for foreboding.

But whatever caused the chill touch fled as suddenly as it had arrived. It hadn't come from the Spae Wife, she was certain, but she had no other clue. A puzzle for another time, Effie thought, as the cottage door creaked open. A balding head popped out. Alpin exchanged words with the man in a hushed tone Effie couldn't overhear. She stepped closer, and the man emerged fully from the cottage to block her path. His shoulders were broad and his neck thick. His glare seemed to pass through her rather than meet her eyes.

"I have instructed Constable Tyne to keep you from the cottage," said Alpin. "If you persist, he will restrain you." The Sniffer waved at the shepherds, who watched the confrontation with slack jaws. Keith's face had paled. "Use these two, if you need assistance," he told the constable before entering the cottage and snatching the door closed behind him.

Effie gently straightened her skirts. After facing what she had the past couple of years, a local constable and an aging Sniffer would not cow her. "Step aside, Mr. Tyne," she said. "I have orders from the queen's own agent."

The man folded his arms across a meaty chest. "As do I, Miss Effie. And that agent is here. Where is yours? Or do you have an actual writ from Her Majesty?"

Her foot tapped, and she folded her arms to match his. But winning a contest of stubbornness wouldn't help anyone. She needed to act. Silently, she reached for the Spae Wife's aura and pushed out an image of warmth, the happiness of children playing in a pile of leaves, and the cozy scent of honeyed tea sipped in front of a fire. *Just hold on*, she sent through the images. *You are safe*. Effie's fey affinity was as a Grundbairn. That tied her to the life force of the land and all its inhabitants, so such sendings were easier for her than other fey.

The Spae Wife managed a crude response. Spae Wives healed the sick and mended the body's humors, just as Star Readers read portents of the future. Their Fey Craft felt odd to Effie, as hers must to them. The woman sent the image of a tree—Muckle Ben perhaps. On it a carved face grinned at her, with strands of moss cascading around it like windblown hair. Effie started. The face was her own. The woman knew her, or knew enough about her to cast her features.

Effie redoubled her resolve. If the constable sought to intimidate her, she would do him one better. She took a wide stance and slowly extended her arms, palms out. The gesture was only for effect. Her Fey Craft blossomed fully in her mind. She remembered the hound they'd passed and sought him out. She searched for others within the village and called to them as well. She didn't control them or force them in any manner. She refused to violate their will. Instead, she begged them to stand with her. She showed them how the constable blocked her path from aiding Miss Teasdale. She nudged their sense of pride and duty, and showed them how respected they would be if they found the courage to heed her call.

An eager howl came from the road. Effie grinned. The constable started and cast his gaze toward the feral sound and back to her. Good, she thought, he sees the connection. She lowered her arms and continued to beg the hounds to come.

An old sheepdog appeared first. It charged around the corner of the cottage and growled when it saw the constable. Its hackles stiffened, and it padded forward, slunk down and ready to pounce. A beagle came next followed by the hunting hound she'd spied near Muckle Ben.

"Chester?" whispered Ewan Keith.

The constable stepped back. "Call them off," he commanded, but his voice had grown frail. "You can't do this!"

"Here, boy, heel!" barked McCreary, advancing on the sheepdog. The dog bared its teeth and snapped at the shepherd, yet Effie felt a flash of playfulness from it.

"Now, Mr. Tyne, I will enter," said Effie. She didn't need to let on she would never allow the hounds to attack. "Step aside, if you please."

Her bluff worked. The constable put his hands up and moved from her path. "There will be consequences for this," he yelped. "I will inform Mr. Alpin. I will write the magistrate!"

Effie waved the sheepdog over and scratched its ears. It licked her palm and nuzzled her. "I will speak with Mr. Alpin, but write your report if you must. I'm sure these good men will bear witness to your account." She gestured at McCreary and Keith, who had pressed themselves against the wagon. It would do him no good. As long as Conall Murray remained Fey Finder General, she was protected.

Striding forward, Effie threw open the cottage door. Fergus Alpin spun toward her. He hunched over an elderly woman, the syringe in his hand filled with a thick, yellow serum. His face scowled in fury at the sight of her. Effie steeled herself and stormed inside.

2

Fergus Alpin growled. Effie remembered Edmund Glover's face when that man had used the truth serum on her. The previous Fey Finder General had been a cruel and vile man. He'd acted out of malice with an intent to injure. She didn't believe Alpin was such a creature. She vexed him, certainly. Her fey blood and upstart position rattled his sense of propriety, skewing the world he recognized. But there was a human side she could still appeal to. His posture held more disdain in it than malevolence. She needed only to craft her argument with care.

"It is all right, child," said the elderly woman, as if reading her thoughts.

Miss Teasdale had a kind face. Her silver hair wound in an unkempt bun atop her head, with loose strands sprouting like weeds in all directions. She wore a smock dress of wool, belted by thick leather. Over a century of wrinkles etched her cheeks, though she did not appear frail of health. She sat straight, her shoulders holding the poise of a matron used to authority, at the least within her own household. Her cottage smelled of wildflowers. Sprigs were tied in bundles about the rafters, their scent masking whatever goods were stored in the pots and baskets crammed on tables, shelves, and racks lining the walls. A threadbare rug covered the floor, and a fire crackled at the hearth, its smoke hovering in the air like a bank of fog.

Effie spied a rolling pin on a table near the hearth and fought the urge to snatch it up. Threatening Alpin would only antagonize the man. Instead, she relaxed the hardness of her gaze and spoke in a gentle manner. "The Fey Finder General bade me come for the very purpose of avoiding such barbaric practices. If you do not treat Miss Teasdale with the respect due one of Her Majesty's subjects, he will hear of it."

"Miss Teasdale," replied the Sniffer, his voice cold, "consented to my questioning methods without any means of coercion." He checked the syringe, swilling its contents about as if it were a fine whiskey. "It is perhaps a subject with much to hide who would do otherwise."

Dumbstruck, Effie's mouth fell open. Her own encounters with the Sniffers had left scars deeper than those of the flesh, but she had forced herself to overcome that fear in order to save those fey she could from the crown's persecutions. That any would willingly submit to such practices rattled her sense of justice. She'd come to Langmire, after all, not to aid the Fey Finder so much as to thwart his cruel ways.

"It cannot be," Effie croaked. "Our kind..."

"Would never stand against the crown, is it?" snapped Alpin, silencing her. "Or do you mean to say your kind would never speak a falsehood? I would remind you of the very murders in Duncairn that thrust you before the crown's attentions in the first place. And as for your arrogance against my handling of this investigation, I would ask if you had any notion of the practices used against human offenders? They are not nearly as pleasant, I assure you."

An image of Muckle Ben, with its carved face, returned to Effie—a sending from the Spae Wife. It soothed her nerves and felt warm and safe. The Spae Wife smiled at her. "I have nothing to fear from Mr. Alpin," she said. "Nor from Mr. Tyne. They only seek to perform their duties as the crown has instructed them. I have no need to stand in their way."

Effie blinked, not believing what she heard. "Fey have been hanged for less evidence than a change of wind," she said. "A Spae Wife of Falkirk was burned three summers ago for telling a laird his horse was lame. The woman suffered the flames and the horse died all the same."

Miss Teasdale shook her head, but her kind smile did not wane. "Langmire is not a large town of strangers, and I have handled its ailments for half a century and more. The village folk respect me. I have delivered their babes, mended their limbs, and broken their fevers. John McCreary is a humbled man whose heart has broken. His words were spoken in anger to the constable. His charges are hollow."

"There, you see?" asked Fergus Alpin. "You understand her heart. Now, if you will excuse yourself, we may conclude this matter and perhaps return to Stirling by nightfall."

Effie's head reeled. She'd prepared herself to fight the Sniffer, but she'd never thought she'd have to force the woman to safety. Her imagination had run wild with thoughts of fleeing the village under the cover of darkness, hounded by an armed mob. She wondered now what she could possibly say to change the woman's mind. Certainly, she was not about to leave and let the Fey Finder have his way.

"Why was Mr. McCreary heartbroken?" she asked, grasping at a detail that made her curious.

"I have no patience for this," barked Alpin. The effort made him hack spittle into his sleeve.

"And no need for injecting your serum," replied Effie. "Miss Teasdale clearly submits to your interrogation, so by your own argument has nothing to hide. So what is the point of raising a stern hand when a gentle one would suffice? Put your serum down and ask your questions as a gentleman, not some superstitious charlatan from the continent." She planted her hands on her hips and defied the man to force her away.

Alpin glared at her for a moment, weighing his options, before he grumbled something in annoyance. He fired the plunger. Yellow serum spewed across the floor in a thin burst. When it was spent, the Sniffer capped the syringe and shoved it into his coat pocket. He'd relented, but only just. Ire masked his features. His brow pulled tight and his neck strained.

"You will stay where you are and remain silent," he said, wringing his hands clean on a handkerchief he produced from his waistcoat. He turned to Miss Teasdale. "Now if you please, tell me of John McCreary's plight."

Effie swallowed down the lump in her throat. The last time she'd stood in defiance of a Fey Finder, it'd taken a regiment of soldiers to keep her from being summarily shot.

"It is the death of his son, James, that has left him so full of vengeance," said the Spae Wife. "The bairn caught a flux and would not eat. The McCrearys brought him to my cottage, as they had a dozen times before, but to no avail. I could do nothing with herb or crystal to save him." She hung her head, as if the loss were still a heavy burden. "What's more, Mrs. McCreary has not kept a child in the womb for years and is unlike to again. And so the once happy couple find themselves without a family of their own."

"There are others who would vouch for this account?" asked Alpin.

"Aye, the whole village knows of it," answered Miss Teasdale. "It causes John McCreary even greater shame, but the village folk ken better than to trust his harsh tongue."

"His perhaps, but what of Mr. Keith or Mr. Tyne? They have also offered evidence against you. They say they have seen you dancing in the woods and calling to spirits, casting spells so that the wulvers would come."

Miss Teasdale snorted at the absurd notion of her dancing anywhere, much less out in the woods. A broad grin exposed a row of stained teeth. A kettle over the hearth began to shrill, and the woman rose to fetch it. The Sniffer stepped aside and watched her pour three cups of tea. It had an earthen scent, like peat mixed with a hint of cloves. Effie gratefully took her cup, not only for the warmth the tea brought her belly, but so that she had something to do with her hands. Her fists kept balling, urging her to speak up and end this foolish charade.

But against whom would she speak? The Fey Finder acted civilly, even if his profession was buffoonery. And, supposing she could convince the woman of such a thing, the Spae Wife could not flee the village without the act screaming of guilt. The whole matter stunk from top to bottom.

Miss Teasdale reclaimed her seat. "Their words will wilt before the eye of the magistrate. I ken them both for good, honest men. They speak now only to appease a friend. They will stand for me in the end, they and the rest of the village. I have done so much for them all these years. Their consciences will not let them see me harmed."

"No," said Effie, not able to contain herself any longer, "you cannot trust in that." She'd heard too many tales of fey suffering at the hands of those they believed good and honest.

"It will be for the magistrate to decide," said Alpin. "The accusations are enough. It must warrant his attention."

Effie shook her head. "There is no need for the magistrate. You have the authority to dismiss the matter." Fey Finders were appointed by the crown for just such a purpose as dismissing false claims against the fey. That they rarely saw fit to do so owed more to the prejudice of their order than lack of commission.

"I do," agreed Alpin. His chin raised, and something of a smirk passed across his lips. "But the matter remains contested. You see now why I use the serum. It would leave no doubt as to whose account was honest."

Effie felt the heat rising in her chest. "Then use it," she snapped. Despite her abhorrence, it was a better outcome than hoping the accusers would reverse their account.

Alpin brought up a hand, as if to hold back her temper. The pacifying gesture infuriated her even more. "There is no need," he said. "I believe Miss Teasdale's account." The Sniffer began to pace, plodding slowly before the hearth. "It is Mr. McCreary's account that must be satisfied. I have much experience with these kinds of things, and these sorts of men. If we were to declare Miss Teasdale innocent and depart with only our decree to soothe his temper, she may well end up swaying beneath Muckle Ben before the day is through."

Effie patted down her skirts, biting hard on her tongue. The man talked in circles, blundering between threats and agreement with her. He wanted her to concede to his will, she realized. She'd wounded his pride, storming in as she had. Or perhaps it had started earlier, when she'd dared to accompany him. Her lips pinched together. Such a frail and decrepit thing the man's pride must be, for him to act so callously. That he would sacrifice Miss Teasdale to claim the better of her, Effie had no doubt.

It rankled Effie, but if she must bow to the man's ego to protect the woman, she would do just that. She swallowed down her exasperation and stared at the floor before her feet. "That is an awful end surely none of us desire. What do you believe we should do? There must be some way to ensure Mr. McCreary recants."

Fergus Alpin studied his nails. "The man is a shepherd. The loss of a child means the loss of income to his family. In my experience, that is the root of a peasant's grief." He turned to Effie. "How much do the mines pay for a child these days?"

Effie's stomach soured. It turned in fits again when John McCreary greedily accepted the coins the Sniffer proffered in compensation. For all he claimed to mourn the loss of his son, it had not taken long for him to change his tune.

Within the hour, she and the Sniffer departed Langmire. Effie watched Muckle Ben as they trundled away in the steam carriage. She noted how its limbs sagged, as if tired from holding up the weight of the village for so many long years. They'd reached a good outcome, she forced herself to acknowledge. Miss Teasdale was safe. Her accusers had recanted. Before Caldwell House, such a thing wouldn't have happened. Neither the Fey Finder nor the magistrate would've listened to the woman's pleas of innocence. Certainly, the crown would not have paid for her absolution. Any accusation at all had warranted a death sentence, regardless of merit.

Yet somehow this outcome didn't feel like progress. It only reminded her there was so much work left to be done, as if an eon of such toiling would barely register as a speck of sand on a vast and endless shore.

3

Glasgow stank like a privy overused after a feast of rotten fish and moldy cheese. Effie pressed the perfumed handkerchief to her nose once again. She'd tried to ignore the stench and act delicately on arrival at Lady Fife's city estate, but the air had only grown worse, stuffy with pipe smoke and the press of warm bodies atop the putrid breeze carried in from open windows. The other guests at Lady Fife's ball didn't appear to notice. London and Newcastle must smell as bad for them not to, she thought.

"You might as well leave that thing dangling from your nostrils if you intend to deprive us of your radiant face," said Conall Murray. The young Fey Finder General grinned. His dark eyes teased. Black curls hung about a cheery face, his lips twitching with an eager mischief. His wit was terrible at times, but Effie couldn't help but blush a little.

"How can they stand it?" she asked. She forced her hand down and clasped it with the other to keep it still, fussing with the skirts of her deep jade, muslin gown. Sleeveless and cut tight around the chest, it hugged her over a rigid corset. White gloves and a simple necklace were her only adornments, a pale showing in comparison to the other ladies in attendance.

Conall leaned closer. His dark, tailed coat bespoke his family's wealth, and he wore a ribbon of office on his breast. It was red with three black stripes. "They have decades of practice ignoring that which is beneath them," he said.

Effie turned and bit her lip, stifling a fit a laughter. She understood the subtext in Conall's words. Dressed up as she might be, she still felt like a stranger in such a decadent room. Stuart Graham, the man who, along with Thomas Stevenson, had taken her under his care at a young age, had tried to coach her on proper etiquette. But not all of the lessons had stuck, and many she still did not understand. At a high society ball such as Lady Fife's, every gesture had its proper place, every step and word a formal meaning.

This particular ball served two purposes—to celebrate the start of formal treaty negotiations between the fey court and the crown, and to welcome the members of Parliament who'd journeyed north to take part in the negotiations. That the negotiations would be held in Glasgow and not Edinburgh was not lost on anyone present. Edinburgh held a royal residence and stood as the capital of Scotland. It was the proper place for a formal treaty with the crown, if not in London itself. That the negotiations would take place outside its boundaries spoke volumes about the opposition the treaty faced.

Glasgow had become a bigger city than Edinburgh over the past century. It had tripled in size and then tripled again since the start of the Industrial Age, and while the capital remained a bastion of learning, science, and the arts, Glasgow had grown in commerce. On the banks of the Clyde sprawled a hive of shipbuilding, iron smelting, and chemical manufacturing. Textiles and locomotives, carpets and cigarettes, along with heavy machinery and a thousand other products all flowed out of the Second City of the Empire.

And the lords from London all had their hands in that giant pot.

Effie glanced about the ballroom. A floral print covered the paper on its walls. A high wainscoting shone white, matching the plaster of the ceiling with its simple yet elegant scrollwork. Music drifted, light and airy, beneath the din of a dozen huddled conversations. *Glasgow and not Edinburgh*. It meant that wealth had trumped whatever designs the Duke of Edinburgh had laid before his royal mother. At Caldwell House the threat of an invading army had forced the duke into an alliance with the fey. And afterward, in the throes of victory, the crown had promised to negotiate in good faith. A procession across the Highlands had demonstrated unity and hope for a civil marriage between the Seily Court and the crown.

But that grand merriment had started to wane. "I don't see the duke," she observed.

Conall sighed. His lithe shoulders slumped. "His Grace found more urgent matters to attend."

Effie read his eyes and frowned. The absence of the queen's son was deeply troubling. Those in favor of the treaty had not the numbers of those opposed. "Without the duke's direct support, the crown's representation falls on Lord Granville," she said.

"It does."

"A man who has twice put forth legislation to formally outlaw any association with the fey and ban the use of Fey Craft." The lord was the last person she would pick to negotiate with the fey. They might as well use the dead wulvers of Langmire. "Is the duke blind?"

With a treaty in place, all fey had a chance of living in peace. Without, they would be hunted greater than before, killed, or exiled.

Conall nodded to a passing gentleman before speaking in a low tone. "The duke knows the worth of Aerfenium, and the tales told of its value have changed the minds of many in London. The substance can mint coin, they are hearing. It makes them deaf to its Fey Craft origins. Lord Granville may not possess such a rigid posture as he once held, and his allies would all like to lay their hands on this new mine of gold."

"They're as bad as the pirates from Robert's book," said Effie. Thomas Stevenson's son had risen in esteem over the publication of his latest book, and at last the two had reconciled.

"Aye, and less trustworthy, too," Conall agreed. His cheeks flashed red, and he started to fidget with his waistcoat. Effie felt the weight of prying eyes and looked across the room to find a gaggle of young women gawking openly at them.

One girl, pretty, with blonde hair and fair features, turned and placed a hand coyly over her mouth to whisper something. Her friend, equally comely but with darker features, giggled, her ringlets bouncing. Amusement gleamed in her eyes. They linked arms and hurried away, yapping in low, excited tones. The rest of the group turned away once the two left, though Effie felt their attention remained fixed on her and Conall.

"It is my position which makes them swoon," said Conall. He sounded tired. "My father and Lady Fife have made it their charge to inform every available hand present of my appointed station. Of course, they do not mention the position is only temporary and that I cannot be rid of it quickly enough."

"One should be flattered by the attention." Effie's voice held more than a hint of mocking. She had no claim over Conall, and certainly no cause for jealousy, yet she felt a stirring in her chest over the attention the other women showed him.

"You know me better than that," said Conall, and Effie knew what he meant. Conall Murray had never chosen the path his life had taken him on. His father had seen to his advancement, pulling him along against his will. Conall would be happier laboring in the shop he once owned, bartering tools for the rail lines.

Effie resisted stepping closer to him. *Let the lasses stare*. She refused to feel threatened by them, stirrings or not. "How goes the hunt?" she asked to change the subject. As Fey Finder General, Conall scoured the countryside, hunting the last of the Sidhe Bhreige, an ancient race of devilish fey. Three had escaped when Aerfenium had first been mined. Its nature as a ward against the fiends had been unknown and lost in time. Two had perished at Caldwell House, but the last remained hidden to them.

"I'd as soon hunt for a particular fish in all the oceans of the Earth," replied Conall. "We comb the Highlands on whiffs of gossip alone. There is no danger we can find. There is no hint of the foulness the Piper of Ceann Rois and Laird of Aonghus delivered. We chase a specter, known to us only because of the sensations wrought among the fey at its escape."

"What a horror that must be," squealed a high-pitched voice.

Effie turned to see the girl with the dark ringlets emerge from the crowd, her blonde friend still on her arm. The excitement on her face belied her words. Her round eyes sparkled with delight. Her lips hung slightly parted. Her figure was slight but barely contained within a cobalt colored gown trimmed with white lace. She stepped closer to Conall. "My father says you are outmatched in every regard. You must be terribly brave to continue on as you do."

"Oh, ah," Conall mumbled. His brow wrinkled as he managed a stiff nod.

The girl pulled her friend a step forward, blocking Effie from Conall. She giggled and stroked the arm of her friend. "Oh, I don't mean to say silly things. My mouth gets me into so much trouble sometimes."

Effie painted a pleasant smile on her face. Now was not the time to call on some songbird to perch on the girl's head, nor a field mouse to run up the girl's skirts. Besides, there was something clever behind the girl's eyes, a shrewdness in the exaggerated way she spoke. She knew perfectly well what she did and how she acted. It was a game to her, a spoiled girl playing at society. Her friend remained mute, her face chiseled into a happy expression like a doll's.

"Mr. Conall Murray, Her Majesty's Fey Finder General," said Conall, bowing more formally. "And this..." He reached around behind the girl and pulled Effie to his side. "Is Miss Effie of Glen Coe."

The dark-haired one frowned, but hid it quickly. "Miss Catherine Granville," she said. She curtsied, her gaze taking in Conall as her head dipped.

"You have no family name?" the other girl asked Effie. "Lord Granville says family names are as important as breathing. They carry weight and a binding to one's place within the empire. I couldn't imagine not having one."

Catherine Granville elbowed her friend softly. "Oh, and I am Miss Margret Godwin, of course," the girl added, dipping into a low curtsey.

Effie felt blood rush to her cheeks. Until the year previous, she had never considered a surname. She had never thought to stand amongst such company as she'd need one. Her mother had named her Aelfryth, after a queen, but her friends had always called her Effie. Stuart Graham had offered the use of his name, but somehow that felt like admitting she still needed his protection. She'd traveled under the name Elisabeth Martins for a time, but that also no longer seemed to fit. It was a name for staying hidden, lost among a crowd. It wasn't one for attending balls and feasts on behalf of the Seily Court. So Effie she remained, as Effie she'd always been.

"I beg your pardon," said Margret Godwin, curtseying again.

Effie nodded in acceptance. She never knew who would become an ally to the fey cause, she reminded herself. And the girl did not seem as shrewd as her friend. She probably did not intend the slight.

"Excuse our boldness. We just had to introduce ourselves to Her Majesty's newest servant," said Catherine Granville. "There are so many boring men here. I do hope your dance card is not yet full?" She laughed and pulled her friend away before Conall could stammer a reply. Their skirts rustled as they fled, disappearing into the crowded ballroom.

Conall took a deep breath and watched them depart.

"Uneasy lies the head that wears a crown," said Effie. His cheeks pulled into a grin, and he turned his eyes on her. The gaze lingered into an awkward silence, and she could only guess what thoughts passed beneath his brow.

"I haven't properly thanked you for your part in resolving the matter at Langmire," he said finally. "Or those at Gallness and Kinross."

"You have," Effie replied.

"Telegrams are a poor substitute for gratitude. I do appreciate your support, Effie, and all that you risk. I don't take it for granted." His face relaxed fully for the first time since she'd joined him earlier. It reminded her of their time on the road to Kinlochy, when despite an armed regiment at their back and warrants for their arrest, they had travelled peacefully across the Highlands, learning of each other and becoming closer than proper society would ever allow.

"I know you do not," she said. She thought to say more but couldn't think of how to say she missed his company without sounding improper. A hundred ears and more could overhear her, and the gossip of her enchanting powers already ran rampant enough. She spied another pair of lasses watching them and sighed in frustration. With luck, they would get a chance to talk in private later. She would have to settle for the possibility.

A hint of roasted pork basted in sage and butter reached her nose, replacing the earlier stink. She all but shoved Conall toward it, anything to remove them from where they stood before some new troop of twits happened by. The food sat on a grand table of polished oak. Silver platters held piles of fish and fowl, cheeses and olives. A raised game pie towered in the center, the pastry pressed with roses and fluted columns, baked a golden brown. It stood as high as a gentleman's top hat. Steam piped from a round hole in its top, letting out the succulent odors of venison, carrots, and onions.

Conall followed a step behind as she glided through the press. "After we dine, perhaps we should take a dance, if you'll have me," he said.

The thought brought a tingling to Effie's flesh. "Perhaps we should take all of them together. Your father would delight at such an endeavor, all his hard work scheming with Lady Fife undone in an evening of reels and waltzes."

"Aye, the scandal! It would be worth it just to see his face."

"It would at that," Effie agreed. The welcome tingling turned to apprehension as the notion of being at the heart of such a spectacle overcame her. But she swallowed down the flash of anxiety and marveled instead at the food. There had been a time in her life when she'd almost starved, and she'd seen the faces of those in the streets as her steam carriage had brought her to the ball. The city was full of unfortunate souls who'd do anything for a tenth of the tabling Lady Fife displayed. Most fared well enough only to keep from dying. It reminded her of how fortunate her life had turned, even with its dangerous and untoward moments.

She'd barely selected a slice of cheese, the piece soft and white with sweet berries running through it, when a pair of gentlemen striding for the back of the ballroom drew her attention. Out of place amongst the merriment, they held in their bearing a determination for privacy. And more than a hint of anger. The shorter one ranted in a sharp, barking whisper at his taller companion, glaring at anyone who dared approach.

Conall caught her stare. "Lord Granville must have some important business to attend with Lord Wilshire," he said. Effie gawked as Conall pointed out Lord Granville, the taller of the men. She had expected some portly blowhard with a red nose of split veins from too much drink. Instead, the leader of the treaty's opposition, at least within Parliament, was a fit and comely man of middle age. His hair was dark and finely kept, his smile genuine and countenance mirthful. Even with

Lord Wilshire blathering in his ear, Lord Granville appeared as if out on a summer stroll.

Lord Wilshire held the weight of too many pork pies in his gut, and he walked while swaying from side to side. Effie knew little of the man besides his familial bloodline, which sprung, in centuries past, from some household knight of the Duke of Norfolk. That, and that he was Lord Granville's man, through and through.

"The pawn must be very cross to address the king that way," she said, plucking up a piece of pork to go with the cheese. She wondered what they discussed. Did it have to do with the duke's absence? Or did it involve some grander scheme now that power in the negotiations had shifted further into Lord Granville's hands?

Conall eyed her warily. "Effie," he breathed. It wasn't a warning as much as a hesitant pleading.

"What?" she asked, feigning innocence as her mind worked out how best to uncover what the lords discussed. "I doubt they speak of game pie, is all I mean."

"We have our roles to play. Let Caledon and Mr. Stevenson handle London. They are more adept at politics than the both of us together."

Effie glowered at him. Caledon, the leader of the Scottish fey, and Thomas Stevenson, Effie's longtime benefactor, had made it clear the treaty negotiations were no place for one of her sex. Still, she didn't need to be scolded like a wee bairn who'd jumped in a puddle. "I don't mean to intrude on them, only perhaps to discover the subject of their conversation. I can certainly walk across the room without making a nuisance of myself."

The rebuke left Conall looking sheepish, and he knew her well enough not to argue once she had her hackles up. Spearing an olive with a delicate fork, he plopped it into his mouth and gestured for her to lead the way. "If you must," he said, though his tone made it clear he'd rather dance with an ornery badger.

His reluctance irritated her. She had no doubt he would risk life and limb for her. He had already proved as much more than once. But she was reminded again that her cause was not his cause. That the boldness of his actions sprang from a purity of morals rather an endearment with the fey, and that he had reached his position through the maneuverings of his father, not from any crusade born in his heart.

The roasted pork suddenly smelled off-putting. She winced at the thought of wasting the remainder of her portion and snatched up a napkin in which to wrap it. She would find some critter to feed it to later.

The lords had reached an exit at the back of the ballroom by the time she started after them. She tried to take an indirect route, so as not to draw any attention, but feared she would lose the gentlemen if she dawdled overmuch.

The ballroom exited into a long hallway ending at a pair of doors, one on either side. Lord Granville and Lord Wilshire slipped through the left door as she peered after them. She listened but could hear nothing beyond the clamor of the ballroom behind her—the quick pull of bows across stringed instruments, a cackle of laughter, and the booming guffaw of some gentleman. The dance floor sounded like a herd of elk marching across a frozen pond, from the click-clacking of dozens of shoes keeping time to the music.

She glanced at Conall. "You'll keep an eye out for me?" she asked.

A grin snuck onto his face, though he tried to hold it back. "As always," he said. He took the napkin from her hand and shoved it into his coat pocket. Turning, he planted himself to block the view of her from anyone watching within the ballroom.

She nodded and crept down the hallway. Portraits of the elder lords and esquires of Lady Fife's bloodline hung on the walls, their hard glares passing judgment on her. Her snooping no doubt broke what they would consider rules of decorum. A central carpet padded her steps, and she feigned as if wandering aimlessly, her interest only in taking a breath of air.

The door the men had passed through remained open, and she could hear their retreating footsteps in the room beyond as she approached. Their heels clacked across a wooden floor that creaked under their weight.

Their movement stopped and Effie paused near the doorway, not daring to peek within the room.

"...the funds to pay those men again," said a gruff voice. Anger filled his tone, though he spoke in a hushed manner.

"So pay them from the crown's purses," replied the second man. His voice was soothing and handsome. "It is all the same, and the Lord Treasurer will make an allowance for it. He is of a like mind for our efforts."

The first man growled. "They should be printing the stories themselves as God's honest citizens."

"Pshaw, nothing is accomplished by honest citizens when there is coin to be had. Now what of the other matter? I want the proposal put forth before my return to London."

The scuff of a boot snapped Effie's attention to the way she'd come, and she all but leaped from her skin. A tall fellow stood not a yard behind her, his arms thick and chest barreled. He smirked at her gasp, and she had the impression he'd made the scuffing sound on purpose. At the least, he'd traversed the entire length of the hallway without alerting her to his presence.

"I did not... Who..." Effie stammered, caught between explaining herself and demanding the man tell her who he was.

Ignoring her, he stepped forward and pressed a finger to her lips. The movement reminded her of a stalking cat, from a man well used to skulking. *Dangerous*—the word sprang to Effie's mind. She took a step back, trying to judge how quickly he could snatch her arm and whether the scheming lords would save her if she screamed.

4

"This is not the place one would expect to find the Green Lady," the man said. His breath smelled of brandy, and his tie hung crookedly. Effie noted a layer of dirt coated his boots.

"What do you want of me?" she breathed. She could see no sign of Conall. The man stood so close, she could barely see anything around his broad shoulders. Opening her fey senses, she probed her surroundings. But no cat or hound lurked nearby, and only three others of fey blood attended Lady Fife's ball. Caledon and his escort, a Sithling named Rose Brewer, stood in the ballroom. Laeth, a Sithling who'd returned from Elphame—the distant realm of the fey—strode toward them. She could sense their auras through the walls. Without thought, she sent them a blast of panic, like an alarm whistle shrilling in the dead of night.

Running his gaze over her gown, the man stepped aside. "Return to the ball before you are caught out," he said. "Spying on lords of the realm is no way for a young lady to conduct herself, and no place for a would-be ally to be discovered." Mocking filled his tone, as if he partook in some jest that she was unaware.

She eyed him askance, wanting to crack open his skull and determine what the jest meant. Yet remaining in place risked too much. The man was a rogue, clearly, and she wouldn't learn anything more from the lords while he stood there pestering her. She gripped the hem of her dress to free her legs. Stepping well clear of the man's reach, she took a few quick strides to add distance between them before slowing her pace and ambling casually back into the ballroom.

She saw where Conall had gone straight away. Lady Fife held him within her clutches, introducing him to a young lady in an amber gown. He met Effie's gaze and shrugged his shoulders. He needed her to rescue him as much as she'd needed him. But she couldn't hang on his arm the entire night. He had social duties to attend, and it would be better for him if she were elsewhere. She smiled at him and shook her head slightly.

No sooner had she turned away, than did Caledon and his companions appear before her. The Steward of the Seily Court of Righm, last Scottish host of the Daoine Sith, looked concerned. Effie knew him well enough to see it, even if others might not. He stood with a stiff and formal bearing. A hooked nose brought balance to his handsome face. His brow furrowed slightly, and his lips pressed together. Yet amusement remained in his gaze.

Effie didn't know Rose Brewer well. She'd only met the Sithling once before, but it didn't surprise her that the woman's countenance mimicked the steward's. The two were a matched pair. Ginger ringlets framed Rose's soft cheeks. A snug gown, devoid of bustle, highlighted her slender frame. Effie guessed it a new fashion from France. It made her stand out amongst the other ladies in attendance, though her elegant features held no arrogance in them. Rose had returned to Scotland the previous year from a small hamlet in the Kingdom of Norway. There, she'd lived among the Huldrefolk, teaching their culled numbers the auld ways of veiling themselves from sight. She knew much of Fey Craft and of fey lore, Caledon had told Effie, more than any Scottish fey remaining within the empire.

Laeth she knew slightly better. He had answered Caledon's call for aid and returned from Elphame to fight at Caldwell House. He wore his formal attire like a child might, as if he wanted nothing more than to rip off his coat and dash through a puddle. He'd pulled his silver hair into a tail that fell below his shoulders.

"You gave us a fright," said Caledon.

Effie glanced down the hallway but saw no sign of the rogue. *Had the man vanished into thin air?* Effie's brow wrinkled in puzzlement. "There was a man who came upon me all of a sudden. I..." She shook her head to clear her thoughts. "I'm sorry for raising an alarm. I am all right now. It was nothing."

Caledon studied her for a moment before speaking. "You have no cause to apologize, Effie of Glen Coe. The gravest threat is that which is ignored."

Rose Brewer burst into laughter. "Do you always offer such a mystical speech?" she asked. "The lass did not ask for your tutelage, aged as it may be."

The steward grinned, but his attention shifted as another man stepped before them and bowed. Sir Walter Conrad's dark eyes rested atop gaunt cheeks. His coat and shirt were starched stiff, and every lock of raven hair was held meticulously in place. Effie's loathing of the geologist hadn't slackened since their first meeting years before, when she'd been a prisoner of the crown and he had sought to exploit her for his own greedy ends. But desperate times had made for desperate allies, and they had come to a cordial understanding of one another.

Caledon bowed in return, as he would to a cherished friend. His civility was well practiced. Laeth followed his lead. Rose and Effie returned rather shallow curtseys.

"I trust you are having a wonderful evening at Lady Fife's expense," said Sir Walter. "Mr. Stevenson appeared so when last I saw him in the drawing room." He smiled at Effie, and she could see his sharp mind at work behind the gaze. "He will stand as president of the Royal Society of Edinburgh. It is as great an honor as a Scottish engineer can receive. A proud achievement for his name, especially for one who would rather debate scientific principles than politics."

"He is honored and the position well deserved," answered Effie as politely as she could, though they both knew it would divert Stevenson's attention from the treaty. Sir Walter's subtle reminder made her stew. The man would riffle through every stone in a desert if it would find him a speck of gold.

She wished Stuart Graham attended the ball. For all his preaching of etiquette, he rumbled like a starving bear around Sir Walter. It made for an entertaining sport, even if a bit cruel for Graham to have to suffer. But Graham's business interests had kept him away. His workers threatened to halt progress on the construction projects he endeavored. They were caught up in the same fervor spreading throughout the empire, their dispute not with Graham himself but with the treatment of other tradesmen. Still, it was a humbling blow for a man who thrived on his respect as an employer.

"How go the treaty negotiations?" Sir Walter asked Caledon.

The steward regarded him calmly. "Negotiations will commence in three days' time," he said.

"Formal negotiations," corrected Sir Walter. "But the heavy work has already begun. Our opposition spins webs in every corner of the empire. Or did you think the broadsheets in London printed themselves? Those incessant accounts of beasts ravaging livestock and a duke enthralled by a fey sorceress?"

A connection clicked in Effie's head. Lord Granville's talk of funding and printing stories. She balled her fists, furious the man spread such vile propaganda. It was one thing to read such hideous things, quite another to know the words were purposefully meant to sway the public mind.

"The Green Lady," laughed Rose. "I'd forgotten I stood near such a nefarious seductress."

Effie snorted. She should never have joined the procession through the Highlands. Sir Walter and Thomas Stevenson had convinced her to take part. She'd worn an emerald gown of silk, spotted with pearls and trimmed with silver lace. And ever since, the tales of her actions during the Battle of Caldwell House had melded with those of the royal procession, becoming a fancy of witless imagination and untoward gossip.

Sir Walter clucked his tongue. "Humor alone will not ensure our issues are addressed," he said.

"You have done more than enough to demonstrate the advantage of our position, Sir Walter," said Caledon. "It will speak for our cause as you know it must."

Effie knew the steward meant Aerfenium, or rather, the uses of the substance the empire could exploit for its benefit. The volatile gas was a product of Fey Craft the fey called Aegirsigath. It bound the Sidhe

Bhreige in the Downward Fields, keeping their kind from terrorizing the Earth. Producing more of it had become the central issue of the negotiations. Caledon had agreed to call it by the name Sir Walter had dubbed it before becoming aware of its nature. Sir Walter had urged him to do so in part because it removed the stigma of its fey origin, but also because, named as an element, it served to remind people of its scientific potential. Already, a scramble had begun to patent uses of the substance. As a highly combustible gas, it burned hotter than coal, burned longer, and was far lighter to store. It would allow steam carriages to travel at higher speeds and airships to carry larger loads, travelling farther distances. The possibilities weren't bound by transportation, either. Radio waves could be exploited for communication, manufacturing increased, and the gas itself sold as a commodity.

"Yes," agreed Sir Walter. "The treaty will pass, but at what expense? The crown will gobble up every ounce of Aerfenium in the name of national defense. To protect our coastline, our cities, they will cry. I can hear them already, squawking in the backrooms of gentlemen's clubs."

"The fey will bear the greater cost," said Caledon. His meaning was clear. Supplying the empire with Aerfenium was tantamount to a tax levied against the fey in exchange for citizenship, and once such a barter existed, how long would it last before more was demanded by the crown and less received by the fey? "It is why we must demand creation of it within Elphame, so we will not become enslaved by such aggressive positions."

"Aye," agreed Laeth. Caledon had placed the Sithling in charge of the storehouse where they stored the crown's measure of Aerfenium. "And so it can be protected. The buggers be halfwits if they think they can use the stuff for long afore other empires come clamoring for it."

"How goes the containment technology?" asked Effie. Curiosity of such engineering feats always begged her interest, and she wanted to change the subject. She had heard Sir Walter and Caledon banter often enough in the past months. "Will they have the valves you suggested for safely releasing the gas into a feeder line?" Such a standardized means of delivering the gas as a fuel would greatly accelerate the development of devices using the substance.

"The tubes are being pressed as we speak," said Sir Walter, "though at a high personal cost."

"We all have our burdens," said Rose. Her eyes danced over to Effie, who turned away to hide her amusement.

Sir Walter tugged at his sleeve. "The crown remains rooted in the past. They should see reason and shove the cost of fey investigations onto those towns who bring charges. Let the accusers pay for the Fey Finders. The empire's funds are better spent furthering the adoption of Aerfenium, and the shift would kill two birds—faced with the financial burden themselves, towns and villages would be less inclined persecute the fey."

"Leaving the crown with enough coin to pay for your tubes," said Effie. "It is a noble suggestion." She kept her tone polite despite the derision her words implied. She'd heard his argument before. It was typical of the man, a solution that didn't address a problem directly but would still feed money his way. "Would the Hostmen of Newcastle agree with it? It is the coal barons' coin you spend, is it not?"

Sir Walter's pressed lips were all the answer she required. He made a mocking bow, conceding her point. She had only a hint of satisfaction before his eyes lit up. "Lord Granville," he said and bowed again, this time deeper.

She started and turned. The lord had come to stand behind her. He had his head bent as he checked his watch, a gold-plated piece scrolled with roses. His gaze rose at hearing his name. She stepped aside to allow him into their group, and a sudden impulse made her study his shoes. They were clean and polished, as they should be. Wherever the rogue had come from or fled to, the lord apparently hadn't followed.

Sir Walter introduced her, and she curtseyed. Lord Granville's smile was infectious, surrounded as it was by the dimples of his cheeks and chin. He bowed low to her and even took her hand into his, lightly brushing his lips across the back of it. "I hope you won't enthrall me as you did the duke," he said. The jest shone in his eyes with no malice intended, yet Effie knew he'd chosen his words with care. She recognized the handsome voice from earlier. His words then had been spoken in the same manner, despite their vile content.

"I had the good fortune of your daughter's introduction earlier, my lord," replied Effie. "She is quite charming, and I believe she has a better chance of enthralling the Fey Finder General than I do, your lordship."

Lord Granville laughed. "Please forgive her. She is only recently out in society, and her mother bade me bring her north to visit with her aunt." He turned to Caledon. "Master Steward, I trust you are finding accommodations to your liking here in this fine city. Glasgow is a model for the rest of the empire, so we may ensure our prosperity in the generations to come."

"We have received a grand reception, my lord," said Caledon simply.

"Good," said Lord Granville. "Now, if you will excuse my abruptness, I have other matters to attend. I trust you will rest and rally your strength. I'm afraid the negotiations will be a trying ordeal for your cause. There are many still in the empire who don't value the details of how your brethren aided the duke against our common enemy. Their minds are closed, and they see what they've always seen, a fey adversary that needs to be put down lest it savage the hand that shows it kindness."

Effie bristled. The man was brazen to threaten Caledon so openly. "Closed minds are rarely changed through the reinforcement of ignorant principles, as you well know, my lord. Perhaps if the newspapers entertained more favorable accounts of our aid?"

Lord Granville's smile only widened. But an uproar from the front of the house silenced whatever he thought to say. A shriek rang out followed by several shouts. The music stopped, and all heads turned. Those toward the front of the ballroom began to press back. Somewhere, a table overturned. The clatter of plates hitting the wood floor sparked a new round of shrill cries. Effie could feel the panic rising in the room.

"Gentlemen! Ladies!" hollered Lord Granville. He pressed forward with his arms raised. "Do contain yourselves."

Effie followed in the lord's wake. She moved without any consideration not to, curiosity willing her forward. Reaching out with her senses, she could feel a mass of bodies gathered outside the house, though she couldn't tell anything more about them. Caledon's empowered steward's blood lent her the strength of a small fey host, but Fey Craft could not tell her everything. She lost sight of Lord Granville as she pushed into the tide of bodies. Most forced their way in the opposite direction.

She had just reached one of the large windows near the front of the house—so much glass, a display of Lady Fife's wealth—when a flaming bottle shattered it. Jagged shards blasted into the room like a hailstorm. A whoosh of flames licked the walls and spread in a wide pool, fueled by whatever liquid the bottle contained.

Effie spun and shielded herself with her arms. Pinpricks of glass stung her flesh, but she ignored them. Reaching for a tablecloth, she yanked it free. Delicate bowls and porcelain cups flew to the floor in a loud crash. But they could be replaced. If the fire spread, the entire house could be lost. With the ballroom crowded as it was, Effie feared how many would be trapped if that occurred.

A woman brushed past. Her arm bled, and she wailed in panic as a gentleman ushered her away. A long cut marred his face from the flying glass. Heat from the fire roasted Effie's skin as she shoved forward and began beating at the flames.

She became dimly aware of a chorus of guttural shouts booming in from outside. Smoke filled her nostrils, coming off the scorched walls. Her arms tired. The tablecloth singed until only a tattered mess remained.

But others joined the fight. A younger man came forward with a pot and dashed the walls with a plum sauce. Someone threw a plate of rice on the floor where the liquid burned, and soon a convoy of cups and bowls were passed to those in front, their contents poor, yet adequate, substitutes for water and sand.

The fire quieted. Effie coughed on the harsh taste of ash and stepped closer to the open air. She had only a moment to recognize her mistake before a rock sailed past her head. Ducking into as much of a crouch as her gown allowed, she spied dozens of masked figures on the garden lawn.

"No treaty!" one yelled, while another bellowed, "Kill the fey!"

Rocks clanged off the front of the house, and she realized they hadn't targeted her as much as anyone and anything moving within the house. Dread overtook her. She had never witnessed such hatred of her kind *en masse*.

A firm hand snatched her arm and yanked her to her feet. The roguish man from the hallway chuckled as she yelped and batted at him.

"Come, Effie of Glen Coe," he breathed. "It seems I must rescue you once more." She pried at his fingers, but his grip was too strong. He marched her through the ballroom, and she shuffled after him, forced to match his stride lest she be dragged behind.

5

Effie snatched a candlestick as they passed a table set along the ballroom wall. Its wick was lit, and she quickly blew it out before swinging it at the man. She saw no need to spread another fire after just fighting the other. But the delay allowed him to spring away, bending back at the waist to avoid the strike.

"Unhand me and tell me who you are at once!" she demanded. Her eyes searched the ballroom for any familiar faces and found none. Barely anyone remained, and those who did hurried about their own business, either fleeing or rushing toward the front of the house. Both groups had blind eyes for Effie's struggle.

"Jack Canonbie," said her assailant. Mirth reflected in his gaze, yet not the cheeriness Caledon's held, but rather that after a crude jest. "Mr. Stevenson bid me fetch you, if you have a mind to see him."

Effie's eyes narrowed. Her employment with Thomas Stevenson was now common knowledge. That the man knew the connection proved nothing. He read her look and laughed. "Do you suppose yourself such a prize that I would devise some scheme to draw you into a dark corner of the house?" He spread his arms, indicating the chaos around them. "There are a hundred safer ways to abduct you, if that be my aim. Perhaps on your carriage ride home to Bonny Law?"

A jolt passed through her. She had dubbed her simple cottage near the Campsie Fells that name as a private joke to remind her of its beauty and isolation. She wondered how the man had known it.

He read her thoughts again. "Mr. Conall Murray told me that name. Did he not tell you of me? Judging by the look on your face, I can't imagine why he would've avoided such a topic. Now, if you please?" He held out an arm for her to take.

"There is no call for such rudeness," Effie snapped. It rankled her she could not see through the man's game.

"Ha!" The man tilted his head back and bellowed. Her face flushed in outrage. "Is it propriety you're claiming now?" he asked. "And I'd have thought yer skirts a clever ruse only meant to play at society."

He beckoned and took a few strides, watching her over his shoulder. She glowered at him and considered. The man had a point. If he'd wanted to bring her harm, he could've done so at a more opportune time. He could've done so earlier. And as crude as he'd been, he had pulled her away from danger twice, albeit in his own uncouth way. Her arm had a dull ache from where he'd grabbed her, but she refused to rub it. She wouldn't show any frailty to him, though she didn't know why she would care about his opinion.

Resigned, she strode after him with her chin held high. He fell in next to her as she passed, this time keeping his hands to himself. They left the clamor behind, as whistles shrilled in the night and footsteps thundered through the garden. Jack Canonbie led them through the same hallway she'd encountered him in earlier. Yet as they approached the hall's end, he suddenly veered a dozen paces short of the doors and came to a stop.

Raising an eyebrow, he indicated the wall before them. Effie's brow furrowed. She could read nothing in the man's expression beyond an annoying level of amusement at her expense. Planting her hands on her hips, she studied where he pointed. Her breath caught. She made out the outline of another door perfectly cut into the wall between two of the family portraits. It was narrow and flush against the rest of the wall, but also obvious to anyone who looked close enough. Hidden from plain view, yet not undetectable. Something built in for the house's servants, it had to be. She'd been so determined to catch Lord Granville earlier, she'd missed it completely.

Canonbie pushed on the wall, and the door swung open without a sound. He held it while she passed through into a narrow corridor beyond. Following, he set the door back into place. The walls within the corridor were bare stone. A cold draft blew between them. Effie's arms pimpled, and she hugged herself for warmth.

"A servant's passage," he confirmed. "Lady Fife believes the blessing of her employment warmth enough to stave off any chill."

Effie cocked her head. Up close, the man's eyes were lighter than she'd first thought, and bluer. It was the scruff on his cheeks that made his countenance seem darker. "Were you spying on me earlier?" she asked.

He shook his head and chuckled. "Spying? Nay. If it were that, you wouldn't have seen me, would you?"

The answer didn't bring her any comfort. "So it was some random act that brought you to warn me away from my...endeavor?"

His grin spread, revealing a bold set of pearly teeth. With dimples and a strong chin, he was a handsome man. She would allow him that. "A woman's curiosity can bring her danger. So Jack Canonbie made his service known. A good timing for it, too. The lords made their retreat not soon after, and you'd have been caught with yer corset in a bind."

Effie took a deep breath. She refused to let the man rankle her. She'd heard cruder talk many times before. The craftsmen at Stevenson's worksites could be as lewd as any in the empire, and Canonbie had aided her, if he could be believed.

"After I left, did they discuss...certain things further?" she asked.

Canonbie's jaw quivered, but he bit back whatever jape had come to mind and simply nodded his head. "Aye, they did indeed. This Lord Wilshire is to make a grand proposal. He will ask Parliament to find a permanent island colony for the fey, where your kind can live in freedom. Well, in freedom but still under the watchful eye of the empire, of course."

Effie gasped. "He means to create a penal colony?" Such things had all but ended with the Australian colonies decades before. Yet for centuries its practice had been a favored solution for political and religious malcontents.

"People fear the fey will mass together and use their Fey Craft against the empire, or so the lords proclaim." He waved toward the front of the house. "And now they have the Sanctity of Empire League to herald their claims."

Jerking, Effie blinked. "You know of those rioters outside?"

"Aye, the brazen louts. They and a few other gangs have been pressing folk on the streets, warning against a fey alliance. Didn't think they'd ever stage so violent an assault, truth be told. They're a cowardly lot, mostly, whispering threats in dark alleys and such, but never forming a visible front. They must've found some incentive, and not a small one at that." He rubbed his fingers along his thumb to make his meaning clear.

Effie thought on that while they moved through the corridor, twisting through the innards of the house before emerging into a private study. A fire blazed within the hearth, its crackling a blissful sound for the warmth it signaled. A large desk sat next to it, cleared of any papers, and a bookcase half full with leather bound tomes was built into one wall. Only the fire and a few candles lit the room, but Effie recognized Conall Murray and Thomas Stevenson immediately. They conversed quietly, turning as Effie entered.

"Effie," said Conall. He hurried across the room. Concern painted his face as he took in the state of her appearance.

She rubbed at the soot on her arms and dress. "I am unharmed. At least, nothing you need worry about. But we must assure the rioters are dealt with."

"They will be," assured Thomas Stevenson.

He came and clutched her shoulders as a father would, taking in her bearing. The man had sheltered her as a young lass, after the death of her mother. When she'd reached adulthood, he'd hired her to render his lighthouse designs in fanciful drawings. He used those to engage funding for the projects. But more than employment, he'd given her a life, one she could call her own, where she lived among family, pursuing a livelihood she enjoyed.

She took his hands and breathed in the gentle hint of wine and pipe smoke wafting from his coat. His face had aged, but it still held vigor. He was a man of propriety and a naturist who blended science and nature into his engineering works. She loved him for all of it.

As he released her, he said, "It is well to see you are unharmed." Their eyes met, and a part of her exhaustion and worry faded away.

"You must accept my apology for earlier," said Conall. "Lady Fife pulled me from my post, and I could not let her see you return to the ballroom." His eyes flicked to Canonbie, and he offered a short nod. He clearly wasn't surprised to see the man. Effie frowned at that as she accepted Conall's apology.

Stevenson raised an arm toward the rogue. "Mr. Canonbie comes well recommended," he said. "You will also have to accept my apology, I fear, for the introduction was poorly done. I had not expected the evening to turn so adventurous and had planned on informing you on the morrow."

Effie turned between the men. "I don't understand. Mr. Canonbie comes recommended for what purpose?"

"I have hired him to protect your person," said Stevenson.

"No!" Effie barked. She cringed straight away. The exclamation sounded like a pouty child, but she couldn't fathom what madness had grasped Stevenson.

"These are less than certain times," he explained. "The attack we witnessed tonight could've occurred just as easily in any town or village in the empire. And you have a penchant for running afoul of such things." He clasped his hands behind his back. "I do not seek to alter your convictions, merely to place a capable defender in the way of any harm."

"A mercenary," cried Effie.

"An associate," corrected Conall. "I was likewise opposed until Mr. Stevenson and Mr. Graham convinced me the matter is no different than when I travel with Lieutenant Walford and Her Majesty's soldiers. Besides, it is better to practice caution than to regret it."

"Then I will choose the good Lieutenant to defend me," Effie snapped. It vexed her even further that Stuart Graham and Conall Murray were involved. Had all the men in her life conspired against her? Did they think her so fragile a thing?

Canonbie grunted. "A lesser man would take offense."

Stevenson politely ignored the comment. "I have other urgent matters and cannot attend to you as I once did. Mr. Murray is likewise engaged by the crown's desires."

Effie studied Stevenson's unwavering gaze and knew she'd have an easier time turning stone to mud than changing his resolve. She would have to suffer Jack Canonbie for at least a while longer, until she could find a means to dismiss him.

With a deep breath, she relented, nodding her consent.

"Good," said Stevenson. He clasped his hands behind his back. "Now if you please, Mr. Canonbie will see you safely from the city. There may be greater danger lurking in the streets over the oncoming fortnight."

"Those rioters..." Effie began, but Canonbie spoke over her.

"The Sanctity of Empire League," he said. "I will inform the constables, if they are not aware already." He mimicked Stevenson's posture. "I am sure by now the crowd has been dispersed."

Effie's fists clenched on her dress, but she managed to keep her voice from rising. "That is all and well, but what of those within the house? We must see that everyone is safe and not in need of aid."

"This is Lady Fife's estate," said Stevenson. He scratched at his chin and turned away. "She will ably see to what must be done. We would not want to overstep our place and give her insult."

Effie swung her gaze to Conall, but the Fey Finder General offered little support. "As you say, Mr. Stevenson," he said. "It is not our place. I will, however, offer our sympathy and pledge assistance for whatever aid she might require."

"I am sure she could not appreciate anything more," said Effie. She almost laughed at the absurdity. Once again, she'd been reminded that despite her role at Caldwell House, and the matters before and after, she held little influence and even less authority.

Color rose to Conall's cheeks at the chiding.

"Fair enough," said Canonbie, taking in the exchange. He clapped his hands and rubbed them together, staring a little too eagerly at Effie's gown. "Where are we staying the night?"

❧ 6 ❧

The steam carriage jostled Effie as it struck a rut in the broad road leading north from Glasgow. Rain pattered the roof in a steady drumming, stealing away the clamor of the crowded city. Fresh pine and sweet heather filled the air, their scents damp and pungent, replacing that of coal smog and human waste. Effie welcomed the changes. Cities could be wondrous places. Full of spectacle, they often harbored the minds that drove forward invention. Yet she would never feel at home in such crowded warrens. They reminded her too much of what she had learned to fear all her life—the oppression of strangers.

She eyed Jack Canonbie at the thought. The man sat on the bench across from her, next to Rose Brewer. He had traded his evening wear for a rugged brown coat and olive trousers. The grip of a small, two-chambered pistol stuck out from a pocket in his waistcoat. A thick cane rested against his knees. The wood was chipped in places and well worn. It had clearly seen other uses besides a gentle stroll through the park.

Rose had also changed. Her aesthetic dress flowed loosely about her body. It had no bustle or gathering of skirts, only a simple belt to pull it in at the waist and give a hint of shape. Such things were currently favored in Bohemian circles. A straw hat held a sprig of flowers that matched the print on the dress's fabric. Rose clutched the hat in her lap, studying Effie. She needed neither pistol nor cane to appear dangerous. There was an ageless void behind her gaze that spoke of power. The Laird of Aonghus had held the same cast, though in a far less pleasant manner. Effie guessed it came from surviving so many decades in a world of hunter and hunted.

"I knew your mother," the Sithling woman said as they trundled along. "Did you know that?"

Effie shook her head. She'd been surprised to find Rose waiting in the carriage. Their sex rather than their fey blood kept them from any direct involvement in the negotiations, though Effie had assumed the woman would remain near Caledon to offer advisement. That the debate over all she desired would take place without them unsettled her, but she could see no way around it. She'd spied the place where the men would gather as she departed the city's center, a domed building of sandstone blackened by years of coal soot. A line of wilted trees struggled for life before its entrance. She hoped the sight not an omen for the fate of their kind.

"I didn't," she replied. "Did you know her well?"

Rose grinned. "No one knew your mother well. She was banished from the Seily Court, and those that would speak with her she rarely received."

Effie frowned at that. "Caledon said she chose to live in isolation after my grandfather's dishonor." The words panged her to speak aloud. She glanced at Jack Canonbie. The man stared out the carriage window, yet Effie became uncomfortably aware of his attention. She didn't trust him.

At Lady Fife's, she'd waited for him to depart—off to arrange their departure—before she'd told Conall and Stevenson what she'd learned of Lord Granville's designs. Conall had given a melancholic groan. Stevenson had grown pensive, pinching his lips between his fingers as he stared into Lady Fife's hearth. He'd bade them both to keep the matter quiet for a time so he could consult with his friends in London. Something might be done to thwart the plots, but it must be subtle, lest tensions escalate openly. A public row would play too much into the lord's favor, and any direct accusation would no doubt slide off him like water from a duck's back.

Rose's brow raised, but she continued to grin. "When one is shunned by their own society, the concepts of banishment and isolation by choice become a mere matter of perspective. But that is not to say your mother was not a strong woman. She followed her own path and wouldn't let anyone dissuade her from it."

Effie's heart suddenly grew lighter as she realized why the woman had asked to join their journey to Bonny Law.

Caledon.

The steward had no doubt instigated the matter. He understood the bulk of Effie's knowledge sprang only from the fading memories of childhood. She had been a mere girl when her mother had passed, at an age when adult considerations rarely kept her thoughts. She hadn't known then what questions to ask, or why. It had left her with many gaps, even when it came to her own family. Rose had lived in the Highlands for more than a century, her blood holding a longevity beyond that of even common fey. That she might fill some of those gaps flooded Effie with a rush of joy and curiosity.

"How so?" Effie asked eagerly.

"There are many tales," said Rose. "But here is one such. During the potato famines thirty years past, Caledon sent for all fey to rejoin the court. That foul man, the Earl of Derby, had proclaimed Fey Craft the cause of the blight and directed funds from Parliament toward a grand Inquiry. Caledon believed if the fey were to survive, they would need to rally together and use their combined strength to veil themselves from the influx of Fey Finders."

Rose paused for a moment, as if remembering. "Not your mother. She ignored his call and took up with a village baker on the Isle of Stronsay. It was said he fell madly for her. Theirs was a secret affair, however, as the crown's agents scoured the countryside searching for fey to hang as scapegoats for their failing economy and blighted crops."

"Were they found out?" asked Effie. She shifted to the lip of the carriage's padded bench, excited to hear such a tale of her mother's adventures. The potato famine had ended a decade before her birth.

"Sadly," said Rose. "The baker supplied food for the local kelp fishermen. One of these men owed the baker some debt, and when your mother's lover came to collect he found one of the Sniffers waiting. He was jailed for conspiring with an enemy of the crown but refused to give up your mother."

"Oh, heavens!" gasped Effie. "What did she do?"

Rose smiled and patted Effie's knee. "Why, she fled, dearie."

Effie blinked. "She left him imprisoned?"

"There was not much she could do at the time. She had no fey allies to lend her strength, and she had chosen to make few friends. It was flight or surrender, and your mother was not one to bend a knee to anyone."

"How awful," said Effie. She didn't know what to make of the story. If it were her in her mother's shoes, she could not imagine leaving a loved one behind, not even to save herself. She could barely imagine leaving a stranger behind in the clutches of the Sniffers.

"In the end, the baker understood. The Earl of Derby's government collapsed, and in time the famine lifted and the Inquiry was put to rest. So many of those on Stronsay defended the baker's character that he was soon released."

"A happy ending, then?" asked Jack Canonbie. He no longer feigned disinterest.

"Aye." Rose leaned back in her seat and regarded Effie. "I believe you know the rest of the tale," she said, with more than a hint of mischief.

"Ha!" barked Canonbie, catching the meaning faster than Effie.

Her jaw worked for a moment before it fell open. She felt like she'd been punched in the stomach. "They reunited?" she asked.

"Some years later, so it is said, though I never met the man. Nor do I know of one who has. He died of an ailment shortly after your birth."

Tears rushed to Effie's eyes, born of a sadness she hadn't known she'd locked away. Her mother had raised her alone. It had always been just the two of them. Her mother's brother had fled to Elphame before she was born, and when she'd asked of her father, her mother had merely said he'd travelled between the worlds and would not return. The answer had felt honest enough for a young girl. Older, she had only known not to search for him.

She'd had so many questions about her mother's family that she'd never thought to ask Caledon, or any of the fey court, about her father. The scandal with her grandfather had blinded her in that regard. Most in the court considered Arnwyrd to be a traitor, and her mother's decision to live in isolation, rather than face the shame of a dishonored name, a continuance of that betrayal.

Canonbie held out a handkerchief. She took it and clutched it in her lap, staring at her hands. She wanted to thank him, but her thoughts refused to connect. Her mind had become a castle of sand, and a giant wave pounded it apart. She felt scattered. A part of her wanted to rush to Stronsay and see where her parents had dwelt. Another wanted her to curl up her legs and close her eyes. The need for rest suddenly overwhelmed her.

Most of all, she wanted to understand why her parents had been taken away. Why had she little chance to know them? She bowed her head lower. Her shoulders sagged. It was a child's thought, she knew, one of dreams better left alone before they turned into wallowing.

A pinprick of heat, like that of a tiny sun, blossomed before her nose. Her eyes widened as its warmth spread to her cheeks and down her shoulders and chest. The curiosity over it lightened her spirit. She reached up but could not touch its source. Her fingers passed through the heat as if they ran over the top of a lit candle.

And then awareness dawned on her.

"Is it Fey Craft?" she asked Rose. The tiny ball of heat disappeared, gone as quickly as it had come. No residue of warmth remained. Like the setting sun, it left no touch. Rose winked, and Effie sat dumbfounded that such a thing was possible. It hadn't been a vision pushed into her thoughts. She had felt the warmth from the outside as it pressed against her flesh.

"But how?" she blurted. "If you can warm the air, can you also freeze it?"

Canonbie's eyebrow raised. He shifted in his seat, his gaze flicking between the two women. Effie caught his confusion. The man hadn't felt anything!

Rose remained silent, regarding her. Like the tale of her father, the woman wanted her to deduce her own conclusion.

"The air never truly warmed," said Effie. She considered what that meant. "I felt it on my flesh, but only because you somehow convinced me of its presence."

"Sight is not the only sense," said Rose. "Such things were once called glamours. Not many fey use them these days. There is not enough strength of blood for most, and the skill of how to craft them requires a practiced hand."

Effie had done wondrous things herself with Fey Craft, sending out vague mental images. But the only time she'd experienced such a concrete sensation was from the Sidhe Bhreige. "The Piper of Ceann Rois used Blood Craft to construct his glamours," she said, remembering. At Caldwell House, the demon spiders he'd made appear, raking her flesh to the bone and dripping their venomous ichor, still haunted her nightmares.

Rose sniffed, as if smelling something foul. "The blunt force of Blood Craft is favored by those without patience. It is telling that his thirst for power outweighed any masterful skill."

"Does that tell us something of his escaped brethren?" asked Effie. "Whatever or whomever it is, it didn't immediately quest for power through the use of Blood Craft. Does that make it more dangerous?" The two defeated Sidhe Bhreige, for all their tricks, had used hammers to carve out their dominance—big, noisy hammers that had drawn the attention of the Highlands and forced the crown to respond with regiments of soldiers. That the third hadn't, had allowed it to remain hidden.

"Perhaps," said Rose. "Or perhaps it is merely too weak or too feeble of mind after millennia imprisoned in the Downward Fields."

A chill passed up Effie's spine. Arrogance had led to the downfall of both the Piper of Ceann Rois and the Laird of Aonghus. Both had compelled their minions by force rather than inspiring any willing devotion, and when she'd stolen that control away, it exposed them to defeat. She didn't want to fathom a more subtle foe.

"None to worry, lass," said Canonbie. "This last devil is not like to come hunting for you. Ye'll be safe abed at home when word comes that the crown has dealt with it."

Effie glowered. *Safe abed?* Why did the man seek to vex her so fully? She took a deep breath and relaxed her grip on the handkerchief he'd so kindly offered her. Perhaps she angered more because the man touched on a solid point. Would she be safe at home when word came? Certainly, she had no intention of hunting the creature herself. She had barely escaped Caldwell House with her life. She was no fighter.

Nor was she a politician. The maneuvers within courts and balls, backrooms and on a grand stage, left her nauseous. The stink of such murky dealings grated her to the core. Besides, it wasn't as if she'd been invited to take part in the negotiations, even if she'd desired it. She had no station of note and no family name. Her sex alone barred her from the table. The gathered lords would rather her fetch them tea than hear her speak.

But that left her without a place. To hang on the arm of Stevenson or Conall, or even Caledon, was not the same as having a purpose. Stevenson's projects had mostly concluded, the bulk of his time spent with the Royal Society. So she had no rendering work to occupy her time. In truth, despite her failings at Langmire, her travels with the Fey Finders, on Conall's behalf, had provided more fulfillment than anything else since Caldwell House.

She glanced at Canonbie. A fighter she might not be, but she had to help the fey cause somehow. The Sanctity of Empire League he had named the gang who swarmed Lady Fife's estate. The man had also insinuated the gang's appearance not a random act. Someone had spurred them on. If she could unravel such a plot, it might give Caledon the leverage he needed to win some point in the negotiations. More so, denouncing the rising anti-fey sentiment as an orchestrated political design might prove to the populace they had nothing to fear from a fey treaty.

Yet where would she start? Her foot tapped. Stuart Graham always said two heads were better than one. But ten heads devoid of wit stood no better than none. She studied her travelling companions. Rose meant to journey onward to Skye after a respite at Bonny Law. She would have to make use of their time together and pick the woman's mind for all she could. As for Jack Canonbie, he certainly appeared to harbor knowledge of dastardly schemes. But could she rely on him? What she needed was someone on her side. Someone tough. Someone who wanted to tear down those who targeted the fey as much as she did.

A face popped into her head, and she smiled. She knew the perfect brownie. Jaelyn of Clan Kae had stood with her at Caldwell House and would aid her again if called. Effie only needed a means of contacting her. Thomas Stevenson had developed a wireless telegram device powered by stardust—a fey substance that burned hotter than coal but not nearly as hot as Aerfenium. But the air broadcasting devices were too expensive to construct for her to have one at her cottage. Only a few were ever built. And besides, even if she had one, it wouldn't do her any good unless the person she communicated with also had one. Yet perhaps Fey Craft provided a better way.

"How did Caledon send for my mother?" she asked Rose. "You said he sent for her during the potato famine, but how did he know where to find her? Surely he cannot sense the location of every fey across the entire empire."

"The steward's blood is a powerful thing," said Rose. She eyed Canonbie and paused to choose her words. "His sending required an intimacy that is beyond what you or I could accomplish, accept for our dearest of friends. Even still, his reach is limited to those within our court."

Effie chewed her lip. She caught Rose's hesitancy and decided to wait before pressing the woman further. There was no need for everyone to hear her plans, even if that everyone contained only a single, loutish man.

The rain had stopped by the time they reached the village of Westley. The hour had turned late. A fog rolled through the streets, obscuring the row of tidy cottages and bringing a chill to the night air. Effie tapped the carriage roof, and a groan sounded from the engine as their driver pulled a lever to disengage the boiler. A jerking rattle started as the brake locked in, and they slowly squealed to a halt.

Canonbie peered out the window. "Looks like an inn," he said. The two-storied building had boxes of bright flowers under a pair of cheery windows. A wooden sign hung on the door. The Swan Inn, it read. A depiction of the bird did the sign justice, though the paint needed touching up.

"Your lodgings while under Mr. Stevenson's employment," said Effie.

He smirked. "And how am I to watch over you if I'm not near?"

"Certainly, you do not intend to stay at my cottage?" countered Effie.

"A single man slumbering unsupervised near an unmarried woman? That wouldn't be proper."

"Aye, what would the neighbors think?" he scoffed. He glanced up and down the quiet street. "It's late. Everyone sleeps."

"You can wake Mrs. Darning. She will see you to a bed. Inform her I apologize for the inconvenience of the hour." Effie locked eyes with Canonbie. "I can give you coin, if you need it."

The man didn't budge from his seat. His eyebrow raised.

Effie sighed. "I give you my word that I will not leave Bonny Law without calling on you to accompany me. But there is nothing more you can do there. It is a simple cottage not a mile up the road. I will be perfectly safe."

Canonbie turned to Rose, who laughed without bothering to muffle it. "Don't turn to me for support," she said. "A woman's cottage is her palace, as the wisdom goes."

Grunting, the man relented. He opened the carriage door and stepped down. The driver had already pulled his supple leather bag from the rack above and left it for him on the ground. Canonbie hefted it. Bowing to both women, he said, "Don't do nothing foolish. Jack Canonbie's got a name to protect."

Effie caught something in his look. The way his breathing deepened and grin wavered appeared like genuine concern. But for whom? She nodded to him as the driver clambered to his perch and reengaged the engine. The carriage shook and the boiler sputtered. Steam clogged the air as the wheels trundled forward once more.

"There is a man I would not play at dice with," said Rose, once they had passed from Canonbie's hearing.

Effie snorted. "Or anything else." When Rose's eyes twinkled, she huffed indignantly. "Don't make me imagine such a thing. It brings a horror to mind."

"And what of Mr. Murray?" asked Rose. "Does he bring on such a revulsion?"

Effie's cheeks tingled from the rush of blood. "I will keep my thoughts on Mr. Murray to myself, if it please you," she said as politely as she could. Her thoughts on that matter were complicated, and time and distance had lessened the urgency of them. She and Conall had no future together while he remained in the grip of his father's designs, and where she had once thought she could find happiness in a dalliance with him, she now regarded him too strong a friend to risk over something so temporary.

"Oh, very well," said Rose, her tone full of mocking disappointment.

Wishing to change the subject, Effie tried to relax the tightness that had come to her shoulders. "If I sought a dear friend with the same means Caledon had used," she started to ask, before the carriage ground to a sudden, jerking halt. The motion threw her forward and almost off the bench. She put out an arm to brace herself.

"What is it?" she shouted to the driver.

"Someone in the road, miss," the man replied. "I could barely see for the fog."

Effie stuck her head out the window and let out a panicked gasp. An apparition stood in the fog before the carriage. Dark eyes glinted in the light of the carriage's front lamps. A pale shock of hair fell around a paler face. Something like horns stuck out from its temples. The white shroud it wore cloaked its form, and it stood motionless except for a single raised arm. A bony finger pointed straight at Effie.

"Finally, I have found you," croaked a soft whisper.

Effie swallowed hard, wishing Canonbie had left her his pistol.

7

Effie's blood raced. Her heart thudded in her chest, threatening to break her ribs. Reaching out with her fey senses, she delved into the aura of the apparition. When she felt it, she relaxed. She saw Rose Brewer had as well. The woman opened the carriage door and alighted onto the rutted, muddy road.

Effie realized how tired she'd become during the long journey. She jumped at ghosts that weren't really ghosts at all. Stepping down from the carriage, she hustled to Rose's side.

Closer, the girl's flesh wasn't nearly as pale. The steam carriage's lamps had washed out her color. A buxom lass, her shift had been white once but had faded into a worn and stained earthy hue. The horns turned out to be sprigs of mistletoe wrapped in her auburn hair. Perhaps she had wanted to appear as a Greek goddess, but the twigs and spots of green leaf only served to give her a feral appearance.

"My parents named me Jane," she told Rose. Her voice sounded frail, like it would break if made any louder. "Jane Porter."

"What are you doing here, stepping in front of a carriage?" asked Effie. "Are you lost?"

"Not lost," said Rose. She eyed Effie. "She seeks the Green Lady." Her lip curled into a playful grin. "She seeks you."

Effie twitched. She studied Jane again and saw what Rose meant. She'd been wrong a second time. The garb didn't mimic a goddess. The girl dressed like tales told of ancient Oak Seers.

She dressed as a druid.

"The Green Lady," Jane croaked. Clutching her shift, she made to curtsey. Only she stopped midway, gulped, and instead lowered to her knees.

"Oh, please, get up," said Effie. She went to rescue the girl from the awkwardness. Or perhaps it was herself she wanted to save.

Rose burst into a fit of laughter. "This is something I have never seen!"

Effie helped Jane to her feet. The girl's arms felt frail beneath the shift, more so than her round face and shape would suggest. It made Effie wonder when she'd eaten last. "I am not some lady to kneel before," she said. "Now tell us, why have you sought me out? Where have you come from?"

"I've come from Bournemouth, on the coast."

Effie's eyes bulged. "The southern coast? How did you come so far by yourself?"

"I am old enough," said Jane. She stood taller, adamant of the fact, though Effie guessed her under sixteen years. "I booked passage on a train. My father's old employer, Mr. Whitlock, took pity on me and gave me some coin." Her chin dipped in what looked like embarrassment. "Though he meant for me to take up work in the laundry. I suppose he'll be shocked when he finds I've gone."

"And what of your parents?" asked Effie.

Jane touched the side of her face. "There was a fire," she said, distantly, and fell quiet. A lump rose in Effie's throat. She reached out and clasped the girl's hand in her own, trying to impart some of her body's warmth into it.

"I heard," said Jane, after a moment, "of a lady who talked to the trees. She travelled with an owl for a companion and tamed savage beasts. She saved the lives of hundreds by charging across a bloody field. She befriended a giant and made him recant his murderous pact with the devil. My Davie saw it. He fought beside her... Er, you. It is you the tales speak of, isn't it?"

Effie nodded, the movement brief and slow. She saw no point in denying the account. She had fought at Caldwell House, doing more or less all of what Jane had described. Her owl companion, whom she named Gwendoline, was probably out scavenging near her cottage as they spoke.

Jane's grip tightened. "Before you turned him to the crown's cause, the giant threw a boulder that crushed Davie's legs. The regiment dismissed him after the battle. He had only recently joined from some town near Newcastle, and they sent him to Bournemouth for a recovery of sea bathing and pine teas. I took care of him for more than a month. My mother and sister and I worked for a spa near Invalids' Walk. The owner was a charitable man who took on such cases as Her Majesty's wounded soldiers. Davie told me of you. He spoke of little else, and he bade me scour the broadsheets for any news of where you had gone. That is how I learned of your involvement with the Duke of Edinburgh."

The familiar look of sorrow returned to the girl's face. "When Davie died—rot festered in his legs, they tried to take them but he didn't survive—I thought of the old tales. Our priest said the druids used to worship the fey and aid them in their heathen ways. But that didn't sound so awful to me. If the fey can perform such wondrous feats, maybe the druids were blessed to aid them as they did. I thought maybe I could do so as well."

Effie's heart pulled as if a great weight yanked it down. "I'm sorry, Jane," she said. "I don't know anything of the druids. I barely know anything of the fey." She looked to Rose for help. The woman was a vast wealth of lore. Surely, she knew.

But Rose shrugged and shook her head slightly. "I'm afraid I don't have much to offer. It used to be village women would study the ways of a Spae Wife so they might assist when need arose, but I don't believe that had anything to do with druid rituals. Their time perished long ago."

Jane blinked. "Spae Wives? You mean Highland Hags?"

Effie snorted. She had never heard the term before, yet it reminded her of the tales of fancy the English told of the Scots. Most were not very flattering. But a more pressing thought entered her mind. "However did you find me here?" she asked. She'd thought knowledge of her cottage a secret. She never entertained guests there besides Stuart Graham, not even Conall Murray.

"After the fire, I didn't have any connections in Bournemouth," said Jane. "Not even my job remained. We'd lived in a loft above the spa, you see, and it's that which burned. I only had the little coin Mr. Whitlock gave me and the clothes on my back. I came north to Edinburgh, and there I heard the tale of a woman who worked for Thomas Stevenson. She had a pet bear. That connection led me to a tinker in the city who said you and Mr. Stevenson would attend a ball in Glasgow presently. I watched Lady Fife's estate from the shadows across the street, and when you arrived, I paid the driver of the coach you'd hired the last of my coin."

She beamed as she gestured at the open stretch of road. "The man brought me here. He said he'd picked you up in the village nearby but that he'd seen you come from the road north."

Effie rounded on the driver of the steam coach. He'd remained in his seat, perched on a bench atop the front of the carriage. Knobs and levers of brass and steel formed a thicket in front of him. The man put his hands up in a defensive manner.

"Don't look to me, miss," he said. "I'm under Lady Fife's charge and not the man who brought you to her estate."

"Well, I know that," Effie snapped, then apologized for her rudeness. The man had nothing to do with the fear that rose in her. She hadn't thought her home so easily uncovered. Its sanctuary had been dissolved by a young, lost girl, and she wondered now if Jack Canonbie had been right in wanting to remain with her.

Despite her concerns, she stifled a yawn, sucking it back lest she have to apologize again for her uncouth behavior. The hour was too late for such fears, and the dark of night already well underway. The girl had been enterprising in her efforts. Effie had to give her that. It reminded her of her own persistent mind.

And poor Jane had nowhere else to turn. She reminded Effie of herself in that way, too.

The decision made itself.

"You may stay with me at least for the night," she told Jane. "My hearth may be cold, but we can stoke it, and I have blankets aplenty." She sighed inwardly. She had a penchant for picking up strays: hounds, cats, and owls. Even Rorie, the bear Jane mentioned, she'd rescued from a cruel life of baiting. But this was her first human.

Rose smiled at the pronouncement, and Effie had the feeling once again that the woman appraised her. She pulled a heavy blanket from the carriage and wrapped it around Jane, while Rose chirped at the driver until he dug into his coat and offered up his flask. Jane coughed as the whiskey ran down her throat, but at least she appeared to warm a little.

Underway again, their journey was short. Bonny Law nestled between the slopes of two gentle hills, not far removed from the winding country road. A copse of birch hid it from passersby, yet in the darkness of night the trees made little difference. Effie kept its garden lively and in good order. Tulips from the continent lined the ground beneath the front window, and an assortment of wild flowers filled the ground from there, melding into the natural forest.

Their lamplight ran over the flowers as they approached. Pinks and violets, ambers and yellows swirled like a rainbow stirred in a giant cauldron. The cottage itself sagged pleasantly in its middle, its plaster fresh and beams sturdy, if only a little worn down with age. Stuart Graham had paid for new thatching on its roof, and the straw still gave off a sweet scent. Everything felt wet and smelled damp, evidence of a recent rain shower.

No sooner had they alighted from the carriage, than a rustle of feathers swooping through the night announced the arrival of Gwendoline. The small, tawny owl hooted her delight at Effie's return, then hooted again for good measure. Effie held her arm out for the owl to perch on and sent it warm images of open fields rife with plump critters.

"Go and hunt," she said. "And we will rest." The owl hooted and took wing. Jane stood rigid in amazement. Effie only smiled and led the girl inside.

Together they lit a fire in the hearth. Rose found something for Jane to eat, and Effie saw to blankets and pillows. Questions remained between them all, but each was more tired than after climbing the peak of Ben Nevis. Silently, they agreed further discussion could wait until the morning. The last thing Effie remembered was the chirping of a night bird as it scavenged over the rolling hills.

8

E ffie awoke to the growling of her stomach. Something smelled delightful, and it took her a moment to recognize the aroma of fresh wild berries fried within a scone. A thick and rich perfume of tea wafted in on the aroma's heels. She yawned and stretched, listening to the clatter of plates and cups. A few whispers followed from the far side of a slatted door.

The sun had crested the hills. Its light poured into her bedroom, the only other room in the cottage besides the main living area. Curtains of white lace caused the light to cast a pattern on the far wall like snowflakes. Four posts of carved spruce supported her bed. A dressing table and wardrobe were the only other furniture, but the plastered walls held a handful of renderings. Not hers, but those she had bought from other artists. She sought to learn from them, the subtle tricks in their charcoal strokes and uses of perspective. One depicted a cantilevered bridge spanning across a tranquil river. And another, recently given to her by Stevenson, showed a tower of iron the French meant to build in the heart of Paris. The Parisian artist community was in a fervor over its construction. Most called it a blight against the beauty of their city. Effie didn't know about that. She'd never seen the French city. But she marveled at the tower's scale and symmetry.

Pulling on her dressing gown, she freshened her hair and joined the others. Jane had found an apron and removed the mistletoe from her auburn locks. Scones sizzled on the griddle over the crackling hearth.

"Oh, good morning, my lady," said the girl. She made to curtsey but almost dropped the cup of tea she carried and had to rescue it before it splashed to the floor.

"Good morning," said Effie. "But please call me Effie. I am not a lady." She breathed in the sweet scents. "It smells wonderful in here. You've been busy, I see."

"Yes, my lady. Well, I am sorry for the poor fare," said Jane. "I would have done eggs and toast, only you had just the single egg and there was no time for baking bread." She blushed. "I slept a bit too long, and once the coal was restocked and floor swept, I mustered what I could. I hope you'll forgive me the liberties I took. I used to cook the breakfast back home, though it was mostly nothing more than oats or potatoes."

Effie felt her mouth fall open as she glanced around the room. Jane had tidied while she slept. The girl had removed a week of dust from the dining table Effie kept under the front window. The pillows resting on a pair of chairs near the hearth were plumped and beaten free of dander. The rugs were clear of tracked in leaves, and the timbered eaves free of cobwebs. The coal bin overflowed, restocked from the larger storage chest outside. Blood rushed to Effie's head, and she became woozy.

"It's too much," she said. "You are a guest here. I feel ashamed."

"Och, work is good for the young," said Rose. "Puts hair on your chest, so the men like to say." The Sithling woman sat at the table, huddled over a steaming cup. She used it to cover her lips as she chuckled.

Effie rolled her eyes and went to help Jane with the cooking. Once the scones had turned a golden brown, they removed them from the griddle and settled around the table. The fare tasted as good as it smelled, sweet but not overly so, with a crisp bite around the edges and a tartness from the berries.

"This morning I can teach you the means to call on your friends," said Rose.

"As Caledon did the entire court?" asked Effie. Thoughts of food left her instantly as curiosity took over. She would have Rose teach her a thousand and one things each day, if the woman would stay to indulge her.

"Aye, if you wish it," Rose teased, clearly seeing Effie's eagerness. She plopped the last bite of scone into her mouth and wiped her fingers on a linen napkin. "You can aid me in the task. It will take some practice before you can manage such a thing on your own. And you will only be able to manage it when other fey are about. It takes some strength of blood."

Effie glanced at Jane, and Rose laughed. "It was not the Fey Craft that I wished to keep secret from Jack Canonbie," said the woman, "but the message you intended to send. The man's ears are not likely his own, or if they are, they can surely be purchased for the right amount of coin."

Effie thought on that for moment and had to agree. She would have to hold a prudent tongue around the man.

"Open your senses," said Rose. She placed her hands atop Effie's. Her skin felt slightly rough, as if it had a memory of calluses from younger years. "Think on this other fey's aura. Remember its details as closely as possible and fix them in your thoughts."

Effie understood. Each aura stood unique, like a calling card for that individual. She opened herself, and instantly Rose's aura pulsed before her like a blinding bonfire. At Lady Fife's, when Rose had stood near Caledon, she hadn't realized the enormity of the woman's presence. It raged like a distant star hurtling through the night's sky. Gases exploded in on themselves. Vapors swirled. A hint of old-growth forest blossomed beneath, teasing Effie with hidden depths of archaic wisdom. She sat transfixed, forgetting herself.

"Focus, child," reminded Rose with a squeeze of her hands.

Effie nodded and brought her shoulders straight. She steeled herself, frustrated she had lost her concentration so easily. Closing her eyes, she tried to conjure what she remembered of Jaelyn's aura.

A chase through fallen leaves; the hope of satisfaction as winter approached and stole all warmth from the hills and glens. A stand against the frigid nothingness on the horizon. That was Jaelyn of Clan Kae. The brownie held no wickedness in her, only a desperate fight for survival against an endless void.

Rose squeezed her hands again. "Good, now I will guide you through the sending."

Effie felt her head nod. It grew heavier until it fell like an anchor, dragging her down into a murky abyss.

Her vision blurred. When it returned to focus, she stood before a giant oak. At first, she thought it Muckle Ben. But the scale wasn't right. This tree dominated an entire glen, its branches as thick as train carriages. Its central trunk stood broad enough to contain a small village.

And perhaps it once had. She had that impression.

Hollows dotted the massive trunk, each large enough for oxen to pass through. Some stood large enough for a steam carriage, though they lofted too high off the ground. Mistletoe sprouted along the rough bark. Pools of green shadow contrasted against the oak's orange and red leaves.

Fall. It must be the harvest month.

Or a waning.

The grassy field around her heaved at that last thought. The sudden violence threw her down, and her knees banged against the rough turf.

A darkness fell over the oak, sapping the beauty of its colors. It turned a cold, awful shade of steel, like that of a tarnished cannon. The earth heaved again. With a deafening crack that made Effie shriek in fear, the oak split down its center.

Massive branches screamed toward her. Dead things, brittle and decrepit. Their time was long past. The weight of their greatness had betrayed them. They'd grown too heavy, too old. She quested with her fey senses but found nothing to save her. Bark tore and snapped. The rush of dry leaves tumbling to the ground pattered like a downpour in the wake of the falling oak. Her heart seized. Her muscles strained and locked in place.

Death would soon find her.

A distant wail echoed that truth. She barely heard it under the crash of the oak. Yet it taunted her, more substantial somehow than anything her eyes could see.

She jolted in her chair just as the tumbling branches struck her and became aware once more of the familiar walls of her cottage. Tea sloshed as she knocked her cup. It burned where it kissed her fingers. She yelped and sucked on them.

Rose lurched to her feet, her face a mask of concern. Jane hovered over Effie. The girl's arms reached for her, as if needing to catch her fall. The girl's cheeks had lost some of their color, and her mouth hung agape.

"What is it?" asked Effie. Coldness bit at her legs, and she found her arms trembling. The oak had killed her. She swallowed as she remembered the heavy limbs crushing her bones.

"Perhaps you should take a rest, my lady," said Jane. "We can lie you down and get some blankets over you."

Effie eyed the girl, confused. She wasn't suffering from a fit. Turning to Rose, she told the woman what she'd seen. "Was it Elphame?" she asked once she'd finished. The fabled realm of the fey was the only thing she could think of that made any sense.

Rose shook her head. "One does not simply dream of Elphame. It is a far and distant place, its secrets well-guarded. If this friend of yours were there, the sending would simply fail." She reclaimed her chair and leaned closer. "I believe you had a foretelling."

"A foretelling?" Effie's brow scrunched. "Like a Star Reader has? How is that possible? I know nothing of how such things work." She studied what remained of her tea. Star Readers used concoctions of herbs to help fuel their visions. Some even inhaled the vapors of burning stardust. But she had no affinity for foretelling. She was a Grundbairn. She trusted in the trees and earth for her knowledge, what little of it there was.

"Such a thing can happen, though it is rare," said Rose. "I began the sending and meant to guide you along, but you fell away and became closed to my reach. I thought I heard some distant screech, but it didn't come from you." Her gaze became vacant, as if she pondered the memory. "Perhaps it was this Jaelyn who called out. Or perhaps a gift of Fey Craft awakened in you. Some are blessed with certain strengths where others are not, and you have already shown an aptitude for feats beyond most. In either case, you are tired and should rest. I will undertake the sending alone. You have shown me enough of Jaelyn's aura to do so. You will have to learn another time."

Effie protested, but her eyes betrayed her. Despite her recent sleep, they felt heavy, as if she hadn't rested in weeks. Her limbs joined the revolt and overwhelmed her desire to try the Fey Craft again. With

Jane's help, she climbed back into bed and rested for the remainder of the morning.

When she woke for the second time that day, she found Rose had gathered her things and awaited a steam carriage to arrive from Westley.

"Surely you don't mean to depart so soon!" Effie exclaimed. She felt she had barely tickled the surface of all the questions she wanted to ask the woman.

Rose rubbed her hands gently together. "I had intended to remain longer, but I sense now there are matters I must attend in the north. Some part of your foretelling troubles me." She eyed Effie a moment before relaxing. A grin returned to her face. She patted Effie's shoulder. "Perhaps it is nothing. But I meant to travel onward to Skye regardless. Caledon needs me to rally support among the fey court, the bare dozens who remain."

"I'll go with you," Effie blurted. She enjoyed Rose's company and could learn a great deal. Besides, she couldn't remain idle as others toiled for the cause for which she'd already risked so much.

"You cannot," said Rose. A bitterness came to her tone, though Effie knew it was not directed at her. "There are still those in the court who would not speak openly while you stood near. They do not trust you yet."

The words stung. The legacy of her grandfather haunted her once more. Arnwyrd had taken the life of the steward before Caledon. The steward had been gravely wounded in battle, and a sweating sickness had come to the daughter of a mutual friend. Arnwyrd found himself with a dire choice. He could watch both steward and girl pass from life, or he could bless one with health at the expense of the other.

He chose to save the young girl.

That the steward would've died regardless mattered little to those of the fey court. Arnwyrd's use of Fey Craft to take the final spark from their beloved leader blocked any compassion they might've had for her grandfather. They banished him and shunned his name.

Effie stood tall and proud. She would not let their judgment shame her. It had been too many years, and she had never known her grandfather, nor the fey who turned their backs on him. "Then I shall earn their trust," she said.

Rose sighed and shook her head. "We have not the time. The treaty negotiations will commence, and we must be ready."

Effie argued further, but found that Rose had an answer for every point she made, and soon she stood watching as Rose's steam carriage trundled northward. It rocked gently on the uneven road while she and Jane remained at Bonny Law.

❧ 9 ❧

The better part of a week passed, and Jane and Effie grew into a routine. Jane would walk into the village each day, seeing to the shopping and to give word to Jack Canonbie that all was well. Effie agreed to give the girl boarding until she could find work on her own. The girl did not pose any threat, and Effie wouldn't be able to forgive herself if she just turned the lass away and thrust her out into the cold. Stevenson had taken her in when he'd had no cause to do so, and she would pay the favor forward.

For her part, Effie spent some of her time in the garden tidying the flowers and shrubs. She checked on Gwendoline, too. The owl liked to sleep the day away in the hollow of a tree at the edge of the garden, and Effie would bring her fresh clippings and leaves for her nest. At night, Effie labored over a thick tome she'd borrowed from Conall. It contained accounts of the crown's attempts to detect fey through the means of alchemy. The science, what little of it the efforts were grounded in, horrified her. It supposed the secretions of fey organs to be the root of their distinction from humans. Attempts to isolate these fluids and create compounds that would react with fey blood had driven the crown's agents to murder and defile dozens of innocent victims. And not all of them had been fey.

Finishing the final passage, Effie slammed the book shut and stewed. It was late, and she sat abed. The moon had reached its zenith. Her candle burned low. She'd hoped to glean something of fey lore from those who'd spent centuries pursuing her kind. But she'd been foolish to think the recordings of the Fey Finders anything but the drivel of murderous barbarians. Besides, delving into such tomes wasted too much time. She had remained at Bonny Law long enough. She needed to act. Her foot thumped against her bedding in restless fury.

A clatter followed by a thump and yelp of surprise jerked her from her stupor. The noise had come from the other room. Casting off her blankets, Effie hurried to see what had caused the racquet.

"Ack, I'll clobber ye!" shouted a voice she recognized.

Effie emerged from her bedroom to find Jaelyn standing over Jane, her arm raised with an empty teacup clutched in her hand. Candlelight danced over their forms. The brownie, though tall for her kind, stood barely above Effie's waist. She dressed in trousers and a jacket, as her kind preferred. The green wool had golden scrollwork at the cuffs, and it fit her slight frame in a snug manner. Sharp eyes and angular cheeks contrasted with the wild crop of unkempt hair atop her head.

Jane shied away from the brownie, scooting back on her rump, but she kept a firm grip on the rolling pin in her hand. Her eyes were wide. Her arms trembled.

"Jaelyn, stop!" shouted Effie. She reached out a hand to grab the brownie's wrist.

"I owe her one back," Jaelyn snapped. She pointed to a red welt at her temple. It looked painful but not serious.

"She crept in!" exclaimed Jane. "She didn't knock. I thought she'd come to harm us."

Effie rescued her teacup from Jaelyn's grasp and set it on the table, trying to contain herself. Despite the tension in the room, the scene before her quelled her earlier frustration. If anything, it made her want to cry with laughter.

"Jaelyn of Clan Kae, this is Jane Porter." She thrust an open hand at each of them. "Jane is staying with me for a while. Now, would you like to explain to her why you snuck into my cottage in the middle of the night?" Effie sucked at her cheeks to keep the humor from her expression but failed.

Jaelyn grinned. Her teeth jutted at odd directions. It gave the grin a feral appearance. "I had no wish to wake ye," she said.

Effie folded her arms and raised an eyebrow. The brownie would've seen the light of her candle through the bedroom window. Had she meant to test her awareness by sneaking inside? It was something the woman was like to do. The thought made her snort indignantly.

"You did send for me over some trouble," said Jaelyn rather defensively. She folded her arms across her chest to match Effie.

The brownie's stubbornness outdid Effie's own, and she knew pressing further might create a stone wall between them. It was better to let the matter go. She had bade Jaelyn to come, after all. What did it matter the hour of her arrival or the manner of it?

"Jane," she said, shaking her head, "please ask for Jaelyn's forgiveness. I'm sure you struck her a well-deserved clout, and I thank you for your stalwart defense of the cottage. But Jaelyn is a welcome guest and a friend." She helped Jane to her feet. Her tone and grin let the girl know she'd done no wrong. "Perhaps some tea would do us all some good."

"I'll make it," Jane squeaked, and she scampered to fetch the kettle.

"So," said Jaelyn, watching the girl, "ye have turned the order of things and have the human waiting on ye?" The brownie cackled.

Effie ignored the comment and ushered her to a chair. "You received the sending?" she asked.

"Aye, I felt it well enough," Jaelyn admitted. "Though I don't ken the sender. It wasn't ye. I only knew to come here from the message, an image of that bird of yers circling the garden."

"Rose Brewer," said Effie. "She aided me before travelling onward."

"Ah, I'd heard she'd returned. A woman of high wisdom, they say."

"Jaelyn," said Effie. Then she paused. She wasn't quite sure how to phrase what she wanted. "You once debated whether to side with the Sidhe Bhreige against the crown. You were prepared to fight on their behalf, to wage war against the hatred London had instilled against the fey. And now with the greater rise of this hatred, I wanted to know..." She ran a tongue over her dry lips. "Well, I wanted to know how you would go about waging such a war."

"Ha!" barked Jaelyn. "I thought such notions beyond your delicate sensibilities. The apple has soured on ye, has it?"

"I didn't mean I'd raise arms against the crown," said Effie. She took the steaming tea Jane offered and stirred in a healthy lump of sugar. "But you have...associates." She took a care to choose the proper word. "I'm sure they have plans other than a frontal assault on the Tower of London. Any open hostilities would end in disaster."

Jaelyn growled. Her eyes became dangerous. "We'd nae stop until every last of our side lay dead on the field." She turned away and gathered herself, leaning back against her chair and waving an idle hand. "But aye, such a thing would be foolish. It would only serve to fill their history books with tales of cruelty painted as heroism."

"So, what then?" begged Effie. "What plans do they have?"

Jaelyn waggled a finger at her. Her stare became hard. "Ye think because we slew the Laird of Aonghus together and survived a giant's wrath, I'd give over all my—what did you call them? Associates?—for a cup of tea?"

Effie bit her lip. She had assumed just that much. She'd thought facing death with the brownie had bonded them close enough for such a favor. But Jaelyn was right. They had never shared intimate secrets. What the brownie knew of her was common knowledge within the court —the betrayal by her grandfather and isolation of her mother. She would have to approach the discussion as a barter. She needed to give something more than a cup of tea.

"Perhaps if there was an exchange?" she asked. "I don't seek names or anything personal. I only want advice on how to best pursue the dismantlement of Lord Granville's schemes. He holds the fate of the treaty in his hands. If the lord can be cowed, perhaps some of the resentment toward the fey would ease, and the treaty would be more favorable for the fey."

"It would ease me better if ye weren't abetting the crown," said Jaelyn. "I ken of yer aiding the Sniffers."

Effie lifted her chin, refusing to feel embarrassed for her actions. But her hands refused to stop fidgeting with her teacup. The slight cut her, as Jaelyn had no doubt meant it to do. "I never encouraged the crown to do harm. Quite the opposite. And I made no effort to keep my actions secret. I did what was needed. Conall Murray asked…"

"The Fey Finder General," Jaelyn sneered.

"Yes," snapped Effie. "You know him. You know he is not like the others. It is better that I aid him rather than he rely on those of his order. He is trying. I am trying."

Jaelyn chuckled. "So here ye sit, asking for advice on how to subvert yer masters."

Effie forced herself to sip her tea. She needed to do something to calm herself, lest she reach for Jane's rolling pin and clout the brownie a firm crack herself. To be insulted so in her own house! Closing her eyes, she took a breath, realizing the rudeness must be on purpose. Another of the brownie's tests. Jaelyn talked her in circles. But if she meant not to help, why come at all? Perhaps she only sought to uncover how far Effie's loyalties leaned to the side of the crown.

"Lord Granville pays for anti-fey accounts to be published in the English newspapers," said Effie. If the brownie needed affirmation of her loyalty, she would give it. Jaelyn slurped from her cup, remaining silent. Her lack of reaction made Effie think she'd already known of Lord Granville's payments. "And he's convinced Lord Wilshire to put forth legislation that would banish all fey to an island colony," she added.

It was Jane who gasped. The girl came to perch on the chair next to Effie. Jaelyn's eyes widened. She put her cup down and smirked. "Will they at least allow us to choose the island?" the brownie asked. "Because I've grown rather fond of the one we're on."

"They can't do such a horrid thing," said Jane.

"They will and more, if we sit idly by," said Effie. She stared at Jaelyn as she spoke.

Jaelyn nodded. A softness came to her gaze, and the sharp tension in the room dissolved. "Aye, I ken ye well enough, Grundbairn. Aid ye, I will, for what I can. Now, yer always one for foolish notions. What would ye do against such a measure?"

Effie pretended to glower at the barb, but the humor of it won over, and she had to snicker. When she collected herself, she considered the question. "Those in power seek to inflame the populace against the fey. This will gain them the public support they need to reject the treaty and push new legislations through." Resting her elbows on the table, she leaned forward and gazed into the dregs of her tea. "So we should act to dampen these flames."

"You can hold a festival at the solstice," blurted Jane, excitedly. "Perform the elder rituals for all to see and demonstrate how peaceful the fey kind are." She shrunk in her chair at Jaelyn's glare.

"It is not a bad scheme, Jane," said Effie. "But most fey would be reluctant to make themselves such an easy target. The exposure is too great." She turned to Jaelyn. "It does, however, bring up a valid point. How are we to counterbalance the tales fed to the public of vile fey acts, if we refuse to show ourselves openly?"

"The newspapers print in ink, but their pages are full of coin," said Jaelyn.

Drawing the conclusion, Effie tapped her finger on the table. "You mean we should pay for our own pamphlets and articles, to show the good the fey bring to the Highlands."

"That is one approach," Jaelyn said. She drew the words out, implying she thought it a lesser option.

"You suggest another?"

Jaelyn waved her teacup at Effie. "Dismantle the machine that feeds their schemes. These lords spend coin like it's shite from a sheep. Cull the flock, I say, and see if what droppings remain become too valuable to spend."

"That is what you plan to do? In some manner, at least?" Effie leaned in.

"Bah," said Jaelyn. "I won't deny it, but my business is mine."

Effie nodded. She thought of Lady Fife's ball and the lavish spending the lords enjoyed. More than a few sheep would have to be culled for them to feel a lacking. Another thought came to her, and she remembered what Canonbie had told her in the carriage. "The Sanctity of Empire League," she said. "They rioted in protest of the fey treaty. I want to know who pulls their strings and how much they are paid."

Jaelyn's lips pulled back. "Now we are speaking of a common cause. I ken only a little of this group. They once organized labor strikes on the docks along the River Clyde, though more and more they sprout like weeds in other cities with their voices turned against the fey. Striking workers are hungry workers, and hungry men have minds easily warped by the promise of food. A fat man named Alistair Weir leads them. It perhaps did not take much for him to have the league blaming the fey for the cause of their growling stomachs."

"But who pays this Mr. Weir?" asked Effie.

The brownie shrugged. "I ken that not. But I have friends seeking out this knowledge."

"I can help," offered Jane. "I'll go to the docks. I came all this way. I want to do my part."

"The docks are dangerous." Effie spoke from experience.

Jane stood. The determination on her face reminded Effie that the girl must have an iron strength of will to have journeyed so far after such personal loss. Anything less, and she would've given up a mile from Bournemouth. "I'm used to the ribald jests of soldiers," said Jane. "The coarse behavior of the docks can be no worse. One of the wounded men pinched..." She blushed and trailed off. "I had a bruise for a week."

"I appreciate your courage, Jane," said Effie. She drew the girl's attention away from Jaelyn's derisive scowl. "But I have another task in mind for you. Something more important." She would need to think of exactly what later. Maybe the girl could put her Davie's tale to paper or commission someone else to do so. They could use the account to combat those printed against them.

Effie turned to Jaelyn. "Suppose we discover Mr. Weir's benefactor and manage to sever the connection. How do we undo the damage already done? It would take more than a pamphlet in our favor."

"Think of Fey Craft, lass," said Jaelyn. "Our kind can soothe the tempers of a mob when we unite our strength of blood. Not enough to change minds completely, not for so large a mass over so large an area. But most don't need more than a gentle touch to remind them how the crown has done them more harm than any fey. We would do as much to sway them now except the persuasion wouldn't last for long and would take all our energy from other endeavors."

Effie blinked as she thought on that and realized the moonlight shining through the window had been replaced by an amber glow coming over the hills. The sun would rise soon, and she hadn't slept a wink. Her belly reminded her it hadn't seen anything in hours, either. Her muscles ached from the earlier tension and prolonged sitting. She stood and rubbed at her arms and legs.

"I might have a scone or two handy," she said. Her mind raced too much to suggest they sleep. "And a coffee to replace the tea."

Jaelyn clutched her belly. "I wouldn't refuse some oats or a ration of pork sausage. I did come all the way from Dalkeith."

Effie smiled. The brownie had shown her a sign of trust, letting her know where she'd come from. The town stood just south and east of Edinburgh. "I will do up a proper breakfast, then," she said.

Dawn arrived as they ate. Effie mentioned her idea of recording Davie's tale to print, and Jane eagerly agreed. More so, the girl suggested they visit some of the mystics' shops in the cities, those who dealt in esoteric oddities and the occult. There, they might find natural allies. A revival of spiritual practices had begun in Germany the previous winter, and it had quickly spread throughout the empire. The ideals it professed blended with those already swept up in a Bohemian lifestyle. Jane talked eagerly of what she'd learned of the movement, and Effie realized how quickly the girl's mind worked when she wasn't intimidated into silence. She had just risen to clear the table when Jaelyn bolted to her feet and stared at the front door.

Gwendoline screeched from her nest in the garden tree.

"Someone comes," said the brownie. She plucked up the knife she'd used to cut her sausage. Juices ran down its edge.

Effie heard Jane move behind her and turned to find the girl had snatched up the rolling pin again and lofted it like a truncheon ready to strike.

"Oh, for heaven's sake," said Effie. She peered through the front window and saw a familiar, if not necessarily welcome, form. "It is only Jack Canonbie, not a hoard of wulvers."

The man crossed the garden and pounded on the door. Effie grunted at the noise. Smoothing her skirts, she pulled the door open.

"You needn't take the wood from its hinges," she scolded.

Canonbie started. His eyes danced in the morning sunlight. "I figured you still abed at this hour." He saw Jaelyn and his face grew tight. His hand changed the grip he held on his cane.

"We are well awake and have no need of your protection," she said with a huff before she remembered her manners. "If you intend to treat that cane like a saber, you can leave it outside. Otherwise, please do come in, and I'll fetch you a cup of tea."

Effie turned to Jaelyn. "This is the man Mr. Stevenson hired for my safeguarding." The brownie made no reaction to the news other than to retreat back toward the hearth. She kept the knife clutched in her hand, though she let it drop casually to her side.

"A telegram came for you in the village," said Canonbie. "The matter could not wait." He stepped inside and gave a curt nod to Jaelyn. He gave a much warmer one to Jane, his face showing something of a rascally grin. Pulling a folded paper from his waistcoat pocket, he handed it to Effie.

"You've read it?" she asked, taking the telegram.

"No choice, was there?" he asked. He pressed his fist over his heart in a mocking salute. His handsome smile was way too effective, making her fluster rather than hold her ire. "I needed to discover whether its contents were worth waking you at the early hour."

Effie eyed him skeptically. Was she to have no privacy anymore? She would have to discuss the arrangement with Stevenson, and soon. But the thought evaporated as she scanned the message.

It was from Conall Murray, and short.

"Incident at storehouse," the telegram read. "Come at once."

Effie's hand shook. She understood the note's meaning, despite its brevity. The storehouse meant the converted distillery where Sir Walter Conrad and Caledon stored the measures of Aerfenium produced for the crown. An explosion or theft of the volatile substance would only serve to highlight its dangers. It would show the gas could be used for mayhem as easily as for powering wondrous devices. Word of such a disturbance would be used to destroy any chance of a fey treaty.

"We must go to Balclune," said Effie. The blood had left her face, making her feel dizzy. "The Fey Finder General needs us."

Jaelyn chuckled. "The Green Lady," she said, shaking her head. "Always with a foot planted in every tussle. Ye'd be wise to remember ye are not a prophet come to save our kind."

Effie glared at the brownie. She believed no such thing. She acted as she thought best, as she thought any with an honest and fair mind would.

"If you will not give aid, I will go alone," she said. Jack Canonbie grunted, and Jane began pleading to accompany her. She smiled at their reactions and gestured to let them know she hadn't meant to offend.

Jaelyn set the knife down. "Follow yer own path, Grundbairn. But do not expect me to abandon my concerns for the meddling of a Sniffer." The stern words reminded Effie of all the suffering that had befallen their kind at the hands of the Fey Finders, and she couldn't blame her friend the refusal. But she couldn't refuse Conall's summons either. She'd witnessed too much good come from the assistance she'd already given him to allow old grievances to stifle the chance of a better future.

❧ 10 ❧

"Lord Granville has declared Aerfenium unsafe and halted its production," said Conall Murray. "When I objected, he saw to it that I have my rank removed. I am no longer the Fey Finder General." He greeted Effie and Jack Canonbie at the Dunfermline train station and ushered them toward a waiting steam carriage.

The train's shrill whistle punctuated Conall's pronouncement. It groaned into motion and carried on down the line without them, leaving a cloud of ashen smoke behind. The weight of its churning engine rattled the wooden planks of the station floor.

Effie blinked. Her concern for Conall made her deaf to all other thoughts. "But the lord has no power to dismiss you," she argued. She studied him as he clambered into the steam carriage and leaned against the inside of the door. She sought some jest but found no indication of one. His wrinkled clothes appeared several days unwashed. His curly locks ran amok across his brow. It made Canonbie's brushed coat and shaven cheeks seem polished by comparison.

They had come alone. Jaelyn had returned to Dalkeith. Afoot, Effie presumed. The brownie scorned riding and considered conveyance in a compartment of steel and wood tantamount to having her legs ripped off by a giant. Young Jane they had left at Bonny Law. Effie saw no reason to place the girl in danger, and even less to have to explain her presence. Jane had protested and pleaded, but Effie convinced her to stick with the plan they'd laid out before Canonbie's arrival. Before departing, she'd penned a note asking Thomas Stevenson to aid Jane's efforts.

"It has become a futile discussion," Conall explained. "Her Majesty has already named a permanent man to the position." He spoke without a hint of sadness or embarrassment, yet Effie knew him well enough to recognize his melancholic state. His mind wrestled with itself.

The steam carriage rocked over cobblestones as they departed the station. The wheels found ruts and stones, and Effie gripped the padded cushion beneath her to keep from lurching. Out the window, a grand medieval abbey rose into view atop Dunfermline's central hill. Several large factories of drab stone surrounded the hill's base, a ring wall defending the town's heart.

"Who is your replacement?" asked Effie. She hoped the news not dire. "Is it that man Sir Walter suggested?"

Conall shook his head. "Sir Walter dared not raise his voice in the matter. His name is at risk already. It is he who pushes the crown most for Aerfenium, after all. Any doubts as to its safety will be laid at his feet more than any other."

"Except for the fey, of course," said Canonbie. Effie caught herself thinking the same sentiment.

Conall waved his hand, conceding the point. "The new Fey Finder General is a magistrate and the son of some southern lord. A Mr. John Billingsley. He travels from London to Edinburgh as we speak. A missive last night informed me of the appointment and my new orders. I am to abandon Balclune and rejoin the hunt for snarks."

The shadows in the carriage shifted as they struck west for the hamlet of Balclune. A stiff wind brought the sharp tang of sheep droppings. A sweetness of wet grass hinted underneath the stench, and soon fields of bleating flocks stretched in every direction from the road.

"It isn't snarks," said Effie. She fought the urge to reach out and place her hand over his. "Uncovering the escaped Sidhe Bhreige is certainly a task worthy of your effort, even if at times it seems a hopeless one." She wondered if the return to that endeavor was the main cause of Conall's mood. He had never wanted the position of Fey Finder General, after all.

Snorting, Conall plucked a bit of dirt from his coat. "I'm sure you would be right, if I meant to remain a Fey Finder. But now that the game of titles is over, perhaps my father will finally relent and allow me to choose a new profession. I can return to law, if that is his preference."

"You wouldn't!" Effie shouted, forgetting herself. She clutched her gut. His words had struck her like a lead shot. She barely dared to comprehend them. How could the man talk of abandoning their hope of a treaty? She shuddered as a lump hardened in her throat. Staring into his eyes, she realized she had assumed too much. All their work together, ever since their flight from Duncairn more than a year before, had led her to believe their wills united. That the same fire that fueled her determination also fueled his support and unwavering loyalty.

But she had been wrong. He had done it not for the fey cause, but for her. Her dreams were not his. He had merely borrowed them for a time. His gaze, flat and full of sorrow, confirmed it. It dropped under her scrutiny, and he turned away.

She melted. She couldn't look at him. She didn't want to hear his voice. And yet, she had no one to blame but herself. He hadn't led her on. He had never professed a greater conviction for the fey cause than to do the right thing. He'd found himself in his position through the puppeteering of his father, not through any self-proclaimed desire. Could she really blame him for coveting a life of his own?

Still, it hurt that his choice would not be her cause. She brushed the corner of her eye and studied the fields they passed. A warm part of her heart grew cold. Recalling that Conall remained the same man whose friendship she cherished did little to rekindle its fire.

Canonbie cleared his throat. "We have other concerns besides your reduction in rank, do we not?" he asked Conall. "We have come here in haste at your request."

"Yes, of course," said Conall. His posture straightened. "I apologize for disturbing you with my own troubles. It was not an effort to gain your pity or cause you discomfort." He waited for Effie to acknowledge him before continuing. "Lord Granville has laid heavy charges against Aerfenium's safety based on an odd account. Two days ago, while I searched near Fort William, Fergus Alpin notified me that a host of fey had assaulted the Balclune storehouse where the substance is kept."

"Assaulted by a fey host?" exclaimed Effie. Her heart thumped. The news grabbed her attention, and she shoved aside her distress at his earlier confession. "The last of the Sidhe Bhreige. It has to be. Only that fiend would be so brazen, and no other fey would have a need to attack the storehouse."

"So I first suspected," said Conall. "But when I arrived, I received a different description of the attack, though no less disturbing in its result. The Aerfenium is secured, yet Laeth and his companion, Hargrund, have vanished. Mr. Alpin now blames them for the entire ordeal and seeks to have them arrested."

"They would never!" Effie barked.

Conall held up his hand. "Of course, I believe the same. And yet, Lord Granville uses this theory to demonstrate the fey cannot be trusted. You see now why I sought your aid."

Effie nodded, though questions spun in her head. "Mr. Alpin accuses Laeth and Hargrund of some phantom misdeed, yet what of this assault by a fey host? What was its purpose? And who—"

"Who was responsible?" asked Canonbie, interrupting her. "If not these friends of yours, perhaps it truly was the last of the fiends." He tapped his cane on the carriage floor as Effie glowered at him. She wished she had Gwendoline for company, or perhaps Jane. The girl didn't vex her the way Jack Canonbie had a habit of doing.

"Lieutenant Walford and his men comb the hillside to the north of Balclune for that very concern," said Conall. "We hurried here from Fort William together."

"Start at the beginning again," said Effie. "Tell us all you know." The details bothered her, and she could not yet see the forest for the trees.

Conall nodded. "Certainly. Mr. Alpin reported that a fierce blaze ravaged the hills near the storehouse. He called for my aid because he thought them under a direct attack, and he knew I had Lieutenant Walford's men with me."

"I would not give a bucket of goat's milk for Mr. Alpin's reports," said Effie. Her memory of Langmire made her nostrils flare.

"I have seen the scorched earth," said Conall. "The fire blazed too close to the storehouse to be a coincidence. And since Laeth and Hargrund disappeared during the unrest, Mr. Alpin assumed they were involved and ordered what men he employed to draw arms and defend the storehouse against a fey attack."

"I would've done the same," admitted Canonbie. He raised a hand to ward her off. "It's nothing suspect against your friends, but a fire like that is clearly meant to draw folk away from the storehouse. The best decision is to stay put and hold fast."

Effie could admit the logic held some speck of sense. Yet, for all she knew of Laeth, it wasn't like the man to abandon his charge without reason. Something about the account didn't sit right with her. She regarded Conall. The man had asked for her help because he still trusted her more than any other. More than Caledon, and certainly more than Fergus Alpin.

And she still trusted him.

She wouldn't fail him, nor the fey, over something as petty as spite. They had much work to do. Fergus Alpin had already poisoned many ears with tales of a fey ambush. She could hear Lord Granville's smug voice as he declared the fey untrustworthy and railed over the safety of Aerfenium. Those fears would cripple any chance of a treaty. The wealth the substance promised was the fey court's main bargaining position. Without it, they were lost.

The steam carriage crested a small rise, and the storehouse came into view. With the hamlet of Balclune to the east and a sprawling copse of woodlands to the south, the massive building dominated a grassy dell before the land rose into steeper hills to the north. Once a distillery, a tall, slender chimney at its heart rose into a low bank of clouds.

A detachment of soldiers hailed them from behind a stone fence. Their red coats stood in stark contrast to the tall, green grass of the dell and the murky, brown mud that surrounded the storehouse. Conall waved to them and received a chorus of cheery welcomes. The carriage carried onward until it halted before the storehouse's large ironbound doors.

Mud squished under her heels as Effie stepped from the steam carriage, and she had to grip Conall's arm for support. He smiled at her, and she saw in it his genuine concern for her. She returned the look, resting her free hand on his arm and giving it a squeeze.

Canonbie grunted behind her. She cursed when she saw where he pointed. Fergus Alpin trudged toward them, a scowl painted on his face. Splotches of mud covered his trousers and boots. Conall headed the Sniffer off, steering them inside the storehouse.

The perfume of whiskey carried from the timbers of the inner walls. Hard packed dirt formed the storehouse floor, though they'd strewn straw about to keep the dust down. A tidy row of cots allowed for sleeping quarters, and a few held slumbering soldiers. Their snores echoed through the open space. One cleaned his rifle, pulling an oiled cloth through its barrel as he eyed them.

"Why aren't the soldiers on alert?" Effie asked. "Do they not fear another attack?"

"Why would they?" snapped Alpin. He hacked into his handkerchief and wheezed from the effort. "All the vile substance has been moved back to the fey lands. Your brethren from the fey realm came to fetch it this morning, answering the alarm sent by your steward. There's nothing but midges and soiled dirt in here."

"A precaution," explained Conall. He sighed. "One that will likely fuel even greater arguments against our manufacturing of Aerfenium. Yet our new Fey Finder General found it a prudent action." He eyed Effie. The meaning in the look meant he wondered whether Mr. Billingsley knew full well the consequences of such a decision.

Effie cursed to herself. With Lord Granville's coin and encouragement, the newspapers were probably licking their chops to print such a scandalous tale.

"Of course he did," said Alpin. "The fey of Scotland cannot be trusted. Honest men can't know fiend from friend, so let those in the fey lands take the risk, I say, and let them fight each other away from here."

"Then by your own admission, not all fey are equally wicked," said Effie. "Have you changed your mind in that regard? Or do you not realize your own confusion?"

Alpin's face tightened. His eyes narrowed, and his lips turned sour. "The Aerfenium is no longer here. The assailants are no longer here. Hence, there is no need for your presence. Return to whence you came, Miss Effie of Glen Coe, or I will see to it you are removed by force of arms."

"She has come at my request," said Conall. He drew himself up.

Alpin rounded on him. "You no longer hold that authority, nor any here. I am tasked with the security of this storehouse, Mr. Murray."

"Pardon me, gentlemen," said Canonbie. "But are those the bodies of trows?" He pointed to the far end of the storehouse where three small bodies lay in the shadows atop a stack of hay. Effie could barely make out their shapes, but she had seen trows up close before. They looked like piglets, if piglets could walk upright and clasp crude tools. Their ears were long and flapped like those of hounds. Their fur was short and coarse. They dwelt in caves and loved music, though in discordant harmonies. The Laird of Aonghus had used them against their will, preying on their greed for precious stones and glittering treasures. The laird had turned them into ferocious imps who stalked the Highlands, and now that the laird had fallen, they roamed the countryside in aimless packs, much like their cousin wulvers.

"Aye," said Fergus Alpin. "We did encounter them during the hunt yestereve, more proof that the local fey were behind this attack."

If that were true, why would they stop at only a fire in the hills? Effie opened her mouth to point this out, but Canonbie stepped in front of her, reaching back to pat her arm.

"I've never seen the beasts before," he said. "Might I beg you show them to me? I always make a point to admire the trophies of great hunters."

Effie bristled as Alpin's expression turned to something of pride. But as the men strode away, Canonbie gestured for her to stay, and she caught on to his ploy. She would get nothing more from Alpin but bluster and quick dismissal. Jack Canonbie had freed her to roam the area on her own. She swallowed down her anger as a grin came to her lips. The man had guile, she'd give him that.

Gathering her skirts, she strode from the storehouse. The wind had changed, and she smelled now a faint undertone of smoke that she hadn't before. Following her nose, she edged around the building and found a small paddock. There, a few horses grazed from a trough. Their tails flicked at flies. One had a blanket across its back bearing a tartan of black striped with green. She recognized it and jolted in shock.

She recognized more than the tartan. She recognized the horse. It whinnied as she approached and stroked its mane. She hadn't felt its aura in some months, but auras were highly peculiar to their owners.

The horse nuzzled her arm. It stamped its front hoof in greeting. "I'm sorry. I don't have an apple for you," she told it. She glanced around, as confused as a daisy sprouting in winter.

Another of the horses came to nuzzle the back of her head, and she laughed as it tickled.

"Do all horses like ye so?" asked the stout man who strode from the direction she'd come. He had a happy belly and a firm chin. White locks curled in ringlets about his cheery face. An assortment of fine tools— brushes and metal picks, mostly—protruded from the pockets of his waistcoat. Their glint showed they'd had better care than the clothing that held them. His boots and coat were covered in mud and dust, signs of a long journey.

Effie's face lit up. "Only the ones who know I'll take pity and bring them more oats," she said in a jesting tone, though she knew it had more to do with her Grundbairn nature. Animals were often drawn to her, whether she willed it or not.

"Come 'ere, lass," said Stuart Graham.

She raced over and flung her arms around the man who, along with Thomas Stevenson, had raised her since her mother had passed. She breathed in the whiskey on his cheeks and hint of leather oil beneath it. It brought a strength to her to have him close.

Still, it made her wonder. "How have you come to Balclune?" she asked, breaking their embrace. "Conall said nothing."

Graham spread his stance and tugged his coat straight. "Bah, Mr. Murray had news to tell more important than to worry over me." He winked. "As for the rest, well, that is a quick tale. I resolved my business matters and found myself in Fort William. There, I happened on Mr. Murray, who told me of the trouble here, and that he'd sent word for you to join him."

"And you thought you'd better come and see I didn't do anything foolish," she said. A wry grin spread across her face.

He barked a laugh. "Aye, I ken ye too well." He shot a glance over his shoulder, and his smile faltered. "Only we've run afoul of this Mr. Alpin,

I'm guessing the same as you." He grimaced in disgust. "The man is a stranger to reason and logic."

"Oh?" asked Effie.

Graham gestured at the hills. "Aye, I've told him twice he has the lieutenant's men searching in the wrong direction."

11

E ffie scanned the hills to the north. The late afternoon sun made it difficult to spy the black scars left by the fire. They blended into the natural shadows left by the patchwork of low hanging clouds. But the scent of smoke still came strong from that direction. It left little room for doubt the fire burned there.

"Aye, the fire," said Graham. "A diversion."

"Meant to draw out the soldiers and leave the Aerfenium unguarded," Effie said.

Graham shook his head. "Only meant to draw the attention of human eyes." Effie cocked her head, quizzically, and he waved her on. "I'll show you something. I told Mr. Alpin, but he growled at me and said he'd have me in chains if I didn't leave the storehouse grounds. He ordered me to leave the security of the place to those men with rifles, the damned fool."

She patted his arm and received a snort in return. As they left the paddock, he said, "The new Fey Finder General is not Sir Walter's man, and the chaos here has left him rather exposed. He is under some strain to demonstrate Aerfenium's worth. He's promised funding for designs of devices using the stuff that he can display to the public." Graham nodded to a passing soldier. "But he also has a need to find and protect the ancient stores of the matter. If he can't prove the stuff's safe, the public outcry will paint him a villain."

"Lord Granville has already started painting the fey with that same brush," said Effie. "The treaty will fail if we cannot find the truth of this chaos before it dries."

Graham mumbled something sour that Effie pretended not to understand. He led her to stand next to the steam carriage in which she had arrived. "I spoke with a soldier called Jolly Ben—a good lad. According to him, a dozen were already stationed here before Lieutenant Walford reinforced them. Now, the fire started at that hillock there." He pointed at a rise to the north. With the storehouse angled as it was, Effie knew the same hill could be seen clearly from the paddock at the building's rear.

Graham next pointed at the stone wall she'd passed on the way in. "At the time it began, three soldiers held that position there, and another half dozen patrolled around here." He made a circle with his arms to indicate the general area. "The men all turned to the blaze, as one naturally would. But no shouts of alarm sounded. No beasts howled or rifles fired, so most just watched and held their ground." He waggled a finger. "Not so the fey. They, according to Jolly Ben, came sprinting out of the storehouse and ignored the fire completely."

Effie's eyes widened. "They searched another direction," she said, catching on.

"Aye," said Graham. He pointed at the woods to the south. "That's where Laeth and Hargrund did stare while the soldiers finally marshaled to storm the hillock."

"But what does that mean?" asked Effie. "Do you suppose they saw something?"

"No, not saw," said Graham. He placed a light hand on her shoulder to redirect her. "Look, it is a matter of angles. These fey became aware of something toward those woods. But from here, they would have to pass by the soldiers at the wall, men who would've had a better sight of anything in that direction."

Effie grinned. "You're right!" She knew she shouldn't be excited by Graham's observation, but the unraveling of the riddle thrilled her.

"This Jolly Ben said he watched from here as the fey stormed off into the woods. But none at the wall followed them. Which means the soldiers probably didn't see anything."

"You assume Laeth and Hargrund sensed something with their Fey Craft."

"That is my guess," said Graham. "But of course, it can't be proved because they never did return."

Effie pondered for a moment. "True, but perhaps they said something to those soldiers at the wall. They were here to protect the Aerfenium, after all. They wouldn't just run off without letting anyone know what they'd found."

"Unless..." said Graham.

Effie sighed. "Unless they were involved with the diversion as Mr. Alpin believes." Effie shook her head. She couldn't believe they were. And it didn't make any sense. If they'd meant to steal Aerfenium for some nefarious reason, they would've just taken it with them when they fled. Fergus Alpin's prejudice blinded him from that one, simple fact.

"Are you aware if any of those soldiers who manned the wall remain on the grounds?" she asked.

Graham shrugged. Effie planted her hands on her hips and turned to study the storehouse doors. They could walk the grounds, begging answers from every soldier they passed, but the process might take all night. She knew an easier way to find her answer, though it left a taste in her mouth similar to swallowing a clod of mud.

* * *

Fergus Alpin blustered in disbelief as Stuart Graham spoke, but the Sniffer fell quiet when Effie informed him Sir Walter Conrad would agree with the theory. Despite his current embarrassment, Sir Walter still held the weight of the coal barons behind him.

They stood with Conall Murray and Jack Canonbie near the soldiers' billet inside the storehouse. Canonbie sipped at a cup of tea he'd managed to scrounge from somewhere. It steamed and smelled as harsh as dirt. The two Sniffers stood apart, wary of one another. Conall's face remained a melancholic mask. He'd had much and more to worry over since he arrived in Balclune, yet Effie wondered how he'd failed to see what Graham had so easily uncovered.

Alpin glared at Conall as if he'd brought a pox on his house. "Fetch Mr. Roth," the Sniffer said to a soldier at rest on one of the cots. The man stood and nodded before hurrying off. Effie noted the soldier did not salute. Her Majesty's Fey Finders might hold an appointment from the crown, but that did not mean the rank mandated respect.

Alpin glowered after the soldier before returning his attention to Effie. "I will not have it said I failed to investigate all possibilities."

"Of course," she said. Graham snorted, and she resisted the urge to do the same. If Alpin needed his ego stroked, she would do just that. Better to draw milk from a cow with a gentle hand than poke it with a spur.

The soldier returned with another of the regiment, a lanky man whose pocked cheeks shone pale behind a red and chapped nose. The man reported to Fergus Alpin with a hint of indifference and stood at attention without meeting the Sniffer's eye.

Alpin gestured to Conall, who nodded to Effie. She pressed her hands together low before her waist in an effort to keep them from planting on her hips. The men before her would steal the last of her patience, and they'd do it with the awareness of a midge. "Mr. Roth," she started slowly, to ensure there was no sharpness to her voice, "we would like you please to give us an account of Laeth and Hargrund at the time the fire spread over the northern hills."

The man cocked his head. A sour expression passed quickly across his face before he remembered he stood at address. "Those fey, you mean, miss?"

"Yes," said Effie. "You were stationed at the stone wall, we were informed. You had a chance to watch these fey pass close by your position during the confusion."

"That I did, miss. I have given my account to Lieutenant Walford." Roth glanced at the two Sniffers. "We were ordered to treat them as proper wardens, you see. We didn't know them for traitors at the time and had no cause to fire on them. Lieutenant Walford said we'd done right when we gave him our account."

Fergus Alpin grunted and shifted his stance. "If that is his opinion on the matter," he said. His tone left no doubt he held a different opinion.

"We have no cause to question it, nor the lieutenant," added Conall in rebuttal. He turned to Roth. "But perhaps there is some detail remaining we have overlooked. Can you tell us, did the fey say anything to you in passing?"

"Anything at all," said Effie. "If they are to be branded as traitors, at least let their own words attempt to defend them."

Roth's nose wrinkled, and he studied the rafters for a moment, as if trying to remember a best forgotten memory. "Aye, I believe they did." His head cocked to the side. "The old one hollered something. I don't recall the words, but it was perhaps about a pack of them trows or the like. But we knew that, didn't we? We was already under attack at the time. The flames were rising up from the far side of the hill."

"Did they say anything else?" Effie begged. *Trows!* And the soldiers did nothing, not even report it to their lieutenant. Was the man daft, or did he lie to them now? Her blood began to boil.

"If they did, I didn't hear." Roth scratched his cheek. "Oh, wait. He may have said something to Hairy Jones. Ole Hairy's got a better memory for such things. He's out with Lieutenant Walford hunting for them fey now."

Effie's hands tightened on one another, fingers interlacing. She tried to keep the anger from her voice as she asked, "They headed south, and no one followed? No one heeded their words or went to find them afterward?"

Roth shook his head. "No, miss. There was no cause at the time. It's a hanging offense to leave our post, and nothing did attack us from the south. It came from the north alone. These fey, they just ran off at the first hint of danger without a 'by your leave' or nothing."

"Bah." Graham waved a dismissive hand.

Fergus Alpin scowled. "I've humored this folly long enough. You are dismissed, Mr. Roth." The soldier jerked his head stiffly, spun on a heel, and retreated through the entrance of the storehouse before Effie could gather her thoughts to object. That the soldiers did not heed Laeth's warning did not surprise her. But that they continued to brand the fey as traitors when all evidence pointed against it made her want to clout them all with a spoon made of iron. And a spiked one at that.

She rounded on Fergus Alpin. "Humored this folly? You abandoned an ally and now assume they can be nowhere else but conspiring with this imagined horde you claim attacked you! Next you will have them as dwarves trying to assassinate the queen!"

Alpin's eyes bulged. He thrust his finger at her. "Guard your tongue," he snapped. "I will not hear such treason, nor will I suffer your abuse. The fact of the matter is your friends ran off and left the Aerfenium unprotected. If they were Her Majesty's soldiers, they would be shot for desertion. I care little for what horde they did or did not join, nor what lies they shouted as they fled. You have no role and no authority here. Nor do your many...attendants." He waved a hand at Graham and Canonbie. "Even your Mr. Murray exceeds the boundaries of his current orders."

Conall made to speak but stopped short and bowed in submission.

Even with her hackles raised, Effie didn't fault him. He had no doubt come to the same conclusion she had and saw any further argument for a wasted effort. Even if they managed to convince Alpin that Laeth and Hargrund had not turned traitor, the man would not lend them any aid in gathering proof. And what did it matter, anyway? No Aerfenium had been stolen. In fact, there was little evidence an attack on the storehouse had even taken place. The fire could've had another cause, despite its proximity.

But that made little sense. If some local farmer or herdsman had caused it, they would've known it by now. Effie's mind whirled.

She turned from the gathered men and ran through what she knew had occurred. A fire raged to the north, yet Laeth and Hargrund had raced south. The elder Sithling had spoken some message to the soldiers, but it had been ignored. Not only had no Aerfenium been stolen, but no person, fey or human, injured. It all had the feeling of a grand show rather than a horrifying assault. Had the entire ordeal been staged? Told in an exaggerated manner from the lips of soldiers, the tale would dissolve Sir Walter's claims of Aerfenium's safety and squash Caledon's efforts with the treaty.

"Thank you, Mr. Alpin, for reminding us of our duties," Effie said.

She smoothed her dress as a means to calm herself. Something had to be done, and she would start with Laeth and Hargrund. Caledon had appointed the fey to the storehouse, which meant the steward trusted them. That meant she would as well, until she learned for certain to do otherwise. She had to believe they were in danger, perhaps used as pawns in some plot meant to discredit the fey. Whether or not the plot was for a grand show or something more sinister was moot.

Alpin pulled a watch from his waistcoat, checking the hour. He at least had the decency not to smile at his small victory. "You are welcome to dine here," he said, "but I fear we have nothing to offer but soldiers' tack and some salted beef. You'll find better fare in Dunfermline, as well as accommodation for the night."

"We will see to ourselves, then," said Canonbie.

He set his cup on one of the cots and glanced at Effie. He'd remained unusually silent, and the look in his gaze made her wonder why. Some rude jest formed on his tongue, she did not doubt. She nodded to Alpin and strode for the storehouse's exit. Stuart Graham strode at her side while Canonbie and Conall followed farther behind.

"The man's a damned fool." Graham growled as he repeated his earlier comment. "A rational mind is needed in his profession, not some buffoon with closed ears."

Effie smiled at him. "It will have to be enough that we are here."

"You mean not to leave?" he asked. The tinge of disdain in his gaze melted away, replaced by wariness. One eyebrow raised slightly.

"No," replied Effie. "I mean to find my missing friends."

12

They had not stepped a dozen paces from the storehouse when Effie waved to Jack Canonbie. "If you please," she said, "take the carriage down the road, out of sight, and wait for me there."

Canonbie stopped short and folded his arms over his chest. "And where do you think you'll be while I'm awaiting?"

Effie planted her hands on her hips, drawing her shoulders back. She knew the storm was coming but had no time for it. "Discovering where Laeth and Hargrund went."

"Without me?" Canonbie raised an eyebrow.

"It is too dangerous," said Conall. "You have no provisions, and what if more trows or worse roam the area?"

Effie scowled at him. "You know I would sense it if any fey blood lurked about."

"Then the lack of it also tells you Laeth and Hargrund are not anywhere near," said Conall, searching her face.

"I will go with her," said Graham. He gave her a quick nod to show his support. "She has the right of it. We won't know what's out there unless we try."

She smiled at Graham and gave him a firm nod. To Conall she said, "As you say, Laeth and Hargrund, wherever they are, are not close by. But we have no other clue to their whereabouts than the trail they might have left. We can at least use whatever part of the day remains to uncover what we can." She lowered her voice and relaxed her shoulders. "You know what the stakes are. You summoned me here because of them. I cannot depart without at least trying to do more. Besides, Laeth and Hargrund are friends. We cannot leave them to the wind."

Conall scraped at the dirt with his boot, watching the clods bounce away. "I know," he said. "I know all of it too well. You are right, of course. I only meant to see you safe."

"The carriage driver can go by himself and wait for us," said Canonbie. "I'll not have you say Jack Canonbie was afraid of shadows."

"I'll go with the carriage," said Conall. "I'll want to hear word of what you find before you depart."

Effie felt her heart tug. She'd expected him to insist on going with her, too. Had his father's will beat him so low? Or had it been the mantle of command pressing on him over the past few months?

As if sensing her thoughts, he added, "My orders remain from Her Majesty's Fey Finder General. I am to return to Fort William as soon as Lieutenant Walford reports." He tried to lighten his tone. "Besides, who's to come looking for you, if you get lost?"

She saw no humor in the quip. He couldn't have it both ways. If he chose to take his command so earnestly, without questioning its lunacy, then she would leave him to it. But she dared not speak for fear her voice would break. She merely nodded to him, held his gaze for a moment, and stalked away.

The ground crunched under her boots. The sun had dried some of the earlier mud. It made walking less treacherous. She glanced at the sky and saw she had a couple hours of light remaining. The clouds had parted, allowing the spring air to provide a small amount of warmth.

Graham and Canonbie caught up to her easily. Their strides nearly doubled her own. "You needn't follow like some love-struck pup," Graham said to the other man.

Canonbie chucked. "It's your coin that keeps me so attached, pleasant as it may be." He glanced at her, and something of a smile passed his lips.

It flattered her, but she was in no mood for such things. If the man wanted to come, she had no reason to refuse his assistance. Yet her thoughts remained on Conall. Had they grown so far apart? She sighed. It was more like they had never been so close to begin with. She reminded herself he had loved another not long ago. He had meant to spend his life with that woman. Did she expect him now to devote his life to her passions when they had barely known one another for more than a year? She'd known Thomas Stevenson most of her life, and she'd barely heard from him in months. Lately, he spent the bulk of his time with the Royal Society.

She missed a step and almost stumbled. The thought made her realize that perhaps her frustration wasn't solely with Conall.

The joy of victory that had swelled after Caldwell House had ebbed. She'd thought a permanent fey treaty so easily attainable then, in the afterglow of the battle. She'd thought anyone with reason, from the simplest of minds to the leading scientists of the day, would rally for what should have been done centuries earlier. An apology to the fey. A treaty that allowed them to live peacefully in the woods and fields that had long been their homes.

But that dream had started to slip through her fingers within days of the victory. Nuance and positioning, and ego and pride, had all sprouted like a malignant mold.

And now her friends seemed to be abandoning her. Even Stuart Graham she had not seen in some weeks.

No, she scolded herself, *do not blame them for living their own lives.*

"Tell me again of it," said Graham, breaking her from her reverie. He studied her face and must've seen her dour mood. "The flying, strapped to a pair of wings with nothing but buckles and leather keeping you aloft. How did it feel?"

Effie smiled, breathing deep as she recalled. It had been a desperate thing, that brief experience. The trows must've found the wing contraption and hoarded it away. That is, until the Laird of Aonghus commanded they use it to hunt her through the village of Duncairn. When she'd won it from them and strapped it on, she'd thought only of her need to flee to Edinburgh as fast as possible. But soaring high above, with the wind buffeting her and the land a distant blur of colors far beneath, she'd felt unburdened by fear, as if it were something chained to the Earth that could no longer reach her.

She tried to express the sentiment to Graham once again but felt foolish. That Canonbie pretended to ignore the conversation served to embarrass her further. The man only did that when he held an interest, keen to hear every word she said. She could feel his appraisal even as his gaze shifted over the landscape.

Still, the matter brought a lighter mood to mind than her earlier thoughts. Graham knew how to do that—changing her temper until her troubles were forgotten, at least for a time. After a short while, she found herself laughing at his pantomimed version of her flight, while she described each movement she'd made and every gust of wind.

They traipsed past the stone wall and into the scattered woods beyond. The tall grass tickled their knees as they waded through it. Canonbie slowed his pace, and she followed his lead, scanning the ground for any evidence of her Sithling friends. Though what she should look for, she had no idea. Broken twigs and trampled leaves lay all around in the patches where the grass didn't grow. None stood out more significant than any other. She quested with her fey senses and found only a few squirrels and birds about. She couldn't search far with only her blood to wield.

"Do you think the wings are still there, hanging from the tree where you crashed?" Canonbie asked once she had finished her tale.

Effie grinned, shrugging. "They may be. The place was rather removed from the road I stumbled on. But they were fully destroyed. Only scraps of wood and tattered canvas remain."

"A pity." His tone sounded oddly genuine, opposed to his normal mocking. When he met her gaze, she found it difficult to break away.

Graham coughed, and when they didn't turn, he coughed louder. Effie raised an eyebrow at him. He pointed at the ground. "That is a clear boot print," he said. "It angles toward that thick cluster of birch trees."

"So it is," said Canonbie. His eyes danced at her. "It appears fresh. No more than a few days old, and at least since the last rain."

Effie glanced the direction they headed, then toward the trees. "Those birch would take us out of sight from the storehouse." A prickle flashed across her flesh as she said the words. She saw Graham's eyes flare as well.

They changed course and hadn't gone a dozen paces when Jack Canonbie stopped and sniffed the air. "Do you smell that?" he asked.

Effie inhaled. Pine and birch intermixed, giving a minty sweetness above the sharper tang of dirt and stone. A hint of smoke remained, but maybe she imagined it. They'd walked far away from the area that had burned. Nothing else came to her.

Canonbie didn't wait for her reply. He set off at a brisk stride, halting every so often to sniff the air again. But his course remained clear to Effie, even if she hadn't caught on to what he'd found.

Halfway to the cluster of birch, she caught a whiff of rank decay. It reminded her of spoiled meat, and instantly a sense of dread overcame her. She stopped short and stared at the trees. Perhaps her imagination played tricks, but they seemed to take on the appearance of sentinels standing a silent vigil. The guardians of a tomb.

Graham remained at her side. They watched Canonbie scramble the last few paces, his burly frame swallowed by the shadows of the trees. When he reappeared, he waved for them to come. Effie's feet felt like lead, but she shook off the weight. She'd known horrors before. She'd smelled death in a sea cave full of rotting selkie corpses. She'd seen it at Caldwell House by the thousands.

Reaching the trees, she didn't need Canonbie to point out the bodies. She heard the midges buzzing. Laeth and Hargrund wore the dress of country gentlemen and had appeared as such in life. Now they lay dead, their eyes vacant and jaws agape. Blood spilled from their temples and pooled on the ground around them. It had dried and crusted black, giving off a scent of burnt copper under the broader rot. Something had bashed their heads. Each appeared to sit, propped up and resting against a tree, their legs splayed out before them.

"Bugger me," cursed Graham. He spat, and his face grew hard.

Effie swallowed the lump in her throat. Now was not the time for sorrow. The slain fey deserved better. They deserved for their assailant to be caught and brought to justice. Effie shook her head. They deserved more, but that was the best she could offer.

A curious thing struck her as she stared at the familiar faces. She stepped closer. The wounds didn't look as barbaric as they first had. They were too uniform, as if performed by a practiced hand. Her brow scrunched. A practiced hand wielding a specific tool, she saw now. Square wounds the size of a large walnut formed a matching pair atop the feys' heads. The two holes mirrored each other in the exact same position, just above the left temple.

"An awl?" asked Graham. He'd noticed the same thing. He bent over Laeth's body and pointed to the hole.

"A large one, if it was," said Effie. She peered into Hargrund's wound and gagged, turning away and gasping for fresh air. But it wasn't from the rot.

"Their heads are hollow," she said. "Their brain matter taken from them." She put her hands to her gut and breathed deeply. Such things rarely affected her, but there was something about the way the open cavity looked. It bore a sadness of loss beyond death. Not only had life been stolen from these poor fey, but part of that which made them who they were.

Canonbie inspected the wounds and wrinkled his nose. He stood straight and searched the direction they'd come. She followed his gaze and saw that the storehouse could no longer be seen, just like she'd earlier assumed. "Something must've lured them out here," he said. "A trap, just the same as the fire that drew the soldiers' attention the other direction."

Effie considered that. They had come perhaps a mile from the stone wall, too far for any direct sound to carry. Out of sight and hearing of human senses, she realized. They stood near the edge of where her fey awareness could roam from a position at the storehouse, yet the pair of fey had had each other to strengthen their awareness.

"I think you are right," she agreed. "But why kill them and leave the Aerfenium untouched?"

Graham nodded, following her thought. "If the fire and this lure were orchestrated, the remainder of the plot seems incomplete."

Canonbie shrugged. "Tell Mr. Alpin of this, and he will only see a pair of fey betrayed by a foe with whom they conspired. He will pass that account onward, and those who stand against the fey will relish the news. They will use it to bolster their rhetoric."

Effie folded her arms to stave off a chill. As the shadows grew longer, the wind had picked up. It rustled the leaves and whispered through the trees. It couldn't be that simple, could it? And done by whose hand? Could Lord Granville have orchestrated such a heinous crime just to defeat the treaty? Slowly, she shook her head, refusing to believe the murder of her friends so callous an act.

"No," she told Jack Canonbie. A detail popped into her head and unraveled the man's argument. "That account holds some merit, but it overlooks the crucial element."

He considered for a moment. "The brain matter," he finally said.

She nodded. "Yes. Why go to all that bother? It would take time." She searched the ground around them. "And look, no evidence of it remains. So the killer took it with them."

"Or consumed it," offered Canonbie.

Effie shivered. This time, it had nothing to do with the wind. "A savage beast would've left evidence of the attack," she reasoned. "Anything more meticulous... Well, I can't image they would tarry here to dine. They must've planned this and known they would take the matter with them."

Graham squatted and studied the wounds again. "I've read there are some who argue the phrenology of the fey brain the key to their Fey Craft," he said. "That must be the cause of the trepanning."

Effie remembered the tome she'd borrowed from Conall and growled. The anger she'd felt learning of all the cruel experiments done to her kind returned. Had one of fey blood done something just as dastardly to her friends? Was it some ritual of Blood Craft?

"The fire creates a diversion for the soldiers," she said aloud, walking through the evidence as a means to steady her temper. "But Laeth and Hargrund feel an impulse stemming from their fey senses coming from the other direction. An impulse that isn't just stagnant. It draws them out."

"Maybe to protect or rescue something from danger?" offered Graham.

Effie nodded. The notion fit. They'd thought all along that the Aerfenium must be involved, but if one took it out of the riddle, a different tale unfolded. "They try to quickly notify the soldiers stationed at the wall, but rush off feeling an urgency greater than their duty to remain at the storehouse. They are lured here, subdued by some means, and slain. The Aerfenium was never the target. They were."

"But what was so special about these fey?" Canonbie asked.

Effie knew Caledon or Rose might be able to answer such a question. Yet she thought it might miss the point. "It is possible Laeth or Hargrund held some special gift, or that they ran afoul of some old foe," she allowed, "but perhaps they merely stood in the only place where the killer knew fey to be? Without a nose for such things, most humans go an entire lifetime without stumbling into one of our kind. To know they are here near Balclune creates an opportunity."

Grunting, Canonbie said, "You assume the killer wasn't a fey themselves."

"We're assuming a lot of things," Effie admitted. "But I prefer to paint a picture with the brush strokes we have rather than leave it to the likes of Fergus Alpin or Lord Granville." She gathered herself. Many questions remained, yet the sunlight had started to fail them. "Do either of you have a means to track where the killer went?"

"In a city, maybe," said Canonbie, shrugging. "I'm not one for fen and forest."

Graham shook his head. He appeared transfixed. His fingers came to his lips, playing at them lightly. She watched him as his mind worked, until he finally spoke. "The bodies stink," he announced, leaning in to sniff.

"Aye," said Canonbie. "Aren't you a clever fellow?"

"Nay." He waved a hand as if searching for a means to explain himself. "I mean yes, but..."

"They stink too much," said Effie. She realized it now that Graham pointed it out. A tang beyond simple decay added to the stench of rot. "There is something foul about it, like soured milk. It's not right."

Graham smirked at Canonbie, but the rogue only chuckled. At a raised eyebrow from Effie, his smirk disappeared. He cleared his throat. "It could be a toxin," he said. "We should check them for other wounds. I'm sure they didn't stand still and allow their killer to land those precise blows against them."

"I'll help," said Effie. Together they checked the arms and legs, stomachs and chests of Laeth and Hargrund. But they found nothing out of sorts, no other wound or bruise. Effie chewed her lip and scoured them again.

"I'll move him to better examine the back," said Graham. He braced himself to heave Laeth over.

"No, there!" Effie exclaimed. She put a hand on Graham's shoulder to stop him. With the other, she indicated the tiny tear of flesh in Laeth's neck. It widened no bigger than a needle point. She'd only noticed it because its rim had turned purple and raised, and that mark stood no bigger than a shirt button.

"It looks like from a syringe," she said.

"Or a dart," said Canonbie. He hovered over her, using his long arms to reach past her head and poke at the wound. She could feel the warmth of his body, the smell of him. Releasing Graham's shoulder, she spun away, rising and straightening out her skirts. Amusement flashed in Canonbie's eyes. She scowled. The man could read her all too well.

Graham played at his lips again, this time tapping the upper one with a finger. Leaning over the needle prick, he inhaled deeply. "The smell comes from here," he said. He pressed a thumb against the tiny wound first, then used both hands to pry open Laeth's jaw.

Effie yelped in surprise. A jolt passed through her, stiffening her muscles. The inside of Laeth's mouth, his tongue and gums, had all turned black.

"Poison," said Graham.

anonbie's throat rumbled something between a curse and a groan. He straightened, and his eyes darted between the shadows formed by the trees. "It grows too late. We should return to the storehouse," he said.

As if summoned by his words, the sky darkened. It took Effie a moment to realize the sun had finally dipped below the hills. Only an amber cast to the horizon remained to light their way. A field of clouds had moved in overhead to hide the stars. The air chilled as well, and she could hear the wind strengthening as it swept across the surrounding hills.

"We cannot just leave them like this," said Effie.

"They are too much for us to carry and return safely," said Canonbie. "Let us tell the soldiers to fetch them with stretchers. They will go nowhere tonight."

"Here," said Graham. He reached into his coat pocket and fumbled through a handful of tiny paper packets. Tearing open two, he dumped their contents on the ground and found a stick to mix the powders each had contained. The mixture started to sizzle and glow with a faint silver light. "I've found these useful a time or two on projects."

Graham found two other sticks, coated their ends in the glowing mixture, and handed them to Effie and Canonbie. Next he took a handful of rocks and dabbed them in the mixture. "We can use these as markers to light the way back. I'll return here with lanterns and the stretchers. I'm sure Mr. Murray will want to see these fey at once."

Canonbie snorted. "I'll put a wager against that."

"How dare you," Effie snapped, whirling on him. "You'll do better to keep your mouth shut than slander a gentleman you know so little about." She tried to silence the part of her that doubted her conviction. It only boiled her anger all the more.

Canonbie put a hand up, but it was more to hold back her fury than to apologize. "Mr. Murray made his intentions clear enough. Oh, if you do the asking, I'm sure he'll come at once. It's the wanting that is lacking."

Staggering back a step, she placed a hand on her stomach. She couldn't face the infuriating man any longer. He uttered aloud too many of her own dark thoughts. "Fetch Mr. Murray from the road and ask him return to the storehouse with the steam carriage," she told Canonbie. "We will turn over our discovery to the Fey Finders and return with stretchers to recover the remains of these poor fey."

She caught Canonbie's nod and gestured for Graham to follow her through the thickets of lowland shrub and tall grass. The going slowed as the daylight failed, but Graham's glowing sticks provided enough radiance that they didn't worry over their footing. On another night, Effie would've asked him about the compounds used, or how often he carried them on his person. She could think of times in her own life when such a trick would've proven more than useful.

Lanterns and a large campfire provided an obvious beacon for them to spy the storehouse, even if its dark silhouette hadn't stood out against the horizon. The soldiers at the wall challenged them but allowed them to pass. If any pondered over her odd comings and goings at the late hour, none voiced it. As a group, the men seemed indifferent and relaxed in their station, as if their detail were meant more for their own recovery rather than the protection of one of the crown's most valuable substances. She wondered how many of them even knew the true worth of what they guarded.

The exhale of a steam whistle from down the road let her know Jack

Canonbie had reached Conall. She found Fergus Alpin watching her from the campfire, where a handful of soldiers busied about with preparations for the evening meal. The man stood with a rather noisy sigh of indignation, followed by a brief coughing fit.

"It is never so easy to get rid of you," he said. His brow raised as Graham bristled, but he didn't allow the other man to speak. "Take this gentleman with you and be gone. I have a mind to write the Fey Finder General as to Mr. Murray's encouragement of your intercession. Then we will see how long you remain in his favor. You may even find yourself the subject of much discussion!"

"We require four sturdy men, some lanterns, and a pair of stretchers, if you please, Mr. Alpin," said Effie. She had no patience to challenge his arrogance. Like in Langmire, she would let the man bluster for all his worth as long as he conceded to reason in the end. "We have found Laeth and Hargrund. They were murdered not far from here while you and the soldiers under your command watched some parlor trick and ignored the real threat." Her eyes narrowed. "Would you like me to write that account for Mr. Billingsley?"

Fergus Alpin's jaw quivered. The soldiers about the campfire had stopped their tasks. They watched in silence. Alpin's gaze danced over her shoulder as the steam carriage sputtered and popped, returning to the storehouse. The Fey Finder found himself woefully outnumbered. She could see the realization in his eyes.

"It is not in doubt you followed the crown's commands, Mr. Alpin," said Graham. He pulled at his coat and widened his stance. "We only seek to offer assistance."

Effie held her tongue. She could tell by Graham's fidgeting he sought to placate Alpin's ego the way she had at Langmire.

"Very well," Alpin said. "You will have what you need as long as it is clear the safety of the Aerfenium is and always will be the chief concern of this posting. I have neither the time nor disposition to follow the frivolities of your fey friends."

Effie thought to point out that those same fey friends were allies under his protection, but she caught sight of the storehouse and the trickling of soldiers who watched them, their uniforms disheveled and postures slack. Caledon had agreed to the location at Sir Walter's suggestion. But it dawned on her now the absurdity of that suggestion. Why not store the Aerfenium in a fortified castle? Why not detach a full company of soldiers to protect it? Sir Walter's private schemes couldn't be so foolhardy as to place the entire operation into jeopardy.

Unless Sir Walter hedged on the treaty's defeat. Then the openness and ease of access for his pawns worked in his favor. Her gut turned to stone. She had taken the passing of a fey treaty for a certainty, the only question a matter of the cost. But everywhere she turned, it seemed she discovered more evidence that the treaty's opponents mounted. Those in favor of the treaty had more than the likes of Lord Granville opposing them. Their own benefactors refused to fully commit to it. Even Caledon feared what the treaty might bring, the enslavement of the fey, bound into producing more and more Aerfenium for the prosperity of the empire.

But without the treaty, men like Fergus Alpin would continue their ignorant bigotry, and she could not stand for that. She could not. She needed to keep fighting. She had to find a way to balance the scales. "And what of the attack?" she asked. "Is it not a crime to murder allies of the crown?"

Alpin pulled out his pocket watch and made a show of dusting its surface. Checking the hour, he barked at the soldiers to hurry about their tasks before returning his eye to Effie. "The crown thanks you for the information you've provided in the matter. I will pass word along to Mr. Billingsley and await his instructions."

"A killer roams free!" she cried.

"A killer, you'll no doubt claim, who is not of fey blood." He shoved the watch into his pocket. Clasping his hands behind his back, he puffed out his chest. A smirk crossed his lips. "That is unfortunate for you. You see, as a Fey Finder I am not commissioned to hunt common murderers. Fetch the constable, if you desire. But bother me no more about it."

* * *

Effie sipped a strong black tea. The lack of honey made her grimace, but she needed something to wash down the hard bread and strip of salted beef Conall had offered her. Both were a far cry from the fare at Lady

Fife's, the last time they had shared a meal. They sat within the storehouse, in a corner away from the soldiers' billet. The hard wood of the bench numbed Effie's backside, but it creaked every time she moved, so she sat still and endured it.

"Trows and wulvers still roam the countryside," Conall said. "Their numbers dwindle, but not the tales of their ferocity. Between each village, they grow larger and their deeds more wicked. The slaying of a single sheep becomes a whole flock before the tale is passed to the cities."

"I know," said Effie. She had heard her share of these tales. She'd heard of the beasts with spiked tails, too, and of those who stole wee babes from their cradles. She'd heard of one devil who breathed frost cold enough to freeze rocks. He froze his victims and shattered them whole. All of it, beyond the few trows and wulvers who only sought food for their bellies, was rubbish. All of it a tide that battered against the truth.

"I will speak with Mr. Billingsley." Conall drained the last of his tea and produced a flask. Pouring a dram into the cup, he passed the flask to Effie. "He may have an opinion on the matter we have not considered."

"That sounds like a prudent action, but one you have no desire to perform," said Effie. Her tone sounded as hollow as she felt. "I mean any of it. Your father still has you dancing on strings." She took a sip from the flask. The whiskey warmed her throat. Its flowery notes were sweeter than her tea. When Conall lowered his gaze, she added, "There is no shame in wanting a simpler life. I want very much the same. It's just, forgive me for saying, but I've often forgotten that you wish it above all else."

"You have a cause," he said. "I have friends who need me, for whom I would risk anything." He shrugged. "But the two aren't the same."

"No, they aren't," agreed Effie.

"So what is a famed pugilist to do?" he asked. The jest reminded her of the feigned bravado he'd displayed when they'd first met. It had worked to calm her then. Now, it only made her long for the road they had shared, their fates intertwined for that brief time.

"Throw punches at the wind and hope the gods hear you roar," she said. "Stuart Graham likes to say that." She glanced around but couldn't spy where the stout man had gone. Most likely, he'd seen the need for her and Conall to share private words.

Conall grinned, but there was little mirth in it. "Wisdom for a fool to follow. I wish I were that strong."

Effie took another nip from the flask and passed it back to him. "What of these murders? Will you speak to Mr. Billingsley on this matter as well?" She had little faith it would do any good. The new Fey Finder General no doubt took his command with pockets laden by the coin of those with interests other than justice for a pair of fey.

"I will," said Conall. "But Mr. Alpin is correct. We Fey Finders have no authority in the matters of murder, or even petty theft, unless the culprit is fey."

"But when we first arrived, Mr. Alpin argued that very thing!"

Conall shook his head. "He only asserted that fey were behind an attack on the storehouse. He had no notion of the murders until you brought the deed before him, and sadly, you did an exceeding job convincing him the culprit must be human."

"The possibility of a fey perpetrator is not excluded," said Effie.

"Of course," Conall agreed, though his tone was conciliatory rather than encouraging.

Movement caught her attention. Graham and Canonbie approached, striding with purpose. "Lieutenant Walford has sent a missive," Graham said, eagerly. "He and his men have uncovered a local crofter who admits to setting the blaze."

Effie scrambled to her feet. "Truly?"

Graham nodded. He could not keep the gleam of excitement from his eye. "At first this crofter claimed it a muirburn to remove some old growth. But a shepherd who seemed angered by the blaze later argued that grazing was already bountiful enough. The crofter had no need to burn anything back. The lieutenant returned to the crofter and forced him to tell them true."

"To what end?" Effie leaned forward, as if to hear the words faster.

Graham folded his arms across his chest and bent his head toward her. A grin spread his lips wide. "The crofter did confess a man paid him to set the fire."

"Is the crofter arrested?" she asked. "Where is he now?"

Graham's excitement waned. His shoulders sagged. "Bah, the local man had rights to set a muirburn. The lieutenant and his men let him on his way."

Effie let out a soft moan. She felt herself deflate. "Did they at least obtain a description of the man who paid the crofter? It must be the killer, or one of them, at least. No one else would pay for such an odd request."

"He did," answered Graham. "A scrawny man and short, with a northern accent perhaps from Aberdeen. He wore a beard and carried a cane of red wood. It bore a strange device seared into it. He approached the crofter at a coaching inn not far from Balclune. The crofter frequents there often, so the seemingly chance meeting might not have been random."

"No doubt the beard is shorn and cane thrown into a rubbish heap by now," said Canonbie. He'd taken up Graham's stance, with his arms crossed, though skepticism showed openly on his face. "The lieutenant stands a better chance growing a tail than trusting in so vague a description in hopes of catching the stranger."

"Lieutenant Walford and his men will accompany me to Fort William, now that this matter is settled," said Conall. His voice carried barely above a whisper.

"Settled!" cried Graham, in disbelief.

"He means the attack," said Effie. "Or the lack of one, since it is clear the Aerfenium was never in danger."

"So the killings fall to the local constable," said Canonbie. He chuckled. "I'd wager better odds for a sow to pen a sonnet than for the constable to uncover this stranger."

Effie planted her hands on her hips. "I'll take that wager," she said. Her glare defied him to find any humor in the statement.

"You mean to do something," said Graham. It didn't sound like a question. His arms dropped slack, and his stare grew hard. "Too right. Laeth and Hargrund deserve it. Something foul beyond murder occurred to them."

"The constables. Surely they will want to know the significance of the trepanning," offered Conall.

"They will," said Effie, catching his eye. "They just don't know it yet."

Jack Canonbie held up his hand to ward her off. "You don't mean to go traipsing about again like some gypsy bloodhound."

"Does Mr. Stevenson's coin not spend as well when you're not lounging about drinking?" snapped Effie. Canonbie's posture shifted subtly. It reminded her of a stalking cat about to pounce. His stare turned to stone. But he clamped his mouth shut.

"I will speak with Sir Walter," said Graham. He ignored their spatting. His mind already worked to solve the problem before them. "If he knows the truth, he may press the local constables into action. Or he may relate the matter to a magistrate. I'm sure once they are involved, this Mr. Billingsley will follow."

A smile crossed Effie's lips. Graham's eagerness to help lessened some of the acid she felt brewing within. "It's a good start, but we will need to act quicker if we are to have any hope of catching wind of this scrawny man the crofter described. Already he has two days on us."

Graham nodded. "Too right," he repeated. "Well, then we'd best visit this coaching inn afore it gets any darker. Maybe the killer was known to someone there."

"Bloody hell," mumbled Canonbie.

Graham chuckled. "It costs us nothing to make a few inquiries." He dipped his head slightly to Effie. "Besides, it's my coin paying you as well."

She laughed at that, grateful one of the gentlemen before her saw reason in pursuing justice for its own sake.

"You'll need more than a few details to interest Mr. Alpin," said Conall. "But maybe if you uncover enough, I can convince Mr. Billingsley to push the local constables into action, just as Mr. Graham suggested."

"You'll have it," said Effie. "I intend to push until there is an arrest. The empire must hear of these heinous crimes as much as they do the tales of fey wickedness. We cannot let Lord Granville have his way, defaming the fey and denouncing Aerfenium based on reports now proven false. He'll doom the treaty if we can't force him to concede the account."

"One needn't make an arrest for word of these murders to spread," said Canonbie. "Truth and diligence are not how the game is played. Or at least, not how the game is won. Lord Granville knows this. He did not wait for proof before dismantling the public's trust in your fey steward and turning the empire against the treaty."

Effie bristled. But the man did have a point. An arrest was not needed to see word of the murders in print. She would telegram Jane and have the girl bring the tale to the printers. It just needed a little seasoning beyond the description of the deed itself.

Seasoning she meant to uncover.

Graham stroked his chin. "The killer is familiar with chemistry," he said. "Perhaps a tinker or an anthropologist. That is how he knows of poisons and fey phrenology. It is not a far stretch from what we know as true. Those burr holes from the trepanning came from a practiced hand."

"It could be the work of a surgeon," suggested Conall. "Or another profession with a similar education."

"Well, that narrows it down to a few thousand suspects," said Canonbie. He snorted and shook his head.

"If you have not the stomach for the hunt, we can part ways," said Graham. "I'm sure Lady Fife would gladly welcome your return."

Canonbie's cheeks burned. He sucked in a breath to retort, but let it out with only a conceding shrug.

Effie caught the reaction but had no time to consider it. She placed a hand on Graham's arm. "Ready your horse," she said. "Mr. Canonbie, please, the steam carriage. Night has only just fallen. The coaching inn cannot be more than two miles from us if it is near Balclune. I'm sure a private room with a soft bed is better for my delicate nature than a rickety cot sprawled amongst a room of Her Majesty's soldiers. Don't you gentlemen agree?"

Graham chuckled and stalked away. A smirking Canonbie bowed and followed on his heels. Conall studied her face as she watched them depart. "Keep an eye on that one, and do not trust him overmuch," he said.

She cocked her head and eyed him. "You helped heap Mr. Canonbie on me, if you'll remember," she said, flatly.

"Effie," said Conall. He plucked up her hand and held it in both of his. A warmth passed between them, yet she could see in his eyes how lost he'd become, forced to choose between his friends, his country, the will of his father, and his own desires. He squeezed her tighter, and she wanted desperately for him to choose her. But that would not be fair to him. It would not be right, and in her heart she knew it wouldn't matter, anyway. She had moved on.

"Don't say it," she said. "Whatever it is. You have no cause to owe me anything. Certainly not an apology."

She removed her hand and leaned in to kiss his cheek, breathing in his musky scent, and letting herself savor the closeness before pulling away. She wished, in part, that he would turn to meet her lips. But he didn't.

❧ 14 ❧

The coaching inn rested within sight of Balclune near a long ditch that had turned into a bog. Several bits of rotting wood stuck up between the reeds and grass, and a mossy film covered the muddy water. It reflected off the steam carriage's lamps as they bounced down the road. Graham followed. He'd donned a heavy overcoat of dark brown wool and a pair of supple doeskin gloves. Effie wished she'd done the same. The night had turned chilly and damp, with low clouds swirling about that seemed to stick to her skin. But she hadn't wanted to take the time digging into her luggage. It was stored on the roof of the carriage, and the process of fetching it down, sorting through it, and re-lashing it afterward seemed overly burdensome for such a short journey. She reasoned she'd be warm enough within the carriage. The boiler sat behind her back, after all, through a thick plank of wood banded by iron.

Canonbie had not mentioned the cold, nor moved for his own coat. He sat in silence across from her. She had often wished for such a posture from the man. Though now that she had it, she found it a bit unsettling. She wondered what thoughts had stolen his tongue, and whether she was included in them.

Clamping her jaw closed to keep it from chattering, she eyed the inn. It had a yard adequate for a dozen carriages and a small stable to one

side. The inn itself appeared in good repair, as near as she could tell in
the darkness. The lamplight reached only a few spans in each direction,
but she thought she spied fresh paint on the gables and on the timbers
framing the windows.

Two boys peeked through the front door at the sound of their
approach. Their heads disappeared for a moment before the lads
emerged with lanterns. They directed the carriage driver to an open
patch of the yard and took Graham's reins. Their manner was well
practiced for their young age. If they thought it too late for the arrival of
guests, they showed no sign of it. Effie and Canonbie alighted, and they
all entered the inn while the driver and boys saw to their things.

The matron of the house wiped her plump fingers on a stained and
worn apron. She greeted them with a cheery smile. Her face had
weathered the better part of her years with grace, but a thicket of gray
hair belied her age. She stood at Effie's height only broader of girth and
fuller of bosom. The inn's common room held only empty tables and
chairs. A fire crackled in a hearth against one wall, and a long bar ran
along the back. The hint of a barley and beef stew remained in the air
along with a mixture of wood polish and stale beer.

Effie inquired after rooms and food for her party. Despite the rations
she'd eaten at the storehouse, her stomach rumbled as she caught a
whiff of the stew. Besides, she'd never known men to turn down good
food, and the display of extra coin might help the matron find her
tongue.

"Is it usually so quiet along this road?" she asked as she and Graham
and Jack Canonbie sat at one of the tables.

"Ye mean in here, dearie?" asked the matron. She wiped the table
down with a rag, though the surface had little need of it. "Och, so it is.
It's these new contraptions what needs no horse. Twenty years ago, all
the carriages would need to stop and rest their teams. But coal needs no
rest, does it? Folks trundle on past without a care unless it's time for a
wee nip."

"Do none of the locals come to drink?" asked Effie.

The matron waved her hand, but her tone remained pleasant.
"There's a public house down in the village of Crossford. That's where
many a go."

"Well, let's see if we cannot make up for that," said Canonbie. "A round of pints, if you please."

The matron glanced at Effie for her approval. "It's none of my business," she added, after Effie gave consent. "But it's been long years since we've had a ladyship in here. How am I to address ye?" She pulled three glasses from a shelf and started drawing them full. The creamy head looked divine over the thick, black ale.

Graham's cheery grin doubled in size. Stifling her own amusement, Effie glanced at Canonbie. She'd done almost all the talking, so the matron had naturally assumed her male companions to be of an inferior rank. As equals, polite society would've had her defer to the men. The flub reminded her of another detail overlooked in a country wayhouse years before, when she was but a girl. That mistake had led to calamity, her capture by a Fey Finder, and a march toward execution in Edinburgh. The memory brought a flutter to her stomach, but she felt no distress over the matron's assumption. She'd come a long way from the days spent hiding in the forest, scavenging for food like a field mouse. And not just in the physical sense. The thought of meeting strangers no longer terrified her as it once had. Her sense of safety no longer relied on anonymity. Caldwell House and the procession with the duke afterward, the balls and society events, had changed all that.

Canonbie leaned his head back and barked a hearty laugh, refusing to contain himself as she had. "Her uncle spoils her to the core, and it's fed her sense of station," he said. "But she is no lady to be curtsied to, or addressed with pomp."

Effie's eyes narrowed. Kicking the man's shins or snapping at him wouldn't help prove she wasn't spoiled. The thought of it did bring a smug grin to her lips, however.

"A lady is made from the company she keeps," said Graham. He rapped a knuckle on the table. "And in some cases, in spite of it."

Jack Canonbie bawled harder, slapping his knee. Heat rose to Effie's cheeks, but her companion's laughter was infectious, and she couldn't help but join him.

The matron looked as though she didn't know what to make of the response. She settled on a short huff, wiping her hands on her apron to dry them before serving their pints. As the woman approached, Effie studied her and decided on a direct inquiry. She saw no cause for coyness, and she guessed the matron wise enough to see through any embellished pretense.

"There was a crofter who came here a few days ago," she said. She took a sip from her beer and relished its rich, malty flavor.

"The one who set the muirburn over the hills to the north," added Graham.

Wiping her hands on her apron, the matron eyed them skeptically. "What of it? I don't go gabbing me gums over other folks' business."

"A Lieutenant Walford, from one of Her Majesty's Highland regiments, has questioned the man. The crofter claimed he set the fire under the direction of another he met here, in this very room." Effie thought it better to avoid mentioning the Fey Finders and the Aerfenium storehouse in case the woman knew nothing of them.

"The lieutenant is a family acquaintance who asked us to inquire after the matter on behalf of the land's owner," said Canonbie. He spoke casually and stopped to take a rather large swallow of beer. "You see, neither party wishes for anything formal to be done, but there is this odd matter of the fire's presumed benefactor."

"A scrawny, bearded man with a red cane, the crofter told the lieutenant," said Graham.

At that the matron's eyes flared in recognition. "Och, that man was odd. I knew something was amiss afore he even sat down. And sit he did, all day long over on that chair there." She gestured at a table in the corner. "He read from some thick tome what had diagrams scrawled all over the pages. It gave me a fright when I first glanced at it."

She paused and wrinkled her nose, planting her hands on her hips. "That was odd, too. Every time I came near, he'd pull that book closer and shut it slightly as if to hide its words from me." She shook her head. "Daft fool. It only made me all the more curious."

"Do you remember its title?" asked Effie.

Shaking her head, the matron said, "No, but it looked right expensive."

"Do you recall if he arrived by carriage or horse?" asked Graham. "Could he be from Dunfermline?"

The matron thought for a moment. "Horse, I believe. But from where, who's to say? There are many an odd folk who pass through that town. Why, it's almost as bad as a city!"

"Can you tell us anything else about the man?" asked Effie. "We do wish to find him."

"Nothing I can think of," said the matron. "As I said, he came in, sat and read all day, and left. I never saw him talking with anyone."

Effie jolted and nearly spilled her pint. "He didn't stay the night here?" she asked. The clue gave her hope the trail had not fully died.

"Nay, he never asked after lodging."

Graham shot a glance at Effie. He had caught on to the importance of the news as well. "If he came by horse and didn't stay the night here, he would've had to store his...instruments somewhere." He raised his eyebrow to ensure she knew what he meant. "I'd wager he stayed in town. He'd stand out too much in one of the villages."

Effie tapped her finger on the table, thinking. If they assumed the man wasn't fey, he either had a companion or some other means of giving off the appearance of a fey aura. It was the missing piece that troubled her most. But Graham was correct, in any case. The man had to stay the night somewhere, and Dunfermline made the most sense. They could start their inquiries at the inns and hotels there in the morning. There couldn't be that many of them, and perhaps the man had left a name or some other detail.

She bit her lip. Assuming he hadn't used an alias or wasn't local himself. Another thought came to her, and she asked, "Do you remember how far into the book the man was?"

"Toward the start, I believe," said the matron. "For all its heft, the thing looked rather new."

"You think he visited a bookseller in town?" asked Graham.

Canonbie scoffed. "It's just as easy the man took a train from Edinburgh or Glasgow, or even Manchester for that matter."

"True," admitted Effie. "But there are fewer booksellers in Dunfermline than there are lodgings. It is a better place to start."

Graham nodded and raised his glass. "Clever," he said, taking a gulp.

"Ah, a return to civilization at last," said Canonbie. He drained the remainder of his pint and slapped the glass down.

Effie hid the bubble of joy that pulsed through her. It made her feel guilty. They sought a murderer, not a cheery place for a picnic. Yet the quest thrilled her, the riddles to unravel and secrets to explore. Even thoughts of Lord Granville's propaganda could not dampen the eagerness of her curiosity.

She thanked the matron for her help, and again when the woman brought them bowls of the piping hot stew. The broth was thick and salty. It took another round of pints to wash it down, and afterward they all sat for a time with full bellies and content smiles. Canonbie lit a pipe and listened as she and Graham spoke of new devices he'd read about.

Despite the macabre nature of their hunt, she laughed easily with her companions. For the first time in a while, she felt her actions might bring justice to the fey cause, and that lightened her heart, regardless of what the morrow might bring.

🦋 15 🦋

Like many Scottish towns, Dunfermline sprawled atop a central hill. Its stone-cobbled high street led to a medieval abbey that had peered over the Fife countryside since the days of King Malcolm Canmore. Effie stared at the abbey's high walls and crenellated tower. She'd come to the town seeking a man who possessed two fey brains. The abbey contained the body of King Robert the Bruce, minus the man's heart, which had been buried in Melrose. There was some morbid symmetry there.

She stood along the high street in front of a butcher's shop, pulling her coat tighter about her neck to stave off the early morning cold. A light rain fell. She heard its patter on the gas lamps that lined the street. A bustle of horses, steam carriages, and locals afoot swarmed around her, their heads turned to morning duties. Graham gestured at a millinery, pointing out the vibrant colors—modern chemistry on display, in the guise of fashion.

Movement above drew her eye to an airship passing overhead. Its large balloon looked like a giant bean, its tail a shark's fin. The carriage lashed to its belly could hold perhaps two dozen passengers, a meager sum for all its bulk and weight. The problem was the heavy store of coal needed to fuel its engines. On such a barge, the coal would consume half its hold.

Aerfenium would change that ratio and allow for a greater storage of cargo and number of passengers. She started to point that out to Graham, but he had gestured and opened his mouth to do the same.

"It's headed for the city," he said, chuckling. The rain had plastered his hair to his head. His cheeks held a few day's stubble. She smiled and nodded, knowing he meant Edinburgh. The city lay just across the Firth of Forth, only slightly more than a dozen miles to the south.

"The pair of you gawk like school children," said Canonbie, appearing out of the bustle. "It's a wonder either of you still hold a full purse. Come, I ken a place to seek our man." He strode past them and indicated with a dip of his head they should follow him down a broad alleyway. His cane clacked against the cobblestones, his stride full of purpose.

"Bah." Graham batted his hand at the air, as if to ward off the jest. But he chuckled all the same.

Effie jumped. She hadn't heard the man approach. He'd left them earlier to make inquiries. He'd argued that a man alone could glean more information about the town's disposition than the three of them traipsing about together. She'd reluctantly agreed. The man was savvy about such things, and it wasn't wise to handcuff him when they worked toward the same purpose. Just the same, she despised waiting around while another took on the challenges she yearned to face.

They followed Canonbie between two stone buildings that rose nearly as high as the abbey, though their foundations rested on lower ground. Globules of rainwater dripped from the eaves, forming large puddles that smelled something awful. Effie stepped around the puddles as best she could. She didn't want to think on what mixture of refuse created the stench.

"The bookseller at Fowler's of Kinross hadn't heard of our man, and he grew rather cross when I inquired after books of an occult nature." Canonbie chuckled at something but didn't elaborate any further. He continued to the alleyway's end and turned them onto a smaller lane that wound down an embankment. Spring flowers blossomed on the slope on the far side of the cobblestones. A row of shops, more worn and derelict than those found on the high street, lined the near side.

"You said you'd wait," Effie snipped. "You were only meant to make a round of the streets, not enter a shop."

Canonbie shrugged. He'd shaved and slicked his hair back with grease. It made him appear polished and rather fetching. He could almost pass for an honest gentleman if one didn't know him. "I saved us some time. From the volumes in the window, I could tell the shop wouldn't hold any answers. The shelves were too tidy."

"Too tidy!" she echoed, though her tone held more bite. "What does that have to do with anything?"

"The occult," answered Graham. "A proper bookshop wouldn't carry those types of books. You're looking for one that hides what it sells."

"Ha!" barked Canonbie. "The man knows a thing."

Graham gave the man a sour glance. "Your employer also knows we should inform the local constables. They have more numbers and might even know the man by his description. But regardless, they will want to know if a murderer were loose in the town."

Canonbie waggled his cane. "Not a murderer of fey."

It pained Effie to agree with Canonbie. She had heard Graham's argument earlier, and despite its good intention, she knew it would lead only to a delay of their own efforts. "We must play our hand correctly, if we are to entice the authorities to act," she said.

"You sound like Sir Walter," said Graham, "as if everything is politics." He cocked his head her way. "Have you come to believe no one ever acts just because it is the right thing to do?"

The irony of his question made her grunt and shake her head. "I believe quite the opposite. But I have found these past years that what is right is not so easily seen by all, nor agreed upon." She thought for a moment before adding, "Even if its truth is blinding."

Graham's gaze reflected a sadness, as if he yearned to reach into her and take that sentiment away, anything for a parent to give a child greater hope.

A few shops down the road, Jack Canonbie slapped his hands together and rubbed them. He'd stopped abruptly before an oaken door. A sign above read: Harrow & Loch. The lone window held frosted glass.

It hadn't been cleaned in some time, and mold crept along its edges. "Here's the place. Keep yer wits about," he said, pushing through the door.

Effie clutched her reticule, a small velvet bag pulled shut by a short drawstring, and huffed a breath of disdain. But she could only follow the man inside. He had left her no chance to retort. Graham stepped in and held the door for her. He had the decency to hide his grin, yet she could see his lips quivering.

It took a moment for her eyes to adjust. Only a few candles burned within the shop, and the darkness turned the shabby room into a squalid dungeon. Several rows of wooden bookcases pressed together in the shop's center, leaving little room to squeeze between them. Books overfilled the shelves. They stuck out at odd angles, some upright, others leaning on their neighbors or stacked in small piles. A cart of leather-bound tomes lined one wall. On another, a glass case contained delicate silver chains and an assortment of crystals.

An earthy incense burned in a bowl that rested on a table near the corner of the shop. Behind the table sat a dour-looking man. He had the weight of two sows, and Effie wondered how his corpulent frame could maneuver through the crowded bookcases.

"Yes?" the bookseller asked in a manner of greeting. A candle near the bowl of incense had burned to a stub. It lit the man's face, revealing a wobbling jowl and a thin pair of reading spectacles.

"We are searching for a man who may have purchased a book here a few days ago," said Canonbie. "A scrawny fellow with a beard and a bright red cane." He held up his own and tapped it for emphasis.

Effie cringed. Had the man no tact? She would at least have traded a cordial banter with the bookseller before broaching the subject. But she kept her mouth shut. Perhaps boldness was what the matter needed. She had long shied from direct confrontation with strangers for fear that her fey blood would be uncovered.

The bookseller pulled the spectacles to the end of his nose and stared over them. "I sell many books to many patrons," he said. "Some of them even have beards."

"This one is special," said Canonbie. He ambled forward until his height allowed him to hover over the seated man. "It may have cost the scrawny man a great deal."

"Hmm, I see." The bookseller leaned back in his chair. "And what was the name of this expensive book?"

Canonbie leaned forward, resting his knuckles on the table, his cane gripped in both hands. The gesture made the muscles of his shoulders and arms bulge.

"Oh, for Heaven's sake," said Effie. She strode forward. "We're not here to put the poor man to the question." She glowered at Canonbie. Turning to the bookseller, she said, "If you could please assist us, I promise you the matter is very urgent. This man we seek may have committed a terrible crime."

"Och, rats," uttered Graham, drawing their attention. He hunched over an object the size and shape of a large chest. It perched atop a stack of books. A black cloth covered it. "I can hear them skittering," he said.

Pulling back the cloth, he snapped his fingers away quickly as a tiny, whiskered snout nipped at his flesh. He yelped and staggered backward into a wall sconce, tipping the candle burning within. Spinning to catch the candle, his foot kicked the stacked books. Melted wax sprayed his hand and coat. The books tumbled over, and Effie gasped. Her feet locked in place as the cloth fell free. The rat cage crashed to the floor.

"No!" bellowed the bookseller. He lurched to his feet as three rats scurried from the broken cage.

The rodents' grey fur blended into the shadows, but Effie could sense them without seeing their darting movements. For a heartbeat, they scattered as if fleeing a sinking ship. Then one paused, rising onto its hind quarters. Graham lowered the candle from the sconce, and they all watched its wee nose twitch.

Slowly, the rat padded toward Effie. She held her breath. Even knowing the other two would soon follow did little to lessen the shock as their silent forms slunk into the light the candle cast. Together, the three rats came to her feet and halted as if they were hounds obeying her command to heel. She was a Grundbairn, and her nature called to them. Such uncanny things had happened to her all her life, though she'd only recently understood their cause. It had to do with her fey aura and her affinity for the land and all living things on it.

Graham cursed. The melted wax dripped onto his fingers and crusted. Canonbie stepped away from the bookseller, keeping his back to the wall. His gaze swept over the rats and back to the man.

The bookseller's jaw worked. He wheezed as his breath labored. His eyes had gone wide in shock, but they narrowed as he regarded her anew. An understanding passed across his face and disappeared behind a toothy smirk.

"They are my gentle pets," he said. He came around the edge of the table and stooped, swiping up all three rats in his pudgy fingers. They squirmed a bit in his clutches. Their whiskers twitched and tiny claws fought for better purchase, but he held them tenderly.

Graham righted the cage and held its latch open for the man to restore the rats to their home. His cheeks flushed as he stammered an apology. The bookseller waved him away. He carried the cage back to his table and plopped down in his chair.

"They are unharmed," he said, inspecting the rodents. They continued to stare at Effie, and he turned his gaze to her as well. "Now, about this patron. A terrible crime you said?"

"Yes. A murder. Two, actually."

"Well, that is most foul." He steepled his fingers. His face took on a pensive cast, as if he struggled to recall a distant memory. "I think I may know of the man you seek. A local apothecary has purchased books here from time to time. He is known to carry a red cane, though I do not remember the last book he procured from me."

Effie traded a look with Graham. An apothecary would certainly know of poisons.

"Is his shop in Dunfermline?" asked Graham.

"Ah, yes, just down from the high street," said the bookseller. "But I do hope I am mistaken. The man has expensive tastes, and I would loathe to lose his custom." His lips pulled into a strained grin.

* * *

Rain turned the cobblestones slick. Effie picked her footing carefully as they ascended to the high street. A frown painted her face. The bookseller was an odd fellow, nothing more, she tried to reason. But the flash of comprehension in his eyes kept coming back to her. He had known her for a fey. The deduction was obvious. Not so long ago, the thought would've made her want to flee the town. Now, it made her curious. How many allies had the fey within a town like Dunfermline? How many enemies?

Canonbie shuffled something in his coat pocket. The motion drew her attention.

"Do you always barge into shops like a rampaging bull?" she asked him. "I thought for a moment you would draw your pistol."

The man stepped around a lady headed the other direction. The tassels of the woman's parasol dripped rainwater. Her bustle stuck out from under its protection, and the dampness left the back of her dress shades darker than the front. Canonbie ogled her openly before glancing at Effie and smirking.

"I barge where I please, Miss Effie," he said. "And I will draw my pistol at my own choosing, though I wouldn't bother for a craven like your bookseller." The hint of mischief in his eyes let her know he only meant to enrage her. It was a game he played, she'd come to realize. The teasing and plucking at her ire. She plodded onward, shocked that a part of her wanted to laugh and return his taunt with a bite of her own. The shield she'd erected against the man had dissolved somewhere near Balclune.

A team of horses drew a wagon down the street. The click-clack of their hooves rang sharply. Bolts of linen fabric were stacked on the wagon beneath a large canvas. The wagon's driver doffed his tall hat as he overtook a smaller wain. The wain's driver returned the gesture. Painted a vibrant green, the wain's golden lettering declared it contained a marvel of electric devices.

"Light from glass and wire," said Graham, whistling. "Small motors that turn cranks, heat plates, and even play the piano." He stared after the wain. "What a marvelous world we live in." He continued to speak of the possibilities, as they carried on down the street. Graham had always taken time to share word of any great invention with Effie, and together they'd discuss how the device worked and how they might improve on it. It was one of her favorite memories from childhood.

Yet she listened and encouraged his insight now, if only to draw her thoughts away from Jack Canonbie. She found her eyes stealing to the rogue more often than they should. If he only played at vexing her, she wondered, who was the man truly beneath?

They found the apothecary's shop on a wynd that sloped away from the abbey. It stood within sight of the high street, its lone glass window large enough to give passersby a view of the entire shop. A counter divided the small room. In front of it a couple of chairs allowed waiting customers to sit, while behind it an assortment of jars and bottles lined several racks built into the wall. The containers held a variety of powders, herbs, and salves, each labeled by a clear and precise hand. An amber curtain of velvet hung gathered on one side of the window, with a braided cord attached to it, meant for pulling the curtain closed. A doorway on the far wall led to a back room.

The man behind the counter wore a telescoping monocle attached to a strap that wrapped around his head. His long sleeves were bound tightly around his forearms by a pair of leather bands. Not altogether plump, none would consider him scrawny. Tufts of grey hair sprouted above his ears, and red splotches etched a pattern across his forehead. But nothing covered his cheeks. If this was the apothecary, he was not the man they sought.

"Perhaps the man has a partner," offered Graham. "He could still have some information we seek."

"He is more like to be the queen's bastard," said Canonbie.

"You may wait outside, if you find our pursuit too tedious," said Effie. She spoke in a teasing tone. He smirked and gave an exaggerated bow, gesturing with his cane for her to take the lead.

When they entered the shop, the apothecary raised his gaze and smiled. He pulled the monocle from his head and collapsed the piece to a third of its original length. It made a clicking sound as it ratcheted back. Effie saw he had been chopping open the pods from some flower. The lenses in the monocle must've magnified the pods to aid in the work.

"Welcome, good sirs. Miss." The man stiffened and dipped his head, but the smile never left his lips. "I have a wide selection of remedies for any ailment, and an even greater library of information than you'll find even in Edinburgh." He tapped the side of his head and winked. "Now, if I may ask, who is the patient?"

"The bookseller at Harrow & Loch has guided us here," said Effie. "We're inquiring after a gentleman who caused some trouble near Balclune."

"Did he?" asked the apothecary. He placed his palms flat on the countertop. "I'm sure I know nothing of it, but who might this unsavory gentleman be?"

Effie provided the description and explained how the bookseller had led them to believe the apothecary himself may be the man they sought. "Is there another apothecary you employ? One who might better fit the description?"

"I am happy to say no, but I'm sorry I could not offer you any better assistance." The apothecary's eyes suddenly lit up, and he cocked his head. His gaze darted between the three of them.

"Yes, what is it?" asked Effie. She could hear Canonbie shift his stance behind her.

The apothecary dug behind the counter and produced a tiny silver bell. He rang it, and a delicate chime sounded. The man's smile widened into something that unsettled Effie. "Bless my thick wit, I nearly forgot. There is something more I can do. I've summoned my apprentice. He may know of the man. He scours the hills and glens regularly for ingredients to sell in my medicines and stumbles on strangers quite often."

"You are most kind," said Effie. An impulse made her quest out with her fey senses. She felt nothing of fey blood within the shop. The nearest fey aura she found was somewhere down the high street. But there was another human within the shop.

A brute of a man entered from the doorway to the backroom. His shoulders spread nearly as wide as the opening. He wore a thick apron that held stains of a dubious nature.

Effie forced herself to remain calm. Some apothecaries were known to perform minor surgeries, especially in smaller towns. The stains could easily be the result of such an action. Behind her, Graham wheezed audibly.

"Effie," he warned, in a sharp whisper.

"The occasion necessitates some privacy, I think," said the apothecary. He gestured, and the large apprentice crossed the shop in a few long strides. The brute drew the curtain shut with a deft yank of the braided cord, and the room darkened. The movement had placed him in front of the main door, blocking their exit, Effie realized. The curtain silenced the bustle from the street, and the sudden quiet made her heart thump in panic.

The apothecary's smile waned. "You came with such a tale, I almost missed the gift Mr. Harrow sent. You'll both fetch a good price." He pointed at Effie and Graham. "Don't damage these two," he told his apprentice. "The other you may silence."

Effie's jaw dropped. "No!" she shrieked.

The brute swung at Canonbie. The blow would've crumpled an ox. But Canonbie danced away, ducking under the swipe and raising his cane into a defensive position. His other hand emerged from his coat pocket with his pistol. The two chambers were aligned vertically and housed one bullet apiece.

Something hissed from behind the counter. Effie spun to find the apothecary holding a slender tube of brass. A thick wire attached it to a metal canister the size of a bread loaf. The canister held a valve and what looked distinctly like a trigger mechanism.

Graham cried out. He slapped a hand to his shoulder, and Effie saw a splotch of red appear just as Canonbie bellowed. "Run!"

16

Graham staggered into the wall. His fingers ran slick with blood from the wound in his shoulder. Canonbie leveled his pistol at the apprentice and barked at the brute to back away. The giant man started to raise his hands, but one of his meaty paws lashed out, snatching the velvet curtain and ripping it free from the rod above. It toppled onto Canonbie in a whoosh of dust and cloth. He stumbled under its weight. His pistol cracked, and a puff of white powder fell from the ceiling. The apprentice lumbered forward and pummeled his fists into the trapped man.

The window no longer obscured, light blasted into the shop. Effie shied away from it, hands raised. Canonbie yelled at her to flee. But she would never leave the man behind. Nor Graham. She realized she'd frozen in place and lunged to the side. The apothecary cursed as his device hissed again. Effie caught sight of something like a dart zip past her head. It clattered against the front window.

She needed to help Canonbie. But that would expose her and Graham to the apothecary. The man pulled another dart from a tin he'd set next to the device. With a snarl, he rammed it into the brass tube. Instinct took over, and Effie pulled on the fey blood she'd sensed on the high street.

Three small creatures. Pixies, perhaps. Their wee bodies held more than enough strength of blood to bolster her Fey Craft.

Deftly, she shoved an image at the apothecary of steam bursting from his device. It seared his hands and choked his breath. She strained to make the scalding heat feel as real as possible.

The man yelped and leaped back before realizing he'd been fooled.

Effie rushed toward him, intent on knocking the man down. But the counter stood between them, and her skirts hindered her movement. He leveled the tube at her, his face scrunched in fury. His fingers sought the trigger. She could not reach him in time.

But Graham could. He stumbled forward and dove over the counter, knocking over the device and sending the apothecary sprawling to the floor. The shooting device clattered and hissed a final time as it struck the ground. The dart thunked harmlessly into the wall. The apothecary grunted as Graham landed on him. He scrambled away, flailing with his arms to win free, but Graham pounded with his fists, beating the man's chest and gut.

The apothecary wheezed and held up his hands. A feral sneer tore across his face. "The salve. It should've knocked you unconscious!" he hissed.

Effie blinked as she rounded the counter. She had no time to decipher the man's ranting. She scoured the racks behind the counter. Snatching up a pair of items, she spun and hurled them at the brute.

A canister of an ochre powder sailed wide of the large man. It crashed against the wall, dispersing its contents in a bursting cloud. A jar of plum-colored paste came closer. It rebounded off the front window, drawing the brute's attention.

Canonbie used the distraction to tear himself free of the curtain. He'd dropped the pistol in the scuffle but brought his cane to bear. Shuffling forward, he skipped out of reach as the larger man swiped at him, only to return and pummel the brute from behind. His cane found the soft tissue under the ribs and struck home with sharp thwacks.

The apprentice roared and lunged. His meaty hands sought Canonbie's throat, but they found only the open space where the man had been. Effie watched in awe. If Canonbie had learned to brawl in a tavern, he'd added to those lessons something of a dancer's grace. She snatched another jar but did not throw it for fear she'd hit her own man.

Canonbie changed his stance and grip. With a hand as quick as a snake, he slapped the brute hard across the cheek. The smack rang throughout the shop, and a blistering red welt rose on the large man's cheek. The apprentice flinched and paused, and Effie saw that was the point of the maneuver. Canonbie didn't slow. He sprang from a crouch, dropping his cane, and with a roar thrust both his hands into the brute's chest.

The apprentice toppled backward from the shove. His hands groped for balance as he fell. One leg rose up, and his fingers almost reached his toes as he strained to remain upright. He smashed through the front window in a shower of glass. His body bounced as it struck the cobbled street outside. Streaks of blood covered his face and arms. He moaned and lay still amid a sea of broken glass.

A shriek rang from the street. Several gasps and shouts of alarm followed. Effie spied a dozen faces watching them as a cold breeze rushed through the opening in the shop's front. She had no time for them. She rounded on the apothecary. Graham had the man pinned to the ground. Neither could see above the counter, but they had both heard the glass shatter. The apothecary's eyes widened in horror. Graham wore a mask of fierce concentration.

"The salve on the darts," Effie spat at the apothecary. Her mind raced to fill in the pieces. "It is some poison that affects only fey?" It had to be why the man thought it would subdue Graham, and why it hadn't. He'd believed Graham fey as well. It had only been luck that he hadn't shot at her first.

The apothecary squirmed but nodded. Graham held him firm, rolling his knee across the man's chest and causing him to moan.

"But why?" Effie begged. "You had no cause to attack us."

The fear in the apothecary's eyes deepened. "I had to." His tone lost its bite, turning into a whimper. "He would know. He has ways. Help him capture fey or be killed. He gave me the choice."

Effie's face drained of blood as she heard the confession. The apothecary had helped the man they sought kill Laeth and Hargrund. He had all but admitted it.

Canonbie moved past her and disappeared into the backroom. "There is another door," he called. "We leave now!"

"Effie," barked Graham, calling her attention.

She ignored both men. "Why?" she demanded again. She loomed over the prone man. "What did you mean we'd fetch a good price? From whom?"

The apothecary's gaze turned vacant. He cocked his head, as if listening to some far-off sound. "The cries, can't you hear them?" he asked. "Always they come, a shrill call beneath the wind." His mouth curled into a scowl, and his attention refocused. His fear melted. "He will come for you," he warned. "You cannot escape it."

"Effie!" Graham hollered. He jabbed a finger at a low rack in the corner of the shop. Effie snapped her head around as doubt bubbled within her. How could the apothecary and this madman hate her so, when she'd given them no reason? But more so, how could a royal treaty, mere words on paper signed by men a hundred miles distant, stand against such blind prejudice?

She followed Graham's gesture and her heart thumped hard. A tintype rested on the rack, propped upright against the wall. The photograph depicted four gentlemen standing in a glen with a rise of hillocks behind them. In the distance, a small town could be seen. One of the men was clearly the apothecary. He stood perhaps a dozen years younger, but the scowl on his face matched the one he wore currently.

Of the other three men, all had beards. But only one leaned on a cane. His cheeks were gaunt, almost ghastly, and his shoulders appeared narrower than her own. Effie had only a moment to study the tintype before Canonbie barged back into the room.

A whistle shrilled from somewhere down the street. Canonbie turned toward the sound and grunted. "We must move!" he growled.

Effie leveled her gaze at him. "We have no need to flee," she said. "The man attacked us. He harbors the murderer we seek and has nearly confessed to taking part in the act. Let the constables come."

"To have them hear how we assaulted the man in his own shop?" said Canonbie. "Do you think it would turn into more than his tale against ours? We are strangers here. Our word means nothing."

Effie huffed. "We will fetch Mr. Alpin, then, or Lieutenant Walford, if the man hasn't left for Fort William yet. They will back our side." She fumed, hating that she would need a Fey Finder to prove her words true.

"Effie," whispered Graham once again. He'd stood and clutched his shoulder. A growing pool of blood stained his coat, yet he ignored it. He stared out at the street in disbelief.

"It's him," he said, pointing.

Effie gasped. An older version of the scrawny man from the tintype stared at her from among the crowd of onlookers. He waggled a long, red cane at her. His eyes were sharp. Predator's eyes, devoid of anything but a cold malice.

She stood. Her eyes narrowed.

Canonbie put a hand on her arm. "No. Wait here for the constables if you must. But I will deal with him." He tugged his coat straight and stalked forward. He'd recovered his cane and kept his head bent, like a bull about to rampage.

The apprentice had begun to rise, and Canonbie kicked the brute's arms out from beneath him as he passed. He kicked again, this time to the gut. "Stay down," he commanded, whipping his cane to the brute's temple. The large man whimpered and did as he was bade.

The crowd parted for Canonbie. An onlooker pulled his wife clear, her face ashen with distress. A cluster of workmen leered eagerly, smelling a fight. The whistles shrilling from the high street drew closer. They were followed now by the pounding of footfalls on the rain-slickened cobbles.

"You there!" boomed Canonbie. He raised his cane and thrust it forward.

The scrawny man's mouth curled into a slack-jawed grin. A chill raced up Effie's spine. The man's teeth gleamed as red as his painted cane.

"Behold," he snapped, almost salivating. "A boon for a faithful servant!"

For a moment, she thought he meant to stay and face Canonbie. A duel in the streets, like in the wild tales of the American West. But as Canonbie approached, he dipped his head in a mocking nod, his eyes staring up at her from a lowered brow. He took a step forward and shoved one of the onlookers into Canonbie's path.

The poor fellow cried out and fell into Canonbie's arms. It cost

Canonbie a couple of seconds to straighten them both, and he roared in frustration. The scrawny man had bolted. His feet churned with a quick pace and only a light touch on the cobblestones. Canonbie's tread was much heavier, for all his grace. He had a long stride but could not dart through the crowded street as easily.

"No," Effie whined. The word slipped from her lips as she watched the murderer gain distance from Canonbie. She gathered up her skirts to race after before she remembered herself. Graham wavered on his feet. His cheeks had lost color, yet he held a foot to the apothecary's chest. She could not leave him.

"Go," said Graham, seeing her hesitation. "Help him. The constables are almost here. I'll send them after you."

"You've lost too much blood," she argued.

He shook his head. "I haven't," he said. "It's all still here on my coat." He pointed at it and smirked as he leaned against the counter. Effie swung her gaze back to Canonbie's fleeing form. It might be their only chance to apprehend the murderer. But could she live with herself if something dire happened to Graham?

"Go," he urged again. "Don't let the bastard escape."

She cast about, her need to protect Graham at war with her desire to bring the killer to justice. Her gaze fell across Canonbie's pistol. It lay amongst shards of glass on the shop floor. She hustled over to pick it up. If the constables discovered it, it would not aid their version of the encounter. She could see the men now, running toward the shop. Three of them approached in their dark uniforms, truncheons in hand.

They would question the apothecary first. The man was a local businessman, and what cause did the constables have not to believe one of their own? Effie knew the truth would win out eventually, but after how long? How would she know of Canonbie's success or failure if she spent hours defending herself against false accusations while a killer ran free?

She growled, the noise every bit as menacing as Canonbie's roar. She wouldn't have it, and she knew deep down, neither would Graham. Picking up her skirts, she nodded at him. He straightened and nodded back.

The constables barked at the onlookers to clear the way. They'd reached the shop's front. The broken glass crunched under their boots.

Dropping the pistol into her reticule, Effie dashed out the back.

17

The apothecary yelled something after her. Or perhaps it was for the constables. Effie couldn't make it out. The backroom held more canisters, jars, and vials, only in larger quantities. A few barrels formed a pyramid along one wall, and against another a narrow table rested. She didn't pause for any of it.

She burst through the rear door and found herself in a narrow alleyway. A drainage gully ran down its middle, acting as a sluice for the rain runoff. And other waste, she could tell by the stench. Water trickled down it now, rolling down the slope that ran away from the high street. Slippery moss surrounded the gully, and she had to slow her pace lest she slip on her rump.

The high street lay closer, but she headed away from it. No doubt a crowd had amassed there from all the commotion, and she had no intention of joining the press. She had seen the madman turn toward the abbey before he disappeared from sight, and she meant to angle that direction and hoped to pick up his or Canonbie's path.

She scowled as she stalked down the alley. *Mad,* she thought, *for mad he must be to expose himself in such an open manner without cause. Mad to attack a storehouse patrolled by the crown's soldiers, and mad for the heinous murders he committed.*

Fog obscured the alley's end, replacing the earlier rain. A low bank of clouds blanketed parts of Dunfermline. The wind that pushed the bank whispered through the stone buildings of the town in gentle gusts. It kissed her cheeks when it found her, leaving a dampness behind.

Shapes appeared in the fog ahead, unformed shadows at first, like a ghostly version of the town. But as she stole closer, the features of men and women sharpened. Their footfalls sounded. Their breath appeared as cold vapor. She emerged from the alley onto a lane busy with foot traffic. The fog thinned here, and she hurried as fast as decorum—and her damned skirts—allowed.

As she went, she cast out with her fey senses. Only the same three auras returned to her. They hadn't moved since the last time she'd felt for them. They were strangers, and she wasn't sure what aid they could offer besides allowing her to tap their combined blood strength, so she decided not to send them anything yet. She already risked the safety of her friends and saw no need to add to that account.

The lane split, and she turned toward the abbey, climbing a small rise before heading up a short wynd. The abbey grounds emerged before her. The original abbey had been destroyed over three hundred years earlier, along with a royal palace on neighboring grounds. The ruins of both remained, intermixed and repurposed within the structure of the new abbey. It gave the place a strong sense of the past and a hallowed feeling. Crenellated tower walls shot heavenward in the abbey's heart, but they fell off to older, shorter walls, crumbled and scorched.

A garden ringed the abbey, and an expanse of woodlands and pasture sprawled on the far side from the town and high street. Effie paused and listened for the sounds of pursuit. She heard the din of the high street and the distant clamor of the textile machines that filled the warehouses near the train station. But nothing of a struggle, nor a chase, came to her.

A clergyman passed her, and she smiled and bowed her head. He returned the gesture and continued on his way. His arms were loaded with a pile of books and papers. Another gentleman strolled down a garden path, passing a hedge blossoming with tiny flowers of purple and yellow. His cane clicked a rhythmic procession. She scanned the other direction and found a couple strolling the garden at a leisurely pace.

She moved on, intent on circling the grounds. The fog thickened on the far side of the abbey. It obscured her vision and forced her to stop and think. Folding her arms across her chest, she tapped her foot. Frustration mounted, and she had to dampen it down before it stole her wits. She hadn't had time to delve into the madman's aura, even if she'd remembered to do so. Each aura was as unique as a face. But like faces it took some familiarity to pick them out at a distance.

She searched for Canonbie's aura and found the man slowly progressing down a path some distance from her. She couldn't tell if he stood on a street or within a building, or even on a roof, for that matter. She knew only his proximity to her, and a vague direction.

She thought for a moment more and realized she knew something else. Something important. He progressed slowly. He moved at a careful pace. That meant he either stalked their quarry, or he'd lost the madman completely.

On the other side of the same coin, it dawned on her that the madman had a cause to hurry. If she couldn't pick out his aura by recognition, perhaps she could seek one that moved at a quick pace. She stilled her body and focused. Opening herself to the full field of auras surrounding her, she gasped and staggered a step back. The jumble of men and women, children, horses, dogs, birds—everything living within a mile of her—made her head swim. It took her a moment to clear the dizziness.

Seeking out a single known aura was much different than trying to examine them all at once. It was much like the difference between fetching out a single carrot from a stew versus holding onto all the ingredients of the pot while trying to spy the source of an unknown flavor. She found she could only focus on a few auras at a time without becoming overwhelmed. Girding herself, she tried again, only this time she cast her senses out to only those in a tight bubble around Canonbie. She closed her eyes to help her concentrate. Yet the strain of even that small effort exhausted her, and nothing hurried more than it properly should.

Taking a deep breath, she balled her hands into fists and scoured the area around the abbey. But it likewise held nothing of interest. Her shoulders slumped. She felt like she could sleep for hours. The skill was too complex for her without the practiced hand of another to guide her. What she wouldn't give for Caledon or Rose's skill to aid her, or even for Jaelyn's bellicose presence.

As she opened her eyes, movement caught her attention. A flash of red cut through the fog and disappeared. She reached out and found the aura of a man hustling toward the woods. A chill raced along her arms even as her heart thumped faster. Her feet churned before she'd decided to follow. It took several paces until she could spy anything but a shadow of the man. But when she did, her heart lurched.

A sliver of red flashed again.

She had guessed correctly. The madman had come to the abbey. Or the grounds, at least. He angled away from building itself. Padding after, she wondered what she would do if the man suddenly charged her. She sent Canonbie an image of the abbey and hoped the man was smart enough to recognize what it meant, or that it even came from her. Next, she sent an image of the woods before her, and one of a red cane. It was the best she could do while stalking forward.

Her footsteps crunched the hard-packed dirt of the garden path. Her heart quickened with each step until her vision swam. The air held a gentler fragrance than it had in the town, with all the spring blossoms filling the grounds.

Her quarry turned sharply to the right, strode a few paces, and stopped. She let the man disappear into the fog, knowing it hid her as well. The smart thing would be to stop, to hold her ground and wait for Canonbie to come. But she had no need of rescue. She had Canonbie's pistol. She also had her Fey Craft. She could at least see what the man was about and observe him from a safe distance.

She crept to a tall tree and peered around its trunk. A broken stone wall rested along the path a short distance away. The man stood beyond, out of sight except to her fey senses. Maybe this man wasn't the killer. The thought flitted through her head. Her quarry couldn't be the only one who carried a red cane, and she had only seen the flash of red and a shadow that resembled the scrawny man's shape. The man before her could be anyone.

She needed more. She needed to be certain.

Fool lass, you deserve a clout to the ears. Her mother's voice came to mind as she stole over to the broken wall.

At one time, the wall must've run a ring around the inner part of the town. Then, it might've towered twenty feet high. The section that remained rose to just above her head before sloping to the ground on either side of her in a jagged pyramid. Some of the stones were cracked and weathered, but most of the wall was merely gone, the stones probably repurposed in other building projects within the town or used to mend some laird's house.

Rising on her toes, she peeked over the wall. The remains of a circular tower lay beyond. Jutting up from the earth like a giant pint glass cracked in half, the tower's base could hold a half dozen steam carriages. The man's aura came from within. He hadn't moved while she approached.

Just one last stretch to the tower's base, she told herself. She would go no farther. One last stretch, and she would be able to see the man clearly enough to know him for the murderer.

He waits for you. The voice from within scolded. She cringed but ignored it. The chance she targeted the wrong man, that she waited for some stranger while the murderer made his escape, outweighed the risk of sneaking a little bit closer.

Crouching low, she slunk forward, around the edge of the wall and toward the tower. Its broken heights had no roof, and the light shining down illuminated an opening in the stones. She angled for the gap. Tendrils of fog crept out of it, giving off a cold feeling like a sheet of ice over a trickling burn.

When she reached the opening, she squatted next to it. Slowly, she drew the pistol from her reticule. Its weight, even slight as it was, helped to calm her racing pulse. Canonbie had fired one shot in the shop, so only one remained to her. But she didn't plan on using it unless she had no other choice. Bracing herself against the tower, she leaned forward to peek within.

The man's voice rang out. "I have searched all my life, but now I understand," he called. His warm voice carried an accent from the far north. "It is plain before me. There is no other truth than to submit to the greater will." His laughter came softly on the wind. "I to it, and you to me. That is the proper order of things."

She froze and suppressed a squeal of shock. Her grip tightened on the pistol. She no longer had a need to spy the man she pursued. She'd found the murderer, as she'd first thought. Casting out another image for Canonbie to find her, she stood and rested her back against the cold stone.

"You will be held accountable," she called over her shoulder. "You will hang for murder."

"I doubt that very much," said the madman. "I am an apostle, come to spread the word. It carries to me in my dreams. The truth above all other truths. We cannot escape it—you, me, anyone." She heard his boots crunch the dirt before she sensed him stalking forward. He meant to slay her. His trap dawned on her in an instant. She had not chanced on him at all. He'd seen her at the abbey, as she'd swayed, lost in a trance. He'd lured her away. He'd shown himself at the apothecary shop for the same purpose.

It had been his plan all along. Her eagerness to bring him to justice had blinded her to the danger.

She struggled to fit the remaining pieces together. But fear won out. Her hands trembled. She fought the urge to flee, to abandon the hunt and seek the shortest route back to Bonny Law and the warmth of her hearth. Who was she to hunt a murderer, after all?

But she fought the urge. She fought it because an instinct even deeper told her that to run was to die. The madman had lured her to the tower on his own terms. He expected her to bolt where he could quickly overtake and subdue her. Yet his plan had a flaw in its design. She had him trapped, and she only needed to hold him for a short while.

Leveling the pistol, she stepped into the tower's opening and took aim. The scrawny man halted his advance and sneered. He'd reached the middle of the tower, only a dozen paces away. He held his cane above his head, in a dueling stance, as if he meant to crack her skull.

"Tell me why," she commanded.

The man's eyes danced with a lust that made her gut twist in knots. "Why anything?" he breathed. "Because I yearn to understand, delving ever deeper without knowing how close I'd always been." He licked his lips. "Because I enjoy it."

Effie's skin crawled. She had seen madness before. The Laird of Aonghus and Edmund Glover, the old Fey Finder General, had both been zealots for their own particular cause. But their madness had sprung from some deep-seated ideology. The madman before her seemed the opposite. He was swept up in a chaos that swirled around him like a buzzing cloud, floating free of any tethers to dogma.

He lowered his cane, planting it firmly before him and resting both hands atop it. "You are more beautiful than the others. Do you think it will make the difference?" He leaned in. "Do you think I will taste it?"

The pistol wavered as her arm trembled. She struggled to force the vile words from her thoughts. She couldn't dwell on them. She had to focus on what mattered, not what horrors she could not fix. "Your accomplice, the apothecary, has confessed. He told us of the darts. They are coated with some poison that renders fey unconscious. The two of you used them to subdue and kill the fey near Balclune."

The man's face soured. His nose wrinkled in disgust. "The man is a coward and a fool to let you best him. He hears the cry but does not understand. He is not faithful. Only I am." He reached into his coat pocket. His lips carried a smirk that didn't reach his eyes.

"Hold still," she shouted. She brandished the pistol, for all the good it did in her shaking hand.

He hurled something at her. She spied the glass vial a moment before it shattered at her feet. Flinching, she sucked in a breath in surprise. An emerald cloud of vapor rose from the ground, dissolving to near transparency as it reached her mouth and nose. She could taste the awfulness of it. Mold-encrusted haggis mixed with rotten eggs would've been better. The putridness of it made her gag, the reaction sucking in more of the noxious fumes.

She staggered back, waving the vapor away as if she could strike it aside. Her head grew fuzzy, her sight losing focus. Her feet numbed, and she knew in a burst of panic that her legs would not hold her weight for very long.

"The vapors do not work as well as the salve," said the madman. "It takes longer to enter the blood, you see. But it will suffice. Besides, my aim in this fog would not be nearly as perfect as it was with your fey friends."

He cackled. "Two shots. Pfft. Pfft." Balling his fist, he flicked out his fingers with each sound to mimic the flying darts.

Effie's knees started to buckle. The fog in her head closed in until she could only make out dim shapes before her. She couldn't flee. She couldn't talk. Even her fey senses had abandoned her. She had only one option left, one that sickened her almost as much as the vapor that stole her wits.

She put both hands on the pistol to steady it. She had but one shot. Sighting down the short barrel, she aimed at the murderer's chest. At his heart.

The action made him cackle anew. Opening his coat, he drew an awl from where it hung on a leather loop under his arm. Dark blotches of dried blood covered the metal shaft. Its handle was a polished wood, bulbous at its top.

"It is foretold," he said. "I have dreamed it. With fey sustenance, I will unlock the lore of the magi." His eyes flashed. "Die proud and embrace your destiny. You may hold a place of honor, one that will echo for eons to come."

She squeezed. The pistol cracked and jumped in her hand. The madman flinched and glanced over his shoulder as the bullet pinged off the tower's stone.

She'd missed.

18

Effie sank to her knees. She fought to blast out with her fey senses, to beckon anyone or anything that could aid her. She sought to trick the madman with Fey Craft, to shock him until he succumbed to fear. But she knew only a groggy haze. She could smell nothing and hear little more than the pitter-patter of some critter winding its way around the tower's base.

As the madman's murky form approached, his cane flashed—a lance of red like a tainted thunderbolt. His boots covered the ground with swift steps. She willed her arms to rise up and protect her head, but they didn't respond.

The pitter-patter drew closer, and a shadow fell on stones near the tower's opening. Some deep part of her told her not to stare at it, that her salvation lay in keeping her eyes locked on the red cane and nothing more.

The madman loomed over her. He placed a gentle hand atop her head, pulling back the hair at her brow. Changing his grip on the awl, he held it point down, with his thumb over its head for greater leverage. Effie stared at him blankly. She couldn't remember how to scream.

Cloth rustled, and the shadow near the tower opening blurred. It flew toward her, morphing as it came into a familiar shape. Effie's hope rekindled, spilling over with joy.

Jack Canonbie slashed with his cane. But the madman had heard the movement, too. He ducked to the side at the last instant, and the blow glanced off his jaw. Wood cracked against tooth and bone. Staggering away, he dropped the awl. It was all he could manage to stay on his feet.

Recovering quickly, a low growl rumbled from him. He put a hand to his jaw, and it came away wet with blood. His eyes narrowed.

"You'll die for one of them?" he snapped.

Canonbie shrugged, smirking. "The coin spends the same."

Raising his cane, the madman sprang forward, slamming down with an overhead swipe. Canonbie brought his cane up to block, but the madman changed the direction of his attack. It struck Canonbie's arm with a loud thwack.

Canonbie grunted. His cane fell from his grasp. Spinning away, he snatched up a jagged rock from the tower floor and crouched into a low fighting stance.

"You lack faith," said the madman. "Your heart is closed, but you will see. She will open the way for us all!"

Barking a hearty laugh, Canonbie tossed the rock at the man's face. The move was clearly meant to distract his foe, and he charged in after it.

The madman ignored the feint, letting the rock sail past him. He tried to leap away and keep distance between them. He needed it to swing his cane.

But Canonbie's strides were longer. He grabbed the smaller man's wrist and grappled for the red cane. The pair strained against each other, their arms locked and boots sliding, searching for better purchase. Yet Canonbie outweighed the madman by more than a sack of barley. His thick shoulders flexed and forced the other man to crumble.

The madman squirmed. His eyes lit fire, seething in rage. He released his grip on the cane and chomped down on Canonbie's neck. Wrapping his arms around the larger man, he hugged him tight.

Canonbie cried out. He used the cane's top as a hammer, pounding at the madman's head. He flopped from side to side in desperation to win free. Blood from both men streamed down his shirt and coat.

Effie struggled to aid him. Her thoughts refused to focus, though she knew she still clutched the pistol. She could feel its weight in her hand. Its bullets were spent, but she raised it anyway, and blinked. She'd raised it. The realization made her blink again, and she filled her lungs with a deep breath to steady herself. Her thoughts continued to swim, but her body had started to respond. Drawing back the pistol, she hurled it.

It struck the madman in the back. With Canonbie battering his head, it must've felt like a fly landing on his coat. He ignored it, and the pistol thumped to the ground.

But she'd thrown it.

Rising, she shambled forward, arms outstretched. She didn't have the strength to pry the madman loose, so she wrapped her hands around his throat and squeezed. She dug her fingers into the bulge at his throat, straining with every ounce of her grip. He wheezed, and she redoubled her effort. She knew if she failed, Canonbie might not survive. And if he went, she would soon follow.

The madman growled, but it ended as a gurgle. He stomped with a heel and struck her shin. She kicked him back, stomping on his calf. The force of it tugged him down. Canonbie screamed in pain and slammed the top of the cane into the madman's eye.

The cane crunched through soft bone and bowled the madman over. He flung an elbow as he went that sent Effie flailing onto her rump. Canonbie recovered first, but he was in no state to press an advantage. Yanking a handkerchief from his pocket, he pressed it against his neck. He held the cane up like a sword with the other hand and staggered back.

Effie scrambled to her feet, staying low and gathering her skirts to charge or flee. She spied the awl on the ground near her and snatched it up.

"Who is he?" Canonbie snarled. He seethed with fury.

"A small man of little note," said Effie. "Nothing more." She meant the words to enrage their foe, plucking at his ego.

If they stirred him at all, he didn't show it. His eye had sealed shut. The tissue around it swelled, and the side of his face swirled in purples, blues, and blacks. His jaw hung at an odd angle and jiggled as he padded back a few paces. Blood trickled from rent flesh. He watched them both with his brow lowered, as he'd done at the apothecary shop. Effie had never seen such malice before. It held no passion in it, only a cold desire for cruelty.

With a flick of the wrist, he flung another vial. It shattered at his feet and burst into a yellow cloud that filled the air before him. Its volume and thickness obscured the man from view, and for a second Effie was terrified he might come charging at them. She shied away as the cloud billowed outward. But it held nothing ominous. It dissolved quickly and left nothing but a faint trace of sulfur behind.

They'd left the tower opening unguarded, and the madman had bolted.

She shuddered. Her body had nothing left. Even if she'd wanted to race after the man, she wouldn't know where to start. He could've picked any direction, and she still didn't have the focus to find him with her fey senses.

Besides, Canonbie needed her. She turned to the man and found him leaning against the tower wall. He'd lowered the cane, but his hand still clutched the handkerchief to his neck.

"Let me see it," she said, coming to his side.

"It's fine," he grumbled. "Needs pressure, is all."

She planted her hands on her hips. "If it's fine, then there's no reason to hide it from me."

He huffed and looked away. But he lowered his hand and revealed his neck, all the same. She swallowed hard and tried not to react any further. She didn't want him to believe it dire, but the madman's bite had savaged the flesh so ruthlessly, the skin hung by only thin pieces. It would need stitching and a hot compress to cleanse it.

More worrisome was the damage it might've done to the man's throat, and only time and rest would answer that. He'd spoken with a slight rasp, but that he'd spoken at all was a good sign, she thought. She pressed his hand back in place and patted his shoulder. Her hand lingered, as the enormity of what he had done came to her.

"That bad," he said, studying her face.

"You'll need a surgeon and some rest," she said, forcing herself to break away. She picked up his pistol and the awl, and shoved them both into his coat pocket. Helping him upright, she started them toward the abbey. Each leaned on a cane and each other, for support. She drunk in the closeness and let it relax her. "The sooner the better, too."

Canonbie smirked. She felt his arm tighten around her. "Pay for a surgeon? When I know where to find a good apothecary?"

Effie groaned. Even now, the man sought to jest? But her groan turned into a smile. "Try not to speak. You need to rest your voice." She glanced around anxiously but saw no sign of the madman. He'd most likely slunk into the same hole he'd crawled into after the murders.

Yet the tide had turned. She knew his aura now. If she had any strength left in her, she'd track the path of his escape. The thought brought on a yawn, as if her body resented the very idea of such a notion. She'd come close to death, and the surge of adrenaline that had flooded her before now served to exhaust her.

She realized Canonbie held his other arm against his chest, the one struck by the red cane she now carried. It crushed her like a ton of stone, the awareness that he'd sacrificed himself to rescue her from her own stubbornness. A lump clogged her throat as she realized how close she'd come to getting them both killed.

"You felt me calling you?" she asked to break the silence.

He looked at her funny. "I heard the pistol shot. The bastard gave me the slip, and I was wandering for higher ground to see what I could when it rang out."

She laughed at that. "Nevertheless, you saved my life."

Canonbie shook his head. "Mr. Stevenson's coin saved your life. Thank him or Mr. Graham if you need to carry on about it."

A grin pulled at her lips. If the man loved to be contrary, she would let him. He had earned the right.

"I feel like we failed," she admitted. "We didn't find the man. He found us, and he nearly killed us even though we had him outnumbered." Heat rose in her cheeks. "We don't even know the man's name!"

Jack Canonbie ran his tongue along the inside of his lips. "We will soon enough," he declared, after a few strides. "I know just where to find it."

19

"The damned fool thinks to become a warlock," said Graham. He growled the words and held open a book for Effie to scan. They stood within Harrow & Loch's. The rotund bookseller watched from behind his table but made no move to stop them as they pulled volume after volume from an old, ironbound chest they'd found in the corner of the shop. It had been locked when they'd discovered it, with a cloth covering it and a stack of books atop its curved lid.

Constable Simon Greysmith frowned. He stood next to Canonbie with his arms folded across his chest. He clutched the leather strap of his truncheon in one hand. The wooden club dangled from it, swaying as the man stepped closer to the book Graham held. The constable had escorted them to the bookseller's after judging the matter urgent enough it couldn't wait for Fergus Alpin. They'd summoned the Fey Finder from Balclune, along with a detail of soldiers to aid in hunting the madman. The constable had heeded Effie's tale with an open mind and scowled over the fact that a murderer ran loose in his town.

Graham had done more to convince the man. While Effie and Canonbie confronted the madman, Graham had pleaded their cause. He'd shown the constables the dart firing device and poison used on the darts. The apothecary had concocted some tale for his own defense, but those who'd watched from the street had sided with Graham's version of events. The brute of an apprentice had erred in that regard. By ripping the curtain free, he'd allowed witnesses to stand against him and his master.

"A warlock?" asked Greysmith. He turned to Effie. "Is such a thing possible?" He'd connected her to the tales of the Green Lady earlier and seemed to view her as an expert on all matters of the uncanny.

"I'm not sure," she admitted, honestly. She'd never heard any fey lore regarding such things. Peering over Graham's shoulder, she glanced at the pages he presented. Diagrams of fey anatomy sat aside complex formulae referring to some chemistry of bodily fluids. In the small blocks of text supporting the diagrams, she caught enough to understand the author's intent. It followed from what they knew of the murderer's actions, and the riddle of the madman started to unravel.

"This book suggests Fey Craft can be stolen," she said, her voice tight. The idea staggered her. If true, it would pose a greater danger to those of fey blood than a thousand Lord Granvilles. But could such a secret have been kept quiet for so long? She wouldn't wager on it, and yet, hadn't Aerfenium seen similar concealment? Running a finger along the diagrams, she flipped the page and winced. A depiction of brain matter and instructions on how to drill a burr hole for its extraction filled the page. "It suggests that somehow Fey Craft's power is stored in fey phrenology."

"The trepanning," said Graham. "I've never seen a notion so revolting."

He moved the book to one flat palm and touched his injured shoulder. Effie thought the gesture reflexive, born of a realization at what the apothecary had intended for him. Dried blood crusted his coat and shirt, though it didn't appear as much as it had in the moments after he'd been shot, when he'd turned so frightfully pale. A local surgeon had come to see to the wounded men from his office up the high street. According to Graham, he'd needed nothing more than a compression wrap of gauze and a stiff nip of whiskey. The surgeon had spent more time pulling out shards of glass from the apothecary's apprentice. But when he saw Canonbie return, he'd waved for the constables to take the brute away and focused his efforts there.

Canonbie had acted in predictable fashion. After accepting a glass of bourbon himself, he'd insisted they come to the bookshop straightaway. Effie peeked at him. She'd had to threaten the fool man and beg him come to his senses. His arm hung in a sling. He'd been fortunate it wasn't broken. Only a severe contusion lay beneath his coat sleeve. The wound at his neck concerned her more. He'd covered the stitching, hastily done by the surgeon, with a cloth. But his cheeks held a sallow color, and he leaned whenever he could. The man was in sore need of a bowl of beef broth, a cup of honeyed tea, and a week's rest in bed.

Effie knew she'd have better luck convincing a sheep to brush itself clean before a shearing. She turned to the bookseller and leveled her gaze. "Did you sell a copy of this book to the man we seek?"

"Or the apothecary you tricked us into visiting?" added Graham. Canonbie had argued the apothecary couldn't be trusted, that he had already lost and had no cause to aid them, especially if he and the madman were close acquaintances. It was why he'd insisted they return to the bookshop instead.

The bookseller swallowed indignantly and raised his chin to peer down at them. "I have a selection for certain clientele who pay a high value for discretion."

Effie sighed. Of course Canonbie had been right. The bookseller wasn't a part of the conspiracy. Not directly, anyway. He was most likely driven by greed alone.

"You procured this selection where?" asked Greysmith. He clasped his hands behind his back and stood taller. "The theft of these books of the so-called occult still count as theft."

The bookseller bristled. "I would never. I assure you I paid a fair price for them."

"Then I would like to see the bill of sale, if you please." Constable Greysmith held out his hand. His face became a mask of stone. "I'm sure you have it written in your ledger of accounts."

It took a moment for Effie to realize his tactic. Books of the occult were largely traded in secret, their authors and printing houses known to only an inner consortium. If the bookseller were to hand over the name of his connection, it would no doubt cost him far more than telling them details of the madman.

Canonbie chuckled as the bookseller blanched. "Counting the coins in your head, are you?"

Graham smirked. Effie put a hand on his uninjured shoulder. "Tell us why you sent us into a trap," she demanded, "and who this madman is who buys books from you and then uses them to murder the crown's subjects."

The bookseller's eyes narrowed into beady orbs that reminded her of his rats. He glared straight at her. "They aren't really, the fey. Not the queen's good subjects. Not them, no matter this recent talk of a treaty. A corruption, it is."

A low growl came from Graham. He sounded something like an angry bear whose food had just been stolen.

Effie stiffened. She felt the hatred coming off the man like a wave of heat. She wanted to delve into her Fey Craft and send him an image of spiders crawling over his flesh, spinning webs from his ears, and biting his nose. She wanted to cross the shop and slap him across the face. But neither would do anything to diminish the man's prejudice. They would only bolster it.

Canonbie reached a different conclusion. He yanked a book from the shelf where he leaned and sent it hurling at the bookseller's head. The bookseller barely had time to flinch before the hard binding smacked into his face. He hollered and clasped his hands over his nose and mouth.

Greysmith eyed Canonbie with disdain, but he addressed the bookseller. "Your obstinacy has carried on long enough. Tell us the information we seek or I will have this shop condemned until you find your tongue."

Dropping his hands, the bookseller glanced from the constable to Canonbie, and then to Effie. His nose had puffed up and turned a dark hue of red. A trickle of blood ran from one nostril. "He is called Cyrus Reed," he began. He sneered as he spoke. "He's a doctor of some sort, or educated as one, at the least. He seeks to blend old alchemy principles with fey brain matter and use Fey Craft as his own. He says the druids of old used to do the same." The man mimicked using a tiny hammer. "Tap, tap, tap a fey's power and ingest it into himself."

The gesture sickened Effie. She struggled not to think about Laeth and Hargrund, or how she might have wound up the same. And how many more? The thought made her shiver. "You told him how to do this disgusting thing?"

Spreading his hands wide, the bookseller feigned innocence. "I have no knowledge of chemistry or biology. Or art or architecture, for that matter. It is all in the books. I am a mere merchant. Would you have me arrested for selling a treatise on warfare—von Clausewitz, perhaps?— when the purchaser goes off to raise arms? Or what of a book on blacksmithing, when a horse throws a faulty shoe?"

"It seems you know this man quite well," countered Graham. "How many books did he purchase for you to be aware of his aims and desires?"

"A few," admitted the bookseller. "But as I said, I don't know what they contained. I only know what the madman told me of them. I see that he is mad, now that you say it. He only did come into town a couple weeks past, and at first I thought him only peculiar. But his rantings have grown recently, and perhaps I erred in believing he read only for his own pleasure."

"What of the apothecary?" Effie spat. "Is he just as mad?"

The bookseller shrugged. He folded his pudgy arms across his chest. "Ask him, if you must. He promised good coin for information on the whereabouts of any fey. It seemed out of character for the man, but who am I to judge? I thought I'd do him one better and deliver you to his door. How am I to know what he'd want, or that he'd intend you any harm? For all I know, he'd never heard of Cyrus Reed. I'd never seen the two together."

Jack Canonbie laughed at the man's blustering. "The problem with learning fey alchemy is it requires quite a few fey to get it right. So what's a man to do when he had no fey friends of his own?"

Effie glowered, but something within Canonbie's words stuck with her. She gasped in excitement as a riddle unraveled in her head. Questing out with her fey senses, her eyes lit up. She knew where the madman hid. She'd known since the morning, though it hadn't registered until now.

"We have him," she shouted. "Constable, summon your men!"

20

"They're letting the killer escape," said Jack Canonbie.

"It's not her fault," said Graham. Frustration strained his voice, and he folded his arms across his chest. They'd hustled up the high street only to run into Fergus Alpin and a detail of soldiers under his command. With them strode Mr. John Billingsley, the new Fey Finder General, along with the superintendent of the Dunfermline constabulary. Mr. Billingsley had leaned on his cane and studied Effie with a cheery smile. His cheeks were rosy, his face full of wrinkles and the dark spots of age.

She'd related all they'd learned in an explosion of words, pressing on the importance of urgency. When she'd finished, the superintendent had turned to Constable Greysmith and asked for a full account. As Greysmith snapped to attention and began retelling the same tale Effie had just recounted, Fergus Alpin ushered her and her companions out of earshot. The gesture infuriated her all the more. Not only did it imply her account couldn't be trusted but that she wouldn't be able to defend any discrepancies.

The superintendent stood of middling height, with a square jaw and thick frame. He clapped the back of one hand into the other as he grilled the constable over some point. The Fey Finder General looked on with barely a peep. He seemed more interested in watching the activity along the high street. Nearing afternoon, the town bustled with activity. A newsboy hawked some broadsheet, and the aroma of fresh pies came from a bakery across the street. Two men collected slop in a hand-pulled wain and swept the cobblestones clean, while a man on stilts checked the street's gas lamps for fuel. Their party attracted a great deal of attention, and the soldiers ringed them to ensure privacy and keep the onlookers moving along.

"Are they still inside?" asked Graham.

"Yes," said Effie. She could sense the three fey auras in the exact location where she'd felt them since earlier in the morning. It had come to her in the bookshop, the oddness of their stillness. They hadn't moved an inch, and their auras were huddled together as if contained in some manner. From that oddness, she had drawn a picture of what occurred.

Cyrus Reed was a madman, she had no doubt. But how did a madman find fey? It made no sense for the man to have fey allies, not if his aim was to use fey brain matter as a mere ingredient in his own nefarious designs. While the possibility existed the man could sense fey blood on his own—all one needed was a slight amount of it within their own bloodline—she doubted it. Laeth and Hargrund had been lured out, and what better means to lure them than three captured pixies placed under duress?

Pixies were never like to remain in one place for very long. They zipped and darted about like midges after downing a pint of coffee. Reed must have drugged them the same way he'd drugged her, leaving them in a stupor, unable to call on any Fey Craft. But their lives had not yet winked out. It gave her hope they were not too late.

From where she stood, she could spy the three-storied building that held the pixies. They were in some room on the top floor. She'd pointed it out to Fergus Alpin as soon as she'd run into the man. The building stood tall and proud amongst its neighbors, with a fresh coat of green paint and white trim. A tailor's shop resided on the ground floor, its name etched in gold in the front window—Franklin's High Street. It hardly seemed a place that would house a murderer. But if the man was a trained doctor—as the bookseller contended—he no doubt knew how to act civilly in polite company.

That she couldn't sense his aura within didn't deter her. The man was a master alchemist. Who knew what tricks he could perform? She'd witnessed auras hidden before, although never one unaided by Fey Craft. The thought made her shiver. Just how close was Cyrus Reed to becoming a warlock?

Effie tapped her foot impatiently. They needed to find the man. "Can we not send some men to watch the building?" she asked Fergus Alpin.

The Fey Finder glanced at the building, then at John Billingsley. She caught a look of apprehension pass his face. "We can see it from here," he replied.

"But not the back," she pleaded. "At least allow Graham and me to go."

"To what end?" Alpin snapped, but there was not much bite to his anger. He seemed a man put out by the situation, and she wondered what had passed between him and the new Fey Finder General before their arrival. "You have no authority to delay or arrest one of the crown's subjects. Not even I have that power."

"You're a damned coward," muttered Graham. "You can order the soldiers to do it, and you know it."

"That is for Mr. Billingsley to decide." Fergus Alpin turned and stepped away. He wrestled with his own pride, Effie saw. She remembered how he'd acted at Langmire, a man of reason clouded by ego. It was why he disliked Conall Murray's presence at the storehouse so much, and why he disliked her altogether. He did not like to be challenged. He did not want to feel impotent, unable to follow the convictions of his own mind.

Effie understood the feeling.

"I can make a dash for it," said Canonbie. He scratched his cheek, eyeing the distance. "They'd follow, mad as hops."

"You can barely stand," said Effie.

The familiar smirk came to Canonbie's lips. "If I don't make it, I'll receive plenty of rest in the tollbooth."

"I'll go," offered Graham. "I'm slower, but they have no cause to keep me here. I can just walk away without a bother." He eyed the soldiers. His gaze was not as certain as his grumbling tone.

Effie smiled, but when her eyes strayed to Billingsley, her shoulders slumped. She didn't know what the man knew of her, or more precisely what he'd been ordered to do with her, but challenging his authority during their first encounter was not likely to encourage his good graces. And no matter his current disposition toward her, all of fey kind would need the man to see he could trust and work with them.

"Damnation," she cursed. Billingsley had come to Dunfermline on his way to tour the storehouse at Balclune, and stumbled into a mess. Willing or not, he might well cause a murderer to run free.

She shook her head. "No," she said. "We stand and wait." Folding her arms beneath her breasts, her teeth gnashed together. She tried not to stare daggers at the superintendent, watching the man confer with Billingsley after Constable Greysmith had finally fallen silent.

It took another five minutes for the men to reach a conclusion to act. Greysmith put his whistle to his lips and shrilled it for all its worth. Without waiting to see if anyone followed, he stormed toward the tailor's shop. Fergus Alpin waved for the soldiers to aid the constable. They formed a tight rank and marched forward, parting the foot traffic in the street like a clipper across open water. Effie hurried after. She didn't pause for Billingsley or the superintendent. If they wished her to remain out of the matter, they would need to hound her themselves.

A crowd surrounded the shop by the time she reached it. Men and women strained to see what the fuss was about and why Her Majesty's army had taken to the streets of their bustling town. To her surprise, Fergus Alpin barked at the press to let her through. She shouldered past a group of boys who wouldn't listen. Their faces were covered in dirt and coal dust, and they stunk as if they hadn't seen a bath in years. When one caught sight of her, his eyes widened, and he nudged the boy next to him.

"See, ah tauld ye!" he spat, his accent almost undecipherable. "Saw 'er, I did!"

"Ha!" Canonbie snorted and ruffled the boy's hair. "That you did, mate. But have you seen her dance under the moonlight? Ho-ho!"

Effie whipped her head around, ready to give the man a good lashing. Blood rushed to her cheeks as one of the onlookers who'd overheard Canonbie mumbled something lewd. Those around him chuckled.

Graham stepped closer, so their shoulders brushed. Casually, he slipped his calloused fingers over hers. But he left his grip loose, and she realized he meant only to restrain her from striking Canonbie. "Ignore him, lass," he said, speaking so only she could hear. "The man compensates for that which he cannot have."

The words sent Effie's mind awhirl. She clutched Graham's hand tighter. He surely couldn't mean that Jack Canonbie thought of her in any manner other than as an unruly charge. Her own thoughts might have evolved of late, but she was not a woman who gave over to roguish churls, no matter how fetching their smiles. No matter if the man beneath seemed more chivalrous knight than uncouth scoundrel.

She glowered. Had she given Canonbie a false impression? His gaze fell on her, and the smirk he wore vanished. Color crept into his cheeks, as he licked his lips and swallowed. Her gut tightened. *Men!* Of all the times, here they went to apprehend a madman who'd subdued and drugged her, battered and nearly killed him, slain at least two fey, and who slurped brain matter in hopes of becoming a warlock, and he lusted for her like a wild hound!

"Go and check the backdoor," she instructed. Her voice trembled slightly, and she lied to herself that it had anything to do with the stirring she felt inside, a slight, almost nonexistent, yearning to pounce into the man's arms and drag him to a quiet and dark alleyway. "He might try to escape that way."

Canonbie nodded and strode off. She watched silently before shaking free of further fancies. She had no time for them.

Turning to the onlookers, she thought to address the crowd. Yet words failed her. To be the subject of so many strange gazes made her want to shrink and hide. What had she to offer them? She settled on a polite nod and embarrassed smile. A few returned the gesture, though most stared glumly back at her. The boys sniggered at some whispered comment, and it felt oddly like a retreat as she stepped away.

Graham held the door for her as she entered the tailor's shop. Bolts of fabric lined the walls. A small, circular dais sat in the middle of the shop, used for the taking of measurements, and a table used for the cutting and stitching of cloth filled one corner. Constable Greysmith emerged from a doorway along the back wall and waved her and Graham forward.

"There is something you should see upstairs," he said. His voice sounded grim.

The doorway led into a short hall that ended at the rear of the building. A door there exited into a small yard. It stood ajar, and Effie saw Canonbie milling about, speaking with one of the soldiers. To her left along the hall, a pair of small storage rooms rested. Their doors were pulled open, giving view to racks of suits and gentlemen's coats in various stages of completion. To her right, a narrow stair climbed to the upper floors. A floral print covered the wallpaper, with a high wainscoting of square panels running beneath it. Two lamps lit the area, casting shadows on the polished floor.

"The matron of the house lets the rooms on the top floor while her husband runs the shop below," said Greysmith. "Her description of the current tenant matches Cyrus Reed, but she hasn't seen the man since this morning's meal."

The stair creaked as they crept up the steps. A sense of dread overcame Effie as she climbed. She had only just met Constable Greysmith, but his cold silence she took for something dire. The way his gaze avoided her and his posture remained rigid made her shiver. She ran a hand along the lacquered banister to steady herself.

From the top floor's landing, the constable ushered her into a ransacked bedroom spotted with droplets of blood. A trunk lay on its side, a man's clothes spilling out onto a thick woolen rug. A stack of books had toppled across a rickety desk. An unlit lamp had fallen from the wall sconce, its glass shattered. The doors of the wardrobe hung open, the drawers within dislodged. The bedding lay rumpled and half-pulled to the floor. Blood left a trail over all of it, telling a tale of a hasty retreat. No doubt, Cyrus Reed had taken only what he could carry on foot.

"Good Lord," breathed Graham, taking in the scene.

The matron of the house hovered just inside the door. She fretted with her hands, her eyes darting over Effie and Greysmith. Her husband, the tailor, slouched against the wall next to her. He wore a smart apron of green wool. Garters held back the sleeves of his starched, white shirt. The dour cast of his face showed the expression of a man whose fortunes had fallen.

"We didn't have any notion the man was a villain," said the matron. "He came into town a fortnight ago and kept to himself most nights. Only..." She drifted off and glanced at her husband.

Effie stepped forward. "What is it? You have nothing to fear, and anything you've witnessed might help in the man's capture."

The matron dabbed her face with a handkerchief and nodded. "It's only, I heard him some nights talking in a low voice to someone. But no one else was here. I am sure of it. I keep a strict curfew."

"And the squeaks," said the tailor. "Tell them of those."

"Och, aye. That be the strangest part. When the man spoke as such, I swear I heard something respond. A quiet, squeaking sound like a mouse might make. But they were having a conversation, or my name's not Betsy Franklin."

Despite the woman's confusion, the account served to confirm what Effie expected to find. Cyrus Reed had held three pixies captive, and no doubt had spoken with them. Perhaps he'd promised them freedom for knowledge of the movements of other fey within Dunfermline. Perhaps he'd tried to learn something of Fey Craft from them. Or perhaps he'd done nothing but taunt the poor, wee things in some cruel manner.

Effie patted the matron's hand. "Will you please excuse us for a moment?" she asked the tailor and his wife. "We need to examine Mr. Reed's belongings."

Once they had departed, Effie crossed to a nook formed between the wardrobe and a corner of bedroom. She'd expected to find a cage there, something similar to what the bookseller had contained his pet rats in. What she found made her flesh crawl.

The dress box had come from a fancy shop in a city. It still held its shape and a ribbon to fasten it closed. Within, three shapes nestled. But they weren't pixies. Not anymore. Sewing pins tacked their wings to the box's bottom—a subtle and cruel ensnarement. They could free themselves if they wanted, but only if they tore their wings apart. An ichor coated their wee bodies, thick and black, hiding any detail of their features. The frizzled hair of one stuck out of the mess, strawberry-colored locks that might've hung to the pixie's waist. None of them stirred. They looked like lumps of tar.

Fury rose in Effie's gut. The ichor remained wet, though she dared not touch it. Cyrus Reed had done this thing after their encounter, as he scrambled to collect his things and flee the town. He had done it while they spoke with the bookseller, or while they waited on John Billingsley to act.

Pulling her gaze away, she studied her feet. She couldn't help but think she'd failed, and her fury quickly turned into guilt. It felt too often like her efforts were never enough.

"What is it?" asked Graham. His face became concerned, and he hurried to her side. His breath caught at the sight of the small forms. "Are they?"

"They still live," said Effie. She could sense their auras, at least. She didn't know what else the madman had done to them.

Graham squatted and reached out a finger to touch the ichor.

"No!" exclaimed Effie, grabbing his shoulder. "We don't know if that's the same substance that dulls fey senses." She placed her hands over her gut. "I have a feeling it is not."

"What then?" asked Graham. "Another poison?"

"It looks to me as such," answered Constable Greysmith. "We found the things afore you arrived and thought you might know better. Or perhaps, what to do with them?"

Effie shrugged. She had no idea how to treat the poor things. The ichor had adhered itself to the pixies' flesh, she could tell. It would take more than a gentle scrubbing to wash it free. It would take a surgeon to cut it off.

Graham returned to the desk and picked up a tome bound by a soft leather cover. It looked to Effie like a journal might. Flipping through the pages, his brow furrowed almost instantly. "The writing changes," he said. "At the start, the hand is meticulous and organized. But the final passages are scrawled in a ranting manner, from a disturbed mind." He turned to the constable and waved at the desk. "May we study these books further?"

"You may not," said a stern voice from the landing. The superintendent strode toward the room. John Billingsley and Fergus Alpin followed on his heels. "This investigation is a fey matter and therefore under the authority of Her Majesty's Fey Finders."

Graham scowled at their entrance but held his tongue.

John Billingsley blinked, as if surprised by the superintendent's pronouncement. "Oh, quite right," he agreed after a moment of consideration. "Mr. Alpin, if you please, collect this evidence." He waggled a finger at the room but stopped short of entering it himself.

"Constable Greysmith, why are these two here?" asked the superintendent.

Greysmith snapped to attention. "Sir, Miss Effie and her companion came at the behest of the Fey Finder General to give what aid they could provide."

A smug grin came to the superintendent's lips. His stare reminded Effie of a hunting cat about to devour some field game. She wondered how much the defiant response had cost Constable Greysmith. "The old Fey Finder General, you mean," he said, "whose commands are no longer relevant."

"Yes, sir," replied Greysmith. He swallowed.

"See them gone, and we will let Mr. Alpin perform his duties unhindered by such a crowded space." The superintendent left no option for Greysmith to do otherwise. The constable nodded brusquely. He raised an arm, palm toward the door, indicating Effie and Graham should precede him out.

Effie stood her ground. "Sir, these poor pixies. They need the care of someone knowledgeable of their kind."

The superintendent eyed her, considering. "Do you know how to mend them?" he asked. When she shook her head, he steepled his fingers before his chest. "Then I suggest you take my gratitude on behalf of Dunfermline for your assistance in this investigation."

"I will ensure His Royal Highness, the duke, hears of it," said Mr. Billingsley. His lips smacked together as he spoke, as if he chewed oats in a field.

Effie's eyes narrowed, but she couldn't think of what to say. She'd uncovered the killer's identity and his motives. She'd even stumbled into one of his accomplices. They had enough proof to counter Lord Granville's tales and defeat his arguments against the treaty. What else could she do? She had already overstepped herself and more.

Her gaze flitted to the dress box, and her hand reached out without thought. Gently, she plucked one of the pins loose. The act gave her courage. The pixies still lived, and they had no other hope besides her. She would not leave them unaided and forgotten.

"I may not know how to mend these poor souls," she said, "but I know those who might." She took up the dress box. She would send word to Rose Brewer. If the woman didn't know what to do, she would know someone who would. "It is more than I can say for any other in this room." She rounded on Fergus Alpin. "Or do you intend to spend the next few days researching how to save these innocent subjects? I'm sure you would not like it known that more victims succumbed while under your dutiful care? The two who were murdered are quite enough, don't you agree?"

Alpin's mouth twitched. She saw in his face a desire to lash out at her, but he choked it back. Despite her assault to his pride, she had offered to rid him of responsibility, and he took to it like moss to bark.

"It is as she says, Mr. Billingsley," he said. "The fey have better knowledge to heal their own. It is better she take them under her own charge."

The Fey Finder General uttered something like a wheeze. His smile began to falter. Effie didn't wait for it to fail, or for the man to give another response.

"Thank you, gentlemen," she said, hustling past them. "I am grateful the matter of Cyrus Reed is in better hands than mine." The superintendent's lips fell into a thin line. She could feel the frost of his gaze as she retreated down the creaking wooden stair.

E ffie found Jack Canonbie sitting on a bench outside the shop. The man appeared dead on his feet—or rump—in his present state. His eyes drifted closed, and his cheeks had drained of color. She handed the dress box to Graham and went to feel his forehead, hoping the man hadn't caught a fever.

Canonbie waved her hand away. "Bah, all I need is a few nips to warm my gut," he croaked.

"You need a bed, a blanket, and a good meal, too," said Effie. She considered that. They had left their belongings with the carriage driver that morning, not knowing where the day would take them. The hour now grew late into the afternoon. The sun dipped low behind the abbey, its rays illuminating the high stone walls in a halo of light. It reflected off the brooding clouds, too, which threatened a return of rain showers within moments. They had neither eaten nor rested since departing the coaching inn, and Effie's feet felt like granite rocks.

All in all, they were in no state to travel anywhere but to a hotel for the night. Still, she needed to tend the pixies and send word for Rose. She also couldn't bring herself to give up the hunt for the madman just yet. Cyrus Reed was more injured than Canonbie. Perhaps he had holed up somewhere close, somewhere where she could ferret him out.

Graham shifted the box to one arm and scratched at his chin. "The apothecary promised to pay the bookseller for word of any fey in Dunfermline, but can we truly believe the bookseller had no knowledge of the apothecary's connection to Cyrus Reed?"

Canonbie shrugged. "The man had no reason to lie on that point. He probably took coin from both and thought no further. He may have other clients who've asked the same."

"So the pixies alerted Cyrus Reed to our presence at the apothecary shop," said Graham, working through the details of the afternoon.

"It is more than likely," said Effie. "Or perhaps the men have some device to forewarn one another."

"Then we should pay another visit to the apothecary and determine how the men communicated," said Graham. He glanced at the windows on the top floor of the tailor's shop. "It is a certainty the apothecary is familiar with Mr. Reed's poisons. The bastard used one on me, after all. He may help revive the pixies and tell us what the ichor is that coats them."

At Canonbie's frown, Effie showed him what they'd discovered upstairs. He cursed and tried to stand. She put a hand against his chest to halt him. "I will scour the town for a trace of Cyrus Reed. I know his aura now, and it is a task only I can complete. Mr. Graham, you and Mr. Canonbie can question the apothecary." She couldn't let the man traipse up and down the streets with her. He would faint or worse.

"You won't find him in his shop," called Greysmith from behind her. The constable marched up to their group. "He is in a cell in the tollbooth, along with that brute of his. We threw them in irons after the disturbance this morning."

Effie huffed a laugh. "Let me presume the superintendent won't allow us to visit him, you'll say next," she said. "He all but had us escorted to the train station."

"Nay, he won't," agreed Greysmith. "But I can go. It is the best I can offer."

"If only I'd made the connection sooner," she said. "Bugger me for a fool, it was right there in front of me the entire time."

Constable Greysmith started at her crudeness. Jack Canonbie chuckled.

As the first drops of rain began to batter them, Effie replaced the lid of the dress box. Cyrus Reed had punctured a few holes in the lid for air to pass through, further evidence he'd intended to keep the pixies alive. Graham held the box out for her to tie the ribbon around.

"Ye can't blame yourself for it," he said. "Who knows whether we missed him by a minute or an hour? He could've watched us while we marched to the bookseller's or fled before you made it back from the abbey grounds."

"What did take the superintendent so long?" Effie asked. "Did he really believe none of my account?"

Greysmith shuffled his feet and glanced at the dress box. "Due to the nature of the crimes, he claimed the matter under the authority of the Fey Finder General. Mr. Billingsley claimed the opposite, that Her Majesty's Fey Finders have no writ or charge that allows them to arrest any wrongdoers other than those of fey blood."

"They debated over who had authority?" barked Graham.

Effie mimicked Greysmith's uneasy stance. "They debated because neither saw an advantage in protecting fey interests. Or fey lives."

The constable put his fingers to his brow and bobbed his head in a salute. From his sullen cast, she knew he meant the gesture as an apology as well as a parting. "I will see to questioning the apothecary," he said.

The rain strengthened as they watched the constable depart. It brought on a cold that seeped into the bones. Effie's stomach gurgled its displeasure. She remembered the scent of the bakery earlier and searched the high street for it. *No*, she thought, *I must continue the hunt*.

The yawn took her by surprise. The force of it made her step back and whip a hand awkwardly to cover her mouth. "Pardon me," she murmured.

Canonbie looked at her with genuine amusement. "There are some who say that if you catch a fey yawning, your luck is about to change," he said.

"I have never heard that," she said. "But it is encouraging you trust in my bodily functions so greatly."

He bellowed a laugh and bowed. When he straightened, his eyes hardened. "Cyrus Reed won't return to the tailor's," he said. "He's too savvy for that. He isn't likely to hole up near the town's center, either. He knows you have a means to find him if he stays within a certain distance. Most likely, he has fled Dunfermline."

"We must do something," said Effie.

"Och, I'd nearly forgotten," said Graham. He handed her the dress box. Reaching into his coat pocket, he pulled out a small, flat object. "I meant to hand it to the constables. Only, we thought we might catch Mr. Reed at his lodgings, and then with the superintendent and Fey Finder General acting as they had—well, we'll make better use of it."

He held out the tintype from the apothecary shop. "If we can uncover what town this is, maybe we can find these gentlemen and learn more of Cyrus Reed."

Effie's face lit up. The clue wasn't much, but it gave her a glimmer of hope. Some of her fatigue wore off. "It is excellent forethought," she said as a rumble of thunder rolled over the hills. She glanced at Canonbie. The man's coat had almost turned sodden. "Let's find a dry place to study it, and perhaps a meat pie."

"I'd go for a pint," said Jack Canonbie. "As long as there's whiskey to follow it."

Graham nodded in agreement. He helped the other man to his feet, and they set off down the high street. They hadn't made it a dozen paces before the clomping of boots drew their attention to a constable rushing toward them. The man held one hand up to steady the watchman's helmet atop his head. His truncheon flopped at his side from its tether at his belt. Effie thought she recognized the man from earlier, but she wasn't certain. Had Greysmith cracked the apothecary so quickly? Or better, perhaps Cyrus Reed had been found in a ditch on the outskirts of town. A mix of apprehension and anticipation filler her.

The constable marched straight to her and thrust a folded piece of paper under her nose. "You are summoned, miss," he said, bluntly.

"To the tollbooth?" she asked. She took the paper and unfolded it.

"To Edinburgh," said the constable. "I've orders to arrest you if you refuse."

22

A steam carriage awaited Effie and Graham at the docks of Queensferry. The driver wore a dark suit of a cut finer than most merchants could afford. He greeted them with little ceremony and even less information. The paper the constable had handed Effie in Dunfermline stated only an urgent need for her assistance and a scrawling signature—Mr. Elias McPherson, esquire. The name was that of a city magistrate, Effie knew. But experience and a warning tickle at the back of her neck told her some other hand prompted the magistrate's summons.

Graham helped her step into the carriage while the driver saw to their belongings. They had left Jack Canonbie across the Firth of Forth with instructions to recover what details he could from Constable Greysmith's interview with the apothecary. Secretly, Effie hoped the man would rest. He'd barely managed to stumble into the hotel they'd found near Dunfermline's high street and had protested vehemently against being left behind. She and Graham had caught the last ferry of the day. The icy waters of the firth swirled and chopped as storm clouds rolled in from the coast. The pelting rain those clouds delivered felt like pinpricks of ice. They pierced the warmth of her coat, and she was glad for the shelter the carriage provided.

She kept the dress box with her. The ribbon dared her to pull it free and do what else she could for the pixies, but she decided that best wait until later. She had no notion of what the magistrate wanted of her, or how safe those with her would be. It was best to keep her wee charges a secret for the nonce.

Graham crawled in after her and sat on the opposite bench. The interior of the carriage matched the affluence shown by the driver. Plush velvet covered its cushions. A hint of rose perfumed the air. Gold paint trimmed the wood paneling of the roof and doors, and a small decanter of wine sat on a railed tray bolted to the front wall of the compartment.

"Someone wishes for your good graces," said Graham, indicating a pair of slender wine flutes. They were etched with a flock of doves in flight.

"A dab of honey does nothing to sweeten a pot of vinegar," she replied. Her lips pursed, but she took the glass he offered anyway. The driver shoveled coal into the boiler before they set out. They could hear him at the carriage's rear. A heavy iron lid squealed open, and a shovel scraped and clanked about. The boiler warmed behind Effie's seat, and she sunk into it, letting the heat unwind her shoulders and back.

"We waltz into a trap," he said. His face was filled with concern. "This magistrate would not have summoned you in such a manner on a lark. It is part of some greater design."

"Of course it is." Effie sighed.

That she should be worried occupied the bulk of her thoughts, but she chose to ignore those concerns. Whatever dangers awaited them would only be added to the ever-growing account she now maintained, and she needed to rest her mind if she had any hope of its sharpness later. Guessing at the trap before the string was pulled would only serve to exhaust her more. She sipped the wine. Its spice burned her tongue, almost like a whiskey. She thought she'd tasted its finish before, but she couldn't quite place where.

Glancing out the carriage window, she breathed deeply. The darkness of night blocked their view of the city as they trundled down the Queensferry road. Edinburgh rose and fell over seven hills, but the surrounding villages made the city seem much vaster than the boundaries of its old heart. Even a mile distant, coal smoke already clogged the air. It blocked out the light of the stars and trapped the heat of the day's sun.

Dark shadows hung above the city from airships tethered to giant towers. They swayed in the wind, warning lamps twinkling from the underside of their wooden hulls. Trams rattled down a track parallel to the road. Their sputtering, and that of the steam carriages, drowned out the din spilling from the tavern doors they passed. Only the driving patter of rain could be heard above the clamor.

"I know you are a woman grown," Graham continued, "but I'll say my peace anyway. Be careful, lass."

She smiled and felt her muscles relax further. His concern warmed her more than either boiler or wine. Graham held her gaze for a long moment before something outside the carriage caught his eye.

"We head for New Town," he said.

Effie shook herself from the stillness that had stolen her away and followed where he looked. "Oh, yes," she said. "I should think whoever summoned us a stranger to other parts of the city." An orderly grid of broad streets gleamed under the halo of gas lamps. Unlike Old Town, which had grown outward from Castle Rock like a creeping mold, New Town had been carefully planned by master architects a century prior. Planned for the rich and affluent who wanted to escape the teeming masses who'd overrun the old city with disease, refuse, and vice.

The carriage turned down a lane bordered by a tree-lined park. At a large house of precisely cut sandstone, the driver engaged the brake and brought them to a rattling, squealing halt. The house stood taller than its neighbors, with an abundance of windows and a pitched roofline. A footman waited for them outside.

As Effie climbed from the carriage with Graham's support, the footman rushed over to hold an umbrella above her head. It blocked her view of the upper windows, but she had the distinct feeling someone watched her. Casting out her fey senses, she felt an abundance of fey blood in the city, but mostly from the direction of Old Town, and none emanating from the great house before her. When Graham reached for the dress box, she brushed a hand on his arm to stop him. There was no need to draw attention to the thing, and it would remain dry in the carriage until they returned.

They were led into an antechamber large enough for a pair of cushioned chairs and a round topiary that smelled of lilac. There, Graham was instructed to wait, while the footman ushered Effie through a set of double doors. He blustered at the command, but she quelled his unease.

"I will be fine," she said even as her heart began to race.

The footman announced her in the chamber beyond. She stepped through the doorway and felt her body turn to stone. Clamping her mouth shut, she stilled her breath. She didn't want to give the man perched on the leather sofa the satisfaction of seeing her shock.

Lord Granville rose to greet her. His lips formed a thin line turned slightly upward in the attempt of a smile. He flicked his fingers, a gesture for the footman to leave them, while never taking his gaze from her. His eyes seemed tired, his coat slightly wrinkled. A few locks atop his head stood out of place, as if he'd continually run a hand through his hair. The chamber was warm with light, a drawing room of sorts, with its sofa and collection of chairs. Lamps ringed the room along the walls. Portrait paintings hung between them, of all shapes and sizes, though their subjects held a similar cast of nose and brow. Effie guessed them familial, most likely that of the magistrate. The hint of an earthy tobacco clung to the air. No doubt someone had conversed with Lord Granville before her arrival. The man himself did not smell of the pipe.

Effie curtsied as the doors groaned and thudded closed behind her. It sounded like a crypt being sealed. She knew of traps, and though she didn't think Lord Granville meant her any physical harm, he would not have summoned her in such a manner for idle gossip.

"I am honored," he said. Dipping his head in greeting, Lord Granville's dimples flared. He was a handsome man with a soothing voice. Both were excellent instruments for a politician, and by all accounts he played them well. He offered her tea and took a brandy for himself before returning to the sofa.

Effie found a stiff-backed chair and sat on its edge, clutching her tea in her lap. "It is proper I should say the same, but the long journey took me away from an urgent matter. A murderer is on the loose and in need of justice, and it appears great slander has occurred against the fey cause."

He waved an absent hand and sipped his brandy. "Ah, yes. Mr. Billingsley has kept me informed of your theories and your meddling."

"Does it anger you that I am good at meddling, sir? Have you pulled me away from Dunfermline because I hinder your designs? Your false proclamations against the fey?" Her voice turned thin. "As for my so-called theories, Mr. Billingsley and the good constables will proclaim the account accurate. So I would warn you to retract your vile gossip and baseless objections against the treaty before they do your honor any further harm."

His eyes lit up at that. "On the contrary, Miss Effie, it is not my honor that we need concern ourselves. For truth, I was not aware Her Majesty employed fey in the ranks of Sniffers. It must give you an unpleasant satisfaction to aid them so."

Effie's lips curled into a polite grin. "Her Majesty does not. But her hounds are in need of a strong leash if you care to suggest such a thing. Or perhaps you already have. Is Mr. John Billingsley a dear acquaintance of yours?" She took a stab, wondering if Lord Granville had pushed for the new Fey Finder General's appointment. Lord Granville studied her without giving away any indication of the fact.

"His manners are kind, if his wits aren't as prime," she continued. "I'd rather hoped the leash would pull the other way. A justice that is not blind is the tool of a tyrant, and I'm afraid Mr. Billingsley can see all too well."

"Truly? Tell me, how blind do you believe your Mr. Conall Murray?" Lord Granville left the insinuation hang for a moment before raising a hand in apology. "We digress. I did not summon you here to debate over the merits of the fey cause."

Effie sipped her tea to help hold her tongue. The man had backed off only when he saw her hackles rising. He prodded her on purpose, she recognized. He wanted to learn how she would react. She lowered her teacup, determined not to give him any indication of her thoughts. She'd grown used to Sir Walter Conrad's manipulations and knew the best means of defeating such ploys was to yank the discourse another direction and see what it uncovered.

"How is Miss Granville finding the city?" She blurted the question before he could speak again.

His laughter barked, filling the room. Rising, he set his brandy on a small table beside the sofa. "It is known within proper society that my daughter travelled to the continent a few days past. She had tired of Scotland already, you see." He paced with his back toward her.

"Oh?" Effie refused to give any hint of interest. *Proper society*. He had meant the odd phrasing as a slight, but she reevaluated the man's disheveled appearance and wondered.

Lord Granville spun on a heel and stared hard at her. "Enough of pleasantries. I will ask you this only once, and if you lie to me, I swear you will hang by the short drop and your fey allies will be burned from their homes." He stalked closer. His warm grin made his words all the more menacing. "A cult of fey infest the bowels of the city. They call themselves *Les Revenirs*. Are they known to you?"

Effie flinched. Lord Granville uttered the threat in such a velvety tone, it took her a moment to comprehend all of its content. "N... No," she stammered, truthfully.

Returning to the sofa, he ran a hand through his hair and plucked up his brandy. She could see his mind working. "But your kind, I am informed, have a means of locating one another. It is one of your little tricks, yes?"

Nodding, Effie kept her lips pressed closed. She saw no reason to correct the man's understanding.

"You will find this cult for me and bring its leaders to the magistrate. They are causing unrest in the city."

"But why?" Effie asked. Her mind reeled, and she couldn't fathom the answer. Any unrest the cult caused would certainly play in favor of Lord Granville's designs. Why would the man seek to thwart that?

"That is none of your concern and not for you to question." Lord Granville waved his brandy at her. "It can go worse for your kind if you refuse. I have read reports from Balclune. When the treaty fails, perhaps funding will appear for those wishing to examine fey phrenology. I am told tapping the power of Fey Craft will be just as powerful as Sir Walter's Aerfenium. Maybe even more so."

"You wouldn't dare!" She stiffened.

"The choice is yours. Turn over the dissident fey. That is what you have argued before, is it not? That some fey deserve to hang while others are allowed to roam unmolested? Now is the time to prove your loyalty to the empire."

Effie studied her teacup. He demanded she act as a Fey Finder and betray her own kind. A ripple of revulsion passed through her before she quelled it. Her eyes darted to him. It could not be that simple. The man hid his true motives, and she knew pressing him directly would lead only to further threats. She needed another tactic to root out anything useful.

Smoothing her skirt over her knees, she asked, "Why do you not call on Mr. Billingsley? You've had him appointed for just such a commission, no doubt. It seems curious to me that you would beg for my meddling when a tool such as the Fey Finder General stands at the ready."

She didn't mean it as a jab, yet Lord Granville bristled all the same. It took her a moment to understand why. Most Sniffers were a boorish lot used to public inquiries. Their use posed too great a risk of exposure, and whatever it was Granville hid, he desperately wanted it to remain that way. The irony sent a tickle through her arms. Fear of exposure had seen her living in anonymity most of her life. That it would cause such distress in one of the great lords of the empire almost made her laugh.

"The methods of Fey Finders are to cleave," explained Lord Granville, echoing her thoughts. "They don't possess the delicacy this matters requires."

She shook her head. "I still don't understand why you have summoned me. To be blunt, we find ourselves on opposite sides of a rather large impasse, one with many lives at stake. You wish me to set aside all your designs to undermine my kind, my very blood, in order bow to the same threats I've heard from your ilk all of my life?"

"Yes," said Lord Granville. "Because I command it, and the empire needs it. Of that, you must take my word." He spoke not with audacity, but with an honest belief that stemmed from every fiber in his being. She could see it in his countenance, the way his posture straightened and his chin raised slightly. The pose resembled those of the portraits ringing the room. He carried an enormous amount of pride, but it didn't stink of arrogance. He had been taught the worth of his family name since his first swaddling.

"There are others you can give this charge, constables and thief-takers." Effie shook her head slowly. "No, you will have to promise more than loose words over my health and that of other fey."

She'd seen through his bold threats. They were smoke meant to mask a desperate need, and it occurred to her that Lord Granville was a man who always plotted with contingencies. He would never allow one ploy to fail for the lack of another. He wouldn't have summoned her at all if he hadn't already considered the offer of some other boon. It gave her a small comfort to know her life now warranted such measures. If she were to suddenly go missing, the outcry from her allies would ripple against him strongly.

"You knew that from the start, and you haven't answered my question," she pressed. "Why do you value my aid over any other?"

"You are a clever one," said Lord Granville. He leaned back against the sofa and brought one leg to cross over the other. Tapping his fingers on his knee, he studied her. "There are many better suited to the task, but you are the fey I know, and I find using such connections more advantageous than employing a common footpad. The promise of coin leads only to greed and mistrust. The promise of something you utterly desire attracts a certain loyalty."

Effie's heart thumped. "The treaty. You would see it succeed?"

Lord Granville sipped at his brandy. "Alas, that is beyond my hand to gift. There are too many who stand against breaking the bonds of history. But I have knowledge of other matters I can offer in exchange."

At his words, the burst of hope melted away. Of course, the man would not change his convictions so easily. He'd rallied in Parliament against the fey for more than a decade. The memory reminded her of how loathingly she'd regarded the man all these years. A feral part of her yearned to smash his head with her teacup, though the act would do little to better fey relations with the crown. No, she couldn't lose her temper with the man. She'd as soon waltz barefoot over broken glass for the benefits it might bring.

She had to keep sight of the treaty's importance. Its success remained paramount to any other concern. To that end, she would do much better to uncover the truth behind his schemes while letting him think her eager to gain his good will. She felt her gut twist in knots, knowing she would need to let him think he had his way.

Still, it would not do to volunteer so readily when Lord Granville would offer more. A bird in the hand, so the common wisdom said. Besides, pushing her advantage would make her consent all the more believable. She set her tea aside, as a thought popped into her head.

"It came to pass in Dunfermline," she said, "that Her Majesty's Fey Finders were powerless to pursue the murderer of five innocent fey." She included the three pixies in her count but felt no shame in stretching the truth. The wee things were in a dire straight, and Cyrus Reed had no doubt killed several fey before his deeds at the storehouse. "They hold no authority to arrest one devoid of fey blood."

Lord Granville cocked his head in puzzlement. "Rightly so. Their charge is given to fey matters alone."

"But you see, the superintendent of the Dunfermline constabulary argued the murders a fey matter and that no non-fey crime had been committed. Surely you see the problem?"

Waving his hand, Lord Granville dismissed the notion. "It is only a matter of semantics."

"One that needs an immediate resolution," she cried.

He pretended not to notice her anger. "I had another thought in mind. I have caught wind of a conspiracy to push forward legislation that would banish all fey to an island colony chosen for their perpetual habitation. It is a foolish plan, of course, but the fey have many enemies in London, and such legislation does stand the chance of passing." He opened his arms wide and smiled. "That is, unless I act to nip it in the bud before it takes root."

Effie's breath caught. The man had no idea she had overheard him with Lord Wilshire. Her mind rushed, seeking a way to use the knowledge to her advantage. Putting forth such a proposal would be an expensive effort for it not to be laughed out of Parliament at its onset. He would've had to work hard for its support. Yet he offered its dismissal to her as if handing her a plate of biscuits. He hadn't wanted to put forth the legislation himself, either. That was something key. All of his other anti-fey proposals had born his name at its head.

She could reach only one conclusion—the man had never fully meant for the proposal to reach Parliament. He'd concocted the scheme as a feint, something to give away during the treaty negotiations. Something to show he acted in good faith. It made her wonder how such a proposal would even work. The penal colonies the crown had created before were filled with captives culled from overcrowded debtors' prisons and other nefarious places. To oust the fey, the crown would first have to catch them all. And that would cost an abundance of money.

The scheme reminded her of something Sir Walter Conrad would do. She smiled, thinking of the similarities between the two men. A snake was a snake, no matter the coloring of its scales.

"What is it?" asked Lord Granville. He smiled back at her, but his eyes scoured her face for the cause of her mirth.

"Sir Walter Conrad," she said, pursuing the connection. "He told you to fetch me, didn't he? He set up this entire meeting in exchange for what? The continued use of Aerfenium once the treaty was defeated?"

The smile widened on Lord Granville's face. He drained his brandy and licked his lips. "A clever lass, indeed. Sir Walter told me I would have to guard my tongue. He is a clever chap, himself." Her eyes narrowed, and he laughed. "Don't worry. Sir Walter still aids Caledon earnestly and yearns for a treaty. He only requested an insurance, like any prudent man in his position should."

"He told you I would do as you ask. Why? Because I would wilt under your dastardly threats? Or because I would swoon for the chance of your good favor?"

"Nothing like that, I assure you. But you see, the constables would create a spectacle, and the Fey Finders would blunder about with even less tact. As for the fey, the steward has other matters on his mind, and I would rather he did not delegate the matter to a stranger." Lord Granville pointed a finger. "That leaves me with you. As I told you before, you are the fey I know."

She nearly laughed at his assertion but caught herself. "Perhaps you'd have better connections if you ever bothered to foster them," she said instead.

"I have made you an offer," said Lord Granville. A coldness crept into his voice. Its bite unnerved her. "It is not for you to scold me like a schoolmarm. I have given into the indulgences of your tongue because of the favor I beg, but please do remember to whom you speak."

Effie steeled herself, knowing his patience had reached an end. She did not believe a word of his arguments, but she felt all she and Stevenson and Caledon strived for hinging on her response. She could needle him no more. She had to consent and find a means to unravel him later.

It would cement the treaty's fate if she did not.

"Let Caledon foil your dreams of a fey colony," she said. Her hands balled as she went against her own better judgment. "Or dismiss the folly yourself. You and I well know the legislation would never succeed, and I won't risk myself over such a weak proposition."

"What?" Lord Granville barked.

"You are right. I am only a commoner, to address a lord in such a manner. I don't even have a family name. Yet have no fear, I will take on your charge. But I won't do it for something as trivial as a cheap trick, and certainly not because you believe my sex too gentle to refuse. I want..." Her voice trailed off. What did she want? She certainly would never join the ranks of the Fey Finders, and yet time and again her lack of any true authority had caused her an impotence that led to defeat. She thought of the tales of the Green Lady, and how much notoriety the simple moniker had lent her.

"I want acknowledgement," she said, then shook her head. No, that wasn't quite right. "I want the crown to formally recognize titles granted by Caledon."

Lord Granville snorted. "Preposterous. Her Majesty would never concede to another creating peers within the empire. If you want a title, I suggest you marry well. Though even if any lord lost his wits enough to entertain the offer, I'm not sure Her Majesty would recognize the union. Such things are not done within proper society. Our blood must be kept pure, devoid of savages."

It was Effie's turn to snort in derision. "I care nothing for your lords and ladies, only a means to ensure crimes against fey are pursued as fervently as those by them. If not me, then grant the authority elsewhere. Form some new body or detail a new policing force. Anything that would show the crown sees the fey as part of the empire rather than counter to it."

"You get ahead of yourself, but I shall think on it. You have my word." Lord Granville brought a closed hand to his lips. His gaze became unfocused, and she could tell he worked through some line of thought. No doubt he sought a means to curb the true intent of her request.

She rose. "If it is only your word I'll get, then you can promise me something else as well. Reverse your accounts of the attack on Balclune. Publicly. You know they are false and that Aerfenium was never at risk." She glared at him, and her fury lent her courage. "Indeed, stop funding your horrendous tales in the newspapers altogether, or I'll let it be known Lord Wilshire raids the crown's treasury to fund them."

If she had shocked him with her indelicate manner before, this new declaration threatened to bowl him straight to the floor. His neck reddened. He dropped his hands to the sofa and shoved himself to his feet.

"I give you three days to turn over these *Les Revenirs*," he said. He stepped closer to Effie, using his height to stare down at her. "But let us be clear. Fail me and I will crush any hope of your steward's success. Fail me, and the treaty won't be the only thing to die."

Effie glared at the man as he stormed from the room. A warning blared in her ears as loud as a trumpet. She sensed the trap clicking into place around her neck.

She needed only to work out what it was, and how soon it might kill her.

❧ 23 ❧

I t didn't take long to cross New Town and arrive at Heriot Row, where Thomas Stevenson held a residence. Effie stumbled out of the steam carriage in a daze. Graham caught her shoulders to steady her. The warmth of his hands made her want to fall into his chest, shut her eyes, and sleep for a week. Patting his arm, she shuffled toward the quaint house built of sandstone brick. The rain had lessened to a light mist, and the nocturnal sounds of the city's merriment had quieted as she climbed the familiar steps to the house's front door.

Neither Thomas Stevenson, nor his son, Robert—who used the residence when his health allowed him to endure the cold winds of Scotland—were at home. But Effie and Graham were known to the household, and the maids had kept the guest rooms in good order. The valet welcomed her with a broad smile. He ushered them inside without questioning the late hour, offering tea and slices of bread with dried salmon.

Effie stifled a yawn, declined both, and soon crawled into a bed in one of the guest rooms. The four-poster bed creaked as she snuggled under a mound of linen sheets and wool blankets. She could hear Graham moving about in the room next door, and she felt a brief pang of guilt that she hadn't told him everything of her conversation before retiring. The thought passed quickly, however. She fell asleep before her head hit her pillow.

In the morning, they set out for the university library. She'd given what comforts she could to the pixies, removing the pins that stuck them to the dress box and adding an extra layer of swaddling. She'd tried scraping off the tar-like substance to no avail. The black ichor had hardened, and she feared doing further harm. She needed knowledge, for the sake of the wee things, and to help her learn what she could of these *Les Revenirs*.

The sun peeked through a blanket of clouds. The light, and the night's rest, rejuvenated her as she strode with Graham through the city. They'd already crossed Queen and Princes streets, and worked their way up the crowded North Bridge in the direction of Old Town. The castle walls rose to their right, the Palace of Holyroodhouse sat to their left. Tenements shot up from the hills and embankments in between, nestled atop one another. They stood so compacted they appeared as if a giant's hand had squished them into a lump.

Airships hung in the skies above, tethered to iron towers. Their shapes were varied by size and function. Some appeared like floating sea galleons, others like giant butterflies, with long tails that flapped in the wind. Some had rudders affixed to their decks, while others sprouted fins from their balloons. But they all were constructed by the same principles. A balloon gave them lift, and a deck below housed a giant boiler driven by coal.

Effie gazed at them and shook her head. When she thought of the revolution in engineering a fuel such as Aerfenium could bring, it stole the wonderment from her. Men sought to preserve their grand empire by diminishing the fey, but they only served to weaken themselves.

Graham coughed beside her. Coal dust rose from the storage bunkers below the North Bridge, where the putrid waters of the Nor Loch once lapped. The loch had been drained to make room for rail lines and Waverly Station, and the area now teemed with coal porters, who shoveled loads on and off the trains in an endless cycle. The coal bunkers serviced the entire city, and parts of the empire beyond, but they came at a cost of noxious air that clung to clothes and flesh alike. Most of the merchants they passed—cart peddlers hawking kitchen tools, soaps, and matchsticks—wore masks of linen over their faces. Their brows and cheeks were black with soot. Thin netting protected their wares, in a feeble attempt to stave off the dust.

"We cannot trust the man," said Graham, once his coughing had stopped. Effie had finished recounting her conversation with Lord Granville for the second time. Graham had scowled while listening, eager with questions both times.

Effie glanced at a woman passing them who'd pulled on a pair of goggles to ward off the coal dust. Brass-rimmed leather flaps hung from the goggles over her cheeks. It gave her the appearance of a Roman gladiator, despite the bonnet and loose-flowing dress.

"No," Effie agreed. She tugged Graham away from stepping in some horse's leavings, catching a whiff of its freshness. "With a certainty, we cannot. He is the enemy, as much as the Sidhe Bhreige."

"Then why play his game?"

Effie had wrestled with the same question in her dreams. She'd envisioned she clutched a bucket with too many holes for her fingers to plug. As soon as she tried to stopper one, another would spout, and all she could do was watch as the water drained away. It had come to her at an early hour that what she needed was an arrest to that which caused the holes. Only then should she worry over the damage already done.

The means of that arrest had to be the treaty. Without it, the fey stood no chance of ever living peacefully, and men like Cyrus Reed would run freely throughout the empire as surely as men like Lord Granville would continue to dominate it.

"Because he has tipped his hand in some manner," she replied. "I can feel it but not yet determine how."

Graham grunted. "He seeks to turn you against your own kind, handing over these fey. He will use the action to paint you against them."

"Yes, but why? What threat do these *Les Revenirs* pose to him, and why draw me into it? Lord Granville has other methods at his disposal, and certainly more important matters to attend to. The entire ordeal feels so much like—"

"A trap," Graham interjected.

"An opportunity," she whispered. "One we must exploit for the sake of the treaty." Her tone sounded less than convincing, but she'd changed her thinking during the early morning. Lord Granville hadn't summoned her away from Balclune merely to threaten her, nor to treat her like an errand boy. She recalled his patronizing tone as she deflected his threats. He thought himself much cleverer than she, and that hubris left him exposed.

Whatever his true motives, they had been enough to draw him to Edinburgh to confront her directly. Lord Granville never spoke with his own tongue when another's might suffice. The whole affair reeked of a hidden fear and grave personal importance. If she and Graham could manage to unravel his scheme, perhaps it would produce enough leverage to force the lord into the treaty's favor.

"Bah," Graham grumbled. He mumbled something unpleasant about a goat but left her to her thoughts for a time.

North Bridge ended at Edinburgh's high street, which cut across the start of South Bridge. The spires of St. Giles' Cathedral, the High Kirk of Edinburgh, rose to one side. The shops of tinkers, tailors, tobacco merchants, and all other manner of goods and wares lined the streets in all directions. The press of the city's denizens became thicker in Old Town, and more fragrant. With the rich situated in New Town, the old streets of Edinburgh were given over to the poor and working class. Coal porters hauled wains down the cobblestones, selling buckets of coal to the shops. Bawdy shouts echoed from a smattering of taverns, their windows thick and tempered as to hide what carried on within. Slop flew from the higher stories of the tenements, to splatter in the alleys, and children ran, screaming and hollering after stray cats, terrifying the poor things.

A layer of filth coated everything. It made the coal dust seem desirable. The children had smudges on their faces and clothes. The men wore suits with torn patches and layers of dust. Their starched shirts weren't as stiff as those in New Town. The oil of their beards and moustaches left a film that stained their collars. The women's dresses had seen the wear and tear of daily labor rather than the efforts of high tea or a stroll in the gardens.

Effie caught a whiff of something pleasant and followed her nose. Her stomach gurgled as she stared longingly at a tray of meat pies that rested in a baker's storefront window. She could almost taste the savory meat

filling and warm buttery flakes of pastry on her tongue, but the sign—No
Fey Allowed—stopped her cold. It rested in the corner of the window,
painted in black ink on a simple piece of wood. She had never seen its
like before. It sickened her and left a bitter taste in her mouth.

Graham's face scrunched in disbelief. His cheeks turned red.
"Bollocks!" he cursed.

Effie glanced into the shop and her heart sank. A line had formed at
the counter. "It doesn't look like their custom suffers for it. It appears
the sour winds of the south prevail here as well." That was something
new. Scotland had long harbored the fey who lived in their lands. Many
saw the fey as kin who suffered at the hands of a common oppressor—
namely, the English. That Edinburgh would openly turn on the fey did
not bode well.

Effie forced herself to turn away. One shop did not a city make. Still,
it reminded her of the dangers the city presented. Edinburgh had a
proclivity for unrest.

As if summoned by her thoughts, Graham thrust a thick finger at a
group marching toward the High Kirk. They hollered and banged at
drums. A few carried signs with slurs against some factory's owner and,
in bold lettering, the word "Strike!" Three of their members, those who
led the march, had their heads wrapped in bandages like Egyptian
mummies.

"It's them that has the phossy jaw," said a man. He stopped next to
them long enough to grumble some curse and spit on the cobblestones.
Effie didn't know whether the curse was meant for the strikers or their
employer.

"They say working with phosphorus is worse than coal," said
Graham. "And if you do it long enough, your teeth fall out, and then
your jaw."

Effie nodded, but her attention had fallen on the crowd around them.
Some continued on their way, as if nothing were amiss. But most stopped
to watch the spectacle. Several men shouted encouragement for the
protesters, while others jeered and made crude gestures. An argument
broke out on the far side of the street. She heard the scuffing of boots
and the echo of grunts, but her height didn't allow her to see anything
through the press.

Yet more distressing was the sense of hostility that rose in those around her. She didn't need fey senses to feel it. It shone through hardened glares and tightened lips, and in the way the air stilled in the silence between the shouting. It felt to her like it had in the moments before the Battle of Caldwell House. There, an army had descended on them, and she wondered if another were about to do the same.

"We shouldn't tarry here," she said. She ducked through the thickening press as the drums and shouting grew louder.

"Other strikers are joining the first group from neighboring streets," said Graham. He followed, his head cocked to peer behind them.

Effie quested with her fey senses as she strode. She found a few fey within the crowd. More roamed beneath them, in the vaults of South Bridge that were covered over by the tenement buildings. Other, older streets were likewise sealed up and used as foundations for newer works. An entire network of warrens and lanes existed under the current city. The "Town Below" the locals called it. It was a favored place for thieves, ruffians, and fey—anyone who wanted to avoid the notice of the city above.

To find those of fey blood so dispersed did not surprise her. In a way, it worked to calm her nerves. It confirmed the rising tensions near the High Kirk had nothing to do with her kind. Simple logic had already told her the same. But the bakery sign had skewed her thoughts, and she had wanted to be certain.

She was so focused on scouring the area for fey auras, she almost ran into a squat man with a thick neck and an even thicker brow. He held his ground as she yelped and jumped aside. His companion glared at her. A boil on the second man's chin radiated a puffy redness. He wore an armband on his coat, a white rag with a crown painted on it in gold.

Effie muttered an apology, yet for a moment she thought the squat man might strike her. His neck tightened and his fist rose. In it, he clenched a slapjack. Her heart thumped. But his companion drew him back, and she received only a silent dismissal. The men brushed past her, slinking through the press like a pack of feral dogs.

"Effie." Graham called her name in warning. She turned and saw a host of other men wearing armbands with the same device. A few glared at her openly, sending a chill racing up her spine. She quickened her step, fleeing down the street.

"Who are they?" she asked once the press had lessened.

"Ain't the foggiest, lass," Graham admitted. He shook his head. "The whole city has an odd feel to it."

Effie bit her lip and glanced about. "The university librarian is a better source for information than anything printed in the broadsheets," she said. "She can tell us what madness has befallen the city and hopefully aid us in the other matters." She had no need to voice the explanation. Graham knew the woman they sought better than she. He'd been the one to introduce her years earlier. She spoke merely to steady her nerve, yet she could still hear the quiver in her tone.

Graham murmured an agreement as droplets began to pelt them. Effie glanced at the thick clouds swirling above. The rain intensified, its patter drowning out the clamor of the crowd behind them. She hoped it would serve to dampen tempers as well.

They reached the university, an imposing building that edged South Bridge, and strode through an archway guarded by fluted columns that stood sentinel to the courtyard beyond. In times past, Effie would've headed to a secret alcove that led to an entrance of the Town Below. There, one could wait for the kindly librarian. The woman often aided the fey of the city—granting them access to the university's tomes and doling out information that the likes of gnomes, pixies, and hogboons couldn't obtain themselves. But Effie now knew the woman's uncanny ability to sense when a fey awaited her was a mere byproduct of her own fey blood. Which meant Effie could find her directly in the library.

The courtyard held a few students hurrying about their business. None paid them any mind, and they entered the library without challenge. The stacks of shelves smelled of dust and decaying parchment despite their constant and vigilant care. Students sat at a row of desks, pouring over volumes while scratching notes on loose sheets of paper. At a large desk near the center of the main floor, an aged woman with gray curls and a proud chin sorted books into neat stacks. She set down each with the loving care of a mother tending her child. The process, for all the movement, gave off no sound other than the soft kiss of leather. Effie slowed her pace and glanced about. The elderly woman wasn't whom she had expected to find. She could see no sign of the one she sought, however. Nor could she sense any fey blood roaming within the area.

As she scanned the stacks and desks, her gaze must've made her appear confused. The woman behind the large desk raised an eye to her. "May I assist you?" she asked. Her whispered voice somehow reached across the room.

Effie shuffled to the desk's edge and clutched it with a hand. "Pardon me, but I am searching for the librarian," she said for only the woman to hear.

"I am she." The woman raised her chin slightly.

Frowning, Effie clarified. "I'm sorry. I meant the woman who held the position before you. The last I heard, she was still employed here."

The woman stiffened. She ran her gaze over Effie once more. "I do suggest you take your business elsewhere," she snapped. "The university doesn't allow for such dealings anymore."

The pronouncement sounded like more than a warning. Graham bristled, and Effie placed a hand on his chest to still him. She swallowed, panicked that something dire had occurred. "But do you know where I can find her? Can you tell me any word on what happened?"

"You've heard my final say on the matter," the woman said. Her gaze flitted to the side of the room, and Effie caught a slight tremble to the woman's hand.

Effie followed the gaze, and her eyes fell on a young man who sat at a desk in the corner of the room. He had no book or paper, no pen or ink. He sat idly, with his coat unbuttoned and one foot casually crossed over the over knee. He watched her from his perch, showing no signs of modesty or decorum. Effie's blood ran cold when she saw he wore the same armband she'd seen earlier on the man with the boil.

She whipped her head around. "That badge, what does it mean?"

"Who is that man?" demanded Graham.

The woman leaned forward and whispered. "The badge is that of the Sanctity of Empire League," she replied. "You must go. The city is no place for fey kind."

❧ 24 ❧

Effie sipped at a light broth filled with turnips and salt. Despite its pleasant flavor, she couldn't enjoy it or the buttered bread that sat beside her tea. She and Graham sat in the small dining room of the house on Heriot Row. Normally, its lace curtains and wood-paneled walls brought a welcome quiet after the bustle of the city. But their winding path from the university had felt like a retreat. They'd stopped only to send telegrams to Thomas Stevenson and Rose Brewer, the first to inform him of the strangeness overtaking the city, and the second to beg for whatever aid she could provide. Effie hoped the woman had lingered long enough at Skye for the message to reach her.

Tearing off a piece of bread, she dipped it absently in the broth. "Where do you suppose she's gone?" she asked. She meant the university librarian.

Graham set down his spoon. "I dunno, lass. Hopefully far from the city to a farm with green fields and fat sows. Wouldn't that be a pleasant thing?" He took a sip of the wine he favored. Stevenson always kept a bottle stocked in the larder for him.

She forced a weak smile to her lips. "It would if it didn't feel so much like a fancy."

"Och," Graham snorted. "Let's have it, then. What's really stealing your thoughts?" One eyebrow raised as he studied her.

She stared at the tabling before her for a moment before answering. "Cyrus Reed escaped. Something fell befalls the city. The people revile the fey more than they ever have, and Lord Granville spins webs around my eyes and ears so that I can neither see nor hear what he plots. Above all, the last of the Sidhe Bhreige roams free, leaving no hint of its whereabouts."

"Ha!" barked Graham. "Is that all? Well, truth to tell, I'd be shivering in me boots to face all that, except for a single thing."

"What is that?" Her cheeks flushed as she asked the question. A part of her somehow knew what his response would be.

Graham drained the last of his wine and pointed the empty glass at her. "I have the Green Lady on my side. Effie of Glen Coe, what bested demons, enthralled giants, and brought the lords of the realm to bear. How could I ever fear anything with her on my side?"

The smile that plastered her lips was genuine this time. She pulled her shoulders back and sat up. "The treaty is the key," she began, ordering her thoughts. "We must not lose sight of that. Everything else means nothing if the fey have no voice in the empire."

"Aye," Graham agreed.

Her mind worked through their options. "If the librarian is not to be found, then we will uncover what we can of *Les Revenirs* ourselves. We will find leverage against Lord Granville there, I am sure of it."

"Do ye intend to hand these fey over to the magistrate?"

Effie barely considered that, shaking her head. "Not unless I absolutely must. There is only profit for Lord Granville in doing what the man asks. His promises, I cannot trust. But we will use his hubris against him."

Graham winked at her. "It's a good start, lass," he said, rising to refill his glass from a decanter. "The man did err in drawing you into his schemes. I've had a thought on that, and I believe his sole intent is to discredit you."

Effie blinked. "But why? I have no name worthy of that effort."

"Do ye not?" Graham laughed heartily. "Think on young Jane's tale and of those boys in Dunfermline. Who knows how far your doings at

Caldwell House have spread? Soldiers do not make for idle lips, and there were hundreds of them that saw you charge the battlefield. Perhaps the tongues of London flap with the same tales, enough that Lord Granville must counter them with an account to bring you low."

"I cannot believe it," she said. "What you say might be true, but my gut says there is something more."

Footsteps sounded in the hall. It gave them a moment's warning before the door swung open. The footman rushed in and begged her pardon. He'd barely managed the words before Jack Canonbie barged into the room after him, jarring the man aside. He had a slight limp to his gait and leaned heavily on his cane. A handkerchief wound around his neck to cover the bandage he still wore. But his cheeks were clean-shaven and his eyes alert.

"Beg pardon," he declared to the room before slumping down into one of the open chairs. As he nodded to them both, his nose caught wind of the broth. "Oh, that's a pleasant smell to end a long journey." He gestured for the footman to fetch him a bowl. The footman glanced at Graham and Effie, and she nodded her consent.

Graham grunted and took up his wine.

Canonbie grinned cheerily. "I suppose this is your house as much as Bonny Law."

"We are all guests here," Effie clarified, though she smiled all the same. She'd grown used to the man's boorish manner and took no offense to his intrusion. On the contrary, she found she had missed his presence. A part of her stirred as she took in his person. "But I am glad you found us at present. Are you hale?"

"Fit enough to ravage a turnip," he replied, accepting a bowl of the broth from the footman.

She laughed. "I am happy to hear it. You will need your strength. Mr. Graham and I were just discussing how to catch a lion by the paw," she said. She told him of Lord Granville's summons, and of what they'd witnessed in the city.

"Aye, the banshee's touch, they are calling it," said Canonbie. "The madness on the streets, I mean. Gentle fellows are turning to thuggery, and all the while raving of a wailing cry clouding their dreams. I heard enough tales of it between Dunfermline and here to fill a loch."

"These are uncertain times," said Graham. "Not just for the fey, but for the laborers of the empire. It is not surprising to see such unrest."

"The Sanctity of Empire League are not common thugs," said Effie. "Nor can I imagine they are driven by a restless spirit. We will need find out more about them and how they've come to hold such power within the city." If Jack Canonbie was correct, the league held its allegiance to coin alone, its ranks filled by dock workers and vagrants. It did not take a great leap to assume something more than bigotry caused them to grow so bold in their hatred of the fey.

She inhaled a deep breath. As she did, a distant murmur swelled in her ears, the echo of a hundred voices garbled together, rising like the tide. Closing her eyes clarified the sound. She cocked her head, trying to pick out one or two of the voices. They weren't clear enough to understand, but their sentiment boomed clearly. Rage and malice spewed forth in a guttural incantation.

Graham heard it as well. He rose and turned to the window, lips parting in surprise.

"What is that?" she asked. Her grip tightened on the table. A prickle of energy raced along her arms. Memories of the fire at Lady Fife's estate flashed through her head.

Jack Canonbie shot to his feet. Raising a finger for silence, he turned in a slow circle. "It comes from Old Town," he said, when he finally stopped.

"Closer than that," breathed Effie.

"A mob," said Graham.

Effie quested with her fey senses and found the mass moving along Princes Street, the long boulevard that formed the southern edge of New Town. Several fey moved within the mob, but a lone fey aura moved at its head.

She met Graham's eye. "Effie," he warned. "This is not your cause."

"You may remain here, if you please," she replied. "I only mean to learn what transpires."

Graham stepped before her, as she strode for the door. "Then I will go, or Mr. Canonbie."

She placed a gentle hand on his shoulder. "There are fey within the crowd. I may be of use to them. I am the Green Lady, after all."

He huffed and planted his hands on his hips. "Bollocks," he cursed. He shook his head. "But I've no place to scold you like a child. I'll grab my cane and coat."

Crisp air shocked her cheeks as they hurried down the lane that led to Princes Street. As they approached, the din turned into a chorus of growling, hissing, and chanting. Yet Effie didn't need her ears to find the mob. The weight of so many boots shook the ground. Failing sunlight cast long shadows down the lane. But at its end, the glow of a hundred torches bloomed like the amber hue of a bonfire.

Graham strode at her side. His warmth helped hold back her dread. Behind, she could hear Jack Canonbie struggling to keep pace. Both men carried canes. Their points clacked off the cobblestones with each stride.

Men rushed down the lane alongside them. Effie eyed each, searching for weapons or the armbands of the Sanctity of Empire League. She saw none, but that mattered little. She could see an eagerness in their eyes, the odd lust for violence that overcame even gentle souls when pressed into an unruly crowd. That bloodlust called to them like a siren's song. *Or perhaps a banshee's wail, as Canonbie had named it*. It infected all it touched, a plague spreading throughout the adjoining streets, summoning men to answer. Only a few trickled the other direction. Those held their heads lowered. They clutched their coats and the brims of their hats. Their eyes darted about in fear as they scurried past.

Effie reached Princes Street as the spearhead of the mob crossed the lane. The swell of bodies forced her to stop short and press into the portico of a stately house. Clambering up a few steps gave her a better advantage of sight, and her gut lurched as her eyes found what her heart had already assumed. At the center of the mob's head a hogboon struggled against the ropes that lashed it to a wooden plank. The poor fellow could pass for a plump child, except for the weathered lines on his face and thinning hair atop his head. A slight sharpness to his eyes and cheeks were all that declared his race, beyond his aura, which only those of fey blood could sense. His height wouldn't reach Effie's waist. His coat and trousers had once been fine, but they hung loose, torn and tattered now. The plank ran across his shoulders, and his stubby arms were stretched out to form a cross. Men on either side shoved the plank forward, forcing the hogboon to stagger forth or be trampled by those who came behind.

"This is madness," she said as Graham and Canonbie pushed against her.

Gentlemen, vagrants, merchants, and thugs filled the ranks of the mob. Even women and children jostled and hollered among the delirious men. Mixed with torches were crude clubs and steel-tipped canes. A fishmonger waved a slender knife, and a woman with flowers in her basket brandished a butcher's mallet. Several men with the shabby dress of the docks surrounded the hogboon. Their faces snarled like starved hounds, and they snapped whenever anyone dared break their circle. Every one of them wore an armband, but not all sported the golden crown. Effie tried to make out the other designs, but the shadows were too thick and the men moved too fast.

Effie rose on her toes and strained her neck before dropping down and cursing. The designs didn't matter, not to the hogboon. The men worked in concert. She could find out why, and who they were, later. What the hogboon needed now was an ally. The ground on the far side of Princes Street fell off into a valley that used to hold the Nor Loch. The long curtain wall of the castle rose over the hill beyond the valley, with North Bridge spanning from New Town to the hill. If the mob meant to dispatch its justice in Old Town, they headed for the bridge.

Reaching out with her fey senses, Effie again found fey auras scattered around the mob. Sithlings, most like, to stand as openly as she did. She could reach out to each of them as easily as speaking to Graham next to her. But her mind raced, devoid of any plan to thwart the growing mob.

As the press surged forward, it ignited everything in its furious wake. The cries and chants became more vicious. The thudding of so many pounding feet numbed her ears. She saw no way to dispel their fervor, no way to swoop in and free the hogboon without herself getting dragged through the streets. She would end up strung from a lamp in Old Town, gurgling her last breath as enraged strangers pelted her with stones and rotten food. She could see it in her head, feel the scratchy rope around her neck. Her body began to shake, and she pressed behind a column of a portico, as if to hide from the horrible fate that awaited her.

And yet, even as she ducked behind the safety of the column, she reached out and shoved her will against the aura of the hogboon. She sent an image of a peaceful glen with a lone hill, perfectly rounded and quiet. Grass and wild flowers covered the glen. They smelled as sweet as honey and swayed under a gentle breeze that rolled over the glen with a soft whisper. She sent the hogboon hope. Hope of freedom and a return to the world his kind cherished.

She could do that at least, until a better plan came to her.

The fey auras around her swelled in response. They joined to her, their touch a vigorous embrace that made her shiver. The linked power of their blood bolstered it in a magnitude greater than the sum of their individual strengths. Effie's apprehension melted away. Her trembling resurged, only this time in delight. The swirling auras, so joined, kissed her mind as they brushed past, giving her a warm sense of companionship. The scent of mulled wine, thick with sharp, wintery spices, filled her nose. A pair of hares darted through the underbrush of a gnarled and ancient woodland. The images and senses were brief. But they came to her like honored greetings from long lost friends.

Graham grabbed her arms to steady her, and she leaned back against his chest. He smelled of turnips and wine, and she breathed him in. Flooded with such delights, it took her a moment to realize her tranquil glen had dissolved. Or rather, it had been wrested away by another. A bubble of energy had formed in its place, like a small pulsing sun.

Effie frowned. She didn't know what the bubble was for, or why it hung before her. It crackled and swirled, begging her curiosity. She eyed Graham, but he showed no sign he saw the bubble. He stared at the hogboon, his face a mask of frustration. The tip of the mob had advanced past them, and now its heart and full might rambled before them.

The bubble of energy shrank down and stilled. Effie felt a flare of warning jolt through her connected fey blood. Or perhaps it was a signal. She reached out to touch the bubble, but her fingers met only open air.

A clap of thunder boomed violently, driving the mob to its knees. Shrieks of panic rippled through the mass, and those at the edges scattered into the shadows. Effie stiffened. She recognized the Fey Craft from what Rose had shown her in the carriage after Lady Fife's ball. But she'd never thought it could be used on so large a scale. Glamours, dozens of them, popped into existence on the thunderclap's heels.

A man roared, pointing, as a volley of fiery comets seemed to blast from the castle ramparts and arc through the night, hurtling toward the mob. Two more claps of thunder had men scrambling with their hands covering their ears. Those that sought the safety of the ground were knocked over and trampled. Fists flew as those in the thick of the mob struggled to flee.

Even knowing they weren't real did little to lessen the terror Effie felt.

"Get down," hollered Graham, tugging at her.

The comets struck the heart of the mob. False flames exploded through the press. They licked everything they touched and turned Princes Street into a searing blaze. Waves of heat rippled in their wake, bringing on greater terror. Men ripped out of their coats, flailing with whatever instruments they held. Bones cracked as noses and arms were met by clubs and canes. In an instant, blood splattered across shirts and faces, everywhere Effie looked. Torches fell from hands, or worse, were used as prods for their owners to escape the crowded press.

Flames, real flames this time from one of the torches, ignited the clothes of one man. He cried out, beating at his chest. Those around him shied away. They cared nothing for his agony. They wanted only the calm sanctuary that lay a few streets away and to leave their memories of the mob behind.

"No!" Effie screamed as she witnessed the devastation. Caldwell House had been a battle pitched between an invading horde of fiends and those who stood against them. Her allies then had a just cause to shed blood. This here was needless.

The false flames and heat of the comets fizzled out. Their illusion vanished as quickly as one of the thunderclaps. But the fear they'd instilled remained. Those within the mob broke and ran as if the devil had been summoned to chase their heels.

Bodies scrambled past the portico, bloodied and bruised. Effie sensed another bubble of energy forming, and she steeled her will against it. She quested out for its source, the fey who directed the glamours, but it was like her hands were slapped away, and a wall rose to block her delving.

She could not sense anything beyond the crackling energy and a few pulsing signals that warned of destruction yet to come.

Graham gulped in a breath and staggered back. His eyes widened in disbelief.

Jack Canonbie stared at the man who'd been lit by torch fire. The man had crumpled to the ground and rocked back and forth, crying out. Effie saw a spark of something in Canonbie's gaze before he dashed forward. His gait remained awkward, but he moved with speed, raising his cane upright before him to shove a path through the press.

"Jack!" Effie cried, her voice lost amongst a hundred others. "Wait!"

Canonbie pushed behind the woman with the flower basket, shielding her from a large brute who stumbled as if drunk. Another man shoved him aside, and he teetered on his feet. Effie saw his cane whip up as the press closed in, swallowing him from sight.

Snatching the hem of her skirt, she bolted from the portico. Her heart thumped hard. A man jostled her as she rushed past, and another stepped heavily on her foot. The pain needled her, but she ignored it. Distantly, she heard Graham's labored breathing, as he forced his way behind her. She led him into peril, chasing after Canonbie. She led them both, but she refused to turn back. Jack needed her. And it dawned on her now how much she had started to need him.

The wall that blocked her from her Fey Craft dissolved, and the thought of a shining silver light came to her. A radiant star, blinding in its magnificence. She thrust the image of the star into the spot where Canonbie had last been. Energy pulsed through her, and her beacon became a searing white blaze.

Those around it shied away, raising hands to shield their vision lest they be blinded. An opening formed where the press fled the light. She spied Canonbie struggling to regain his feet, and she dimmed the silvery star so it glowed only as a gas lamp would.

The effort gave him only a moment of reprieve.

"*Schützen Sie sich!*" bellowed some coarse voice. Effie thought it came from her right, in the shadow of the building across from her.

"Down!" hollered Graham, shoving her to her knees.

She landed hard on the unforgiving cobblestones as a volley of pistol fire cracked along Princes Street. Bullets whistled through the remains of the mob, pinging off stone and thumping into flesh and wood. Graham rolled next to her, wrapping a protective arm around her back.

Jack Canonbie sprawled flat on the street and used his hands to cover his head. Once the volley had passed, he bounded to his feet and ducked behind an overturned cart, where a handful of others hid. The poor man who'd caught fire lay still. What remained of his clothes smoldered like a spent campfire.

They hadn't reached him in time.

Effie traced where the bullets had come from and found the ring of men surrounding the hogboon. Almost all had a firearm of some kind aimed down the street. Their volley had progressed into a series of single shots. As each man drew level and fired, she saw the jerk of their hand and puff of smoke a brief instant before she heard the crack of the shot echo through the city.

"What are they firing at?" she begged of Stuart Graham. The man had no answer. He swung his gaze all around, puzzlement cast over his features. Huddled behind the cart, Canonbie peered over its edge, and she could tell the man sought the answer to the same question.

"We must leave them to it," said Graham. "There is nothing as can be done for the captive. We'll only find ourselves shot or burned or worse. Perhaps on the morrow there'll be another way."

Effie shook her head. Thoughts of the Sithling guards at Balclune, and of the cocooned pixies, weighed heavily on her shoulders. Abandoning the hogboon to a short and cruel fate brought the tally of the week too high. "There has to be more. Would you see others give up on me so easily?"

Graham's arm tightened over her. His nostrils flared as he huffed. "What then?"

"There are others. They have come to help. It is they who broke the mob." She glanced at where the warning shout had come from, but shadows obscured the area. She could spy nothing beyond the dim outline of the building.

"Aye, and did a one of them attempt a rescue?" asked Graham. "Did any of them do anything beyond adding mayhem into a press of human flesh? Don't trust in allies merely because they attack our enemies."

Effie bit her lip at that, falling silent. A lone pistol shot rang out. It pinged down Princes Street and thudded into the door of the building across from her with a sharp crack of wood. In the quiet after, she heard the shrill of whistles. The constables had finally come.

They had perhaps stood idle while the mob raged. There were too few of them to have done much good against it. They marched in a tight rank now, rifles and torches held before them, whistles blowing in a fury from their lips.

The mob leaders, those with armbands who'd remained with their prize, hurried their retreat. But instead of taking the North Bridge, they slunk down a wynd toward the great coal bunkers harbored in the valley beneath the castle.

Effie found her feet and scrambled forward. The street had cleared enough so she could run without fear of being trampled. The pistols had fallen silent as the mob leaders disappeared into the shadows of the wynd. A mob she could not stand against, but perhaps against its leaders she stood a chance.

The thought strengthened her resolve for a few paces, until a sudden gust of wind flung her into a stretch of grass that ran alongside the street. She grunted, bouncing as she struck the ground. When she tried to rise, the wind gusted again and pinned her down. A warm sensation, like the sun's kiss, flowed along her flesh, and she realized what created the wind.

She lay dumbstruck. Fey Craft. The glamour had flung her!

No, she realized, recalling. It had startled her, and she'd stepped awkwardly and lost her balance. That was all. Her mind had tricked her into thinking the gust's force real. It buffeted her now, but as she steeled her thoughts against it, it unraveled.

She quested again for the fey who directed the glamours, and the wall that blocked her sprang back into place. She strained desperately against it, gritting her teeth. She had to uncover their plan to aid the hogboon. Why else would they have stopped her unless it hindered their own designs?

But her hope unraveled. The fey host slowly dispersed. The wall that blocked her dropped, and she could feel the fey again as single auras hustling away like rats scurrying into dank holes. She slumped. Disillusionment tore apart what remained of her energy. Graham had been right. These fey had no intention of rescuing the hogboon. They had only used the mob as a means to wreak what havoc they could.

"The fight is not over," said Graham, coming to crouch next to her. "It only pauses for the night."

"The hogboon," she began.

"No, lass." Graham broke her off. "It's a bloody fate, but it's not your fight. The constables come, and if you're taken, Lord Granville won't need a trap of his own. Word of your capture will be enough to defame you, and all of this destruction and death will be thrust on your shoulders. You can believe the lord would do such a thing."

Effie shook as the truth of Graham's words settled on her. A bubble of laughter swelled and escaped her lips. "I am a hare chasing a carrot within a pit of wolves and dogs."

Graham had no answer for that. He helped her to her feet, regarding her with a mirthless grin. The streets had mostly emptied. The injured had been carried away or were tended to by those who'd returned to see them safe. The dead lay still and spent. Effie could see three others felled besides the man who'd burned, though the night had darkened and she couldn't tell what had caused their wounds.

She swung her gaze to the overturned cart, and her heart skipped a beat. Jack Canonbie had gone. She scanned the few who shuffled along the streets, but she did not spy him. The street had quieted as a frigid mist rolled in from the sea. It rose until she could barely make out the constables who prowled toward them, inspecting the damage the mob had done.

"Come, lass," Graham begged.

She spun in a circle. Yet scouring the street accomplished nothing. The mist dampened her coat as icy fingers crawled up her spine. She could no longer see beyond a dozen feet.

Jack Canonbie had disappeared.

26

Canonbie staggered into the house on Heriot Row in the wee hours of the morning before the sun had crested the rocky crags that ringed the city. Effie rushed to him and reached out, wanting to bring his hands into hers. Yet she stopped short. She didn't know what impulse drove her other than the sudden swelling of joy that throbbed in her chest. It was silly, really, the immensity of the feeling. She could not say what warranted it. She knew only that her thoughts had not strayed far from the man in the hours of his absence.

The footman silently closed the front door, bowed to them, and departed into the backrooms of the house. Canonbie's coat hung disheveled about his shoulders. Dirt marred his shirt collar and coated his hands and arms. A day's worth of whiskers sprouted from his cheeks, which pulled his lips into a tired grin.

"I did not expect to find you awake at this early hour," he said. His eyes flared with what she could only imagine as happiness.

"I couldn't sleep," she admitted. A flush of shame sent her gaze to the floor. "I tried searching for you, but the constables started rounding up anyone who refused to leave the streets. They declared a curfew in the city until the morning."

"You wouldn't have found me. I saw the strangest thing, a miniature being like a small child but with the snout of an elephant. It wore armor plates welded into a thick leather hide. I would've thought it a cousin to the hogboon if I could see its face clearly. But it slunk into the shadows as soon as the pistols started firing. I chased it for a while before it ducked down some hole and vanished. By then I had crossed to the base of castle hill."

Effie frowned. A fey in armor? She couldn't make sense of it. She held out her arm for him to take. She yearned for his touch, as if she needed it to be certain he had returned safely. "There is still some bread and tea in the dining room," she said. "Unless you want to rest?"

"Whiskey," he said. He placed his arm under hers and stepped closer. Warmth radiated from him, his chest a furnace despite the coldness of the night. Her fingers dug into his arm. She didn't care about the filth on his coat sleeve, or the stench of the streets that wafted from the wool. He had come home unharmed, and the tension in her body could finally relax.

She led him the short few steps into the dining room and fetched him a dram of whiskey. Canonbie removed his coat and sat in the same chair he had earlier. He stretched at sore muscles and stifled back a deep yawn.

"You charged into the mob to help that poor man," she said. "You cannot claim it was because of Mr. Stevenson's coin this time."

He shrugged sheepishly.

"Tell me," she begged. "I saw something in your eyes."

Canonbie coughed into his hand. "A memory from my youth, that is all. Another man I did not save." He stared blankly at the wall.

She sat beside him. "I'm sure you did then all that you could, as well." She curled her fingers over his. She knew it had taken an effort for him to admit the little he had.

"They have taken the hogboon to the castle," he said. His voice grew deeper and more firm, changing the subject. "I saw the constables usher him in with some of those that wore the armbands." His brow furrowed. "It didn't look as if the two groups cared much for one another, but they worked together all the same."

Effie grinned at the news. She would not let it deflate her. To find the constables working with the Sanctity of Empire League was not unexpected, and her thoughts turned back to the armored creature. Most likely it had played a role in the glamours that had wreaked havoc on the mob. She'd never felt such Fey Craft before, and the strange energy they'd summoned no doubt stemmed from practiced hands. Hands attached to bodies that wore armor and knew how to coordinate an attack, knew when to run, and weren't afraid to do either.

"We need allies," she said, more to herself than Jack Canonbie. "Allies who are steeped in fey lore and know where to find things in the city." Perhaps Rose Brewer would come, but they could not wait on the woman. The pixies could not wait, nor could *Les Revenirs*. She needed no clock to tell her time grew short on both matters.

The man nodded. He drained the last of his dram. "Then why are we sitting here?"

Effie's grin intensified.

* * *

The Town Below was a maze of warrens that nestled beneath the city. Segments of older streets, boarded up and paved over, joined with the undercrofts of buildings, the vaults beneath the city's great bridges, and earthen tunnels dug out of the volcanic rock that gave the city its hills. The maze gave the fey a home within the city, a place where they could hide from sight and roam as they pleased. Gnomes and hogboons, brownies and pixies, all the fey races who couldn't pass for human dwelt within its confines, embracing its isolation from the world above.

But that same isolation attracted its own dangers. The Town Below had also become an underground highway for cutpurses, thugs, and hunted men. Opium dens sprouted up in the basements of tenement houses. Gangs carved out secret enclaves. Vagrants wandered about seeking shelter, or perhaps to pilfer someone's hidden stash of food or riches. The constables raided the Town Below every few months and cleared out the worst of its denizens. But the ruffians and thieves always returned, creeping back like weeds to befoul the bedrock of the city.

Effie knew the perils well. The Fey Finders had often prowled the Town Below before the talks of a treaty. One had ambushed her once, attacking her savagely. The memory gave her chills. And as she and

Canonbie made their way down a dank, earthen tunnel, she saw the Sniffer's shadow at every turn. Yet she forced herself not to jump. Fear born of memories would not serve her, no matter how unnerving they were.

They had entered the Town Below as the city began to wake. She knew Graham would be cross with her for leaving him in his slumber, but she thought it better to not have so large a group traipsing about underground. In an oddity of the place, they were more likely to be challenged if they came in numbers. The gangs who'd settled below would view such an incursion as a threat and might seek to assert their authority.

The fey below would also run and hide from a larger party, even if Effie's fey blood numbered within it. And that wouldn't do. She and Canonbie had come to find the fey she'd sensed the night before, but she would need guidance from all if those they sought were to be found. They had already stumbled across one brownie who'd slept in a small cave near where they'd entered the Town Below. The brownie's gaunt cheeks highlighted the sharpness of his features. It made his eyes and ears appear almost pointed, like that of a fox. A dark tuft of hair topped his head, and a grey cloak wrapped his wee form.

"Let me alone! I keep me gob shut and mind me own self," the brownie had told them, when Effie asked after his health. "Ye'd best to do the same."

Another pair of fey had fled at their approach, bolting down some steep passage so narrow, Effie doubted if Canonbie would fit shuffling sideways. She'd waved him back from the passage's entrance and planted her hands on her hips, questing out with her fey senses and finding another group nearby.

But reaching the group proved no easy task. The route led them beneath the high street and under the Tron Kirk before winding back along an old and decaying set of stone steps that were once part of a wynd to the Lawnmarket. The earthen tunnel they now passed through held evidence of picks and chisels. Some enterprising hand—or hands— had no doubt carved the tunnel as a means to short cut two open areas of the Town Below.

Canonbie raised the lantern he carried so its light spilled over Effie's shoulder. The air had grown thin and stale. The shadows felt like heavy stones crushing down on their chests. Effie heard his breathing begin to labor, and she quickened her pace so they could find better air.

The tunnel ended in the backroom of an abandoned shop. Whatever evidence of the shop's former owner had long since been picked clean. Only a few broken shelves clung to the walls. A shattered trunk lay on its side in one corner. Effie led them into the shop's front and found it in the same disorderly state. The remains of an old campfire rested in the middle of the floor. The broad windows held no glass and were open to the street beyond, a dirt lane that stretched half a city block.

At some point the city had outgrown the lane, and instead of rebuilding they'd simply sealed up the row of shops and built atop them. The shops now formed the foundations for the buildings aboveground, their original purpose long forgotten. A mix of earth and stone filled the ceiling, with thick timbers running beneath for support. The air freshened, though not enough to hide the stench of refuse and waste left by the Town Below's inhabitants.

The crackle of a fire drew Effie's attention. It came from the same direction that her fey senses told her the group she sought resided. She stepped through the open window and crossed the lane, searching carefully for any other denizens hidden nearby. But she found none. Only the fey auras in the shop before her gave off any sign of life.

She padded to the shop front and waited. She knew full well those within the shop could sense her as easily as she could sense them. A harsh whisper called out, followed by the scraping of feet across a dirt floor. Effie watched the dancing of firelight coming from the backroom of the shop. A shadow in the doorway to the backroom suddenly moved.

"Good morning," she said, in a cheery but firm tone.

The shadow moved again. "Is it?" barked a deep voice. "The coal fog here is not so good for the health. So they say."

Effie smiled and held her hands out in front of her to show them empty. "I wondered if my friend and I could share your fire. We've brought food to offer and some drink." She pointed at the bundle Canonbie carried, slung over his shoulder. She'd thought a gesture of hospitality might loosen a tongue or two, and had brought with them bread and cheese, along with a few slices of salted pork and a bottle of whiskey.

Laughter boomed from the shadow. "We are not kings and queens you need make an offering to, Effie of Glen Coe. You may come and share the warmth of our fire as you please."

A chill rushed through Effie. She took a deep breath. That they knew her aura meant nothing nefarious, she reminded herself. She had become known to many after her association with Caledon. These fey were still as likely to help her as harm her, and even more likely to stand somewhere in between.

She gestured for Canonbie to shine the lantern into the shop so that its beam lit their path. The large front window was devoid of glass, but Effie chose to use the door. Somehow it felt like a courtesy. The shop held a broken chair and small pit filled with scraps of splintered wood. The shadow in the doorway to the backroom resolved into that of a squat and burly gnome.

The gnome's bulbous nose clung to a wizened face framed by dark eyes and a crop of white hair that fell to either side of his plump cheeks like a horse's mane. He waved them into the backroom. "Heh, welcome then. Come find yourself a toasty seat."

Effie followed and found four more gnomes huddled around the crackling fire. A pot hung over the flames, giving off a sweet flavor of oats and honey. The gnomes were wrapped in great leather coats in the style of the continent, with high collars and low hems that fell to their knees. Each had the round nose and pale skin common of their race. The tops of their heads barely reached her chest, but they stood proud and straight. Besides the first, all had dark locks closely cropped about their ears. Dust covered their clothes and boots. Gnomes were known for their stone lore as much as their ornery temperament, and they often travelled within the hills of Edinburgh.

The group nodded to her and Canonbie as they entered, shuffling closer together to allow the newcomers space around the fire. "Good morning," Effie repeated. "I am called Effie, and this is Mr. Jack Canonbie."

Five sets of eyes regarded her. The way the gnomes pressed together reminded her of ducklings waiting for their mother to take the lead. The white-haired one obliged. "Sit, sit. We have porridge made fresh, though the coffee is gone. I can make more, yes?"

Effie held up her hand. "That is quite all right. We do not mean to impose. Perhaps you would like to share the whiskey we have." She hoped Stevenson wouldn't mind her taking the full bottle. She would need to remember to replace it later.

Canonbie squatted and set down the lantern. Unslinging the bundle from his shoulder, he'd pulled the whiskey bottle halfway out when his gaze caught on something in the corner of the room. He froze for a moment before starting and remembering the bottle.

"This'll put some armor between yourself and the morning chill," he said, handing the whiskey to the gnome.

Effie caught his meaning and glanced at the corner of the room. A mound of rucksacks piled there. Short-hafted shovels and hammers were lashed to their sides, along with a couple of mining lanterns. But she saw right away what had given the man pause. A mask of black leather sat atop one of the rucksacks. It would cover a gnome's entire face and wrap around the wearer's head. Thick goggles protruded like bug's eyes from its center, and where the nose would fit, a long, soft tube hung limp, dangling a foot in length.

It looked like an elephant's trunk.

Effie reached out with her fey senses and ran over the aura of each gnome once again. Earlier, she had felt them as a group, probing only as she needed to determine their location. But now she examined each, inspecting them like she might horses lined in a stable. Her memory caught on the third one, a younger fellow whose girth wasn't as formidable as the others.

She remembered his aura from the previous night. He had joined to her from somewhere along Princes Street. His aura resembled that of an iron warship crashing through the waves of a choppy sea. Hard and stern it pressed, carving a path toward a rocky shore.

She had found the fey who'd assaulted the mob.

"Effie *von* Glen Coe," he said. He gave her a crisp nod. "*Ich bin geehrt.*"

"He says he is honored," said the white-haired gnome. "Though you are not of the Seily Court, you require our good behavior."

Effie blinked at the odd phrasing, before she remembered her manners. "I am honored as well, good sirs." She dipped into a more formal curtsey. She realized they waited for her to sit, and so she did so, tucking her legs beneath her. The coldness of the hard dirt made the warmth of the fire all the more welcome. Canonbie sat as well, and the gnomes mirrored them.

Their leader unstopped the whiskey bottle and poured a healthy measure into a tin cup before passing it along. "I am called Freiherr Jörg, and we are of the *Orden der Freiwald*. You wonder why we are here, *ja*? Or perhaps you have come for our aid?"

"*Die Elfe von Clan Kae hat uns gewarnt*," said the gnome closest to Freiherr Jörg. It sounded like a scolding, yet the other gnomes all nodded their heads and mumbled their agreement.

All except Freiherr Jörg, whose lips pursed as if he'd bitten into something sour. He glanced among his companions and turned to Effie. "They tell me to be careful with you," he said.

Effie blinked. She felt like Alice, having fallen down a rabbit hole. But she latched onto a word she recognized, the name Kae. She knew only one member of that clan. "Do you speak of Jaelyn of Clan Kae?" she asked. "Is it she who warned you against me?"

Freiherr Jörg's bottom lip turned down, and he waved a calming hand at her. "Nay, nay, not against you. She gives you high praise and warns only against your meddling."

Effie bristled. Canonbie exploded into uncontrolled laughter. His whole body shook. He tried to apologize, but he couldn't contain his glee. The gnomes watched him for a moment, quizzically, before tittering fits stole them as well.

She couldn't help but join them. Yet her mind returned to Jaelyn. She knew the brownie plotted something near the city, and now she knew something of its scale.

"You risked much, then, exposing yourself last night," she said. She took a stab that their intentions within in the city were not to chance on a mob.

Freiherr Jörg's gaze flicked to the gnome whose aura she'd recognized, and the younger wilted back. "You are right. The Erbgraf, our leader, did not send us here to play tricks. But our purpose is our own, and I will say no more on the matter."

"And Jaelyn?"

"You may ask her yourself," said Freiherr Jörg.

Canonbie leaned forward. "They took the hogboon to the castle. His captors handed him over to the city constables. I saw it."

"The men with the armbands, yes?" said Freiherr Jörg. "They are friends of Magistrate Elias McPherson. This you should know, and also that they have all scuffled between them. Theirs is not a friendly bonding."

"McPherson," Effie whispered. Lord Granville had used the man's house for their meeting. Her blood ran cold. He had used the house of a magistrate now linked to the Sanctity of Empire League. She had assumed the lord's involvement but wondered now if the connection would be enough to turn public opinion against him.

"Will there be a trial?" asked Canonbie.

Freiherr Jörg shrugged. "Hard to say. They have many prisoners at the castle. Not all have we heard from in some time." He slurped whiskey from his tin cup. "It is better to forget this hogboon. He slew two sheep and the son of a shepherd, in the north. He should've known better."

Effie's eyes bulged. "He's a murderer?" She hadn't considered the hogboon guilty. She'd assumed the tales spun against him false.

"He protected his home when the flock came to graze." Freiherr Jörg spoke calmly, as if they discussed a recipe for plum pudding.

A part of Effie wanted to learn more of the hogboon's plight. But Graham's voice sounded in her mind, and thoughts of Lord Granville and the treaty shoved everything else aside. What plot did the man play against her? How steeped into the city's unrest was his puppeteer's hand?

"Have you heard of a troop of fey called *Les Revenirs*?" she asked.

This brought a small jolt from Freiherr Jörg. Leather coats rustled as some of the other gnomes shifted uncomfortably. One spat and mumbled something she couldn't understand.

Freiherr Jörg glanced at the gnome. "Yes, we have heard the name. We have a disagreement with them. You may have seen them too, last night, yes?"

When Effie shook her head, he continued. "We thought a sudden storm might cause the mob to disperse, but no sooner had we sounded thunder when those *Revenirs* did come and fling their comets."

Understanding came to Effie. The gnomes' attempts to aid the hogboon had been thwarted as surely as her own. "So you had no desire to harm anyone?"

"Nay, not at least in that crowd."

"And the gust of wind?" she asked. "The one meant to knock me back?"

Freiherr Jörg's eyes twinkled. "That you may ask of Jaelyn of Clan Kae."

Effie snorted. She would remember to do just that.

"What else can you tell us of *Les Revenirs*?" asked Canonbie. He took a long swig from the whiskey bottle.

Freiherr Jörg grimaced. "It is best you stay clear of them. They are led by a Sithling called Cecily McCray. She is dangerous, and her—what is the word? *Jünger*? Ah, yes. Her disciples, they are even more dangerous."

Effie frowned at the word. "Disciples?"

"Are you unaware? Cecily McCray grooms her flock for rituals of Blood Craft. They are a foul cult who keep, ah..." He paused again, searching for a word. "*Hunde und Katzen*—ah, pets!—as they consider them, chained within their lair."

"Pets," said Canonbie. His gaze grew hard. "Do you mean humans?"

"Yes," replied Freiherr Jörg. "Though some may not be called as such anymore."

"Where is this lair?" demanded Effie, perhaps too sternly. The more she learned of this cult, the more her gut twisted into knots. If what the gnome said was true, it mattered little what games Lord Granville played. She would not let anyone suffer so cruelly.

"You would not find admittance," said Freiherr Jörg. "The lair is well protected. Only those invited may roam within."

"Tell me." Effie heard the frost in her voice and realized her hands had balled into fists.

Freiherr Jörg studied her before nodding his approval. "This is why Jaelyn of Clan Kae gives you praise, Green Lady. For all the warning of danger, you are eager to rampage through the affairs of this cult like a fox gone mad in a hen house." He gripped his coat at the breast with both hands. It gave him a dignified posture. "Find a young Sithling in the Haymarket. He wears the motley of a fool and spins tales in a canvas tent. He can grant you the invitation you seek. But I warn you most strongly, death hovers around *Les Revenirs* and all they touch."

The gnome's gaze softened. He rubbed his hands together and extended one toward the pot over the fire. "Porridge?" he asked.

"Whiskey," Effie rasped. She snatched the bottle from Canonbie. Her throat had suddenly run dry.

❦ 27 ❧

Stuart Graham waited for them on the steps outside the house on Heriot Row. He tried to scowl at Effie as she and Canonbie approached, but she could spot the concern coming through his eyes. The morning sun had come, and with it a little bit of warmth to push back the chill breeze that rustled over the hills. The sunlight kissing Effie's cheeks made her eyes heavy. The lack of sleep had caught up to her, as well as the drams of whiskey she'd imbibed with the gnomes of the Order of Freiwald.

"You needn't worry so," she told him. She patted his arm.

"As well tell a hound to quit wagging its tail," said Canonbie, smirking.

Graham snorted. "It is good to see you safe," he said, as he led them inside. "Come lass, we have a visitor."

Effie's face lit up as she recognized the aura of the woman who waited for them in the drawing room. Her exhaustion melted away, and she hurried into the adjoining room.

There, Rose Brewer sat on a couch that bore a floral print of greens, pinks, and reds. Her dress bore a similar design, though the flowers were her namesake rather than Highland flora. A pair of chairs sat opposite the couch, with a sturdy table in between. A fireplace protruded from one wall, and a large, curtained window let in light that made the room gleam with warmth. Rose had pulled her hair into a tight bun atop her head. It gave her the bearing of a school mistress.

Effie stopped and gave a polite curtsy, which brought a barking laugh from the older woman.

Rose set her teacup on a table and stood. "Come now, child. Do you think I rest on propriety the way the stuffy men of this country do?" She waved Effie over and embraced her in a hug. "What are arms for, if not to feel and touch?"

Effie breathed in the sweet scent that perfumed the woman. It held a note of lilac and something spicier, maybe nutmeg. "You received my telegram?"

"Yes," Rose replied. "And just in time, too. There's only so long a woman can take the endless whinging of the Seily Court. That lot understands no other way than to squabble amongst themselves. I took the next ferry from Skye as soon as I'd read your note, and travelled through the night."

She nodded to the men as they entered. "Mr. Graham gave me an account of your adventures in Dunfermline, and of the riotous evening."

"Aye," said Graham, in a playful huff. "Then she shooed me from the house like dog who'd made a mess on the carpet."

Rose's eyes twinkled. "You wore the carpet thin with all your worried pacing." She reclaimed her seat and patted the couch next to her for Effie to sit. "Now tell me of your morning stroll. I trust you and Mr. Canonbie did more than take a turn in the garden."

Effie blushed at the insinuation. She made to sit, but her fey senses suddenly flared, and her head snapped toward the dining room. Three fey sat within, their auras unfamiliar to her. It took her a moment to figure out what had happened, and when she did, she gasped.

"What is it?" Canonbie asked. He peered out the drawing room door.

"Fetch me the dress box from the dining room," she said. Canonbie traded a look with Graham but did as she bade.

When he returned, she knew for certain. The auras of the three pixies had changed. She could feel now only a slight familiarity to those she had sensed in Dunfermline, but it was like that of a distant cousin.

"Do they live?" Graham asked, catching her reaction.

Rose's examined the cocooned forms, and her expression soured. She reached out and tapped one lightly. It clopped like hollow wood.

"Yes," said Effie. "I can feel them. Only, they aren't what they were before. Or who they were before. I don't know how to best explain it."

"You mean they go through some sort of metamorphosis?" asked Graham. His brow furrowed as he leaned closer to study the cocoons. "Can such a thing truly be done?"

"You must start at the beginning, lass," said Rose. She patted Effie's hand. "Tell me everything."

Effie nodded and did so. When she finally fell silent, Rose drew herself up and stared out the window. Tapping a finger to her lip, her gaze became pensive. "There was a man called Charles Bracken at the turn of the past century. He murdered a pair of boys in a village to the south of Berwick. A heinous crime. The locals found him in a shepherd's hut. There, they locked him in and burned him alive before the constables could reach him." She shrugged. "Perhaps he deserved that fate."

"Was there any doubt of his guilt?" asked Effie. She had never heard of the terrible crime, nor its perpetrator.

"No," said Jack Canonbie. "The lunatic confessed to anyone who'd listen, as I heard it. He smiled about it, too, like he was proud, if the tales be true. It's a local legend told by the southern folk to ward their younglings away from the borderlands."

"So they say," said Rose. "But even dead, the constables had to fetch the gravedigger to clear out the body and put it to rest. It is this tale not many know."

Effie leaned in, and she caught Graham do the same from the corner of her eye. He perched on one of the chairs, hands capping his knees. Canonbie guarded the doorway. He leaned against the wall with his arms folded across his chest.

"Within the shepherd's hut," Rose continued, "which most had thought long abandoned, the gravedigger uncovered evidence of devilry. A singed tome, jars of dissected body parts, and the dried heads of all manner of forest critters filled the warren. Some the gravedigger did not recognize. He could not recognize them, for they had been transformed through some means into horrors. This gravedigger saw enough of the tome's pages to realize that was its intent."

"Hadn't the fire destroyed everything?" asked Effie.

Rose shook her head. "The fire had not been large. Bracken died inhaling the smoke. His body had not been scorched at all."

"How do you know these things?" Effie wondered at the tale, and of how similar it sounded to that of Cyrus Reed.

"The gravedigger was a Sithling," said Graham, with a knowing nod to Rose. "He would've had to be, to keep his discovery quiet. Most men would've shouted for all to come and bear witness. But he didn't, did he?"

Rose's eyebrow raised. "He knew better than to let word of Bracken's alchemy spread. He informed the Steward of the Seily Court, and all the evidence was destroyed." She turned to Effie. "I only wish I had convinced Caledon to let me read what remained of the tome before he burnt it. Still, knowing a thing has happened before allows one hope."

"Huh?" Graham blinked. "How do you mean?"

Effie thought she understood. She answered for Rose. "That if men like Cyrus Reed and Charles Bracken can learn this alchemy from a book, perhaps a solution is contained within one as well. These men performed no Fey Craft. They mixed fey blood in their compounds to reach the chemical reactions they sought, and the knowledge of those compounds are passed in books."

"Aye, but more than that," said Rose. "Think of the wonders told in fey lore, what the ancient elders were said to have wrought." She pulled Effie's hands into hers. "Lore says that Grundbairns once tended the forests and glens of the land. Have you ever thought on what that means? What wonders they might have performed?"

Effie nodded. "Often, and yet I still understand little of it."

"The tales of Grundbairns muddle with those called Oak Seers, but all hold within them a single element—rebirth. Aidan Bough Grower is said to have raised a forest on the spot where a great battle had been waged. And when Cormac the Sapling whispered in the ears of straying wives, they would wake to find their homes filled with vines."

"Ha!" barked Canonbie. "You'll have to tell me the full of that one, sometime."

Rose gave the man a chastising glance, but she grinned all the same.

"There are dozens more, too many for their roots not to hold some manner of truth. A rebirth. A growing."

"You think every time a miracle of Fey Craft is rediscovered, be it a perversion or not, it gives credence that these elder tales hold merit. That any, or all, are possible." Effie considered that. In the past two years, she had witnessed wonders beyond her imagination. Even the past night had proved to her she had much to learn.

"You must teach me of glamours," she said. "How to conjure them and how to force them away."

"I will, lass," said Rose. "When there is time. A dear friend is in danger, and I must see to her safety first." When Effie cocked her head, she continued. "Abigail Salisbury. You sought her at the university library."

Effie's eyes widened. "The librarian. She is in danger?" Another thought came to her, and she blurted, "But, if you are friends, how can— is she aware she holds fey blood?"

Rose roared a laugh. "Of course she is. But that doesn't mean she'll let anyone know of it, even those she aids from time to time."

Blood rushed to Effie's cheeks in embarrassment. Of course the woman knew! She conversed with hundreds of fey and held access to thousands of books. How had she not considered that?

"Do you know where to find her now?" asked Graham. He rose and pulled his coat straight. "I also can claim her as a friend, though not as closely as you."

"I do," Rose admitted. "With all the fey blood roaming the city, I can cast a wide net with my senses. Abigail's aura is known to me as I know the back of my own hand. She is held within the castle, and I mean to see her released."

"I'll go with you," said Effie.

"That is appreciated, but you have our leverage to collect." Rose stood and smoothed her dress. "The treaty cannot wait, and its fate may rest in uncovering Lord Granville's designs. Caledon does not send details of the negotiations, but from what I gather, our cause will need every bit of barter we can grasp. An opportunity has fallen into our laps. We must seize it, and we must seize it now."

Effie's heart sank. "Does it go so poorly?"

"There is impasse after impasse," said Rose. "It is expected. The lords of London wish to dominate the fey. The Seily Court pushes Caledon to obtain a freedom such as our kind hasn't seen since before the Roman occupation. Without the backing of the duke, or a reversal from Lord Granville, the talks will soon breakdown."

Effie stood. Her bones ached, and her arms and legs felt like lead. She could curl up in front of the fire and sleep for days. But Rose was right. An opportunity had come to them and time grew short. She must choose this battle and see it through, lest she find herself spinning in circles while all threads of hope dissolved around her.

Rose must've seen the resolution in her eyes. "I will see to Abigail and do what I can for the others within the castle. Caledon's word will open doors others would find impassible. If they don't, I have other relationships to draw on within the city." She winked and jutted out her hip, resting a hand there for emphasis. Effie caught the meaning and laughed.

"As do I," said Graham, "though not in so charming a manner. I will aid Miss Rose, and Mr. Canonbie can accompany you, Effie." He turned to her. "It pains me to say it, but Mr. Canonbie is younger and better equipped to protect you from these *Les Revenirs*. Still, I would advise not to engage with them unless you absolutely must."

"Aye, she'll be safe," said Canonbie. "You have my word."

Effie grinned at them both before the dress box caught her eye. "What of these poor pixies?" she asked.

"Abigail and I will endeavor to cure them," said Rose. "The warlock we must let roam for the nonce. From your account, he is most likely too sorely wounded at the moment to carry on with his experiments."

"We must also see to these thugs with their armbands after all the rest." Effie felt her strength return a bit, as her path gained clarity. She hadn't realized how much confusion could sap one of hope. Thrusting aside all other concerns, she focused solely on a fool's motley and the best way to reach Haymarket.

❧ 28 ❧

J ack Canonbie scratched absently at his neck. Rose had shown Effie how to make a healing salve, and together they had redressed the man's wound, wrapping it under a fresh pleated tie that went well with his coat. The salve had taken an hour to concoct, and that had allowed Effie time for a short rest. It had served her well. Her mind had sharpened, and as she and Canonbie strode down Princes Street, her feet felt as if she had slumbered an entire night.

Haymarket lay in the opposite direction of North Bridge, at the far end of Princes Street. A crossroads at the western edge of the city, the area's rail station, access to ferry ports, and the starting point of roads to Glasgow and Stirling had given rise to warehouses and a small market. Taverns and inns had followed, and the area now supported a thriving, if eclectic, community.

Men walked on stilts, like those used to light gas lamps, barking out rude jests and handing out flowers to those they deemed worthy. A row of orators pronounced judgment on passersby or espoused on the virtues of some political philosophy. Most were at odds and tried to shout over another until all their voices were lost in a clamor. Boys ran through the crowd selling jewelry most likely stolen from other parts of the city, and Effie saw one boy enticing a couple to follow him down an alley where he promised to show them a hunk of gold from the Americas that dwarfed his head.

What women Effie saw were of two sorts. Those who lived in Haymarket mirrored those of Old Town. Poor and hungry, exhaustion clouded their eyes, as if they spent every waking moment scurrying after coin for food and shelter. Only here, their dresses were a soiled and threadbare version of what Rose had worn. Flowing garments with bold and colorful prints ruled the streets, along with wide-brimmed straw hats and high boots that clacked as they struck the ground. Little Bohemia, the folk of Old Town called Haymarket.

The other women strolling past dressed as Effie, though she could not see many who weren't attached to a gentleman's arm. Their dresses were pressed and clean, their hair neatly done and fingers freshly washed. As Effie watched, she got the impression the denizens of Haymarket regarded these women as prey.

"There is a fey aura in there," she told Canonbie, pointing at a canvas tent at the side of a triangular courtyard. It stood at the end of a line of similar pavilions. A plump man with a long beard hawked iron and leather trinkets from the first. The second held racks of jars filled with thick jam, and clay pots of milled corn. Crows' feet hung from the ceiling of the tent at the center of the line. The dried skins of snakes and painted skulls of animals sat on the shelves inside. A stench, like that of a moldy French cheese, wafted from under its canopy.

Chimes sounded from the next tent. Some clinked of metal, while others had the hollow clack of wood or bone. Effie thought those of the latter appeared frightfully like human fingers. The master of the tent dressed in a long black cloak and a tall top hat. His moustache drooped on either side of his lips like wilted reeds, and his polished nails gleamed.

But nothing drew the eye like the tent at the end of the line. The canvas bore bold stripes of a deep red interchanging with midnight black. A haze of smoke billowed from within. It gave off an overpowering scent of burning peat mixed with hazelnut. A carpet lay before the tent. Its design depicted the gruesome slaughter of a herd of sheep by a boy with furred feet. At the side of the rug, a placard rested on an easel. "Countess Lereveur, the Everliving," it read in a fine script. The tent's flaps were partially closed, obscuring whatever occurred inside. But rather than discourage interest, it stoked Effie's curiosity.

As she made her way to the tent, the fool emerged. The man's motley was shabby and tired. A checkered pattern of gold and black adorned one side of his tunic. Solid green filled the other, with a heart of red cloth sewn into the breast. The tunic hung limp about his slender frame, soiled with stains and torn in several places. His red trousers fared no better. Something had spilled down one leg, and Effie guessed the clothes had been slept in and not washed in some time.

The fool locked his gaze on Effie as soon as he emerged. She nodded to him, and he smiled. His eyes had a yellowish tinge to them. It matched the pallor of his cheeks. His hair fell in a mop about his ears, as dingy as a bog.

"Welcome, Green Lady, and her brave companion," he said. His tone held a hidden laughter that made Effie's skin crawl. She caught Canonbie shifting the grip of his cane, but she kept her pace all the same. It did not shock her that the Sithling knew her. It seemed every fey did within the city. She would need to keep her wits about her. It was not likely the fool would do her harm in broad daylight, but one could never be too certain.

She sensed no other fey within the tent. Stopping before the fool, she studied his face. Up close, his gaunt cheeks had not the frailness of a starving man, but rather they held a firmness to them, as if his skin were pulled tight over a steel skull. His eyes bore through her, but they had no focus or spark of life to them. They carried instead the crazed flatness of a man steeped in opium. She caught a whiff of the stuff on him and guessed his use of it frequent.

The fool stepped aside and gestured for them to enter. "I am Jonas. Won't you come and hear my tale?"

"Does it involve the slaughter of sheep?" asked Jack Canonbie. He widened his stance and stuck out his chest. "Because I'll warn you, I like sheep." He waited for Effie to enter, glaring down at Jonas.

The fool's mouth dropped into a gaping, toothy, grin. "No sheep today," he said.

The inside of the tent held a row of wooden pews that faced a dais.

Instantly, the strong tang of blood met Effie's nose. It lay under the smoke she'd smelled earlier. A pole stood in the center of the tent, raising its pitch to a point. Candles hung from the ceiling atop iron sconces that caught the dripping wax. A brazier sat on the dais with a large oil lamp burning beneath it. It was from the brazier the smoke wafted, and from there Effie knew the whiff of spent blood had also come.

A handful of dirty urchins and a pair of rough looking men sat in the pews. The benches creaked as some of them turned to regard Effie. She felt their eyes wander over her. The tent was no place for a proper lady, and none of them held respectful thoughts, she was sure.

She took a seat in the last pew. Canonbie perched next to her. The man looked ready to batter anyone who came within reach of his cane. "Be wary," he whispered under his breath. She nodded in return.

"Come on, then," shouted one of the boys, once her party had settled. "Let's hear us a bloody story."

Jonas marched to the dais and stepped up next to the brazier. "Good gentlemen and lady," he began. He held up both arms, palms facing his audience. "I tell you today of the Countess Lereveur, known to all in infamy as the Everliving. Hers is a tale of blood and murder, of love and sacrifice, and of the spirit world."

Effie shifted on the hard pew as the fool wove his tale. The countess began her sordid life as a lusty young lass, bedding first one gentleman and then another, until she had tallied more than she could count on a single hand. But her manners, looks, and wit were such that she always found herself in good company, and in time she found a match worthy of granting her father's dowry.

The boys in the pews cheered and made rude jests as Jonas recounted each bedding. Such coarseness didn't bother Effie. She'd heard worse among the workmen during the construction projects of Thomas Stevenson.

"And so the countess found herself atop society, in a rich bed surrounded by a rich house of good esteem." Jonas pantomimed the tale as he spoke, making broad gestures with his hands. His voice rose and fell and changed in pitch as he intoned the various parts. "But she found no happiness in idle days of whist and turns in the garden. A greater purpose called to her from the beyond, an unlocking of secrets long shunned and forbidden."

The tale turned to feature a young footman who, infatuated with the countess's beauty, was lured into his master's bedchamber while the count hunted in a nearby forest. There, the countess made a fountain of the footman's neck, using a dagger gleaming with the runes of Queen Makeda, the great djinni who corrupted Solomon the Wise.

"The blood spilt into a chalice of resurrection," exclaimed Jonas. His hands grew frantic with energy. "The spirits called to the Countess Lereveur, and she drank from the chalice, all the while whispering the words of power. Her body, already shaped by God, blossomed into a creature succulent to the eye and enthralling to the passions of men."

Jonas raised his arms and stood like a snarling bear. "Her husband found her thus, abed with the footman's blood soaking her chin and chest. He could've arrested her then or banished her from his house, but her gaze enticed him. He could've picked up the chalice and joined her, but he knew not the words of power, and she refused to speak them to him. Instead, she enslaved the count and his entire household. As they grew old, she remained ever young and hale."

Jonas started in on other parts of the countess's dark escapades. He spoke of cruel murders and wicked rites that called on the spirits of the dead. Those who approached the countess were quickly held under her thrall. Those who somehow resisted found themselves dismembered or their memories befuddled and their families slain.

Effie had heard similar tales from the continent. She had never given them any merit. The terrors of her own life outweighed those of some creature who lived only from the lips of a raconteur. But the manner in which Jonas spun his tale gave her pause. She heard not in it an eagerness to believe but a disdain, as if the man loathed speaking aloud that which he would rather cherish as a secret. It came to her the man truly believed in the tale of the countess. He was not a fool retelling a falsehood meant to frighten its audience but a zealot preaching a holy account of what he held sacred.

"How'd she die?" asked the boy who'd shouted earlier. "They lop her head off and burn her?"

Jonas slowly shook his head as he grinned at the youth. "She never did. Finally bored of the count's home, she slunk off one day never to return." Stepping off the dais, Jonas came to hover over the boy, bending at the waist. "But now and then, there are tales of a fair lady who appears from nowhere. Death follows at her heels, and if you look closely you can see a stain of blood marring the beauty of her chin."

As he said the last, a droplet of red spilled from his lips and ran down his jaw. He pretended not to notice, and the boy shied back.

"Rubbish," grumbled one of the men in attendance. He rose and staggered from the tent. Effie could smell the whiskey on him as he passed. Slowly, the others made their way out, though none dropped any coin into the hat Jonas held out for that purpose.

"Quite the interesting tale," said Canonbie, once the tent had cleared. He rose and stalked forward a few steps. It put him between the fool and Effie.

Jonas sneered at the empty hat. He flung it onto the dais and made a dramatic bow. The dribble on his chin had crusted over and darkened. "It does not need the flair I impart. Our flock must come willingly and not be tricked by a false arousal of the senses." He lowered his head, shoulders rolled forward, and stared up at Canonbie. In the shadows of the tent, it gave his eyes a fevered cast, like that of a starving wolf stalking for the kill.

Effie caught his meaning. Jonas used his performances to entice victims for *Les Revenirs*, but he could not use any Fey Craft. If the audience somehow became aware their host was a fey, the ruse of the countess would be broken.

"Are we to believe Cecily McCray is this Countess Lereveur?" she asked.

The fool gave a hearty laugh. "Mother is whom she wills." He produced something from his pocket and tossed it into the brazier. Rounding on her, his mirth dissolved. He shook his head slowly. "You should not have come here. It would've been better for all if you had fled the city."

Effie stiffened. She heard a ruffle of the canvas behind her just before a flash of searing light blinded her. It came from the brazier, a silent explosion—lightning without the thunder.

Yelping, she flung her arms before her face, pressing her eyes shut.

Stars swam in the darkness behind her closed lids. She heard Canonbie curse and stumble into one of the wooded pews.

"We mean you no harm!" she shouted, jerking to her feet.

Mocking laughter filled the tent, echoing from all sides. The newcomers flooded in from the front and back. Members of the flock, she could tell, from the lack of fey blood.

Blinking to clear her vision, she gasped. The fool had sprouted horns. Thick and curled, they protruded over a blunt snout. His companions were beasts, though they stood like men. One had tusks and a pelt of coarse fur. Another had a long, pointed beak, and a third the beady eyes and whiskers of a rat.

This last hopped forward in a crouch. Canonbie swung his cane but fell off-balance as a second blast flashed from the brazier.

Grabbing the back of the pew, Effie tried to steady herself. A wet smack came, followed by a thump. *Canonbie!* She tried to scream. But as she opened her mouth, she inhaled a cloud of dust. She only vaguely saw the head of a fox peering over her shoulder, as she hacked to clear her lungs. The thing's hand whipped around, and more of the dust showered her face.

"No harm?" asked the fool. "Pray tell, where is the fun in that?"

Her vision darkened. She felt herself falling. *Falling and failing.* She growled against the thought, and laughter rolled over her again. Gentle hands caught her, helping her to the floor. She smelled a mix of stale wine and spent gunpowder as the world faded away.

❦ 29 ❦

Effie's head swam. She fell deep into a darkness that enveloped her like a crushing sea of inky black. She fell for so long, she no longer remembered how'd she'd come to this place. She fell until stars flared to life overhead, their light distorted and murky, as if veiled by a thin fog. Shadows sprang from the starlight. The figures who cast them howled and cackled. They danced around her, flitting from sight whenever she tried to move her head.

Grass tickled under her, and she knew suddenly that she lay in a field.

The face of a young girl popped into view, her nose almost pressing against Effie's, though turned upside down. Effie sensed the girl's body crouching just beyond the top of her head. The girl had tucked her auburn hair behind ears that stuck out from her face like butterfly wings. Almond-shaped eyes and slanted cheekbones gave her the appearance of a pixie, though she was much too big.

"Wake," she trilled like a songbird. "Wake, for you sleep."

"I am awake," said Effie. Her voice sounded like it echoed down a long metal tube.

The girl shook her head violently, and her tresses bounced free to cover her face. "No, you slumber and only dream of what once was. Wake, and let loose that which you have lost."

The stars flared. Effie blinked and found herself standing in a clearing ringed by tall trees. A chorus of drum, pipe, and flute echoed the whistling of wind through the boughs. It was a song of harmony. Around the trees, the Seily Court thrived. Pixies buzzed through the air, wings flashing like glittering comet tails. Gnomes, hogboons, and brownies sat and danced and caroused. Their chatter hummed beneath the music, light and full of gaiety.

Effie thought they appeared odd at first, until she realized how they were different. Instead of the dress of man, they wore simple tunics of a shimmering cloth. Some wore nothing at all. It stole from them the appearance of children and enhanced their otherworldly features—their angled faces and sharp ears, the hogboons' hairy legs and feet, and the gnomes' protruding noses. Joy swelled in Effie's heart at the sight of the mighty host and at their antics and frivolity. She felt weightless and free, wanting nothing more than to twirl and laugh without a thought for the morrow.

So she did, for a time. Gleefully, she sank her bare toes into the undergrowth of the forest floor. She gulped in the scents of moss and leaf, soil and flower. The drums made her sway, the pipes bounce and hop. She spun for a time longer than she could remember, until she came near an elderly fey whose beauty reminded her of a fierce lightning storm.

"This is what the fey should be," said the fey. She sat in a large hollow in one of the trees. The perch gave her a vantage over the entire host. Her eyes crackled with power as she regarded them. Like the girl earlier, Effie could not quite tell to what race of fey she belonged.

"This is what was, ages ago." The fey's voice turned to frost. The scene before them blurred, and when it came back into focus it had changed. A mighty oak sat at the edge of the clearing. It was familiar to Effie, though she couldn't fathom why. Around it the Seily Court gathered to bear witness. Three men knelt in unadorned robes of white. As they supplicated themselves, they made offerings to the fey—a basket of fruit and nuts, another bearing coils of fine rope, and in the last, a slender silver dagger.

Effie hadn't noticed the boy at first. He lay on the ground with his hands and feet bound. After their offering, the robed men rose, and one of them plucked up the dagger. He raised it high and uttered some words in a harsh language Effie couldn't understand. The incantation complete, the man reached to an oak branch and cut off a clump of mistletoe. To this he spoke another incantation. The other men picked the boy up and held him as he squirmed. The first struck the boy with the sprig of mistletoe—on the brow, the shoulders, and the legs. He held up the sprig and the dagger and turned to the great oak. As he did so, the Seily Court hushed and leaned in. They expected what came next, and with a dread that threatened to rip her to shreds, Effie screamed.

"It is their place to bow to our kind. You will learn," said the elderly fey. "Without death, there is no rebirth."

The man with the dagger faced the boy and stepped closer.

"No!" Effie shrieked and surged forward. Vines sprang from the undergrowth to lash around her. Their kiss of prickly thorns burned where it met her flesh. She squirmed and yelled. She twisted and fought, struggling against the vines, but they held her tight. She closed her eyes as barking laughter filled her ears.

She coughed and rolled onto something soft and spongy.

Music rang out. Harsh strings pulled in an awkward semblance of a merry tune. Bells chimed along with the strings, and for a moment Effie recalled the cacophony of the trows' warren near Duncairn.

A putrid stench filled her nose.

She opened her eyes, and found she sprawled over a mound of cushions within a vast chamber. Vaulted stone formed the ceiling. Thick rugs covered the dirt floor, overlapping and giving off a dizzying swirl of interchanging patterns. Candlelight flickered about the chamber, bolstered by a fire that crackled in its center. The light danced off the bare flesh of a dozen half-dressed men and women who lounged atop piles of cushions that were strewn about the floor without any semblance of order.

They wore the masks of animals. The deer. The badger. The rat. Most were crudely constructed from leather and wood, though a few held a shocking likeness. They'd left their mouths exposed, and Effie saw enough of them to tell man from woman.

Her head was groggy. Her arms felt heavy. A haze thickened in the chamber. It gave off the stench she'd smelled.

"Opium," said Jack Canonbie. She found him sprawled behind her. When they met eyes, he nodded toward a pan nestled in the fire. "They burn it to fill the room." Effie glanced at the ribbed vaulting above and saw how the smoke gathered in a haze.

"How long have I slept?" she asked.

"Not long," said Canonbie. "They danced before moving on to other activities."

A soft moan came from the corner of the chamber, as if to clarify what he meant. Effie glanced and saw a woman shudder as a man ran his fingers along her arm. She wore the mask of a field mouse. He, a red fox. Her shirt had been pulled to her waist, and she stiffened as the man's hand wandered across the expanse of her chest.

Effie turned aside. Heat rose to her cheeks.

A mocking laugh sounded from another woman. A jackal, Effie guessed. She lay next to a man who appeared asleep, his eyes closed and mouth agape. A bear mask sat crooked, half-pulled from his head. The jackal rose slowly and approached, leering at Canonbie. Effie couldn't tell if it was in lust or hunger. Perhaps both. She felt the woman's fey aura and swallowed. It had something in it of a night bird tormenting a field mouse, basking in its fear before it swooped in and ate it. Effie cast out her senses and found the other fey in the chamber exuded similar sensations, a thirst for consumption and frenzy for release.

But not all the occupants were fey. The man who slept and the moaning woman were not. Effie scanned the chamber and saw a handful of others too. The chamber had a score of exits, proper stone-lined archways, deep alcoves, and a few roughly cut openings. She sensed auras stemming from each. She wondered how large the warren sprawled, and whether they would be able to find their way out of the maze unaided.

"I adore fresh blood, especially when it comes from a bull of a man." The jackal drew out the words, touching her lips in a suggestive manner. She knelt and placed her palms on Canonbie's chest, burrowing them under his coat. "I can smell it on you."

Effie half rose. Her hand clenched into a fist.

The jackal cackled with glee.

"A formal announcement is needed before you can claim this one, Tallia," said Jonas. He stepped from the shadows, still wearing his motley and mask. A ram's head, Effie recognized now. He waggled a finger at the jackal. "You have heard Mother's words."

Tallia pouted. Her bottom lip jutted out. "Oh, but this one already bleeds," she whined. She reached for the bandaged wound at Canonbie's neck. He slapped her hand away, and she squeaked in excitement. It turned into a purr. "I need a new pet. My last one is almost spent."

"Tallia," Jonas warned. Effie saw his shoulders tense. His eyes hardened beneath his mask.

The jackal head spun to face him. "You may choose the weakness of constraint, mooning over your precious darling, but I will take as I please." She spat the words and moved into a threatening crouch, as if she wanted to ravage the fool with rake and bite.

"Enough," boomed a husky voice. The discordant music screeched to a halt. Only the crackling of the fire filled the heavy silence that followed. A figure moved along the wall, and Effie startled to find an ogre of a man dressed in a gray cloak that blended into the stone behind him. He carried a stout wooden staff. A thick blade hung at his belt. He wore no mask, and his eyes stared hard at Tallia. Effie searched the walls and caught sight of two more brutes glaring at them.

"Bring them forward," came a new voice, this one female and scratched with age. Effie realized it came from one of the larger alcoves, a recess left entirely in shadow.

Tallia glared daggers at the fool before stepping away. Spilling herself onto a pile of cushions, she propped onto an elbow and studied Canonbie. A lecherous smile crept onto her lips. Behind her, the fire sizzled as a bare-chested man trickled water over the clump of dark muck he'd set in the pan. Tendrils of thick smoke crept across the room, replacing those that had faded away. Canonbie coughed and held his sleeve against his mouth.

Jonas bowed toward the alcove. Snapping his fingers, he bade Effie follow him. She did, and Canonbie strode at her side. He patted his coat pocket, and a grimace passed across his face. Effie knew what the look meant. They'd taken his pistol as well as his cane.

The shadows receded as Effie approached the alcove. There, a figure rested on a high-backed, cushioned chair. A throne perhaps it was meant to be. Its wood was painted gold. Its cushions were a red velvet. The trim held scrollwork befitting a rich lord's estate. The woman who perched on the chair had raven hair that plummeted to her waist. Only part of her face peeked out from behind the strands, a delicate nose spotted brown with freckles, lips almost as pale as the cheeks that held them, and eyes so heavily veiled they appeared as dark lines beneath her forehead. Cecily McCray wore a gypsy's gown, loose and swirling with different colors. A russet shawl hung over her shoulders. It draped to her knees.

She raised a bony finger at Effie. "The Green Lady, Effie of Glen Coe. I knew you would seek me out eventually. Some bade me not to allow you an audience. Some argued for a more violent repulsion to the dangers you bring. But I wanted you to come and witness our truth."

"I have come to discuss the treaty negotiations and nothing more," said Effie. The words struck near the truth. She had to uncover why the woman and her cult were so important to Lord Granville and use that leverage in favor of the treaty.

Cecily McCray cackled. "You must lie better than that. You come to collect me for your master. I have hearing beyond my ears. I know this thing."

Effie swallowed. Glancing at Canonbie, she found the man swaying gently. His eyelids drooped. The opium! It hadn't affected her more than a pint of ale might do. That had to be a trick of her fey blood. But it mattered little. She needed to hurry.

"I... I tell the truth," she stammered. "Lord Granville did command me to bring you to the magistrate, but I have no intention of doing so. I seek only why he has such an interest in your affairs."

Jonas hissed. "Any who deal with that man cannot be trusted."

Cecily McCray raised her hand. Effie caught something in the calming gesture, a connection between them that passed a meaning unspoken. "You would have me believe you innocent?" she asked of Effie. "You have betrayed our kind before. It is well known your murder done at Caldwell House. Why is now any different?"

Effie felt her anger rise but refused to be goaded. "I strive for what all fey covet, to live in peace."

"Peace!" Cecily McCray barked the word as if it brought a distaste to her mouth. "That is a foul word when it comes at such great cost. A rebirth is needed, a return to the old ways. You have seen it. I know you have."

"The old ways where you treat men and women as pets, as playthings to discard on a whim?" Effie spread her arms and gestured at those spilled over the cushions. "Tell me how such cruel indulgences are a rebirth. Tell me how they are a better peace."

"We honor our guests who give us the path to Everlife," said Jonas.

"Before the days of kings and queens," said Cecily McCray, "when man was but a child, we cherished our human friends and helped them survive this cold, dark world. In return, they honored us, giving what lifeblood they could so that we, their betters, could prosper. Or did you believe Blood Craft could only be done with one's own blood?"

Her lips pulled back into a feral grin, and she gave a slight nod. The gesture made Effie shrink back. She spun her head at a soft groan behind her that sounded almost like a moan of ecstasy. The shirtless man in the bear mask staggered as Tallia bit him with a short, hooked knife. The blade didn't plunge deep, but it drew a bead of red. Tallia ran her finger along it before lapping up the blood with a long lick of her tongue.

Effie cringed but forced herself from turning away. She would not let them destroy what hope she had of a peaceful and harmonious bond between fey and human. "This is not the way," she said. Her voice steeled. "I will not let the murder of innocents stand."

"Innocents. Murder," Tallia drawled, mocking Effie. "Our friends offer themselves of their own accord."

"Yes, mistress," breathed the man. Welted lines crisscrossed his chest. Some leaked blood. Others appeared caked over and partially healed, perhaps days or weeks old. He grabbed Tallia's breast and pushed into her, his lips pressing against her neck. She kept her eyes locked on Effie and laughed.

He is in an opium daze and does not feel the life weeping from him. Effie's hands pulled into fists. A truth sank heavily into her gut. It would not be enough to negotiate with Cecily McCray. She would need to see an end to *Les Revenirs* and damn the consequences. She felt Lord Granville's trap pulling tighter around her neck. The man knew she could not witness such atrocity and stay her hand. She would act, betray her kind, and he would destroy her for it. He had planned that all along.

"Give her the banshee's touch!" called the man in the rat's mask. He howled, and a chorus rose in response, filling the chamber.

The banshee's touch. Effie's eyes widened. Her head whipped to Canonbie, but she found the man staring blankly, jaw agape.

Jonas stepped forward. "That is not ours to give," he said, but his voice was lost amongst the fervor of his brethren.

"She is the Oak Seer foretold." Cecily McCray's harsh whisper came out as a hiss. "Its touch already beckons her."

"Show her! Show her!" Tallia cried, and the host took up the call. She lashed out with the knife once more, and the bear-masked man crumbled to his knees. Blood poured from a gouge at his neck. Rat Mask bellowed in excitement. He pulled a young woman from the cushions and stroked the flat of her stomach.

The cheer came again, a deafening clamor. "Show her! Show her!"

"Stop this madness!" Effie screamed. She took a step toward the girl and froze in shock. She recognized the blonde hair and doll-like features of her face. In a heartbeat, Lord Granville's entire scheme fell into place.

"The Piper of Ceann Rois was a fool," said Tallia. Blood dribbled from her lips and spilled down her chest. "We make our own Horned Host, and it is mightier than his." She gestured at a pair of men wearing the masks of stags, who slumped together against one wall.

Effie startled in horror. The masks were no masks at all. Antlers had been affixed to their skulls, driven in by thick nails. The tips of the nails protruded through their eyes. Her head swung back to the blonde girl. Rat Mask had wrapped his arms around her. He whispered in her ear as she gasped. Her breath came in deep heaves that quickened.

Around the chamber, those of *Les Revenirs* writhed against their prey. Wails of lust rang out, befouled by cries of pain and malevolent laughter.

Effie started for the girl, scouring the ground for anything she could use as a weapon. Her mind whirled, searching for anything to placate the crazed horde. She had little hope, but she could not stand still.

Jonas snatched her arm. His nostrils flared. A panged look etched his face. "You cannot have her. She belongs with me."

Effie reacted without thought, drawing on her Fey Craft to summon a flash of light. But a shield snapped before her, ripping away the energy she pulled. It was the same shield she had felt during the riot of the mob.

Cecily McCray rose from her throne. "We *Revenirs* no longer constrain our true natures. We are the apostles of what should be, the ghosts of what was. Of what is to be reborn." She chuckled. Her eyes glazed over, staring at something far off only she could see. "And there is no rebirth without death. It has always been thus."

"Bollocks." Canonbie grunted and staggered forward. He made only a few steps before dropping to his knees, overcome by the opium fumes.

Tallia danced forward with her knife. "We need warriors for our brave host. If I cannot have this one as a pet, then I will send him to fill our ranks."

We are the apostles. Apostles. The word struck Effie as odd. Cyrus Reed had used it. Both held the madness of this banshee's touch, but they could not possibly strive toward a common cause.

Unless...

Effie's heart lurched. "You are being tricked." She cast her gaze around, taking in the depravity within the chamber, before returning to Cecily McCray. "Once your host may have joyfully imbibed in the pleasures of flesh and smoke and drink, but to turn to sacrifice and murder—these must be far from what was."

A flash of sadness touched the woman's face, and Effie knew she had been right. She wrenched against Jonas' grip, but the fool held her tight. "I beg of you," she pleaded, "tell me what hand twists your heart. Is it the Sidhe Bhreige? Has it come to you?" She strained to sense the auras of those around her. But she could sense only a trickle beyond the shield. It felt like a weight of stone had crashed on top of her, battering her wits and crushing her bones to dust.

"Take our guests to the cellar," said Cecily McCray. She flicked her hand, and one of the ogre-sized guardsmen stepped forward from the wall.

Effie didn't see Tallia's blow until it smacked her across the cheek and sent her reeling to the floor. "She stands against us!" she called. "She must be destroyed!"

"Let me kill her for you," said the bear. He crawled on his knees and wrapped his arms around Tallia's legs. "Oh, please, let me give you this service."

Cecily McCray snarled. "It is not your role to beg a gift from my child," she snapped.

"The cellar, but Mother, you can't," Jonas pleaded. He tore off his mask and dropped it at his feet.

Tallia laughed. "Coward." She spat the word at the fool, but that she meant it for Cecily McCray, as well, was clear.

"Tell me," demanded Effie. But even to her ears the command felt hollow, like that of a fly ordering a spider to loosen it from the hunter's web.

Tallia shoved aside her pet. Her bloody knife gleamed under the flickering light. Another of her brethren, a gaunt figure wearing the mask of a sparrow, rose from the carpets and stalked forward. He clutched a butcher's cleaver, broad and flat and heavy.

Effie snatched up a square cushion and brandished it. Yellow daises covered its fabric. Laughter rang throughout the chamber.

"Get up," she begged of Canonbie. She nudged him with her boot. "Get up, or we die." He grunted and blinked, running a hand over his face.

"I will strip the flesh from you both," said Tallia. She licked her blade clean.

"Enough," barked Cecily McCray. "You will do as I say! She is foretold!" But Tallia did not turn aside. The sparrow hovered next to her, awaiting her command.

Cecily McCray flicked her hand at the guardsman. He'd not moved from the wall.

Panic coursed through Effie. Whatever the discord existed within the cult of *Les Revenirs* mattered little to her and Jack Canonbie. They would find death in a heartbeat if she could not wake him from his stupor.

Squatting, she shook him hard. Sweat flowed down her back. She held the cushion aloft in a trembling hand, hoping it would turn aside Tallia's knife. At least a thrust or two. Enough for perhaps one last breath. Her eyes darted about the room, questing for anything she could use to help her.

"Take your Green Lady, if you please," said Tallia. "But we will kill her companion. The man has no use to you."

The sparrow stepped to loom over them. A fat hand reached down and grabbed Canonbie's boot. Effie swung the cushion at him. He swatted it away with a swipe of his hand, and it tore free from her grip to land a dozen feet away.

Canonbie moaned. Tallia laughed and sprang forward. She shoved the knife against Effie's cheek. Effie felt a sting as the blade gave her a light kiss. She fell back onto her rump and grabbed another of the cushions. She meant to heave it, to hurl it and lunge after before they could drag Canonbie away from her.

But as her hand found purchase on the supple cloth, she caught the expression on Jonas' face. The fool had his head cocked. He listened, and from the surprise on his face, he did not like what he heard.

Effie strained and heard it too, a moment before she felt their auras approach the far side of one of the chamber's archways. The feeble trickle she could sense allowed her that much. It was enough to rekindle hope.

The Order of Freiwald burst into the chamber, led by a brownie of Clan Kae. Jaelyn clutched her favorite dirk in a gloved hand and held up the other, palm out, as if to push back all in her path. Effie could tell it was she from her aura alone. She saw only a figure wrapped in a heavy, black leather coat that covered her from the top of her boots to the nape of her neck. One of the masks with the long snout covered her head.

Freiherr Jörg followed her into the room. He wore similar dress, but instead of a dirk he toted a blunderbuss gripped in both hands. Its short barrel had a bell-shaped tip as wide as Effie's fist. Its length was etched with an interlocking set of runes that glimmered under the candlelight.

The gnome tugged the trigger, and the blunderbuss boomed thunder. Dust and stone exploded from the ceiling and rained down over the crackling fire. Effie's hearing numbed, but she scrambled to her feet all the same.

Tallia hissed and spun to face the newcomers. The sparrow dropped Canonbie's boot as Jonas planted himself before Cecily McCray. The guardsmen scrambled from their positions along the walls, glancing at one another with uncertainty. The rest of those in the room shrank back, either with growls of defiance or meek silence.

Eight more of the Order of Freiwald stormed into the room and fanned out behind their leader. All carried a blunderbuss and wore the mask and coat, though some had short-hafted woodsmen's axes clutched in a hand or tucked into their belts.

"Elephants?" asked Canonbie feebly. He rose to his elbows and licked his lips.

"You masked your approach," said Cecily McCray.

"I have that skill," said Freiherr Jörg. His voice echoed through the mask, making it sound more hollow and distant.

"We have masked much more," said Jaelyn. She strode over to Effie, forcing Tallia back with a feint from her dirk. She dug in a pocket and thrust a vial into Effie's hand. "Make him drink," she commanded. She kept her head swiveling around the room.

The gnomes stood rigid. With a militant precision, they'd each leveled their weapon at a different foe. In the cold silence that gripped the room, Effie heard their breath sucking through the long snouts of their masks.

Unstopping the vial, she raced to Canonbie and dripped some of the amber liquid into his mouth. He choked and coughed, clapping a hand to his throat. But when he recovered, he shot to his feet, blinking his eyes.

"We leave now," said Jaelyn.

"No," said Effie. "Force them to tell us of the banshee's touch. Force them to let free those they've ensnared."

"There is no time," said Freiherr Jörg. "Already it begins."

Effie frowned. What had begun? Tallia stepped closer to Canonbie, jutting out her hip and chest. He growled, and the reaction drew out a coy smirk.

Effie whirled toward the blonde girl. "Do they have Catherine? Is she here?" She'd drawn the connection between Lord Granville's odd behavior when she'd asked after his daughter, the presence of the girl's friend in the chamber, and the begging of the fool.

Margret Godwin nodded and burst into terrified sobbing.

30

"What?" Jack Canonbie blinked some more. He stiffened at the girl's reaction.

"Lord Granville has played a rather personal game," said Effie, "though no doubt he is unaware of the grave peril his daughter faces, trapped here by these monsters."

"She never was!" Jonas flinched. He staggered back a step.

"The time," said Freiherr Jörg. "We must go."

"We leave through the Town Below," said Jaelyn.

Freiherr Jörg raised a fist, and the gnomes of the Order of Freiwald formed a column behind her as she marched across the chamber. Their blunderbusses never wavered from their targets. Those of *Les Revenirs* snarled as they passed, and cursed. They crouched, ready to spring. Some eyed their Mother, Cecily McCray, for a sign to let them loose. Others, Tallia.

"Take us to Catherine. We will not leave without her," Effie demanded. But neither Jonas nor Margret Godwin moved.

Tallia laughed. "You see? Our pets desire their place in the natural order."

Jaelyn jerked her head for Effie to follow as her companions disappeared through an archway on the far side of the chamber from whence they'd entered. Effie knew they would not wait. Whatever they'd planned, it had cost them time to rescue her, and they would do no more. She wished she could recognize Catherine Granville's aura and find the girl herself, but she had made no effort to remember it when she had met the girl at Lady Fife's ball.

That left only Margret Godwin, whom Effie had no intention of leaving behind.

She strode toward the girl, Canonbie at her heels. "Come lass, we will see you safe," she said.

"She is mine," said Rat Mask. He stepped in front of the girl and crossed his arms. The girl wilted back. Her sobs came in feeble squeaks.

"Your guests are here of their own accord," snapped Effie. She spun to Cecily McCray. "That is what you argued, is it not?" Turning back to the girl, she offered her hand. "We will see you safe," she said.

A long and heavy silence passed, before Cecily McCray spoke. "Allow them to pass," she said, at last. Her head turned to Jonas as she sank back into her throne. "When they return to us, groveling that we should protect them against the torments of man, then we shall show our displeasure."

Tallia growled. It reeked of a crazed hunger. But she eyed the blunderbuss leveled at her and stood her ground.

Jack Canonbie stalked around Rat Mask and put an arm around Margret Godwin's shoulder. Slowly, he pulled her away. "I am ruined," the girl mumbled into his coat. He whispered something to soothe her, and she leaned her head into his chest.

As they picked their way across the chamber, Effie raised her voice. "If there are any others among you, fey or not, who wish to join us, come now." The fire burned low, casting the room in deep shadows that flickered along the walls. Jonas stood by Cecily McCray's throne, the guardsmen lined before them. Tallia and her companions crept forward, malice clear in their heated stares. But no others stirred.

Effie studied them, trying to remember as many auras as she could. A part of her sickened. For all the hatred and prejudice that stemmed from men like Lord Granville, she had never believed the tales spun of devilish fey who chose to torment when they could befriend. She had seen the cruelty of the Laird of Aonghus and the Piper of Ceann Rois, and the viciousness of wulvers and trows. But their natures bent them apart. It did not come from such willingness to abandon goodwill.

The way beyond the chamber split into a web of passageways and small recesses the size of stable pens. She could tell why Jaelyn knew the archway would lead them to where they sought. All the passageways connected in a beehive of laid stone and chiseled rock.

Only the occasional sconce contained a lamp, and fewer still were lit. The gnomes of the Order of Freiwald struck torches at the head and tail of their column. Their glow allowed Effie to better see the recesses. Most were empty, though some contained a padding of cushions and blankets. They passed a slumbering woman, whose soft snores never faltered as their procession of boots crunched past over the uneven dirt of the floor. Effie spied dark stains in the dirt, and muck, and for once was glad of the scent the lingering haze provided. It masked whatever other smells the passageway contained.

She thought to wake the woman and beg her to follow them out, to save her and not allow Cecily McCray's cult to prey on her flesh any longer. But when she stopped, Jaelyn barked at her to hurry along.

"No," said Effie. "We must gather those we can. I will not have another death on my hands for a lack of trying."

Jaelyn's shoulders heaved. "Other lives are at stake. We save theirs over these who've already made a choice. Come now or stay behind. That is your choice."

Effie could feel Tallia's aura creeping after them. She knew she and Canonbie would not fare well unarmed and outnumbered, and their deaths or capture would do no one any good.

"We will come back with fire and steel," said Canonbie, reading her thoughts. She forced a tight-lipped grin to her face. Shoulders clenched in frustration, she nodded to the brownie.

"Do you know where Catherine is kept?" she asked Margret Godwin, as they set off again.

Margret shook her head. "The cellar, they call it. But I was never taken there." The girl bit back a sob. "They wouldn't let me see her."

Moans of pleasure replaced the woman's snores as Freiherr Jörg led them through a series of turns, first left, then a right, followed by another right. The moans echoed around them for a time before receding. The column of gnomes moved faster now, snaking through the maze of passages, almost at a jog.

Effie hurried behind Jaelyn. She kept her eyes roving over everything they passed, searching for Catherine Granville or anything that resembled a cellar. But the way quickly became empty, rising up a slope and descending a short stair, before dumping them into a long, covered-over street. They had reached the edge of the warren.

"How did you come by us?" she asked Jaelyn, as Freiherr Jörg took them down the street and into another tunnel.

Jaelyn tsked. It sounded like a cricket's chirp, coming through the mask. "Freiherr Jörg came to me as soon as you left him," the brownie replied. "The stink of *Les Revenirs* is well known to us, as is their decay. I knew at once you'd stumble into harm's way when I heard you'd asked after the cult. So I set a member of the Order to watch." She turned her head, and Effie could imagine the smirking expression she wore beneath the mask. "You did not disappoint. We came at once when we heard you'd been taken to the inner chamber."

Effie swallowed and tried not to take offense. "Thank you," she managed to say. "We owe you more than a debt of gratitude. But why are you here in the city? What is it you mean to do?"

The brownie pulled up her mask, flipping the long snout over the back of her head. Her eyes narrowed. "A certain magistrate you know. Elias McPherson. He passes coin from the lords of Parliament to those men who drive hatred against our kind. We will let him know he will no longer fund such acts."

Effie started. Her eyes went wide. Did they mean to attack Elias McPherson with only their small party? "There are not enough of you!" she blurted.

The brownie's lips tugged into her familiar smirk, snaggled teeth poking through. "There are others. We have created a diversion. The timing of it is why we must hurry now. When you reach the open air, you will see it for yourselves."

Freiherr Jörg pointed to a rickety, wooden door. "That way leads to Canongate," he said. "Take it, and do not follow us." He and Jaelyn started to trot away, the gnomes of the Order of Freiwald at their heels.

"Wait!" shouted Effie. Only the brownie stopped and turned. Effie felt her heart tug. She wanted to go with her friend and protect her. She wanted to go with the Order and help strike down the magistrate who funded the Sanctity of Empire League, the man who'd been responsible for so much unrest within his own city.

But all she said was, "Good luck favor you." Jaelyn gave a curt nod and tugged her mask into place. Her dirk gleamed in the torchlight as she scurried to catch up with her companions.

Effie watched them march away before heading for the wooden door. Passing through it felt like another defeat, but they had learned a great deal she reminded herself. Cecily McCray had revealed a plot that might lead to the last of the Sidhe Bhreige, and Effie finally understood the extent of Lord Granville's designs. Either might save the treaty if she could pull loose the threads a little more.

Her resolve turned to steel. Pull she would, indeed. She would yank on them with all her might, even if it cost her everything.

Beyond the door, the way out climbed steadily into an abandoned cellar and from there through a door into a back alleyway attached to a narrow wynd. The bright, cloudless sky blinded them for a minute, and they had to rest and regain their vision before pressing onward.

As Jack Canonbie placed his coat around Margret's shoulders, they heard the crackle of rifle and pistol fire. Cries followed. A large shadow crept over the wynd, turning day into night. Effie stared skyward, and her jaw dropped. An airship drifted overhead. Its shape mimicked a Norse long ship, with a steep prow and a wide, flat bottom. An engine of steel and brass formed its stern. A pair of smokestacks leaned at an angle on either side so that the black smoke they puffed curved around the giant balloon tethered above. The balloon's canvas was a patchwork of gray and white canvas.

Bullets pinged off of its hull. Yet its propeller turned idly, in no rush to outrun the assailants on the ground. The airship dipped low and corrected. As it climbed, thousands of papers were dumped over its gunwales. They scattered and separated in the wind, blowing over Old Town and rustling down among the tenements.

"Come on!" Effie shouted and hurried down the wynd. They reached a short road that connected to another that wound up onto North Bridge. From their new vantage, they could see the airship turn in a lazy circle over New Town, coming around again toward the castle at the heart of the city.

Onlookers crowded the bridge. Their necks strained. Some wore alarm on their faces. Others laughed and traded jests. Whistles could be heard shrilling up the streets, and with them the continued report of gunfire.

Effie grabbed a man by the elbow. "What has happened?" she asked.

"It started near Calton Hill, they say," he said. "Some group of thieves snuck in and what stole that airship. They were armed with grenades and crank-guns but managed not to kill nobody. Ever since, they took turns around the city dropping leaflets." The man chuckled and shook his head. "Leaflets! Never seen anything so strange."

The man's mirth brought a slight smile to Effie's face as well. "But why are they firing at the airship? Surely, they are only causing greater danger."

Jack Canonbie roared in laughter. He'd picked up one of the leaflets that had blown near their feet. He thrust it forward for her to see. "It's your young Jane's tale! Or parts of it, at least, along with other denouncements and accusations."

Effie sucked in a breath and clutched her throat. Snatching the leaflet from Canonbie, her blood hummed in her ears as she scanned its contents. There, in a fine print, was Jane's tale, or rather her Davie's. A variation of it, at least. It extolled the heroics of the Green Lady and her warrior band of fey who saved countless lives at Caldwell House, including that of the royal duke. It went on to tell of bands of fey bringing harmony to the Highlands. A third section called out those lords who preyed on the poorer classes, offering coin in return for fabrications against those who sought only a peaceful treaty.

Lord Granville. Lord Wilshire. The names were struck in bold type.

Effie giggled. She couldn't help herself. Jaelyn had heard Jane's tale at Bonny Law. She had known why Effie sent the girl to Glasgow. The crafty brownie had managed Effie's own plan without her. She knew now why Jaelyn had refused to tell her anything of what transgressed. She would've forced her friend to let her in on it.

A cannon boomed from the castle rampart. The concussion shook the stone bridge and sent its occupants into a flurry. Shrieks and panicked shouts mixed with ribald cheers. A ring of smoke billowed from the castle, its tail giving a clear indication of the gunner's target.

"The fools," said a man near Effie. "They're firing on their own city!"

"Nay," said Canonbie. "A missed shot would land in the Firth of Forth from here. They fire on some poor boatmen."

The airship banked and dipped. A new batch of leaflets fluttered from its deck. As it lowered, the random pistol and rifle fire increased. Tiny puffs of smoke blinked across the city like fireflies. The canon boomed a second time, and the airship shuddered a moment before the resounding thwack reached Effie's ears.

Chunks of wood and steel rained from the hull. The debris landed among the great coal bunkers amid the shouts and cries of coal porters. The airship wobbled and veered over North Bridge. Its engine had caught fire. Flames jetted through the breach in the hull and ran up the ropes that tethered the balloon. Black smoke billowed from its hull.

"Get down!" shouted Canonbie as the airship sank toward them. The warning was not for fear of the dirigible, which cleared their heads by a hundred feet, but for the rifle fire it drew in its passing.

A bullet zipped over Effie's head, and she dropped to her knees. Canonbie hauled Margret down beside her, shielding them as another bullet cracked into the passing hull. A third bullet pinged off the stone of the bridge. It brought a squeal from a woman who huddled against the bridge's parapet.

Effie watched in horror as flames engulfed the airship. They licked across the bottom of the hull, crackling and popping. The wood scorched and burned. Embers drifted in its wake. The smoke brought a sharp tang to the air. She spied several figures scurrying about the deck, their heads visible over the gunwales. They cast ropes over the side and followed after them, sliding down as the airship teetered and slipped hard to port.

At first, Effie thought the airship would crash into South Bridge near the High Street. But as the airship swung over, its tethers failed. The hull separated from the balloon. A collective gasp echoed from those around her. The woman at the parapet wailed.

Effie's leg were already churning. The thieves, whoever they were,

were allies of Jaelyn and the Order of Freiwald. She would not leave them
to their fate, if any could be saved.

"Effie, wait!" shouted Canonbie as the flaming hull crashed into the
base of a tenement building with a rumbling concussion. The balloon
floated free. Now devoid of weight, it rose toward the heavens. The
flames had licked its belly but not taken root.

Glancing over her shoulder, Effie saw Canonbie struggling to keep
pace. His wounds and the exhaustion of his opium daze were exacting
their toll. She didn't slow. The man could defend himself well enough,
even with his body worn.

She drew up her skirts and increased her pace. The wreckage of the
hull had drawn a crowd. Already a bucket brigade had formed to squelch
the flames before they caught the tenement building afire. Charred and
crumpled timbers lay in a smoldering heap there. A debris field of
twisted metal, bits of rope, and coal scattered down the street.

It was not likely any of the thieves survived the crash and fire. But
there had been those who'd escaped by sliding down the ropes. Effie
spied one at the end of the bridge. The figure wore a brown coat with a
high collar, and a pair of bandoliers crisscrossed over the chest. The
helmet it wore was shaped like a hawk's head.

A small handful of onlookers watched as the figure tried to rise only
to be kicked to the ground by a tall, bearded man who snarled as he
lashed out. Effie's gaze hardened as she raced over. Skidding to a halt and
gasping for breath, she had half a heartbeat before Jack Canonbie
streaked past and tackled the bearded man.

31

Both men grunted from the impact. As they toppled to the street, Canonbie bounced over the bearded man's chest and rolled to his knees. The man cursed. Scrambling to his feet, he reached for something at his belt.

Effie didn't let him find what he sought. There were ample fey in the city, and she called on the strength of those nearby, sucking in the power of their blood. Her own hummed from the effort. Energy crackled along her arms, raising the hair and numbing her flesh. Shaping her fingers into cones, tips pressed together, she summoned to mind images of icicles, frigid and jagged. She rammed those images at the bearded man, forcing it into his thoughts.

The icicles pelted him. He flinched and cried out, raising a hand to protect himself. Canonbie gained his feet as two men wearing the armband of the Sanctity of Empire League emerged from the gathered onlookers. One had dark locks and a bent nose, the other a freckled face pinched into a sneer. Bent Nose raised a pistol and pointed it at the figure from the airship.

Effie screamed in warning. She flung her icicles into the thoughts of the two men. Freckles ducked and threw his arms over his head to protect his face, but the man with the pistol barely flinched. His hand stiffened, the tendons there popping into view as he started to pull the trigger.

She redoubled her efforts against him, enlarging the pelting ice. The trigger squeezed, but just before the hammer fell, Effie sensed a calm hand envelope her Fey Craft and guide it. The figure from the airship, she recognized.

The guiding hand warped her image until she no longer imagined mere ice. From a cloudless sky, the icicles grew into a raging tempest. The flurry barraged the end of North Bridge, coming alive beyond a simple image. The figure helped her shape a glamour. Effie followed the skill of the Fey Craft. The cold of it ripped the heat from her body. Ice shards whistled in her ears as they bombarded the street. Sharp barbs whipped about delivering tiny bursts of agony.

Effie's blood pulsed, and the storm's fury pressed into the minds of all around. It scattered the onlookers, who fled with their heads ducked and arms raised, desperate to ward off the violent assault.

Bent Nose's eyes widened. His hand jerked as the pistol fired, its crack hidden by the deafening rush of pinging ice. The bullet whizzed into the distance.

Canonbie sprang forward and smashed his fist into the man's jaw. Bent Nose pin-wheeled his arms to keep his balance as he staggered. The ice beat them both into a hunkered squat. They squinted at one another through the driving cascade.

The pistol trained on Canonbie. Effie's heart froze.

A cane snapped down on bent nose's wrist, shattering bone. The pistol clattered on the stone and skidded away. The hailstorm had hidden the newcomer's footsteps. He wore a ragged coat, and a leather patch covered one eye. A deep, snaking line of a scar ran from brow to ear, beneath the patch. His cane didn't stop. He twirled it around and smashed Bent Nose's face.

"Run!" he shouted, moving to the man's companion. Freckles recovered enough to dance away from this newcomer's reach. But he'd forgotten about Jack Canonbie. He grunted and spilled to the cobblestones as Canonbie's fist drove into his gut.

"Flee, ye cowards!" the man with the eye patch and cane bellowed.

"Harry, they come!" called a voice behind Effie. She whirled to find a slender boy barely old enough for whiskers storming toward her. On his heels were a trio of men sporting armbands. Two held rifles. They'd most likely been drawn to the crash of the airship.

"Behind me, Green Lady," commanded the man called Harry. He raised his cane as he would a saber.

"We cannot stay here," said Effie. She let the hailstorm drop from her thoughts, and it dissolved. That the man recognized her would matter little if they were all shot dead.

Canonbie snatched up the fallen pistol and swung it between the first trio of assailants. The bearded man bolted. Bent Nose and Freckles moaned and squirmed on the cobblestones. A smirk flashed on Canonbie's face before he cursed and nodded to where they'd left Margret Godwin.

The girl was gone.

Effie barked a curse as well. She scanned the bridge in futility. But only Canonbie's coat remained, laying in a heap against the parapet.

"You there!" shouted one of the newcomers. He held a rifle. He and his companion leveled the weapons at the figure in the hawk-shaped helmet.

Effie didn't hesitate any longer. "The Town Below," she barked, and darted for the wynd they'd emerged from only minutes before. The figure jerked a nod and hurried after, something beneath the brown coat clinking with every step.

Canonbie bowled over the bent-nosed man, whose face had swelled red and bloody. He'd started to rise, and the impact hurled him into a somersault. Harry and the boy followed, each flinging curses over their shoulders as they went.

A single shot rang out. The report of the rifle was lower pitched and heavier than that of a pistol. But its bullet made the same pinging sound as it kissed the cobblestones and ricocheted off into the distance.

Effie kept her feet churning. Reaching the wynd, she ducked around the corner and stopped at the building's edge. She peered back at the bridge. Their assailants milled about there, helping their injured brethren. One scanned along the path they had taken, yet none had dared follow them into the shadows. She breathed a sigh of relief that none of them had been zealots who would've pursued them into danger.

The other onlookers returned to the bridge, shaking their heads and staring at the sky. Effie swung her gaze to the wreckage of the airship. A small crowd remained there. Flames no longer licked the smoldering mess, but the stench of it hung in the air. She could sense no fey within thirty feet of the wreckage. Whoever had crashed with the airship had either fled or breathed no more.

"This here's fey royalty, lad," said Harry quietly to the boy. The boy's eyes widened in wonder. The figure in the hawk helmet regarded her with something she thought might be amusement.

Goose pimples rose on Effie's arms. "You do me too great a kindness," she said, turning her attention to the man who'd come to fight beside her and Canonbie. He was older than she'd first thought, but still in the prime of life. Whiskers stubbled his chin. Coal dust and perhaps a week's worth of grime made his coat and trousers smell. Yet she had to fight back the urge to embrace the stranger, all the same.

He put his knuckles to his brow. "Not so, my lady. Ye inspired me. I owe my life to you and the others that came to the duke's aid. I'll not let these bastards soil yer name, nor yer honor, as long as I can stand."

Her gaze flickered to his eye patch and scar, and she thought she understood. "You served at Caldwell House," she said.

"Aye, and survived the day unscathed until one of them trows flung a grenade what blasted in me face."

"I am sorry for your injuries," said Effie. She recalled the great loss suffered that day, yet the man's faith in her brought a warmth to press back the sadness. "In any case, Mr. Canonbie and I must thank you for aiding us today."

"It's never no mind," said Harry. "I am blessed to have served you again. You must know there are those would follow you anywhere. For the courage you showed and lives you saved." He put a hand on the boy's shoulder. "I tell all who'll listen the tales of it, and they tell their mates. They all wish to hear of the beautiful Green Lady and how she tamed giants and slew a demon."

She laughed at that. "I was not alone. We all did those things. Every one of us there that day." Harry's chin raised. He tugged on his coat, shoulders drawn back. A measure of pride shone through, clear as day.

Jack Canonbie cleared his throat softly. "Effie, we must get out of sight for a time," he said.

She nodded. "Yes, and we have matters to attend. Our day is far from finished."

Harry knuckled his brow once more and bowed. They took their parting, the boy still mooning over her in wonder. Her expression probably mimicked something similar, as she watched Harry's retreat. For all the enemies that plagued her, he'd reminded her of the hearts she'd won.

Effie followed Canonbie as he marched them through the door that entered the Town Below. The brown-coated figure followed them silently, the hawk helmet vigilantly scanning their path until they reached the covered-over stretch of street. There, the figure pointed.

"This way," came a light and pleasant female voice. Her other hand pulled off the hawk helmet to reveal long ginger tresses. She'd indicated the direction Jaelyn and the Order of Freiwald had gone earlier. "There is a storeroom where we can rest just a short distance farther."

The Sithling woman smiled. She stood just above Effie's height, and as Effie peered closer, she saw the stout frame of the figure was nothing more than a ruse. A swath of padded cloth beneath the brown coat gave her bulk, hiding the wearer's slender frame. Her eyes sparkled green, and for all their kindness, they held an iron strength behind them.

"I am Ana," she said. Spinning on a heel, she tucked the hawk helmet under her arm and marched them up the enclosed street. "I am a Sky Dancer."

"Your accent sounds French," said Effie as they walked. The stillness and cold air of the Town Below felt strange after the excitement above.

"Yes," said Ana. She led them at a determined pace. Effie noticed after a time a slight limp to her step, but the woman gave no complaint nor mention of fatigue.

"Are you a member of the Order of Freiwald?" asked Effie.

The woman laughed. "No, of course not. But I have—what do you call them—attachments? There are many from the continent who came to aid your Scottish fey after we heard of the treaty negotiations." She stopped and studied Effie. "But none of us wield the power you do. It is the mightiest of weapons."

Effie jerked back, confused. "What?"

Ana tapped Effie's chest, and not too lightly, but she grinned all the same. "The ability to inspire devotion."

Effie swung her gaze to Canonbie, to see if the woman jested with her. But the man didn't laugh, nor did he make some biting jest. He merely planted his hands on his hips and nodded.

"It will be a great victory for all fey, this treaty," said Ana. She started off again, though at a slower pace. "The eyes of Europe watch you closely, or do you think the gnomes of the Order of Freiwald would jeopardize three months of planning to rescue any lost Sithling?"

Effie didn't know what to say to that. She thought of Harry and of Jane's Davie. There had been the boys in Dunfermline, too, and a few other places. Graham had tried to point them out earlier, bless him, but she had doubted the merits of the argument. She had never thought of the encounters together, what they meant as a whole. Her mind started to work at that, and she remained silent for a time.

The storeroom held only dirt and the remnants of a well-used fire pit. A weathered door hung limply on rusted hinges. Ana closed it behind them.

"Have a rest," said Canonbie. "I'll go and find some kindling."

Effie sat, and fatigue suddenly hammered at her. The effort to call on so much fey strength and hold onto the glamour had sapped her as if she'd run rings around the entire city. Besides, she had slept hardly an hour over the past day, and as hard and cold as the dirt floor was, her bones sank into it eagerly.

Her eyes closed of their own accord. She forced herself to blink and take a deep breath. "Catherine," she whispered, trying to focus her thoughts.

* * *

Her eyes snapped awake to the sounds of a crackling fire. Its heat kissed her flesh. Dread filled her instantly. "No," she whispered, trying to stand. She felt Canonbie's warm hand press against her shoulder. The man sat next to her with his legs crossed.

"There will be time," he said. "If Cecily McCray meant to kill the girl, she'd have done so the moment we left. If not, an hour's rest will do us better than storming back into that chamber dead on our feet and unaided."

Effie saw the logic in his words, but it did not appease her. From the small size of the fire and how little the twigs and splinters of wood had burned, she hadn't slept long. Still, the warmth on her cheeks eased the fatigue from her. She glanced around the storeroom and noticed Ana's absence.

"She warmed herself for a minute and left," said Canonbie. "She never said much more, and I didn't ask." He chuckled. His body shook from it. "She clambered over the side of a burning airship in the middle of the city, was attacked by men she didn't know, and fled with us without a question. I didn't want to intrude on her privacy."

Effie smiled. A hundred questions raced through her over how Jane's story had wound up on leaflets dropped by strangers over the city of Edinburgh, but none of them were pressing.

"Catherine Granville is the center of it all," she said. "It is why Lord Granville fixated on *Les Revenirs* above all other foes, enough to draw him away from Glasgow in the middle of the negotiations."

Canonbie scratched his stubble. "But why send you? He commands the Sanctity of Empire League and no doubt scores of trained thugs and thief takers, not to mention Her Majesty's agents."

"Because the promise of something one utterly desires attracts more loyalty than coin. He told me that when we spoke. He seeks to take advantage of my desires and defeat me at the same time. I've been an annoyance to him at Caldwell House and Balclune. Even at Lady Fife's ball I drew attention, demonstrating that not all fey are the wicked creatures he would paint them to be. He wants to defame me, so he plucks me for the task. He cannot risk the honor of his family's name to a mercenary, bought and paid."

Canonbie grunted. "Seems like a gamble, with his daughter's life in the balance."

Effie shook her head. "I've thought on that as well. I do not think she is one of *Les Revenirs'* pets, not in the same way as Margret Godwin. They kept the girls separate, and the way Jonas reacted tipped his hand.

He didn't rage over a threat to his property. He worried for her. He loves her, I think."

She brought her hands before the flames to warm them while considering. "Lord Granville doesn't know of the rift between Tallia and Cecily McCray. He must only know that Jonas, a Sithling man and member of this cult, steals away with his daughter. So he thinks her honor more at risk than her life. He wants her back and the matter kept quiet. If I fail and it becomes known his daughter is with the fool, the lord would blame me publicly for drawing Catherine into the affair."

"And if you succeed, and it became known anyway, he'd do the same," said Canonbie. "Either way, the tarnish against his family name becomes a taint festered by your hand. Aye, it would not take much doing for him to spin that tale."

Effie nodded. "It is why he did not tell me of Catherine at the start. He could not allow me to spread my own tale from afar. My only hope is to rescue Catherine and keep the matter forever silent. That is his trap. He thinks I would do this for some promise, something I desire more than any man desires coin."

"Arrogant bugger, isn't he?" Canonbie chuckled and shook his head.

"It is to our advantage. But there is more. A greater enemy lurks in the shadows." She told him what she thought of the banshee's touch and how it connected to Cyrus Reed. "I'd thought the last of the Sidhe Bhreige hiding, gathering its strength in secret. But what if it's made its presence felt all along? What if this banshee's touch is its doing? The madness of the city, the ease in which violence comes. We must ask ourselves, why did Cyrus Reed act now? Why do those of *Les Revenirs* suddenly thirst for blood?"

Effie bit her lip. "I must send for Rose and Graham. We need them here and do not have the time to go and fetch them. A creeping hand pulls the strings of this madness, and it is not Lord Granville's. A more sinister game is afoot, one plain before our eyes that we have been blind to this entire time."

❈ 32 ❈

E ffie's foot tapped as she sat by the fire. Her patience for sitting
grew thin. She'd found Rose's aura easily enough and used her Fey
Craft to send the woman an urgent series of images, beckoning her to
come in all haste; a fawn running as a forest fire raged around it, closing
in from all sides. It found a cave and waited there until its mother could
lead it to the safety of a tranquil glen.

The woman had sent back something that gave the impression of
relief, followed by a conviction of her own haste—two doves chirping in
happiness before taking wing to dart over rolling hills. Effie followed
Rose's progress. She could sense the woman was not alone. At least five
others travelled with her across the bridges and streets of the city.

"You're like to tap a hole clear through to Hades, you keep that up,"
said Jack Canonbie. He smirked at her. He sat a respectable distance
away in the corner of the storeroom. He rubbed at his arms and she
remembered his abandoned coat.

"Come closer and warm yourself," she said. She patted the dirt next
to her.

Canonbie swallowed. The mirth on his face swelled, bolstered by
something like hunger. He pulled in close, his eyes dancing over her.

"What is it?" she asked. Embarrassment flushed her cheeks. "You've gone quiet."

"I'm thinking about you," he whispered. "How brave you are."

"Oh," she said. Her mind went blank. *He thinks these things now, of all times?*

"Tell me how you came into your roguish employment," she said, avoiding his eyes. Still, she felt the distraction calming her, the deep timbre of his voice removing the worry that spun through her bones. "No," she reconsidered, "tell me of your life before then. Tell me of your family."

The grin increased. He ran a hand lightly along her arm. She felt his warmth pulse against her, and her heart quickened.

"My aunt raised me," he began. "My father and mother had seven children and could not afford so many after the mill in our village closed. Two brothers went to another uncle in the south, the other four with my parents on a ship bound for New Orleans. I receive letters from them, from time to time. They made their way to Chicago, where my father found work in a slaughterhouse. My mother has learned tanning and makes dyes for the vats."

Effie intertwined her fingers into his. She was shocked by the abruptness of his tale, but he spoke without any hint of sadness. If anything, he sounded proud that his family had found success after a time of hardship. It reminded her that to have family, even if separated by vast distances, bettered the isolation she had felt in her youth, the years before she had met Thomas Stevenson and Stuart Graham.

"My aunt was a generous woman and a young widow. She welcomed me as her own and at once set me to the life of a coal porter. The work was honest, but sadly it never took. There was too much excitement in the city for a young boy."

"You must tell me of your adventures," said Effie. Suddenly, she wanted to draw him close and keep pulling until their bodies intertwined. Leaning forward, she nuzzled her head into his chest. He wrapped an arm around her and pulled her tight.

"I will tell you them all, someday," he whispered into her ear. She smiled and closed her eyes. She inhaled him, the coal smoke, opium haze, and the warm musk beneath that reminded her of autumn fields after a sun baked day.

"Do it now," she said. She didn't mean his adventures. She meant his hands. She wanted them to roam her flesh, for his hard shoulders to crush her in, and his lips to find hers.

He understood her perfectly. She shivered, as he trailed his fingers lightly across her back.

"You are not a gentleman," she mumbled, as he used a hand to lift her chin. He pressed his lips to hers, and she pushed into the kiss. Canonbie responded. His touch found her willing, and her own gripped the firmness of his shoulders. He breathed a heavy sigh and shuddered before redoubling his explorations.

Only after some effort did she tear away.

A foot scratched the dirt behind her. "Ahem," Graham's voice rang out. Effie whirled and found him standing in the storeroom doorway. Her face burned and throat tightened in embarrassment. Canonbie barked a laugh and rose to greet the man.

Behind Graham stood Rose Brewer. The sight of her raised eyebrow and knowing smirk made Effie's cheeks burn even hotter. Effie stood and smoothed her skirts as her friends funneled into the storeroom. Her gut lurched, confused by the mix of passion and propriety.

"Hi'ya, Effie," said Abigail Salisbury. The librarian of the university appeared much older than the last time Effie had seen her. Perhaps it was her recent troubles that brought a tiredness to her dark eyes and the sag to her slender shoulders. Black ink stained her finger tips from long years scratching out missives at the university. Her raven hair held streaks of gray. It paired oddly with the freckles on her nose and cheeks.

Effie greeted her warmly and introduced her to Jack Canonbie. She was grateful Rose had found a way to rescue the woman from the castle, though Effie stopped short of asking any details. Their urgency suppressed her abundant curiosity, at least for the time being.

The same stood true for Jane Porter's tale. The girl trailed Abigail into the room with a short man and a bony lass at her heels. Both were about fifteen, Effie guessed. Jane had traded her soiled white gown for a clean, simple one of light blue, but Effie noted a patch sewn over one breast, a sprig of mistletoe done in white cloth.

Jane quickly explained she and her companions had come from Glasgow after Effie telegrammed Thomas Stevenson. They'd already been handing out their leaflet there on the streets. Stevenson had funded the endeavor.

"So you see," said Jane. "Mr. Stevenson told us of your note, but he couldn't come himself." She clasped her hands in front of her and studied Effie's chin. "We thought to come in his stead. You needed help, and we had three of us."

"But how did Jaelyn's allies get ahold of it?" Effie asked. She couldn't help herself. "And how did you become three?"

To the first question, Jane could only shrug. But to the second, she turned and waved forward the lass. The girl's brown hair fell straight to her waist, but she'd pulled it into an orderly tail at the nape of her neck. She barely filled the skirt and blouse she wore, and she stepped forward with the hesitancy of a field mouse entering a roost of falcons.

"Maggie comes from York," said Jane. "Her mum works in the parsonage there. She found Edgar and me passing out our leaflets in Glasgow. She'd come north to find work as a scullery maid."

"I am Edgar Talmadge." The short man stepped forward and bowed. "I hail from Greenock, from a clan of fishermen. But Jane won me through with her tales of heroic fey. I've come to serve you and her, on my honor." He bowed again and smiled at them both. His cheery cheeks looked like they had never heard of whiskers.

Canonbie snorted. "So a cult of wee scroungers, is it?"

"Wheesht," hissed Effie, though she had to hide her own amusement. She greeted Jane and her companions kindly, if not in a hurried manner. She assumed the milk had spilled, and they already knew enough about her to make no never mind over what they discussed next.

"It is too important to stay ourselves, despite the risk," she said after relating what had happened to her and Canonbie, and what they had learned. "It is connected, the madness of Cyrus Reed, the bloodlust of *Les Revenirs*, this banshee's touch plaguing the land. The last of the Sidhe Bhreige plays a game with us. I've grown ever more certain of this." She leveled her gaze at Rose and Graham. "We have not found another whiff of this creature. Not us. Not Conall Murray. Not the queen's regiments.

We must uncover what secrets we can from Cecily McCray, and we'd best hurry."

"Tallia," said Canonbie as a way of explanation. "A murdering wench with godly aspirations."

Effie drew her shoulders back. "The banshee's touch has driven her madder than her brethren. She will break with Cecily McCray and soon. We must save Catherine Granville and the others before they are slaughtered."

"And if they won't come?" asked Graham. "You say many were enthralled, either by opium or this taint of the mind."

"We will save those we can," said Rose. She nodded to Effie, offering encouragement.

"We must fetch the constables," squeaked young Maggie.

"No." Edgar spoke before Effie could, though he echoed her thoughts. "They are commanded to see nothing but a fey enemy to round up and hand over to the magistrate. Even the good men among them cannot offer the aid we require."

"The lad is right," said Canonbie. "A different strategy is needed."

Edgar drew himself up. "We are ever ready and willing to aid you."

Graham smirked. "Easy there laddie," he said, patting Edgar on the shoulder. "Clubbing a man is far different than a fish flopping on a boat deck." He raised an eyebrow and met Effie's eye. "You know the dangers better than us. How do you mean to free Granville's lass without any great harm?"

"The Order of Freiwald?" offered Jane.

"Aye," agreed Edgar. His cheeks had flushed at Graham's words. "Hit the lair fast and overwhelm them."

Rose shook her head. "They fled the city. The magistrate, Elias McPherson, has put a bounty on their heads. Many desiring his coin search for them."

"Even if I could beg such a favor, that way would lead to a violent skirmish with too high a risk," said Effie. "We need to secure Catherine and learn what we can first."

"There are many passageways in and out of the warren," said Abigail. "I know them all. If Catherine Granville is in this cellar, we can rescue her before confronting Cecily McCray."

Canonbie crossed his meaty arms and grimaced. "What happens when the alarm is raised? Do you think they'll let you wander about poking under every blanket?"

"No," said Graham. He eyed the fire, considering. "We'll need a distraction. Good for us, I might have one or two with me." He patted the pocket of his coat.

Effie bit her lip. "But my aura. They'll know as soon as I approach." She gestured at Rose and Abigail. "As soon as any of us approach. Most likely, they can sense us now, here as we stand."

"We can handle that," said Rose. She nodded at Abigail. "We have that skill, and we old bats aren't meant for skulking around tunnels. An obscuring veil is what little aid we can offer, though it'll cost us some strain. Masking auras is challenging work for a host, much less for the two of us. And keeping track of you on the move, to boot. But they'll never sense you've come. Ye can trust in that."

Effie grinned. "You really must teach me these tricks of yours."

"In time, lass, in time." Rose winked. "Ye just need to keep your foot out of the fire a moment so you can learn."

Canonbie chuckled. "Och, a fight it is, then. Give me some coin, and I'll roust a few strong arms from the docks," he said. "We can come in the front and cause some mischief, while you come in the back way and grab the Granville lass. Once she's safe, we'll meet in the chamber and have a word with Mistress McCray."

"I'll go with you," said Edgar. "I grew up on the docks."

"Not these kind," said Canonbie. He shook his head. "No, for these sort of men it's best if I go alone."

Effie fought back the urge to object. She'd thought to have Canonbie's strength at her side. But the fewer number they had sneaking through the passageways, the better chance they had at remaining unnoticed. And the man was right. He excelled at vexing people and causing a disturbance. His place should be to create the distraction. If he came in the front like a roaring bear, it might well give Graham and her the time they needed. She nodded to Canonbie, and his lips pulled into a toothy grin. She caught herself wishing to taste those lips again and had to shake herself free.

"Then may I join you and Mr. Graham, Miss Effie?" Edgar asked.

"Yes, what of us?" asked Jane. "You must let us help." She had a pleading look to her eye. Edgar leaned forward, equally as eager. Maggie pressed her lips together. Her shoulders rose slightly.

Effie thought for a moment as an idea took root. A smile blossomed on her lips. To win a game of chess, one needed to plan a few steps ahead, and too often lately she had ignored that fact. "You'll have the most important job of all," she told them. "The fate of the treaty will depend on it."

※ 33 ※

Effie and Graham stole through the Town Below. Due to the veil that obscured her aura from detection, each step felt like she marched through a thin layer of jam. She carried Graham's cane. He, a worn, wooden lantern. He'd affixed a leather flap to its front and allowed only a slim beam of silvery light to spill onto the ground before them. They'd given Jack Canonbie a half-hour start on them. The minutes had worn at Effie's nerve until Rose had instructed her to sit so they could go over more of glamours. Effie had thanked her for the distraction, and again when she'd finally managed a fiery blossom the size of an egg that sizzled and warmed her face.

She could use that warmth now. The cold of the passageways at night bit at Effie's flesh. She shivered, yet the palm she held the cane in grew moist. "It's just like a shillelagh," she whispered, trying to bring herself comfort.

Graham eyed her. "Conall Murray should know of this," he said. "He can bring Lieutenant Walford's men into it."

"He will, but there is no time for it now. He is off at Fort William." Effie shifted her grip on the cane.

"Aye, and is that the only reason you do not run to tell him?" He shook his head and raised a hand. "Och, never mind. That was clumsy of me, and you're right. Now's not the time."

She pressed her lips into a tight smile but said nothing. She knew Graham didn't believe her petty enough to risk lives over her rift with Conall. He liked the man and thought him well matched for her. His words had come solely from a desire to protect her and see her happy. *He's just as anxious and afraid as I am*, she reminded herself.

When they reached the edge of Cecily McCray's warren, she used her fey senses to seek out Rose and Abigail. They remained in the storeroom and returned her sending with a brief flash of their own—her tawny owl, Gwendoline, taking wing over a forest. She still felt the obscuring veil they raised, and she nodded to Graham that she was ready.

He crouched, producing a couple of tiny paper packets from his coat pocket. "These will burn a bit fiercer than at Balaclune," he said. He tossed the packets into the lantern's flame and closed the flap. She heard the chemicals begin to sizzle.

"Do you think they've remained, even after your intrusion this morning?" he asked, when he straightened.

"Yes," said Effie. "They would've heard of the airship and events of the afternoon. Now is not the time for so large a group as theirs to slink around the city. But more so, the way Tallia challenged Cecily McCray's authority, I believe admitting a need to fear us would ruin whatever hold she still maintains."

"That we should use to our advantage," said Graham.

"Let's see if we can," said Effie. Wiping her palms dry, she clutched the cane with both hands so she could swing it in the narrow passageway. Her heart thumped faster, and she forced herself to take long, deep breaths to settle her nerve. It took all her concentration to avoid scratching her boots on the dirt floor.

The passageway forked almost immediately. Parts of the walls were cut stone and old layered brick. The remainder had been carved out of the volcanic rock that formed Edinburgh's central hill. At a second fork, they found a pocket of recesses in the walls, similar to those she'd seen before. Candlelight flickered in one of them. Soft and rhythmic breathing sounded from it.

Effie stalked closer, testing with each step that the occupant did not stir. When she reached the section of stone wall that divided the recess from the one next to it, she gestured for Graham to cover his light. Once he did, she peered around the dividing wall and found a pair of eyes staring at her. The reflection of the candlelight made them sparkle gold.

Their intensity made Effie start. She almost ducked away but managed to keep her wits. The eyes belonged to the woman she'd seen before as she'd retreated from the main chamber. Her hair was a rat's nest, and her face filthy. Spots covered her nose and chin. Thin red streaks, evidence of sharp blades, ran over her neck and shoulders.

One side of her lip raised, though her eyes remained stark. "She said you'd come." The woman tittered at the pronouncement.

Fear clutched Effie's spine, swallowing it in an icy grip. "Tell me where the others are, and we will lead you from the Town Below. You will be safe."

The woman's tittering redoubled. "I know the secret," she uttered, trilling the words up and down as if it were a song. She swayed as she spoke. "Lean in, and I'll tell it to you."

Effie's breath caught for half a beat. The woman read her hesitation and lunged, hands outstretched. Her long nails had crusted blood and muck wedged beneath them. Effie smelled something of a privy as well. She dove aside and flicked up her cane.

The woman's swipe raked her skirts. Graham leaped forward and hissed the single word they'd prepared. "Shield!"

Effie snapped her eyes closed at once and raised an arm to cover her face. Even with those protections, the searing silver light that lit up the recess illuminated the veins on the back of her eyelids. To the woman, it caused a shock of pain that sent her shrieking.

The woman scrambled away. Effie heard the sounds of it. As soon as the burst of light vanished, she reopened her eyes. Spots danced in her vision, but she knew the poor woman suffered far worse.

"What do we do with her?" asked Graham. He stood back with his hand on the leather flap, ready to let loose another blast of light. He'd come up with the idea in the storeroom, a non-lethal way to subdue anyone they encountered in the dark passageways.

The shriek the woman let out took the decision away from Effie. She would've left the woman to her own will, but she couldn't allow their presence to be uncovered so quickly. If she'd learned anything over the past fortnight, it was that serving the greater good was not as simple as right or wrong. Stepping forward, she cracked the wailing woman across the temple.

"Forgive me," she said, as the woman slumped and fell silent.

Effie lowered her hands as guilt rolled over her. Graham pulled her into his chest and patted her shoulder. "It is not for us to save everyone," he said. "Let us do what we can for those who want it." His words did not make what she had done right, but his warmth and caring brought from her a small nod.

Hearty laughter sounded from the direction they'd come. Effie whirled and spotted the familiar mask of a rat. The man waved a tall candle at them.

"Hurry," he boomed. "Before every drop of blood is spilt."

Effie's gaze narrowed.

"Don't," Graham barked, but she could not hold herself back. She sprang toward the foul man, legs churning, boots pounding across the dirt. She would not let him escape. She would not let him harm another.

Rat Mask waited until she had almost reached him before dashing away, down the passageway and through a series of turns and forks. Effie charged after, trying desperately to keep track of the path he took, until she rounded a corner and smacked into the chest of a rotund man who staggered back and belched at her sudden appearance.

She yelped and leaped aside, scraping her arms against the stone wall. Graham's boots thundered to a halt behind her.

The rotund man licked his gums. His head tottered on his neck as he asked, "Have you seen my pocket watch? It were a good device. I had it from the continent and all." He slurred his words. A blast of stale beer enveloped her as his breath reached her.

Effie shook her head.

"Look," said Graham. He indicated with a flick of his head. The passageway beyond the rotund man widened on one side, large enough for a table and chairs. Two men and a woman sat there drinking and playing at cards. The fourth chair was pulled away and turned out, and Effie guessed its recent occupant stood before her. A candelabra sat in the middle of the table. Its light allowed Effie to see the haggard appearance of those around it, the way the opium daze transfixed them. She could also spy the web of cuts on their flesh.

One of the men set his mug down with a deliberate thunk. He eyed Graham and Effie like a cutpurse might, judging the ease at which he might have his way.

"There are other passageways we passed," said Graham.

"They now know we are here," said Effie. She weighed the danger. "There are more of their victims ahead, and less behind."

"Too many. If we stop for every one of them, we'll only mire ourselves in a bog."

Effie nodded reluctantly. "We must find Catherine first."

"Aye," said Graham. He pressed forward, placing himself between those at the table and Effie, as they passed. He kept both hands ready to flash a burst of light, but the drinkers remained in their seats and returned to their game without a word.

The passageway on the far side snaked around a long curve before dumping them into another wider stretch. Here, mounds of moldy straw held a pair of slumbering forms. A pool of vomit smelled fresh near one of them. The other snored loud enough to wake the dead. Effie crept between the forms, noting each one's face. Graham glanced over his shoulder with every fifth step. His chest expanded and collapsed in a steady and deep rhythm.

The passageway narrowed again, bending hard to the left before running straight for the length of a church's nave. Light flooded the end of the stretch. Effie recognized the candle Rat Mask had held. It sat on the floor casting a flickering halo.

The body of a young woman lay next to the candle. Effie's heart sank as she took in the delicate arm protruding from the sleeve of a fine dress. The arm bent at an awkward angle. Blood smeared cloth and flesh, and pooled in the dark ringlets atop the girl's head.

"Catherine," she whispered.

34

E ffie approached the girl's body. Dried blood matted the hair that covered most of the face. Effie brushed it aside and found the girl's lifeless eyes. Guilt tormented her instantly for the relief that flooded through her. It wasn't Catherine but another young lass meant to look like her. Someone had driven a knife between her breasts. A score of deeper cuts displayed greater atrocity.

"Bah, ye can't blame yourself," said Graham.

"It's not her," said Effie. "It's not Catherine Granville." *Just another I could not save*. She didn't think she could manage those final words aloud.

"We drank a part of her before she soured too much." Tallia's voice drifted through a narrow defile at the corner of the passageway's end. It echoed around corners and down passageways. How far away it truly was, was hard to tell. A taunting chortle came after. Effie felt Tallia's aura reveal itself, the night bird circling its prey. "We'll do the same to your other friends. The rich girl and her lover. You can watch, but we won't let you join. The prize our true Mother offers is for us alone."

"Show yourself," Graham demanded. He raised the lantern before him as if it were a pistol.

"Come and find us," answered Tallia. Her voice purred coyly. "And hurry. I am ever so hungry."

A woman screamed. Its terror echoed through the defile and down the passageway, only to be cutoff abruptly. The silence that followed hung in the air like a thick mist that froze Effie's bones.

Graham touched her arm. "We can't be sure that was Catherine."

Effie gave a slow nod. Her gaze returned to the girl's body at their feet. "Does it matter?"

"No." His voice had turned to steel. "But it will come to more than parlay, playing that one's game. She means to kill us, and we'd best be ready to do what needs be done in return."

Do what needs be done. His words echoed within her. After Caldwell House, she had hoped and dreamed. Hoped that others would create a fey treaty that would cement an everlasting peace, and dreamed of an empire that thrived because of it. Nowhere within either had she considered that her hand would have to turn against another fey. Nowhere within either had she considered she might have to kill again.

Had she been so naïve? Or had a part of her known all along, hiding from her as a shadow on a starless night? But she would not budge from her hope and her dream. They were honest and pure. Her hands gripped tight about the cane. The cost would have to be paid.

Silently, she counted the minutes since they'd entered the warren. Jack Canonbie should have created his distraction in the main chamber by now. That part of the cost she already paid. She had hired human thugs to assault a fey host, and she had done so as easily as any of the lords in London. *Because it had to be done.*

"Give me the lantern," she said to Graham. "You swing harder than I do."

The lantern felt heavy in her hands compared to the cane, but she could manage it with one arm if needed. She peeked inside and saw that only half of Graham's fuel compound remained; potassium nitrate mixed with charcoal dust.

"We have a quarter of an hour at most," said Graham.

Effie nodded. She squeezed her eyes shut for a moment, until the residue of the silver light faded. The backs of her fingers tingled. Her knees threatened to lock in place. But she would not let a fiend like Tallia defeat everything she strived for.

Forcing herself into a crouch, she stalked toward the defile. Graham snatched the candle from near the girl's body and raised it before them. Its light revealed a small section of rock hewn out of the wall leading into another passageway beyond.

Graham shrugged through first, his shoulders scraping against the rough stone. Effie followed. The way for her was easier. She barely touched the walls. The passageway opened in both directions. One way ran straight for a short distance before curving. The other descended a couple of feet and made a sharp turn. The air had warmed slightly, and Effie caught a whiff of the putrid tang they'd smelled in the main chamber. They were close to it.

She sensed Tallia's aura and led Graham down and toward the sharp turn. A pillar formed the corner of the turn, the foundation of some structure above, or perhaps of one long forgotten. She leaned against the stone and ducked her head around it.

An open chamber as large as a village kirk spread in a roughly oblong shape. Dozens of candles burned atop a pair of boulders that sat in the middle of the floor, about an arm's span apart. Dark splotches along the walls revealed several alcoves too deep to see within. A larger opening exited the chamber on its far side.

Tallia stood facing Effie at the rear of the room. She held a knife to the trembling form of Catherine Granville. They'd shorn off part of the girl's raven locks, leaving limp strands to pepper her scalp. Her cheeks still held the nourished complexion of the privileged, but her eyes and shoulders sagged from the terror coursing through her. Her hands were bound, her dress torn in several places and stained in shades of filth.

"We have taken the fool's pet." Tallia sneered as she spoke, running the knife blade along Catherine's neck. "He is weak and does not deserve such a prize."

"Nnn...no." Catherine whimpered.

Effie stepped fully into the chamber. Her boot met with something soft, and she risked a glance at the pool of wine spilled from an overturned cup. Goblets, tankards, blankets, and other implements of mirth rested along the walls or lay scattered across the dirt. Abandoned in haste, Effie surmised. She saw a violin near one alcove and a dice cup near another.

The chamber was meant for merriment, an antechamber for the

heart of the warren, where the cult could indulge without the watchful eye of their Mother. That Tallia had led them to the chamber confirmed Effie's notions about the failing grip Cecily McCray held over *Les Revenirs*. The jackal acted without her Mother's blessings, no doubt.

She and the fiends who followed her.

Glaring at Tallia, Effie guessed at the trap the woman would spring. Tallia had never kept her mouth closed for more time than it took a sheep to soil a field. Her silence now alerted Effie to the danger lurking in the darkened alcoves.

They masked their auras and waited for her and Graham to come closer.

"The alcoves," Effie warned. She strode forward. If Tallia ran, they would find who was quicker. If a horde rushed from the alcoves, she held an answer for that as well.

Graham stepped clear of her reach but remained a pace behind. She heard him stoop to pick something up from the floor, a rustling of his coat and scratch of the dirt.

They had reached the first boulder when the auras of those lying in wait popped into her senses.

"Shield!" Effie yelled. But she didn't need to. Graham had already ducked his head away and covered his eyes. Effie squeezed hers until it hurt, before flipping open the lantern's leather flap.

Silver light flared before her. Sudden against the dim flicker of candlelight, it might've been the sun. Effie kicked at the candles standing tall on the boulder and sent several spinning across the floor. The buffet of wind extinguished them before they struck the dirt. She kicked again and stamped until she could find none of the candles upright.

A husky cry rang out beside her. Effie chanced a peek and saw Graham rushing forth, swinging his cane at the candles on the second boulder.

The silver beam bursting from the lantern became the only light in the chamber, and a surge of inspiration reached her. She slammed down the flap, sending the chamber into darkness. She waited only a heartbeat before flipping it up again and snapping it down once more. The beam flickered in a rapid cycle, as she kept the flap moving.

The effect was blinding. Even with her eyes squinted, the silver beam burned into her vision. Removing it left only smeared shadows before it came to blind her again.

"Slay them!" Tallia screamed. Effie could make out the woman's arms flailing.

A blur of dark shapes streaked from the alcoves. The light flared against the fiends too fast for Effie to clearly define any of them. But she didn't need to. They emerged with their arms raised against the pulsing light. The fearsome masks they wore, for all their horns and fangs, did nothing to protect their eyes. They shied back, staggering about under the assault, the thunder of their charge stolen.

Effie used their hesitation to dash toward Catherine Granville. The girl had jerked from Tallia's grip as the blinking light flooded the chamber. She'd turned away and put her bound hands to her face, bent at the waist.

Tallia reclaimed her wits. She spun around and stumbled, searching to reclaim her purchase on the girl. Snatching part of Catherine's shirt, she yanked the girl upright just as Graham reached the pair. He ducked and swung low, lashing out at Tallia's knees. The Sithling woman leaped back. She swiped with her dagger and drove Graham away.

Effie darted in and thrust the lantern before her like a spear. As she did, something whistled toward her and smacked against its wooden frame. A rock, by the clack it made. She yelped and lost her grip but managed to snare the lantern before it tumbled to the dirt.

"Take Catherine," shouted Graham. He swung the cane wildly to keep Tallia's blade away from them. "Run!"

But Tallia's grip was iron. As she swiped and thrusted, she tugged the girl along with her. Graham could do little but dance away from the attack, and Effie even less. Catherine Granville fell to her knees. She raked her nails against her captor, but she had not the strength anymore. Her struggles might've been a child trying to cling to its mother's skirts for all the good it did.

A watch ticked in Effie's mind. She could feel the seconds draining away, not only until the burning compound was spent, but until the shapes streaking from the alcoves reached them. Another rock sailed past her. It scratched her cheek and clattered off the wall.

They were outnumbered and could not win the fight. They needed to fell Tallia. And they needed Jack Canonbie to win them free.

Effie could see no other way. The trick of a fey glamour would only buy her a moment of reprieve, if it worked at all. Pulling back the lantern's flap, she flung what remained of the fiery compound into Tallia's face. The Sithling woman realized too late what Effie had done. She shrieked in agony as the chemicals splattered over her. Her flesh sizzled. Her hands clawed at her cheeks and came away smoldering and bloody.

Graham cracked her on the temple and ended her screams.

Searing pain raced along Effie's wrist and fingers. The chemicals had sloshed onto her flesh as she flung them. But she had no time for it. Whirling, she hurled the spent lantern at the closest of Tallia's horde. It smashed against the snarling face of a wolf. The fellow wearing the mask yelped and jarred back a step.

"Into the main chamber," Effie yelled. Canonbie awaited them there, if all came to plan. She had to trust in that. It was the only hope they had. Snatching Tallia's dagger, she shoved Catherine Granville before her. The sting at her wrist brought tears to her eyes, but the footfalls at her heels drove her like a leaf hurled by a windstorm.

Catherine stumbled toward the opening at the rear of the chamber. She whimpered, and Effie hoped the girl had recognized her, or at least had the wits to realize she and Graham meant her no harm.

"I'll hold them back," said Graham. He put his back to the opening, brandishing the cane.

"No!" cried Effie. He would not last for long. The chamber was too large, their pursuers too many. Sacrificing himself would do little good. "We flee together!"

Graham slashed twice with the cane at a dark form that prowled his flank. The beady eyes of a rat mask reflected off the chamber's dim light —the same that had taunted them in the passageway earlier. Another masked figure stalked head-on, this one a lion, and Graham jabbed at him before hurrying to the opening and Effie's side.

Together they dashed down the passageway that led out of the chamber. Catherine Granville found her legs and raced with them. Her squeaks of exertion echoed against the pounding of their feet. Graham slowed several times to hack at the beasts that raged after them. Effie could barely see those that hounded their heels. But their howls and curses rang in her ears as if uttered only a hand's-breadth away.

The opium haze grew stronger, and Effie followed her nose. She snaked them around a quick turn and through a narrow defile that emptied into a forked section of tunnels. She recognized the intersection. The main chamber lay beyond. The light stemming from it was warm and subtle, yet it dazed her vision all the same.

Effie's heart thumped. Her lungs ached. The salt from her sweat seared her burned flesh. A sense of panic rose in her, but she didn't slow. She leaped into the main chamber, Tallia's dagger raised before her.

But her snarl turned into a whimper at the sight that greeted her. Confusion set in. Jack Canonbie had come, as he'd promised he would. He'd brought a dozen men with him. They stood by his side with their pistols and cudgels raised. They'd taken their armbands off and tied the white cloth to cover their mouths, protecting them from the opium smoke.

Each cloth displayed the sigil of a golden crown.

Graham halted at her side and growled. "Och, ye bastard."

"Jack," whispered Effie, reeling as understanding dawned. She crumpled to her knees. Jack Canonbie had come all right, and he had betrayed her.

35

Effie blinked, unable to make sense of the deception. Her gut seized and hardened into stone. Canonbie tried to flash a grin, but it fell from his face the moment his eyes locked on her. He could not meet her gaze.

"Are you one of them?" she demanded. "Have you always been?"

Canonbie flinched. "I... No..." He had no time to say anything more. Those of *Les Revenirs* flooded into the chamber, boots skidding to a halt when they saw what awaited them. A heavy silence fell. The eyes of the men of the Sanctity of Empire League widened as they took in the fangs and horns and snouts of *Les Revenirs'* masks. More than one stepped back and glanced at his companions, at anything but the wicked host that had stormed into the chamber.

The wolf-masked man howled and thumped his chest. In the dim firelight, he could've passed for a wulver grown to monstrous size. His brethren took up the call, snarling and yapping behind their masks as they ducked into low crouches and stalked forth.

Graham dove into Catherine, driving the girl into a mound of pillows as the league men jarred from their stupor. Their pistols cracked. Bullets whizzed past Effie's head to ping off stone and thwack into flesh. She jerked at the sounds. Swiveling her gaze, she spied the bodies of Cecily

McCray's guards, three of them lying in heaps by the entrance the intruders must've used. Two of the league men were bloodied as well. But they held control of the chamber.

Jonas stood near the makeshift throne. He shielded his Mother against Canonbie and a trio of the league, lashing out with a cane. A terrible cry came from his lips when he saw Catherine, and his slashes became more furious. He tried to press toward her but was beaten back.

The chamber had been otherwise empty. Tallia had stolen from their Mother the remainder of the host, leaving her undefended. That was until Effie and Graham had led the host into the fray. Not all had followed, but more than a dozen spilled into the chamber. A few were fey, the rest their human pets. It mattered not a whiff to the league men. Their pistols barked and cracked like yapping hounds. Those with cudgels surged forward.

The assault threw Tallia's cohorts onto their heels, but the fey among them would not bend so easily. The boom of a cannon rattled the chamber. Dazzling bursts of starlight rained down over the league men, and a fissure opened in the floor, a gaping maw plunging into a black abyss. It made a couple of the league men leap back before they realized the trick.

The glamours impressed Effie. But they were not coordinated the way the Order of Freiwald had managed. They only served to confuse the league men in pockets. One league man with a cudgel brought it down on the man Tallia had suckled from earlier. Bone crunched, and the man's arm fell limp. A second blow cracked the man's temple. The bear mask he wore did little to protect the skull, or the tissue it contained.

A grunt sounded behind Effie, and a knife whirled through the air. It smacked into one of the league men who'd stopped to reload his pistol. Thunks and thwaps overtook the barks of pistol fire as bullets were spent. Cries rang out. Steel flashed, catching firelight in a glittering dance across the chamber.

Boots staggered around Effie as she found her feet and slunk forward. The stench of opium swirled with that of spent gunpowder. Graham and Catherine choked on the haze. His dive had brought them near the central fire pit. Its flames had almost gone out, but tendrils of the thick smoke still wafted from the embers. Patting his pockets, he yanked out a handkerchief and pressed it to Catherine's face.

"Bloody bastard!" Graham snarled at Jack Canonbie as Effie reached him. The large rogue whipped and slashed his cane at Jonas. If he heard Graham's curse, he gave no reaction.

"It doesn't matter." Effie forced the words from her lips. The man's betrayal had brought them an opportunity to escape. She would let her fury rage about it later. "We need to get Catherine from here."

"The ways are blocked," said Graham. Effie glanced. The league men held one side of the chamber, and those of *Les Revenirs* the other. Some had already fled, and the ticking watch in Effie's mind came again. The league men would soon win out, and if she and Graham and Catherine weren't killed outright, they would surely be thrown in irons.

Her gaze darted about the chamber. They could risk one of the other exits, but they had no way of knowing where it would lead. Any of them might end abruptly at a stone wall and trap them. She hadn't seen any of the *Les Revenirs* choose the other ways, and they knew the warren better than she.

"A pair of gates bar a passageway behind the throne," said Catherine Granville. The girl hacked into the handkerchief, shoulders shuddering. But she'd recovered her wits and stared at Effie with desperate eyes. "Jonas has the key. The cellar, they call it. It is where Mother allowed us to...to stay."

For your protection. The girl had not seen the danger she was in, Effie realized. Her feelings for the fool had clouded all judgment.

Jonas bellowed as Canonbie's cane cracked him on the shoulder. His own cane spun away to clatter against the wall. Effie lumbered forward, calling on Fey Craft. Her mind shaped the glamour without thought, and a pair of trows popped into existence on either side of Jack Canonbie. Their piglet forms and large, floppy ears, clutched mirrors of the dagger she held. They hopped and snapped their teeth, drawing his attention.

He started and swiped, but no sooner had the trows come, than Effie felt her fey senses ripped away. Something blocked her power, as it had the night of the mob. Canonbie's cane whiffed through open air. He stumbled and growled, eyes darting about.

Jonas regained his feet and pressed back against Cecily McCray. His gaze found Catherine, and he yelled for her to run to him. Mother had her eyes closed. She was lost in a trance, a sadness hanging heavily on her slumped shoulders and downturned face. But the shield blocking Effie from her fey senses hadn't come from her.

A foul cackle echoed throughout the chamber. It raised the hairs on Effie's neck. She turned and stared at Tallia. The flesh of the Sithling woman's face had blackened in patches and come apart. Rivulets of blood streaked down her cheek, a vile echo of the gashes she had given her pets.

"Oak Seer." Tallia snarled. "Your meddling ends."

Thrusting her arms at Effie, her hands dissolved into a slithering mass of withered roots that sprang across the chamber. Offshoots sprouted as the roots enlarged, entangling all they touched. Mold and ichor coated their surface. They stank of bloated corpses left to rot in a putrid bog.

The league men fired into the mass. They hacked with cudgels and knives. Effie saw one open his mouth to scream, and the roots shot down the man's throat, choking him until he fell lifeless to the ground. His belief in the glamour allowed it to steal his breath. Those of *Les Revenirs*, the humans among them, fared no better. Roots tore into crusted over wounds and wrapped around ankles. They pulled and constricted. They rubbed until the flesh bled.

Effie slashed with the dagger, as she hurled her will against the shield Tallia raised. The taint of decay filled her nostrils and mouth. She felt Tallia's glamour surging, the power of it distant and unreachable. She growled, shivering from her exertion. Even knowing the roots weren't real did little to stop their assault.

Graham slashed his cane against the fetid things, but already he gasped. His cheeks glowed red, and sweat poured down his face. A root lashed out and buckled his knee. He crumpled, roaring as the mass ensnared him.

"No!" Effie yelled, gritting her teeth. She had to save him. Her head snapped to where Cecily McCray sat on her throne. "Is this the rebirth you speak of? The old ways? It is only death!"

Tallia's cruel laughter came again.

"You are right, child," Cecily McCray's voice rasped from the alcove. "It is not the way I sought. But it is too late for me. Too late."

Effie could no longer see the woman. The roots were too thick, the chamber too dark. Roots entwined her calves. She tried to cut them, but they snapped at her hands and crept up her thighs. She couldn't move. She could barely hold her balance, and when she fell, there would be no one left to save them.

"Resist the hand that grasps your mind and warps your thoughts," Cecily McCray's voice came again. "Resist it, or all you love will die."

"Silence!" screeched Tallia. "Doddering fool! I have taken everything from you. I am the apostle! The chosen one our true Mother speaks of! She will see me live in glory, as all bow down to her will!"

"No!" Effie shouted again. "The fey will have peace!"

"A dream. A lost dream." Cecily McCray's voice drifted off. A whine escaped Effie's lips. Her thoughts could only dwell on the way the roots constricted, so much like that of a noose. Her knees shook. Her arms could no longer move.

She had lost sight of Graham, and the pain of it hammered at her heart.

"Mother." The whimpered word came from Catherine Granville. She had lain near Graham, the last Effie had seen.

Effie ripped and battered at the shield. She clung to the hope that Rose and Abigail might sense her peril, that they might offer some answer she could not fathom. Sweat flooded her brow. Her head pounded from the strain. She grew dizzy, the shapes around her dimming and closing into darkness.

"Child." A strength returned to Cecily McCray's voice. Effie felt the unspoken bond that passed between the woman and Catherine, and suddenly the filmy impression of her obscured aura vanished. The shock of being dunked in a frozen pond ripped along her bones. Unseen tendrils followed, delving beneath her flesh and wrapping around her in a light caress. Effie grinned at the sensations. She knew what they meant. Cecily McCray offered her a clue. Effie had felt the ice and tendrils before, when Jaelyn had linked with her during the Battle of Caldwell House.

The linking of auras. The shared blood of the fey, from which sprang all of their Fey Craft. The shield had something to do with that. She stopped her struggling and allowed the tendrils to guide her. She could feel the hatred pulsing from Tallia and grasped on to it. As if pulling herself up a long rope, she inched her way toward her awareness of the woman.

Delicate and slow, she crept until the pulsing began to clarify. It broke into dark and twisted tendrils, much like those of Cecily McCray, only Tallia's did not caress. They held barbs and stuck themselves firm into Effie.

The shield wasn't a shield at all, Effie realized. Tallia consumed the strength of her fey blood, leaving her nothing. She had linked them without Effie's knowing. Effie thought to rip the barbed tendrils away but stayed her hand. Instead, she surged forward with her senses, racing along the tendrils with ones of her own. They were shaped like vines with green leaves, hale and firm.

Tallia sensed the attack. Her tendrils lashed out. But Effie gripped onto those as well, snaking her own around the barbs and questing forward. Linking worked both ways, and Tallia had left herself open, her arrogance blinding her to the threat Effie posed. She screamed and flailed her tendrils, cracking them like whips.

Effie grasped as many as she could, gathering them into a tight bundle. Her own vine-like tendrils thinned and hardened into steeled wire. She yanked, and the wire sliced through Tallia's tendrils, severing the link.

Her fey senses flooded back into her. Instantly, she called on a glamour of frost to gust over the entangling roots. Where the frost touched, the roots cracked and crumbled to dust. Effie whipped the frost into a frenzy, hurling it about the chamber.

Tallia seethed. Her eyes narrowed to tiny slits that locked onto Effie. She let her glamour fade, and gasps of relief sounded throughout the room. As the league men stirred and recovered, Tallia gestured to a pair of her brethren. The man in the rat mask leaped forward and slammed a mallet into one of the league men's knees. The man howled as he crumpled to the floor.

Another in a bird mask—a hawk, perhaps—rushed at Graham. He raised a short, rusted sword high above his head. Effie hurled Tallia's dagger at him. It spun hilt over tip and smacked against his chest. But it didn't bury in. It bounced off the skin, leaving only a line of red.

Graham rolled aside, struggling for his feet. He raised his cane to block the first strike of the sword, but Effie could tell he would not be fast enough to block them all. She darted forward but jerked as a pistol shot rang out.

The hawk-masked man dropped in a spray of blood. Jack Canonbie marched up to hover over him and fired again. Hawk Mask's body lurched and lay still.

Effie swung her gaze to Tallia, and her eyes widened in horror. Tallia's brethren had afforded her a moment's respite, and she had used it to produce a slender stick from some hidden part of her clothing. She held it aloft, its wick barely longer than her arm. From a pocket, she drew a match, struck it, and flourished it for all to see. A wicked grin spread from ear to ear, as she touched match to wick.

"Dynamite!" hollered Graham. The league men bellowed the same and scrambled back as the wick sprang to life, hissing and spitting sparks. They frantically called for someone to shoot the woman.

Jack Canonbie leveled his pistol. But Rat Mask sprang at him. He charged the ground between them with shoulders lowered, smashing into the rogue as the pistol cracked. The impact sprawled them both to the floor, where they grappled, arms and legs thrashing for purchase.

Tallia cackled as she hurled the dynamite stick into the middle of the chamber. She didn't wait for it to land but fled into the darkened passageways from whence she'd emerged.

❧ 36 ❦

E ffie took a step to follow Tallia. The woman's taunting laughter echoed from the passageway. Some of her brethren had taken it up as well. They hurried after their new Mother, leaving behind their wounded and dead.

Graham reached Effie's side and grabbed her arm. "Hurry, lass!" he urged. He pulled her toward the throne. His eyes darted to the crackling wick. It had almost spent.

"Catherine," Jonas cried. He stretched out an arm as the girl dashed toward him. Their embrace held a longing in it, but quickly he pulled away. Together, they helped Cecily McCray to her feet and disappeared in the recess behind the throne.

Effie started to hurry after. But Jack Canonbie moaned, and she turned to him. The Rat Mask straddled him, pummeling his head. Canonbie kept his arms in front of his face, but the defense did little good. The blows landed with dull smacks of flesh and bone. Both men bled. Their clothes had torn and flesh flushed to a searing red.

She could not abandon Canonbie. Even if he hadn't come to save her life. Even if he'd betrayed her to the Sanctity of Empire League. Even if he had led her to believe something blossomed between them. It was not in her heart to be so callous.

Snatching up his cane, she thwacked Rat Mask across the temple. It sent the man sprawling, grabbing at his head. Canonbie didn't let him recover. He sprang to his feet and stomped his boot into the man's neck until something crunched.

Stooping for his pistol, he whirled on Effie, snarling. Welts covered his neck and cheeks. The flesh there had swelled and split, trickling blood and turning black. His eyes narrowed to tiny slits. But he saw her and flinched. Remorse clouded his gaze.

Effie wasted no time on words. She bolted after Catherine. Graham and Jack Canonbie stuck to her heels as she dashed behind the throne. The darkened recess opened on one side, and she hurried into it. Her shoulders brushed stone, and she knew the larger men would have to shuffle sideways, slowing their progress. Ahead, she could barely make out the fleeing forms of Cecily McCray, Catherine Granville, and their Jonas.

There has to be time, she willed. *Just a few seconds more.*

At the far side of the recess, a rusted iron gate clanked shut. Jonas stared at her through the bars. The rattle of the gate's closure sent a lead ball into Effie's gut. She threw herself at the gate. It didn't budge. Her shoulders jarred from the impact. Panic flooded her. The space was too tight to let Graham or Canonbie pass forward and use their strength. She rammed the bars again to no avail.

They couldn't flee back into the chamber. They couldn't go on. Effie glared at Jonas as the fool stepped back into the tunnel that widened on the far side of the gate. His features slowly vanished into the shadows, but he did not watch Effie. His gaze had turned to another.

"Jonas, please," begged Catherine. The girl pushed against him. Effie could hear the hurt in her voice. "They came to aid us."

"Let them pass." Cecily McCray called from the darkness behind them. "She has proven herself worthy, where we have not."

Jonas glanced over his shoulder. He whispered something to Catherine and dipped his head. His hand found an iron key on a chain about his neck, and he stalked forward.

The lock clicked open as the explosion thundered from the chamber behind them. The walls trembled from the blast. Chips of dirt and stone rained from the ceiling. Effie jerked into the gate, banging her head against the bars. But it gave way and flew open. She stumbled and caught herself, her hands scraping along the stone walls.

A cloud of smoke and dust billowed through the recess from the main chamber. Shrieks of agony came with it. Effie could barely make out the sounds. Her hearing dimmed, replaced by a high-pitched whine. She tasted blood in her mouth. She had bit her tongue and cheek.

She found Catherine's hand reaching for her and took it, coughing against the dust. Light flared ahead. Jonas unhooded a lantern, and as the smoke and dust cleared, Effie saw that Cecily McCray slumped in a small alcove atop a bed of straw and blankets. The tunnel continued onward beyond. The alcove was just large enough for the bed and an old iron-bound chest.

Reaching the space, Effie stepped aside and eagerly scoured Graham for injury. "Bah," he mumbled, raising a hand to let her know he was fine. Catherine had a gash on one cheek, and Jonas tore off a piece of bedding to press against it.

"I instructed them to bring you no harm, but they didn't care," said Jack Canonbie. He crawled into the space the alcove afforded them and tried to place his hand on Effie's shoulder. "I couldn't tell them about Miss Granville. So I didn't. For all they know, she's just another moppet enthralled by the fey."

"Portrait of valiance, ye are," growled Graham. He slapped Canonbie's hand away.

Effie's fists balled. Her nails gouged her palms. The strain of it made her arms shake. "But why?" she demanded. "I want to hear you tell me why."

Canonbie wiped blood from his chin with the back of his hand. He stared back toward the gate. "My employer bade me, and I had no recourse to decline."

Effie's eyes narrowed into daggers. "I am your employer, sir." The truth struck her only after the words had left her mouth. He had come well recommended to Thomas Stevenson, she recalled, no doubt from a person with a measure of influence over her benefactor. She could think of one in particular. One Stevenson had been eager to defer to when they'd dined at her ball. Effie's face flushed as she made the connection.

"That was how you knew the secret ways within Lady Fife's estate," she said. "You've been hers from the start." When he didn't deny it, she jabbed a finger at him. "Why does she expose your betrayal now?"

"The treaty wavers and Lady Fife believes it will fail," said Canonbie. "She seeks to forge new alliances with the opposition. Lord Granville would grant her a large boon for the same service he requested of you. You know the man has no loyalty."

"Ye've told her everything?" asked Graham. Fury shone in his eyes, and hurt. Effie knew he wouldn't forgive himself for his part in putting her in Canonbie's path.

Canonbie shrugged and forced a grin, as if to steal some of the awkwardness away. It only made him appear all the more guilty. "I had to," was all he said.

Effie seethed. She had known from the start not to trust the man. She had known it, and yet, somewhere along the way she had let him in. She'd included him among her friends. She wanted to scream until she passed out. At the foul man, at herself, at the walls and the air in between. Her shoulders throbbed from the strain her anger pressed against them. But she kept her tongue. The man did not deserve to behold so violent a reaction from her. She would rather he saw that he meant nothing to her.

"You have done murder." Cecily McCray's voice carried to them as a feeble whisper. Fatigue painted her face, which had paled to a bone white.

"From a young age," said Jack Canonbie. He did not boast, but nor did he sound ashamed of it.

"No, this is something more. It shames you. We are kindred spirits, you and I, full of regret." She closed her eyes. Her head slumped.

"Mother," Jonas breathed. He rushed to her and brushed aside the russet shawl she wore. Effie saw the dark wetness behind it. She'd been wounded grievously and would not long stay among the living.

Catherine shrieked, pointing at the gate. Boots scuffed the ground behind them. A pistol shot cracked. The bullet pinged off the wall near Jonas' arm. The fool whirled and bared his teeth. In the lantern's light, he seemed more wolf than man. Graham pushed Effie and Catherine further into the alcove, while Jack Canonbie pressed against the wall and readied his pistol.

Effie caught a glimpse of a pair of league men skulking their way from the main chamber. Dust coated them in shrouds of white. Their eyes formed dark orbs beneath, making them appear as wraiths.

"Go. I will hold them here," barked Canonbie. He jammed bullets into his pistol and peered at the league men.

"We can't trust him," snapped Graham. "He'll save himself and turn on us again."

Canonbie's gaze swung to her. "Effie..."

"Don't," she warned. She glanced at Catherine and squeezed her eyes shut. "They can't find her here." She felt her hopes spilling through her fingers. Lady Fife's reversal of support for the treaty would start a tide of rats scurrying from the sinking ship. They needed to stop that damage as much as they needed Lord Granville's favor.

Canonbie's pistol popped. Effie flinched, but her feet had already started moving.

"Is the next gate locked?" she asked Jonas. Blood smeared his hands. It soaked Cecily McCray's colorful dress, running slick and wet.

"Yes, and I have its only key." The fool regarded Effie with sad, vacant eyes. "But Mother breathes still. I will not leave her."

"Och, move then," said Graham. He handed his cane to Effie and grabbed Cecily McCray's legs, looking to the fool.

Jonas nodded. He hauled his Mother against his chest, and together they carried her down the tunnel. Effie fetched the lantern and made Catherine march before her. She didn't bother to check whether Jack Canonbie watched her flee. She heard his pistol covering their retreat.

She scoured the area with her fey senses as they went and found the auras of Rose and Abigail. The women stood above and behind them, almost a quarter mile distant. *Flee,* she urged them, sending the image of a deer scrambling away from a pack of slathering wolves.

An exchange of pistol fire echoed along the stone walls. Grunts and shouting followed, but by the time they reached the second gate, the tunnel had fallen silent. The second gate was as rusted as the first, though the lock appeared new. It made sense. Cecily McCray must've had the locks repaired when she'd first taken residence in the warren. Effie could only guess at their original purpose.

Jonas set his Mother down carefully and slipped in the key from the chain around his neck. Cecily McCray's eyes fluttered as the gate creaked open. A moan escaped her lips.

"Rest now, Mother," said Jonas. He reclaimed his grip under her shoulders.

Effie closed the gate after they'd all passed through and tugged until she heard it click. She didn't give a thought to Jack Canonbie. The man was a survivor. She had every confidence he would find his way slithering out of the Town Below, and she had no desire to see him again.

The tunnel carried on for a minute before they came to a fork. Jonas took the left passage without slowing a step. The air began to stink of the privy, and Effie noticed the roughhewn stone of the walls had become sturdier masonry. Ahead, she heard the rush of running water.

"We'll need to put out the lantern if the stink gets any thicker," said Graham. He reshuffled his grip on Cecily McCray's legs. "The fumes here are worse than the opium."

"We are almost free," said Jonas. Shortly thereafter, they reached a steep stair set into the wall. A slimy moss coated the stone steps at its base.

"Set me down," rasped Cecily McCray. She wheezed, her breath sounding wet and weak. Effie could barely make out her words.

Jonas and Graham solemnly obliged. The fool sat on the first step and rested his Mother's head in his lap. She gave a meek cough. Blood trickled from her wounds onto the mossy steps to pool at her feet. Catherine Granville sniffled and turned away, though not before Effie caught the tears rushing down her cheeks.

The wounds were clearer now that she had a chance to study them. She thought of Tallia's dagger and grimaced. She had been too late in her rescue efforts, but not for whom she'd imagined.

"You have felt her touch, haven't you child?" Cecily McCray asked. Her eyes remained shut, yet Effie knew the question had been directed at her.

"The freed Sidhe Bhreige," she said. She came closer and crouched next to the dying woman.

Blood spittle bubbled from Cecily McCray's lips. "Aye. She was...a mistake. We were not always so, our lust for death. We loved, as of old. But she called, and her will was too great to resist."

"We have lost our way these past months," said Jonas. He traced a hand through Cecily McCray's hair, trying to soothe her. "Your victory at Caldwell House led us to believe the city safe again. Talk of peace sprang from every tongue. We returned, ready to restore our band of merriment, a life free to indulge and live as our wills desired. But our way darkened somehow. A subtle pressure warped our manner, and we found ourselves growing ever more hungry for the taste of another's life."

Effie's heart froze. "Is it here in the city?"

"Nay," said the fool. "Her cries haunt us from afar. We can tell by the sending."

"You've heard them, haven't you?" croaked Cecily McCray. Her voice fell to barely a rush of breath. "The whispers. The cries in your dreams. The banshee, Jonas took to calling her, for her voice carried death on the wind."

The banshee's touch—somehow the name had spread. An image came to Effie of a dank and sickened hollow dug at the base of a large tree. A giant oak tree, the one she had seen in her foretelling at Bonny Law. She had seen it again, in the fleeting instant when she'd severed her link with Tallia. A shiver ran up her spine.

"Where then?" she asked, voice cracking. Her throat had run dry.

"Search the stars and find the darkest crypt beneath a shadowed hill," said Jonas. "An oak tree sometimes mounts its top. Sometimes a ring of standing stones. The details change, but the stars, they are always the same. It is the best we have to offer."

Effie's brow furrowed at the riddle.

"I read your coming from the stars," said Cecily McCray. "The Oak Seer foretold. My downfall is deserved. You are stronger, to resist her call. I failed... I failed us all." Her eyes grew vacant, and her lips parted in a final exhale. It passed like a meek rustle of leaves.

"It was not your burden to carry alone, Mother," said Jonas. He brushed his fingers over her eyelids to close them and kissed her forehead. Turning to Effie, his face full of sorrow, he said, "I will take her and see she is laid to rest."

"No, no, no." Catherine Granville whimpered. She brought her hands to her chest and clutched them together. Her face paled.

"They knew," said Graham, in a low tone of disbelief. "They knew, and they let it happen to them. How could they not turn aside? To know and carry on makes their deeds a fouler thing."

"Not many would argue against your judgment of us," said Jonas. He rose and hefted the limp form of Cecily McCray, hugging her to his chest. "But not all are as strong as they once hoped to be."

Catherine stepped to him and clutched his arm. Her expression pleaded for a kindness, and Effie wondered how far shattered the girl's mind had gone.

"Go with them, my sweet," said the fool. "They will see you safe, a task at which I have failed." He stepped away from her grasp and bowed his head. The tenderness of his tone did not match the torment in his gaze. But he turned his back all the same as she fell to her knees. He left her sobbing.

🌿 37 🌿

A still and somber evening had settled over the city as they made their way to Heriot Row. The wreckage of the airship stood abandoned. A light waft of smoldering timber and coal smoke thickened the air. North Bridge barely held a soul, and the plain sky of the day had been replaced by a dark bank of clouds that threatened a downpour at any moment.

As Effie strode next to Graham, she forced herself from dwelling on what they'd learned of the last Sidhe Bhreige. The banshee, the fool had dubbed it. The corruption the thing had spread from afar terrified her. The Laird of Aonghus and the Piper of Ceann Rois, for all their might, had ensured all bore witness to their machinations. That this creature wielded such a perverting influence and remained hidden made it a far more dangerous foe.

Graham made grunting noises as they walked. "This beast will have us all fighting ourselves until the whole bloody empire is in chaos. Times are dire, lass, and getting worse," he said. "The peril the city has faced the past two days must give us some grave concern."

"I know," said Effie. "But we must focus on the treaty before we see to the other." She had come to that conclusion as they'd emerged from the Town Below. Lady Fife's reversal of support meant there was little time before its failure.

Cocking her head to the side, she studied Catherine Granville. The girl followed them, lost in a reverie of her own. They would return her to her father, though already Effie felt a bubble of guilt when she considered using the girl as a bargaining position. She did not deserve to suffer more at the hands of those who should be protecting her, and Effie would not bring herself to such a base level.

Besides, she had a different plan in mind, to force Lord Granville's hand.

They reached Heriot Row as the gas lamps lining the cobblestone streets of New Town flared to life. A small crowd gathered outside Thomas Stevenson's house. They lounged on the steps and huddled in groups.

Graham put a hand on Effie's arm. "I'll see what they want, and if need be, drive them off," he said.

"No," Effie replied. "I was expecting them." More, actually. She surveyed the gathering, as Graham eyed her quizzically. Jane had roused perhaps a dozen. Most were young, in worn, if not tattered, clothes. Not so long ago, Effie would've shied away from approaching so many strangers at once. But the time for anonymity had ended.

It had dawned on her in the warrens of *Les Revenirs*, the masks the fey wore. Their kind had learned to hide, and hide well, to survive. Even village Spae Wives, such as Miss Teasdale, limited themselves, lest they appear presumptuous. Yet hiding also disconnected them from society, from fostering relationships and demonstrating their worth. Lord Granville and his cronies knew this and had taken advantage of it for far too long.

Effie strode forward. She would not allow the tales spread of devious fey to reflect the entirety of their kind. The Green Lady wielded more power and influence than she could ever hope to achieve toiling about in the shadows. She would embrace the moniker, and damn the fear that had held her captive from a young age.

That fear no longer served her as it once had.

"Welcome," she said cheerily. She knew she must look a state, bruised and soiled, with her hair a frazzled mess and hands swollen red from the chemical burns. It mattered not. Those gathered fell silent. A few of the men bowed their heads and women curtsied. Effie saw one tremble excitedly and others cross themselves.

Effie didn't care what reason had drawn them to her, only that they had come. She ascended the steps to the house and opened her mouth to speak. As she did, something clattered against the door from the inside. A muffled shout followed and the quick tramping of feet. Effie started and shoved open the door.

Inside, pandemonium had taken root. A toppled chair lay in the middle of the floor. A dented silver platter sat near it, with a collection of spoons spread all around as if they'd been thrown.

"Close the door!" hollered Edgar. He wore no jacket, only a tweed waistcoat over his white shirt. He ran with a wooden spoon clutched in one hand and a kitchen pot in the other. He flew past, disappearing into the drawing room before she could utter anything in response.

"Effie," squealed Jane's voice from the dining room. Her head popped into view from the doorway. Disorderly locks of auburn hair fell across her eyes.

"Jane?"

A thunk followed by a crash of glass came from behind the girl. Jane cringed and whipped her head to spy over her shoulder. "They've escaped!" she squeaked. "Close the door, please hurry!"

Effie blinked, unable to make sense of the commotion. Graham nudged her into motion. He shut the door behind them as Stevenson's footman hurried to them and made a quick, if anxious, bow. His eyes swung between them. "Miss Brewer assured me you would consent to these guests. But the destruction of Mr. Stevenson's effects..."

Effie raised a gentle hand to stave him off. "I will see to it," she said. She hurried toward the dining room, as another thump and clack of furniture overturning sounded.

"Ha, got you!" came Rose's voice from within the room. "That's two. What happened to the other?"

"Edgar followed it into the drawing room," said Jane, pointing from the doorway of the dining room.

Reaching her, Effie stopped short of entering. Rose clutched a squirming creature no bigger than her hand. It had the large, round eyes of a bug and small, floppy ears. Its hairless skin was ashen, its head overlarge for its wee body.

Rose's gaze swiveled to her. Her hair and dress were as disheveled as Jane's. Amusement flared across her face. "Well, we know what the goop does to the pixies now," she said. "It turns them into goblins."

Effie's jaw dropped, and Graham made a choking sound behind her. She could see it now. The creature still claimed a delicate nose and the lithe body of a pixie. Its wings were gone, and its fingers and toes were tipped in tiny claws. It was like a majestic cat who, once shaved, resembled more of a drowned rat.

"Hi'ya, Effie," said Abigail. She stood in the corner of the room holding a second of the goblins. "Devious buggers, these. They'd turn over every last thing if we let 'em."

Rose's gaze flicked to Abigail. "Come, let us find a cage for these two. There will be time for tales later, after the last it caught."

"Oh, yes," said Jane. She curtsied and waved to Effie. "I did as you asked. You saw outside. But Edgar... Come on!"

Effie allowed the girl to lead her into the drawing room. There, Edgar stalked the last goblin in a low crouch, the kitchen pot held out at the ready. The couch sat askew from its normal resting place. An end table had been flipped upside down, and broken shards of glass spread around it. The goblin stood atop the fireplace's mantle, thrusting a lit stick of kindling at the footman every time the man tried to snatch the creature up.

"Ack!" he cried out, as the goblin struck the flames against his hand. He snatched his hand back and shook it out.

Effie laughed. "Oh, just grab the critter, won't you?" She marched forward, intending to do just that.

Edgar waved with his spoon-clutching hand. "No, wait," he hissed.

Effie found out too late the cause of their hesitation. As she neared, the goblin sprang from the mantle with lightning speed. "Squeeeeeee!" it hollered as it zipped past her shoulder, struck the back of one of the chairs, knocking it over, and tumbled to the ground.

Edgar dove for it with the pot and missed. The footman banged his shin against the chair's leg trying to stamp out the cushion that had started to smolder where the flame kissed it. Effie leaped aside. She kept her gaze locked on the goblin. It scurried about the room, under the couch and around Edgar's prone form. It clutched the lit kindling against its chest with both arms. The flame at its top trailed a line of smoke.

The goblin screeched as it went, a high-pitched call that its brethren echoed from the other room. Effie stumbled after it, trying to shoo it toward the front corner. When the wee creature reached the curtained window, it spun and regarded her. She squatted down, and it mirrored her. She laughed and pulled her face into a stony glare. It did the same.

"It's trying to play," she said. She raised both arms wide to block it from darting past.

"Tricksters, they are," she heard Abigail say behind her. "But devious."

The goblin backed against the wall, and Effie gasped as the flame brushed against the dangling curtain. She lunged forward from her crouch, just as Graham stepped behind her and sloshed a bucket of water onto the creature. The water splashed against the wall, doused the flame, and soaked her shoulder and the side of her head.

But she managed to slap the goblin against the floor, pinning it beneath her palm just long enough for Graham to reach in and grab it.

He had just regained his feet when splotches of light burst all around his face, ranging in color from searing white to deep reds and blues. Graham blinked against them and fell back onto the couch. Effie shied away. She felt the tiny creature pulling on her fey blood, using it to craft the dizzying lights.

"Oh, no ye don't," growled Rose. A surge of energy flared in the room. Effie sensed it snap across the goblin and tear away from it the glamour it shaped. Graham struggled as the goblin squirmed, until Abigail leaned over his shoulder and spritzed the creature with perfume from a glass diffuser.

The wee thing took a full blast of sweet, floral mist, and could do nothing else but cough. Its face scrunched up in disgust, and its jaw worked, tongue trying to rid itself of the residue. Calmly, Abigail took the goblin from Graham.

"We found a birdcage to contain them," she said, hurrying out of the room.

Effie sighed and sank back onto her rump as the footman and Edgar straightened the couch and overturned chairs. Gazing at the mess, she shook her head and giggled. *Could nothing be simple anymore?*

Rising, she set about appeasing the footman and the rest of the small household staff. Despite the bedlam, only a couple of items could not be salvaged, and nothing of importance. In no time, they had the house back in order.

Effie laughed once they had all gathered in the drawing room. "This is not how I thought we'd begin." She turned to Jane. "I see from the crowd outside you've been at work. Is all else prepared?"

Jane curtsied. "Yes, my lady."

Rose snorted, and Effie shook her head, grinning all the while. "Please do call me Effie. I have no rank or title within the fey court, nor any other."

"But you do mean to lead us?" the girl asked.

"Against Lord Granville? Yes, I do." Effie caught Catherine's eye. "But it will not be a battle won from steel and blood. We must show the lord and those in Parliament something else. Something long forgotten. A harmony betwixt fey and man."

Catherine's lip tugged, almost into a smile, though her eyes remained saddened. Effie quickly related to the others what had transpired within the warren of *Les Revenirs*. When she spoke of Jonas, she spoke of him well, for Catherine's sake.

Rose clucked her tongue at Jack Canonbie's alliance with the Sanctity of Empire League. When Effie had finished the tale, she asked, "If Lady Fife has thrown her support to the other side, and the safety of Aerfenium is called to question, just how do we save the treaty?"

"I might ask a different question, one that's occupied my thoughts ever since that horrid mob raged against the hogboon. What do we do after the treaty has passed?" Effie replied. "Young Jane told us something days ago at Bonny Law. Something important. I should've listened to her then, and I intend to now."

Effie surveyed the room as she spoke. "The fey of old did not hide in the forests. They did not dwell in dark warrens, afraid of the sunlight. They lived alongside man, tending the land and celebrating life. A treaty is merely words on paper, for all its significance. It will mean nothing if the people believe only in the wicked tales spread of fey kind, if they only see pain and suffering from it. They must see more from the fey. They must know more from us, and of us. Only then will they realize the boon our harmony can bring. Only then will they relish our company and delight in our nature."

"You suppose men like Lord Granville will buckle to public sentiment if you get enough voices hollering for you?" Graham's tone was skeptical.

Effie shook her head. "There will always be men like Lord Granville. Our only hope is to make it harder for him to enact his schemes, that the cost of such plots will fall heavier than the benefit."

"Aye'ya, Effie, that's true," said Abigail. "So how do ye plan to start this peaceful revolution?"

"With a demonstration," said Effie. "One to make all the tongues in the empire flap." Her face lit up as she turned to Rose. "I will need you to show me a bit of Fey Craft, but first I must see to our guests outside."

❄ 38 ❄

Effie wore the emerald gown, with its pearls and silver lace, as she marched through the streets of Glasgow. Gwendoline rode on her shoulder. The tawny owl's head twisted and bobbed, taking in the city with faint unease. Graham strode beside Effie, with Rose and Abigail trailing a step behind. Jane and Edgar and Maggie had donned white robes, thin and billowy, belted with hempen rope. The girls had mistletoe woven through their hair.

A trio of gnomes marched with them from the Order of Freiwald. In place of their heavy coats and elephantine masks, they wore fine coats of a steel color, with high collars and onyx trim. Freiherr Jörg had refused to come, but he'd allowed any of his company to answer her call, at their own peril. Jaelyn had refused as well. The response soured Effie, but it was one she'd expected.

Rose and Abigail had called on friends of their own. A pair of pixies buzzed around their procession. Their vibrant dress and darting speed made them shimmer in blurs of green and gold. Two brownies and a handful of Sithlings came next. The brownies strode with purpose, their height half that of all save the pixies. Angular cheeks and wild crops of hair were at odds with their bespoke dress. Their wee canes clinked on the cobblestones in contrast to the thumps of those around them.

Those Jane had raised rounded out the party. They had gathered a few more along the way, though in all the host remained meager. But it was a start.

"Will this work?" Graham muttered the question. Those they passed stopped and gawked openly, whatever task they'd been about forgotten. Most from the city had only heard tales of pixies and brownies. Their knowledge of the fey races stemmed from penciled drawings in the newspapers.

"I don't know, but I trust it is the right thing to do," said Effie. When they'd first alighted from their steam carriages, her heart had fluttered so furiously, she thought it might break free from its cage. Her shoulders had begged to buckle forward, and her head to duck. She'd wanted nothing so more as to run away. But she had learned to hide her fear of late, and she managed to stand tall and proud, bringing a smile to her cheeks.

She saw that strength reflected in her brave companions as they crested the hill at the north end of the high street. There, the old cathedral of St. Mungo's stood sentinel over the heart of the city. Coal soot had blackened its stone and clouded its windows. Its mighty spire was lost in a haze of smoke. The stench of it hung in the air. The haze spread over the rooftops as far as the eye could see, pumping from factories, shipyards, and carriages.

From the higher vantage, they could hear the clamor of industry. Engines shrilled steam from valves; giant hammers pounded at steel and rock; and rail cars creaked and groaned as they trundled down rattling tracks.

At a newspaper stand across from the cathedral's entrance, a group of boys hollered as they played at a game with sticks. One looked up and caught sight of Effie's host. He jerked rigid, his jaw dropping slack. The others caught his gaze and did the same.

Already some of the gawkers the host had passed followed their procession: a coal porter covered in black smudge, a footman in a fine suit, and a woman hawking chestnuts from a basket she carried. They trailed a dozen paces distant, curiosity overwhelming them. The boys ran to join their ranks. They skipped and whispered to each other as they ogled Effie's host.

Others took absent steps toward the procession, drawn toward the wonder of the sight, before reclaiming themselves. An older woman barked a coarse laugh, while her younger companion blushed in embarrassment. A couple rough-looking men bellowed crude taunts as they staggered along, deep in drink.

A fellow in an apron glared out the front of a confectioners. Effie met his eye and nodded kindly. She'd sought out those who'd shown signs of hostility since their arrival. That was the point of their procession, after all. She didn't mind that many would continue to loathe the fey. She never had any hope of eradicating bigotry or hatred.

She wanted to demonstrate the profit of harmony despite those things.

"It is time to conjure a greater spectacle," she said. The shadow of an airship swaying high overhead cooled the air. She watched its propeller spin lazily and cleared her mind. Pulling on the fey auras of those in the host, she expanded her senses and felt her way through the city. She called on all the fey she could find and begged them to come join her. She called on horses to gently plod her way, and for hounds and cats to gather as well. She did not force them. She had no need. Her call was soothing and teased at a primal need—the fellowship of a pack.

Rose raised her hand and golden lights flickered into existence. The lights ringed the host, bobbing on the wind and trailing tails of glitter. Bells began to chime, and under them came the soft thump of a drum. The gnomes and the pixies, Effie felt. They added their Fey Craft, linking their auras and becoming stronger.

Pipes and a fiddle joined. The music pressed back the clamor of the city. A hound padded to Effie, tongue lolling. She stroked its ear and started down the hill along the center of the high street. Gwendoline hooted and watched the hound as it followed at her heels.

None could ignore the host's march. Horses clopped from their path, edging to the side of the street. Neighing and flicking their tails, they greeted Effie and ignored the clucks and urgings of their masters. Those on foot shuffled aside. Some cheered and clapped. Others paled or turned away or simply watched in uncertain silence.

A Sithling man in a drab, brown suit was the first fey to answer her call. He wore a short, flat hat, and muck splattered his trousers to the knee. He bowed deep and grinned at Effie. "Oak Seer," he said. He took the hand of a girl who stood, clapping to the music. Twirling her, he passed her into the arms of a young woman before grabbing another partner.

The golden lights brightened. The pixies zipped about in a twirling dance. Laughter echoed around the host, infectious and light. Glimmering bursts of colors raced skyward to explode around them. They formed beacons for the denizens of Glasgow.

Effie's heart thumped. She had never been so bold, not even charging the field at Caldwell House. Here, she did not face the fang and claw of wulver and trow, but the darkest fears of her childhood—the scrutiny of man.

The host grew, as did its gaiety. Dancing and singing, merriment and cheer, blossomed in their wake. They rounded a bend in the street, and the grand chambers that held the treaty negotiations came into view. The shadow of the building's dome loomed over a cobblestoned square.

Effie sensed Caledon's aura pulsing within. The steward's blood was strong and vibrant. He would feel their approach, know their intent, and act, she trusted. She had no need to forewarn him.

She heard Graham curse a moment before she saw the men of the Sanctity of Empire League. Their armbands made them easy to spot. They emerged from the crowd milling about the square and stormed toward the host. One raised a pistol and fired into the sky. The crack echoed along the cobblestones and brought a jarring stillness to the street. The music stopped.

The hound at Effie's side growled, padding in front of her with its hackles raised.

Calm, she pulsed, using her Fey Craft. *Calm*, she reminded herself, drawing a deep breath. It was time to gamble and hope luck landed on her side.

With her palms open, she strode forward. The men brandished cudgels, canes, and pistols. They formed a line across the street, barring the way to the square. The one who'd fired the pistol spat on the cobbles. He had a dimpled chin and dark eyes full of wrath. His dress proclaimed him a man of the docks.

"Those of you fey, come 'ere and don't cause no trouble," he hollered.

"The rest of ye can bugger off." He glanced at the brownies and gnomes, and sneered.

Effie stopped a few paces short of the man and curtsied. She smiled at him. Gwendoline hooted. From the corner of her vision, she caught the face of a young girl who stood transfixed. She could not allow the confrontation to turn violent, not like the mob in Edinburgh. Her entire plan rested on the day remaining peaceful.

She raised her voice so all could hear. "You are welcome to join us. We are a joyous host and would have all indulge in our song."

"It's the witch." A burly man hissed the words.

"I am the Green Lady of Glen Coe," Effie replied. "Oak Seer and child of the forests, the hills, and the sea." The proclamation didn't taste as odd to her tongue as she thought it might. She stood steady.

"You'll be quiet," snapped the first man.

"You have no authority and less cause to stand in our path. Your masters might give you coin and buy your loyalty, but that is a pale substitute for your enslavement. Let me free you from the poison that twists your hearts, and let you see the truth."

She delved into them, her Fey Craft a gentle caress across their thoughts. It did not take long to find what she sought. She had found the same in Edinburgh. Withered branches, roots befouled by disease, and gnarled stumps of rotted trees had all crept into the auras of the men. The banshee's touch. The decay and corruption of their wits, the same as she'd glimpsed in Tallia's aura.

Effie ripped these fetid things out. Rose had shown her how. The cleansing was easier for a Spae Wife, but Effie had mastered the skill well enough. The burly man exhaled and staggered. He glanced around at the gathered crowd, and his cheeks flushed. He let the stout club he carried drop to the cobblestones. A smile came to another man, and he blinked as if waking from a long nap.

Not all reacted as favorably. Effie could remove the banshee's touch, but she could not alter the men's natures. The group's leader seemed oblivious to the change she had brought him. His scowl deepened.

"What witchcraft is this?" he demanded. He cocked the pistol and leveled it at her.

A gasp bit though the air. "No!" someone shrieked. Effie reacted without thought. Her glamour turned the pistol molten, its metal scalding to the touch. Vapors wafted from its glowing surface, searing into the man's flesh.

He yelped and dropped the pistol. As it clattered to the street, she let the glamour fade. The man's eyes widened in disbelief. He snarled and stooped to fetch it, and as he did, his burly cohort kicked it away.

"Me village had a Spae Wife, an' she did heal our wounds and ails," said the man. He folded his meaty arms across his chest. "Healed me hound a time, too, when he'd put his gob in a badger hole. But then men came an' hanged the woman. Said she were some trickster, as foul as William Burke." He shook his head. "She never done nothing save good. So let's hear the lass speak, I say."

"Aye, let the fey speak!" someone shouted.

"Aye, aye, aye!" a chorus of agreement rippled through the crowd. The hound bayed in agreement, sitting on its rump and pointing its snout to the sky.

Effie raised her hand and waited for the crowd to quiet. "Good people, our host has come to your city in good faith to demonstrate that the fey are not your enemy."

One of the league men, scrawny and sharp-eyed, stepped forward. "Dancing lights and ghost pipes. Bewitching animals. The coin our betters give us puts food in our bellies and coal in our hearths. What is it you have to offer that isn't some trick?"

Effie drew her shoulders back. "We offer the same as a miller, as a shepherd or a cook. We are seamstresses, porters, and shipbuilders."

"We don't need more of 'em," said the man. He waved a hand to cut her off. "The city is crowded as it is. There's no jobs for more. No food, neither."

Effie glanced at the crowd and saw eager faces hanging on every word. But she also saw the soot and filth that speckled their clothes, and the gauntness of many of their faces. She had seen the same in Edinburgh and Dunfermline. The country villages fared no better.

"Then give us a chance to provide our share," she said. "To provide and live in peace, it is all we ask. Come, let us hear what the lords have to say to that."

She strode past the man before he could respond. The crowd parted for her, and she sensed her companions following. The trill of a pipe started. If not as spirited as earlier, it still held a cheerful cadence. They reached the open square that led to the city's grand chambers. Along the square's two sides that ran toward the chamber's entrance, wilted trees struggled for life. Effie had gazed at them from a steam carriage on the night of Lady Fife's ball. They seemed no less sad now than they had before.

She went to one of the trees and felt its trunk. Gwendoline hopped from her shoulder onto a dry and cracking limb. The crowd gathering around her had grown to a size that rivaled the mob that'd hounded the hogboon in Edinburgh. But they did not chant words of hate, nor brandish stones and blades. Not yet, anyway.

The league men shoved their way forward. Graham stepped into their leader's path, and the men glared at one another. A low growl came from the hound.

"Steady," Effie whispered to them all.

A door banged open at the chamber's entrance, and a slap of boots on stone drew the crowd's attention.

"What is this?" boomed Lord Granville's voice. He stood flanked by a pair of fluted columns at the top of the chamber building's stone steps. His coat and stiff shirt looked as if he'd come from a formal dinner. His dark hair and clean cheeks had returned to their polished manner since their last meeting in Edinburgh. A lanky fellow with a tightly trimmed mustache hurried to his side. A constable, Effie guessed from his uniform. Caledon followed, along with the portly Lord Wilshire and two other gentlemen.

Effie regarded them. *The fate of an entire race lay in the hands of those men.* The absurdity of the notion brought a grin to her lips. She glanced around the square, remembering those who'd been caught up in the procession, clapping to the music, and laughing at the display of lights. Even signed and sealed, a treaty would do little good until the denizens of the empire learned to trust and love the fey once more.

Treaties are mere words on paper. It reminded her she had much work to do.

Lord Granville's face echoed her amusement, yet she could not fathom it was for the same reason. She caught his gaze dancing over Jane and Edgar. He whispered something to Lord Wilshire, and the men chuckled.

Effie stepped toward the center of the square. "Lord Granville, it is well you have come to hear our concerns. I fear they have become grave."

"I have come for a breath of air, as your steward bade me," said Lord Granville. "Another fey trick, I see." His lips pulled into a toothy smirk, his manner as charming as it had been at Lady Fife's ball. He gave no sign of inconvenience or distress at finding so large a crowd amassed outside the building.

He gestured at Caledon and at Jane. "I do admit, you inspire a certain loyalty. Perhaps Her Majesty should find work for you in the royal kennels."

Gwendoline screeched at that and took to wing. Effie soothed her with a flare of Fey Craft. She ignored Lord Granville's taunt. "We must discuss the empire's need for our alliance. A madness besets the cities. The banshee's touch, the gentle folk call it. It is a taint of the last Sidhe Bhreige, and this creature will use it to bring ruin to us all."

Lord Granville bellowed laughter. He turned to the other lords to ensure they did the same. "Yes, there is a great danger lurking. But it is a fey creature you speak of, correct? Just like the hordes who assailed the Highlands, bringing death and destruction." He shook his head. "That does not show promise for your argument."

"I have learned to cleanse the infected of this touch," said Effie. "With an alliance, the fey who hide in fear can freely join our cause and bolster our resistance."

"Tsk, tsk, Effie of Glen Coe. We have danced this waltz before." Lord Granville clasped his hands behind his back. His voice took on the tenor of one delivering a practiced speech. He addressed the crowd. "The fey would have us believe they are our only hope. But our empire is strong. It has withstood far mightier enemies. It will not shrink from defending itself, nor cower before invisible threats. It will stand until the end of days, as it has for thousands of years."

Effie barely heard his words. She delved into him, searching for the corruption of the banshee's touch. But nothing fell presented itself. The man gave off the sense of solid stone, of a pinnacle grasping for the clouds, unhindered by gravity, and casting the surrounding hills and streams in shadow. She shouldn't have been surprised, but a part of her had hoped she could lessen his malice toward the fey with a deft swipe of Fey Craft. It would've made convincing him to reverse his political position easier.

"As a demonstration of good faith," he was saying, "I bade you to turn over the dissident fey of Edinburgh. We have all received word of how that turned out. An airship stolen and a magistrate's house attacked." He waved a hand at the gathered troop of fey. "Are these the criminals? Have they come to surrender themselves?"

A murmur spread through the crowd. Effie struggled not to cringe. Lord Granville tried to paint her as one of his stooges and defame her companions. She kept the bite from reaching her tone, but her chin lifted all the same.

"Your memory does not serve you, my lord. You begged me confront *Les Revenirs*, and that cult alone. It appears you have some personal vendetta against them, yet you must know by now their leader is dead at the hands of your henchmen. The cult is no more, the remnants fled."

Lord Granville's smile faltered for a heartbeat. But an understanding dawned in his gaze, and his mirth quickly returned. "A convenient tale, to be sure. I'd ask you to bring me the hag's body if I thought you'd manage the task without any trick or twist of words."

"I'll vouch for her account," said Graham. He planted himself next to Effie, hands on his hips. "That is, if the word of a Scotsman holds any merit with a fine and dandy lord of the far south."

Effie nodded to him, listening as the sentiment of the crowd swung back into her favor. It was one thing for them to hear of her exploits for and against the fey, quite another to be reminded of Lord Granville's English blood.

"I will stand for Effie as well," boomed Jack Canonbie. He emerged from the crowd to stand near Rose. An angry welt marred his temple. Bandages wrapped both his hands. "And if my word is not enough, you may take that of Catherine Granville. Surely you trust your own daughter, my lord?"

"Jack," Effie breathed. Her heart caught at the sight of him. He'd snuck up on her as he had when they'd first met only a few weeks earlier.

She didn't know what to tell him, how to thank him when she'd wanted never to see him again.

Canonbie turned to her, his gaze full of remorse. "He knows you will not degrade Catherine's honor and takes advantage of that fact. I am not burdened by such scruples, and besides, I've heard from her own lips her desire to make public her love for Jonas."

"You dare!" Lord Granville's face grew hard. His composure wilted. "Arrest that man," he barked at the constable. "He has no place here. This foolishness is at an end!" The lord whirled to storm inside, but Jack Canonbie did not let him.

"She loathes you and your foul schemes," shouted Canonbie. "She chose a vile cult over your company. She has a fey lover, and she means to run off with him still."

"Silence!" Spittle flew from Lord Granville's mouth. He grabbed the constable by the shoulders and shoved him down the steps. The constable barely caught his balance. Putting a whistle to his lips, he blasted a long shrill.

"Do you know the other things I've heard?" said Canonbie. He slowly stalked forward, his cane clacking with each step. "Miss Catherine did have a thing or two more to say. Something about debts your family quietly purchased after the Transvaal War." He chuckled, the sound full of scorn. "Keeping the old guard afloat, are you? I wonder at what kind of leverage those debts procured?"

The whistle shrilled again. Lord Wilshire turned beet red. Effie saw him say something to Lord Granville, but she couldn't hear what.

"Let him speak," someone shouted, and the chant was taken up by the crowd. The constable reached for Canonbie, and the larger man danced aside. The crowd cheered. Someone threw an apple. It sailed high and splattered on the steps.

Effie felt the fervor rising. The crowd had come for a show, and it made no matter to them whether it was the one she intended. She glanced at Rose and Abigail. The women were being jostled, as the crowd surged to and fro. It had doubled again in size, and Effie saw a crush of bodies clear to the bend in the street.

She had to do something to quell them before the mass rose to a violent pitch.

"You hold the newspapers in your pocket." Canonbie leaped through the press, shouting over his shoulder. "Spinning lies with Her Majesty's coin." The constable shoved after him, but he'd sooner lift the chamber building on his shoulders than catch the rogue.

More fruit flew. Effie heard the wet smack of it on the cobblestones. The hound pressed against her legs, its tail tucking from the clamor of raised voices.

"Put him down!" screamed Lord Granville. He waved his arm at Effie and pointed at Canonbie. "An extra year's wages for it!"

Effie frowned, comprehension coming a step too slow. The lord hadn't waved at her. He'd waved at the leader of the league men. The man stood a dozen paces behind her, his pistol drawn and leveled.

"Jack!" she shrieked, as the man fired into the crowd.

❦ 39 ❧

Her glamour came too late. Three shots cracked before the pistol turned into a snake that bit the league man on the wrist. He flinched, giving Edgar enough time tackle him. The gnomes of the Order of Freiwald joined the scuffle and subdued the man. Panic washed over the crowd. A young girl wailed. A man grunted as another slammed into him. The scrawny league man balled his fists and swung at the Sithling man who'd come to dance.

Jack Canonbie slapped a hand to his throat, as if he'd been stung by a wasp. He staggered into an older woman who wore a shopkeeper's apron. A trickle of red began to paint the back of his fingers through the handkerchief he wore.

Effie's breath fled as he slumped to his knees. She couldn't scream. She couldn't budge her legs. She could only watch in horror, knowing she would never reach him before the press swallowed and trampled him. Gwendoline screeched, swooping to perch on her shoulder. Her talons bit into Effie's flesh, and she jerked. The tawny owl screeched again.

Move! The wee thing seemed to tell her. But Effie's mind raced. She couldn't fix on a plan. She didn't know what to do, how to save Jack Canonbie, nor how to rescue the peace of the afternoon. So she acted on instinct, from what her gut willed.

Thrusting her hands to the sky, she summoned a fiery globe. It burned pure white, shimmering with molten heat. Those around her shied back, raising their arms to block the brilliant light, and turning away from the intense fumes that brought sweat to their flesh.

Effie spread her hands slowly apart, warping the glamour into a flat disk that stretched over the crowd. Rose was the first the join her. She felt the woman's aura link to hers, the bolster of her guidance and strength enlarging the disk faster, so that it rushed over the crowd like a crashing wave.

Abigail added a low-pitched hum to the glamour, that of a bee hive the size of a tenement building. The pixies and brownies linked and added their strength. And finally came Caledon. His steward's blood dwarfed them all, and the disk crackled with blue lightening.

The panic of the crowd did not lessen, but its movement stilled. Those in the press were forced to hunker down and turn away from the blinding light. Only those of fey blood, linked to the host, remained on their feet. A quiet fell over the square, until only the hum and crackle remained.

Effie strained to maintain the glamour. Already, her arms felt like chiseled stone. She saw the girl who wailed staring at her in fear. Her heart panged, but she needed to hold the blazing disk a few seconds more.

Until the crowd fully stilled. Until their tempers quelled. She didn't know where the impulse had come from, only that a mix of pain and guilt and sadness rushed through her. A part of her knew she was making things worse. She was failing those she'd hoped to charm.

Go to him. The sending entered her thoughts. Rose caught her eyes and tipped her head toward Jack Canonbie. The woman raised an eyebrow, and the blue lightning sprouted bolts of reds and purples and greens. The heat evaporated and the disk raised higher into the sky. Those in the crowd gawked at the display of lights.

Go to him, while there is still time. Effie let go of the glamour and felt Rose take control. She hurried to Canonbie's crumpled form and fell to her knees. The man wheezed wet breaths. His hand remained pressed on his neck, but the blood there had started to turn thick and sticky. A pool of it ran over his shirt and coat, and seeped into the cobblestones.

It reminded her of Cecily McCray, another she'd failed.

His eyes locked on her, and he grimaced. It took her a moment to realize he tried to smile. "I came looking for you," he whispered, "and found Catherine...at the house. Margret too, and Jonas."

Effie gripped his other hand. It felt clammy and cold. She had left Catherine Granville to recover at the Stevenson house, but she should've guessed the girl's friends would find her. She never considered Jack Canonbie would return there.

"Shhh," she breathed. "Save your strength."

His body trembled. His eyes closed. "I came for forgiveness. You were right. I am dead because I didn't see it early enough. I betrayed the wrong lady." His wheezing grew faint.

"Jack, no." Effie pressed her ear to his chest and heard only silence. *Help me! Show me how to heal him!* She blasted the cry through her linked fey senses.

He is too far gone, lass. The sending came from Rose. *He joins his ancestors.*

Ancestors. The word reverberated through Effie. She knew so little of the man's past, not even where he'd been born. And now she'd lost the chance to ask him. Would his family, if any existed, be proud of his sacrifice? Would they blame her for its futility?

Her gut clenched. Her head swam. She couldn't swallow. She couldn't speak. Her mouth had no moisture, and her tongue had turned to sand.

Ancestors. Had she failed her own as well? She thought of her mother, the man of Stronsay who was her father, and of her grandfather.

Arnwyrd. The tale of his supposed betrayal. A spark flared in her thoughts. Her gaze whipped to the frightened girl, and to the line of withered trees framing the square. Could she bring herself to do it? Had she the strength?

Her lips pressed firm. She would find out. She would not let Jack Canonbie die for nothing. She would ensure the tale of his sacrifice lived on far past her own life. She had come to make a demonstration, one to wag the tongues of the empire and show the fey could bring harmony to its citizens.

And so she would make one.

Raising her head, she placed both palms on Canonbie's chest. His blood covered them. She felt its fading warmth as she brought to mind the image of a young lass stricken by a wasting sickness. To the image, she added another man. Felled by a battle wound, the Sithling held the visage of Caledon.

Show me, she begged the steward.

For half a heartbeat, she thought he might refuse, until his linked aura pressed into hers. The icy chill of the touch made her shiver. Her fingers numbed. He pulled at the tension in her shoulders and made her relax.

With the steward's immense will guiding her, they delved into Canonbie and found the last ember of life. Effie brought to mind her vine-like tendrils and carefully plucked up the ember, pulling it free of the deadened shell that enclosed it.

She struggled to keep the full weight of what she had done, what it meant, from crushing her. She almost let slip the ember, but Caledon was there to steady her. If the ember had winked out, she knew she would never have forgiven herself.

She still might not.

When Arnwyrd had used the life force of Caledon's uncle to save the young lass, he had done so with the skill of a Spae Wife. But her affinity lay not in the healing of flesh. Her nature lent itself to the hills and lochs, the fields and rivers. And the trees.

The trees along the square were withered, not yet dead. Two lines of hazelnut anchored a pair of sturdy oaks.

She took the ember and poured it into one of the oaks. She felt the roots of the tree failing and stoked the ember with an imagined flutter of wind. The warmth of it rekindled. With Caledon's help, she tugged at the water far beneath the earth's crust. She prodded the soil and reminded the tree of how it should be.

The boy beneath the oak tree. The dagger. The sacrifice. All from what seemed a fever dream. The Sidhe Bhreige had shown her. Or had it been Cecily McCray? Blood Craft was needed for what she did, and blood was spilt. It mattered not to the tree from whence the power came.

The oak tree stirred to life. Its limbs wiggled and started to straighten. Effie strained, her will exhausted. But she carried on, pushing and prodding, not knowing how to work the Fey Craft of the Grundbairns, but feeling her way through.

Caledon's strength overmatched hers. He was an ocean to her pond. The heat of the ember leaped from the oak and danced from tree to tree. The stand responded, with Caledon's force and Effie's urgings. Coal soot trickled to the street as limbs flexed and broadened. Leaves sprouted, green and hale.

Effie heard gasps and a stir amongst the crowd in the square. She glanced at the swirling colors of the disk floating above and rent it into millions of glittering flecks that showered the cobblestones. Where they kissed the ground, they melted like snowflakes on a sunny winter's day.

Hazelnuts pattered to the stone of the square. They filled the sprouting limbs of the trees, round and hearty. Effie weakened, and Caledon's will diminished. It passed through her mind, giving her an overjoyed sense of encouragement, before receding completely.

Effie slumped to her haunches. Tears streaked her cheeks. The trees had become a grove once more, vibrant and strong. Their growth had not been a glamour. She and Caledon had altered them, and they stood now without any need of Fey Craft.

"Oak Seer," said Jane, bowing in reverence. The word echoed as it was whispered through the crowd and carried throughout the city. Those in the square rose, their panic forgotten. Jaws slack and eyes bulged, they gazed on the rebirth she had wrought.

They gazed on the final gift of Jack Canonbie.

40

The hound licked her face. It was a sneak attack. She hadn't seen or heard him pad next to her. She started, and he wagged his tail and licked her again, tickling her cheek. The hound's breath stunk of rotten fish. Effie stroked behind his ear. Around her the crowd had parted. The Fey Craft that had restored the trees had not been visible to them, yet somehow they knew it had come from her. They did not eye the brownies or the gnomes, or even the pixies who zipped about the square, flitting from branch to branch.

They eyed her.

She didn't know what to say to the faces that studied her in awe. She forced a polite smile to her lips. It felt out of place compared to the numbness within.

"He knew what he was about," said Graham, coming to help her to her feet. "He chose to come, lass, and it doesn't serve his memory to wallow in regret."

She latched onto Graham and hugged him tight. Her thoughts steadied, and she thanked him for all he had done. For all he had risked. Swinging her gaze over the rest of her host, she knew she would have an endless amount of thanking to do over the next few days.

But the thanking would be for later.

Overhead, Gwendoline screeched as she swooped in front of the chamber building. Effie saw straight away the owl's meaning. Lord Granville shoved past the other lords, retreating into the chamber building.

Effie snatched her skirt and hurried after. She caught sight of Rose hustling her way and waved her back. "See if there are any in the press who need your healing skill," she said. She left unspoken the need to spread the tale as far as they might, to the edges of the empire.

Gwendoline fluttered to her shoulder as she raced up the stone steps and barged through the ironbound doors. The chamber beyond spoked into several hallways. Oil paintings of city elders hung on the walls, and a tiled floor formed a mosaic that spiraled in a Celtic knot. A man in a military uniform stepped to block her path, his boots clacking on the tile, but the hound leaped before her and bared its teeth. A vicious growl rumbled from its throat.

"Allow her to pass," said Caledon. The steward seemed bemused by the hound. He waited for her just inside the door. "She is with me."

The uniformed man nodded hurriedly and waved her on.

"Lord Granville," she intoned. Her voice filled the chamber. The lord didn't turn. He kept his pace, angling toward one of the hallways. Lord Wilshire hovered at his heels.

She kept bellowing his name until he finally turned. When he laid eyes on her, his face scrunched in distaste. "I should have you in irons for inciting a riot," he snapped.

"I will join you in a cell, my lord. But not for long. Murder is a much graver offense. You may hang before the winter comes." The other lords parted for her. Caledon strode at her side.

Lord Granville snorted. "Murder? The man had no rank. He was a common rogue, and you will find no pistol in my hand. Now, be gone. We have matters to attend. The formal dissolution of these negotiations. I'm afraid after the mayhem we just witnessed, we have no choice other than to squash this foolish treaty. You have cemented your own fate."

"No," said Caledon. He clasped his hands behind his back and planted himself before the other lords. "She has merely reminded our kind that we have no need of you, nor your rank and title. Dissolve the negotiations. We will stay and fight the last of the Sidhe Bhreige. We will protect the Aerfenium stores, and we will become the Good Neighbors we once were. We do not need your permission."

One of the lords Effie didn't know cleared his throat. He had a shock of gray hair and kind, brown eyes. "A moment, Master Steward. Let's not be too hasty. I believe Her Majesty would very much like to hear of this banshee's touch. All reports had led her to believe we were no closer to capturing the last of the demons than we had been a year ago."

He turned to Effie. "I would like a full report of what you've uncovered, how you came to learn it, and whom else can confirm that information."

Effie's gaze spewed fire at Lord Granville. It was all she could do to keep from smacking the man. That he shunned any responsibility for Canonbie's death burned her to the core. She watched in delight as this other lord spoke. Lord Granville's face remained a hardened mask, but she saw the fear creeping into his eyes.

"Lord Barnet," said Lord Granville, not allowing her to speak. His tone had a slightly higher pitch to it than normal. "As my daughter's safety is a concern, I beg you allow me to discuss the matter in private before any public discourse."

The men stared at one another, each silently calculating, before Lord Barnet dipped his head. A wry grin came to Lord Granville's lips, and Effie knew the exchange, though won, had cost him.

Lord Granville waved her at a door. "We will speak in here," he said. "You may leave your menagerie to wait outside."

Effie kept her head tall, though her heart thumped in anticipation. She said a soothing word to Gwendoline and set her on a bench along the wall. The hound watched the owl with curiosity, tail wagging. Effie sent him an impression of guarding and followed Lord Granville into a small room sparse of decoration.

"I'm sure you believe you have done some great service to the empire," he said after she had settled in a chair opposite him. Exhausted as she was, its plush fabric made Effie want to burrow into it. But she sat rigidly on its lip.

"I believe I have done a great service for your family," she replied. She kept her tone soft and her face pleasant, to match his, though she seethed to be so close to the vile man. "A service the empire would survive with or without."

"You hold my daughter hostage." He did not ask a question, and Effie knew he sought to provoke her.

"She is free to leave as she pleases," she replied, remaining calm.

"You hold her good name hostage. It is one in the same."

She laughed at that. "It is your good name you care about. Good names are all you care about." She idly brushed a bit of dirt from her skirt, ignoring the blood that stained her hands. "It took me a while to decipher your scheme. You sought to defame me, and I couldn't fathom why you would go to the trouble. I didn't consider myself so large a threat that I should merit your interest. But I was wrong, wasn't I? You kept hearing tales of me, of my actions at Caldwell House, and they became a thorn in your efforts."

He remained silent, his eyes taking on their calculating bent, as they had with Lord Barnet. He waved at her to continue.

"When Catherine ran off, you learned of Cecily McCray's cult. Or perhaps you were already aware of them, it makes no difference. Rather than having a father's concern for her wellbeing, it angered you she would risk her honor and your name in such a scandal, so you decided to use her as a disposable tool. If she were harmed or uncovered while I blundered about in the cult's warren, you would lay all blame on my villainous influence, no doubt. And if I managed to rescue her in secret, you would still defame me for betraying other fey."

She tilted forward. "Names, Lord Granville. They are your vice."

His eyes twinkled, as if he enjoyed the jab. It reminded her he still lived on the younger side of middling age, despite his rise to power. He enjoyed being called out. It allowed him to trap her in some other manner. "Now is not the time to chide an enemy," he said. "With unrest in the cities, I will see the crown thinks it prudent to remove all association with the fey."

The threat might've frightened her once, but no longer. She let a grin play on her lips.

Lord Granville's eyes narrowed. "Eight bodies were dragged from the warren beneath Old Town. That is not counting fey, of course. Another dozen lay injured by the stunt your friends pulled with the airship, and a magistrate's house was sacked." His voice rose with each accounting. "What will Her Majesty think about that? The crown will have no choice but to act."

A part of Effie wanted to deny Granville's accusations, to argue that tales of fey wrongdoing were exaggerated, or a just reprisal for the harm done against them. But she had seen otherwise with her own eyes. With the Order of Freiwald, she might retain her high ground. But Cecily McCray's cult stood no better than Cyrus Reed, and she would not defend them.

"You have me," she admitted. "Not all fey want a treaty with the crown. Not all fey deserve one."

She watched him gloat for a moment before continuing. "But that does not pardon us from seeking a higher standard for the betterment of the empire, and you have left out the most heinous treason of all."

Gripping the cushion on either side of her, she watched his mirth dissolve. "The actions of the Sanctity of Empire League are abhorrent. In Edinburgh, they've fired canon and pistol in the streets with no regard, and incited riots. In Glasgow, they almost burned your lordship alive along with Lady Fife's estate, not to mention the murder that just occurred in front of a thousand honest folk. It seems to me the crown ought to become aware of what hand guides them. It is not well for lords to maintain private militia, especially when their aim is to attack Her Majesty's subjects."

"You may only pull that string so far, you will find," said Lord Granville.

Effie smirked, taking his meaning. "Oh, I have no doubt Elias McPherson will make for a noble sacrifice. But how certain are you that your name won't become despoiled? It is so easily caught up in the same affair. With Catherine's scandal—tell me, how many generations do you think it will take to restore the Granvilles to a place of honor? How much personal coin will it cost you?"

Lord Granville relaxed back into his seat. Turning his head to the side, he tugged on his shirt cuffs. His silent contemplation brought a weight to the still air. When he returned his attention to her, he spoke with a softer tone. "You have made my life difficult. There is no point in denying that. Over the past days, I have thought on your earlier argument and come to the conclusion you are correct. I would indeed have better connections if I'd taken the time to foster them."

She blinked rapidly, searching for some trap. He took her shock for reveling.

"Oh, do not celebrate overmuch." He intertwined his fingers and rested them in his lap. "The strength of the empire depends on the will of the great lords and their ability to form the bedrock of our society. We would have nothing of culture or invention without our esteemed gentlemen who take root from centuries of tradition. It is we who matter, above all."

"No, it is there I fear we will always disagree," said Effie. She leaned in. She felt him teetering. She had exposed a weakness, threatening his honor and coin, and realized she need only nudge him with his heart's desires to claim her own. "But let us speak plainly. The league and newspapers both cost coin. Your resettlement scheme would've cost even more, enough to cripple your standing in Parliament, and without me your daughter would've fallen prey to an atrocity far worse than a soiled name—one I will give you the benefit of knowing nothing about."

She forced the tension from her shoulders. Now was not the time to lose her nerve. She raised an eyebrow. "You want me to believe your efforts are all for ancient names and grand houses and honor, yet you go to great effort to sway the opinion of the commoners who mean so little to you."

He grunted, conceding the point. "We both have found use of them, it would seem. But your tricks will not gain you any privilege. You nor any other will receive a title, nor can the steward bestow one without the explicit approval of the crown."

"Trifle considerations," she said. "If that is all you intend to offer, I will have to make an appeal to Lord Barnet. Or perhaps I should visit with Lady Fife. I'm sure she would like to know whose hand has cost her the use of her estate. She has a rather large contingent of friends in Parliament, does she not? They might make inquiries on her behalf."

"I have powerful friends as well, you'll do well to remember."

Effie shook her head. "No, you have cohorts bought with coin. They will do you little service other than to drain your coffers when pressed. Between them and your other foolhardy schemes, it'll be a wonder if you manage to keep the coat on your back." She leaned toward him. "I have no need to defeat you, Lord Granville, for you to suffer. My position is clear. Continue to defame to the fey, and you will find it a very expensive and very personal proposition."

"Such a tactic would expose you, as well," said Lord Granville. "You will no longer be able to hide behind Mr. Stevenson, nor your steward. I will see to that."

Effie steeled her gaze. "I would rather be known to every soul in the empire than allow your schemes to continue. So do as you must."

"Bah, so be it." He waved her away. Sucking on the inner part of his cheeks, a battle raged behind his gaze. "There are other tides of unrest that need my attention far greater than your concerns. We can be friends, for the nonce, if that will keep your pestering at bay."

Effie cocked her head, not believing her ears. "Do you mean?"

"Aye, the rampant accounts in the newspapers will stop. They will have to for this treaty to pass. Otherwise, the crown might question my good judgment."

For this treaty to pass.

The man had conceded.

Relief flooded through Effie, making her legs tingle. She had won the day, though Lord Granville would never admit as much. Already, he deflected to other matters and other schemes. She had no doubt he would continue to make life difficult for the fey and would see some profit from his turn of face. But for now she had saved the hope born at Caldwell House.

She studied his gaze and worked out the unrest to which he alluded. "You've empowered the dockworkers, banded them together, and now they aim to strike, the same as the miners and matchmakers. Better wages and safer working conditions, is that it?" The irony of it made her want to laugh at his expense, but she kept herself composed.

"They will turn away when their empty bellies growl. They have not the heart for anything but grumbling. Yet the timing of their uproar comes at an opportune time. There is that, at least."

"It will allow you to save face," said Effie. "I assume you will use the distraction to forge some pact with Sir Walter Conrad and the Hostmen of Newcastle? With a treaty in place, Aerfenium will have its day and shower coin on those who have gained position over it."

Lord Granville snorted. "You are too clever for your own good. Yes, Aerfenium will change the world. But then, so did the longbow. The lowborn wielded it, a devastating weapon, and yet their betters remained in command. It is the way of things."

Effie considered that as he stood and straightened his coat.

"I have tarried with you long enough," he said, "and in this city longer than I had any desire. I will pass your treaty and take my coin, but you must pledge two things. First, you will not encourage Catherine in her debauchery, nor speak of what occurred to her with any other. I will see that she is brought back in line, obedient and silent."

Effie's shoulders tightened. "And second?"

"You will hunt this last demon and make a spectacle of proclaiming the empire safe after its defeat. It is a brilliant tale you fey have spun of these so-called Sidhe Bhreige, but I will not have its threat continually held over our heads."

As he turned for the door, a sour taste came to her mouth. Her great victory had suddenly taken on a hollow feeling. "No," she blurted.

Lord Granville spun. His eyes widened.

"No, I do not agree to those terms." She drew up her bearing. A twinge of guilt returned to her as she thought of Jack Canonbie. She could not let Lord Granville prosper so easily. She would not let him go unscathed.

"It is not enough. What you offer, words on paper, for all the cruelty and death you have wrought. It will never be enough." Her blood boiled, and she heard the hound stir outside the door in response.

Lord Granville's nostrils flared. "I would remind you of your position, and to whom you address. I have been more than generous to allow your familiar tone."

Effie balled her fists. "You have taught me something this fortnight, my lord. Did you know that? I used to cower when addressed as the Green Lady. The recognition brought me embarrassment because I had learned to hide all my life."

Standing, she leveled her gaze at him. "But you showed me how dangerous that hiding could be. You took advantage of it, with your fictions and fear mongering. You had no one to oppose you as you twisted public opinion." She leaned in, raising to her toes. "No longer. The fey will have a champion. They will have their Green Lady, the Oak Seer, and she will see that justice is served, no matter the birth or blood of their enemy."

Effie's whole body lightened. It dawned on her that she had never wanted to slink back into obscurity. That notoriety persuaded her little did not lessen the desire that gripped her to have a voice, one that would rattle the empire and shake free the parasitic hold of its prejudices against the fey.

"The treaty will pass because it is better for the empire," she said. "I will see our common enemy brought low because I cherish our home and would see it safe. But do not believe I regard you as anything more than a loathsome parasite. We are not friends, and you will have no promises or pardons from me."

Her boots clacked on the tile as she stormed past. She felt his seething glare, but she ignored him. She had work to do, and a rather large crowd to address.

❧ 41 ❧

Fergus Alpin grumbled. The noise made Effie grin. He could bluster all he liked, just as long as he kept his word. They stood before a cottage just beyond the edge of Inverness as the morning sun warmed the air. A rise of hillocks rolled southward behind them, and on the far side of the cottage the waters of the Beauly Firth lapped against a stony shore.

They had uncovered the place from the tintype Stuart Graham stole in Dunfermline. It had not taken them long to determine the small town in the background of the photograph was Inverness, but it had taken diligence to connect any importance of the cottage to Cyrus Reed.

Edgar Talmadge strode to them. The short man had watched the cottage for the better part of a fortnight, while Effie convinced the Fey Finder General to dispatch Fergus Alpin to make an arrest. Jane's friend had eagerly volunteered for the task. Conversely, the Fey Finders had greeted their new authority the way a plow horse might a field of granite.

At the urging of Caledon, the crown had granted Fey Finders the discretion to pursue and arrest those who perpetrated crimes against the fey. No doubt, Lord Granville thought the matter trivial. Mr. Billingsley still danced on his strings, and the Sniffers were not like to abuse the power. But for the fey, it was as if a giant stone wall had suddenly cracked and allowed the breeze to whistle through.

"He rests in front of his sister's hearth," said Edgar. "Just staring at the flames and whispering to himself."

"I should see this man for myself and judge whether he took any part in the murders at Balclune," said Alpin. "To attack him unaware and throw him in chains is not justly done. Think of the panic it will bring the man's sister."

A derisive snicker burst from Effie's lips. She couldn't contain it. For all her dealings with lords and gentry, it was men like Alpin who baffled her the most. He saw no profit in disparaging her other than to justify a position he already occupied. "You can console the sister as you please, Mr. Alpin, just as long as you execute your charge. As to the man's guilt, you will have to take my word, paps and all."

Edgar swallowed and glanced away. A bit of color rose to his cheeks. Fergus Alpin hacked into his handkerchief. When he recovered, he folded his arms across his chest. "I'd tell ye to wait here if I knew the stone between your ears would listen to any form of reason."

Effie raised an eyebrow but stood her ground as Alpin waved to a pair of constables he'd roused from the town. They'd remained a short distance apart, near the steam carriage they'd all ridden in from the Inverness rail station. One held a rifle and the other a bludgeon. Their expressions were almost as sour as the Sniffer's.

"Should I join them?" asked Edgar as Alpin and the constables marched toward the cottage.

Shaking her head, Effie said, "You've done your part brilliantly. It is for the crown's men to see it through." Not for the first time, she wished Jack Canonbie stood beside her. She touched her lips absently as she thought of him. But she wouldn't let herself be sad. He had brought her too much hearty laughter to remember him with any melancholy. It was far better to think of some crude and vexing jest than to wallow in his absence.

The constable with the bludgeon used it to pound on the door. It opened and a woman's face popped into view. She shrieked as the constables barged past her, flailing at them until Fergus Alpin pulled her away. The shadows swallowed them as they moved farther inside, but

Effie heard the clamor. Cyrus Reed growled some curse and must've thrown something heavy and wooden. The boom of it was dwarfed only by the screams of the man's sister. A grunt and whimper followed a wet, slapping sound, and then another heavy something clattered to the floor.

Effie's foot tapped. Her fists rested on her hips. She wanted nothing more than to rush in and see the madman in irons. But she thought better of it and resisted the urge. She needed to earn the trust of Fergus Alpin, however begrudgingly he gave it, if she was to call on the man again. And she intended to, along with all of the Fey Finders. Even Conall Murray.

How she had come to the position, she still could not fathom. The turn of tides that had brought her to associate with the very souls that had once summoned within her such fear was a mystery as perplexing as why some trees wilted whiles others took root.

It took only a few minutes longer for the constables to emerge from the cottage. They dragged Cyrus Reed between them. Irons locked his wrists together. His scrawny frame had turned skeletal and sickly. He'd shorn his beard and wore a strip of cloth wrapped around his damaged eye. When he saw Effie, he bucked against his captors. But they held him tight.

"You stole from me," he cried. "The shrill cry, I hear it no more! The way, the path, it was laid before me, but now I am blind to it." Spittle flew from his lips at his manic ranting. His one visible eye refused to focus, though his attention did not waver from her direction.

One of the constables slapped the back of his head. "Shut yer gob," he commanded.

Cyrus Reed cackled. He dropped his head back and roared.

"No, no," Reed's sister called. She'd broken loose from Fergus Alpin and ran toward her brother, begging of the constables. "He never meant to do so foul of things. It weren't him but the Lord's will. He heard the calling, he says. He's told it to me all. You can't blame him for it. Let him free!"

"Yes!" shouted Cyrus Reed. "I was summoned to the great oak. I danced in my dreams. I saw her there, rejoicing." His eye finally fixed on Effie. It pierced her like a dart. "And you, Oak Seer. At her command, the mighty limbs will crack and strike you down. You know it for the truth. You have seen it!"

Edgar whirled his head toward her, but she kept herself from flinching. She had expected the man's loose tongue to tell her more of the banshee's touch. It was part of why his capture was so important. They would bring him to justice, but they would also use him to uncover the last of the Sidhe Bhreige.

Effie claimed a measure of satisfaction in that knowledge. For the first time, they had a thread that might lead them to the enemy. A hunt for snarks, they no longer waged.

She remained silent as the constables shoved Cyrus Reed into the carriage. The madman continued to squeal and froth, but his words had turned to nonsense. She would have to wait until he calmed to learn anything of use.

Glancing back at the cottage, her brave face melted. Her blood turned to ice. A thicket of ancient, gnarled bramble entwined all before her. Its shoots snaked round the hills and across the stony shore. Its barbs were sharper than steel, some reaching longer than a sword. A pressure grazed her thoughts, and the barbs sprang at her.

She flung her arms against them, and they danced aside, needle tips piercing her flesh in wicked stings that left her crying out. *I can touch you anywhere, Oak Seer.* The impression formed in her head of a feminine lilt, a threat whispered from Cyrus Reed's master—the creature who stole *Les Revenirs* from Cecily McCray, and the source of the banshee's touch.

Jerking back, Effie thrashed against the assault. She refused to let dread overcome her, despite the strength of the Sidhe Bhreige. She would give her last breath here and now, if forced.

But the creature only taunted her. The barbs and bramble dissolved, as did the pain of their bite. Yet rushing over the hills and across the waters of the firth, a mocking wind wailed.

THE END

Thank you for reading! Did you enjoy?

Please Add Your Review!

Don't miss the beginning of the Fey Matter novels with book one, THE LAIRD OF DUNCAIRN and discover more from Craig Comer at www.craigcomer.com

* * *

The year is 1882 Scotland, and the auld alliance betwixt king and fey has long been forgotten. Men of science, backed by barons of industry, push the boundaries of technology. When Sir Walter Conrad discovers a new energy source, one that could topple nations and revolutionize society, the race to dominate its ownership begins. But the excavation and use of this energy source will have dire consequences for both humans and fey. For an ancient enemy stirs, awakened by Sir Walter's discovery.

Outcast half-fey Effie of Glen Coe is the Empire's only hope at averting the oncoming disaster. Effie finds herself embroiled in the conflict, investigating the eldritch evil spreading throughout the Highlands. As she struggles against the greed of mighty lords and to escape the clutches of the queen's minions, her comfortable world is shattered. Racing to thwart the growing menace, she realizes the only thing that can save them all is a truce no one wants.

* * *

Please sign up for the City Owl Press newsletter for chances to win special subscriber-only contests and giveaways as well as receiving information on upcoming releases and special excerpts.

All reviews are **welcome** and **appreciated**. Please consider leaving one on your favorite social media and book buying sites.

For books in the world of romance and speculative fiction that embody Innovation, Creativity, and Affordability, check out City Owl Press at www.cityowlpress.com.

ACKNOWLEDGMENTS

An overwhelming thank you goes once again to the great folks at City Owl Press for their guidance and enthusiasm for this book. Thank you to Heath McCorkle whose editing insight continues to make Effie's tale stronger and more cohesive.

To Ahimsa Kerp, who read an early draft and pointed out the things I could not see, I thank you, as always. Who knew our many walks to Cameron Toll all those years ago would turn into this? To Garrett Calcaterra, your friendship and advice have always put me in your debt.

Thank you to my family for supporting me with my weird tales.

Last, this book would not exist without the sacrifice, patience, and encouragement of my wife, Martina. She read and gave notes on many early drafts of the book, and not only shaped and improved it but allowed my writer's brain to wander while she supported us both. I could not have done any of this without her, and she deserves more than I can say in words.

ABOUT THE AUTHOR

CRAIG COMER is the author of the gaslamp fantasy novel THE LAIRD OF DUNCAIRN and co-author of the mosaic fantasy novel THE ROADS TO BALDAIRN MOTTE. His shorter works have appeared in several anthologies, including BARDIC TALES AND SAGE ADVICE and PULP EMPIRE VOLUME IV. Craig earned a Master's Degree in Writing from the University of Southern California. He enjoys tramping across countries in his spare time, preferably those strewn with pubs and castles.

www.craigcomer.com

Facebook: www.facebook.com/craigscomer/

Twitter: www.twitter.com/CraigComer